AMBULANCE GIRLS

Deborah Burrows

AMBULANCE GIRLS

EBURY
PRESS

1 3 5 7 9 10 8 6 4 2

Ebury Press, an imprint of Ebury Publishing
20 Vauxhall Bridge Road,
London SW1V 2SA

Penguin
Random House
UK

Ebury Press is part of the Penguin Random House
group of companies whose addresses can be found at
global.penguinrandomhouse.com

First published in the UK in 2016 by Ebury Press

www.penguin.co.uk

A CIP catalogue record for this book is available from the British Library

ISBN 9781785034602

Typeset in India by Thomson Digital Pvt Ltd, Noida, Delhi

Printed and bound in Great Britain by Clays Ltd, St Ives PLC

Penguin Random House is committed to a sustainable future for our business,
our readers and our planet. This book is made from Forest Stewardship
Council® certified paper.

For the 'Williams Girls': my beautiful nieces, Jessamy, Susannah and Esther. And also Annabelle and Bethwyn, who came into the world in 2013 and 2016 and made me 'Great'.

CHAPTER ONE

Tuesday 15 October 1940
London

Blood, warm and sticky, was trickling down my forehead. Something sharp must have nicked me as they pushed me through the narrow gap. Never mind, I was inside.

'Hullo,' I called out. 'Anyone there?'

The words disappeared into the darkness as my torchlight flicked over the mess of plaster, wood and debris. In the fug of soot and dust and ash, my breathing was shallow and unsatisfying, which added to the sense of impending doom that had gripped me the moment they shoved me inside.

The trickle of blood on my forehead had become exquisitely itchy. When I lifted my gloved hand to wipe it away, the leather was harsh against my skin and felt gritty. Now my face was bloody *and* dirty; I probably looked like any child's nightmare.

Whatever was I – Lily Brennan, schoolteacher from Western Australia – doing here, crawling into the ruins of a bombed house, playing the hero, when the children were most likely already dead?

But what could I do? Really, there was no choice.

I had arrived with my ambulance partner, David Levy, to find a familiar scene of devastation, bleached to aquatint by the moonlight. Piles of rubble stood in the middle of what had been a row of Victorian dwellings. They towered in gaunt ruin against the sky, between shapeless wrecks of masonry that showed the signs of a direct hit. Men's voices, brisk and business-like, emerged from the gloom, between whistles and the occasional shout. Short flashes of torchlight appeared and vanished in the darkness, as rescue workers sought doggedly for signs of life in the ruins.

When I emerged from the ambulance, the warden had looked me up and down as if I were a prize cow at the Royal Show. As he did so, the letters on his tin helmet had stood out brightly in the moonlight: 'ARP'. They stood for air raid precautions, and I had felt inappropriate laughter bubble up in my chest when I got a good look at him. How could this small man protect anyone from the destruction London had suffered in the past five weeks of air raids? And yet there was a quiet authority in his slow nod to me, and in the way he had then turned to throw a cryptic comment to the men standing behind him.

'She'll do; she's thin enough.'

Levy, who had come to stand beside me, laughed at that, saying, 'I think she might prefer to be described as slim.'

There had been no answering smile from the warden. Instead, he gestured at the ruins of what had been a house. 'We've got two infants buried under the rubble there,' he said. His clipped, precise voice did not at all obscure the horror of those words. 'At least one's alive – or was alive until a half-hour ago – because we've heard a baby crying. We understand they were left sheltering under a solid kitchen table before the bomb hit. Problem is, the place is just holding together. If we disturb the site too much it'll bring the rest down on top of them. It looks like someone slim – as slim as you, miss – could squeeze through. You'd need to crawl through to the kitchen at the back, find the kids and bring them out. Think you can do that?'

Levy knew I had a horror of tightly enclosed spaces. 'I'll go,' he had said. 'I'm good at squeezing through ruins. I've done it before.'

'There isn't the room. You'd never get in.' The warden sized me up with another quick glance and challenged me with his eyes.

I had always been small for my age. Even now, at twenty-five, I could still be mistaken for a schoolgirl. I always suspected that was because I had been born too early and never really caught up. I was so small when I was born that I really should have died, like the three tiny babies who had slipped away in my mother's arms in the years before I arrived in the world. And that was why my mother took one look at my little wrinkled body and turned her face from me, unwilling to engage in another losing battle for a child's life. That I survived was due to my father. He was a fighter, and he fought for me.

A woman who had helped at my birth told him the best chance to keep me alive was to carry me next to his skin, where his strong heartbeat would teach my heart to keep beating when it forgot. So Dad fashioned a pouch for his tiny joey and for two months, until I could suckle and had grown into my skin, he carried me everywhere, pressed against his heart, just as the woman had said. I was no bigger than his hand and he fed me my mother's milk from an eyedropper, like a little bird. When I was old enough to hear the story he told me that the moment he saw me he knew I would live, because he could see that I was a fighter too.

Most people cannot see that in me. Because I am small and slender people often mistakenly assume that I am fragile. Not the warden.

'I think you could get to the children,' he said to me. 'Get them out. Willing to chance it, miss?'

I had smiled and said, 'Of course.' What else could I do?

Now on my hands and knees, crawling over the rough, debris-strewn floor, I took comfort in the thought that, after five weeks of driving an ambulance in this relentless Blitz, I had learned to push fear aside when attending an incident.

Served me right for being smug. Without any warning, my torch dimmed and failed. Darkness enfolded me. My heart thumped painfully and my chest tightened. I tried to breathe my

3

way out of the almost overwhelming panic, but my breaths were shallow and too rapid, and my thoughts would not stay still, so that I couldn't settle into a plan of action. Snatches of a song, a poem, memories of home came unbidden and left as quickly to resolve into one, dreadful realisation. *I'm entombed. I'll die here, alone in the darkness, far from home.*

Then there was anger at my own defeatist thoughts. I pushed them away and shook the torch violently, once, twice, and on the third shake it flickered back into life. As the beam strengthened I exulted in the simple fact of light.

My slow crawl began again and optimism reasserted itself. I would find the children alive and I would get us all out of here. They would probably be afraid of me, with my dirty face and goggly eye shields under the steel hat, but in my three years as a country schoolteacher I had learned how to soothe frightened children. The important thing is to keep calm, speak with authority and show a sense of humour. I used the same tactics in dealing with the injured adults I transported in my ambulance.

The air was dusty, and I sneezed. That immediately reminded me of home and I let my thoughts drift into childhood memory, anything to take my mind off this interminable crawl into darkness. It was always dusty in Kookynie, the tiny gold-mining settlement on the edge of Western Australia's Great Victoria Desert where I grew up. It was dusty also in the Wheatbelt town of Duranillin, where I had taught in a one-room school and saved the money to make my escape to Europe. My students had been bush kids, independent, cheeky and often rambunctious. I had loved teaching them, probably because I had been just like them myself – until my mother took note of that fact and sent me to boarding school in Perth.

'Lily needs to learn how to live in *society*. She's thirteen and it's time she learned how to act like a *lady*,' she had said, as if Perth were some cosmopolitan centre of civilisation, and her own grandfather had not been convicted in 1850 of stealing a cow, and transported to Western Australia for ten years of penal servitude.

My mother hated people to know of her grandfather's convict past, but I was proud of what he went on to do with his life after such troubled beginnings. After receiving his ticket of leave, he became a government schoolmaster and a respected member of the community. His son became a bank manager and his grandson – my Uncle Charles – was a judge. Life is often ironic in Australia.

A sharp pain in my knee brought me back to the present as I bumped into something that gave a loud crack. My entire body jerked, and I froze, heart pounding, praying I had not disturbed the precarious jumble around me.

Silence and, except for the narrow band of my torchlight, darkness. I sneezed again and I crawled a few feet more, slowly and more carefully. I wished I were not so alone. My hands were sweaty and sticky inside the thick gloves. I stopped to stifle yet another sneeze as best I could, and I gazed at the destruction exposed by my torchlight.

Splinters of cabinetry, shards of glass and crockery, and pieces of plaster with torn wallpaper attached. The wallpaper was a cheerful yellowy colour scattered with a design of orange berries, the sort of paper that would brighten up a kitchen. Small children would barely notice it as they drank their milk and ate their meals. It would have been there in the background in a room they had thought was as permanent as the Rock of Gibraltar, but was now a shattered mess.

'Hullo? Are you there?' I called out again, making my voice calm and firm. 'Please tell me if you are. I'm Lily and I'm here to help you.'

There was no reply. If the children were alive I did not blame them for hiding from a stranger who was waving a torch around in the ruins of their lives. It would be better if I could call them by name, but I did not know their names. So I listened hard for anything that might be a sign as to their presence: a whimper, a sob, a moan. Silence pressed in, broken by creaks and groans from the settling ruins. I could not see the kitchen table they were supposed to have sheltered beneath.

It occurred to me to recite some poetry. My students had loved Edward Lear's poetry, which is nonsensical enough to surprise and delight small children. A frightened child might be intrigued.

'Those who watch at that midnight hour,' I declaimed, 'From Hall or Terrace, or lofty Tower, Cry, as the wild light passes along,' – and here I let the torchlight play around me – '"The Dong! – the Dong! The wandering Dong through the forest goes! The Dong! the Dong! The Dong with a luminous Nose!"'

'That's silly.'

It came distinctly, the piping voice of a small child. *Oh, God, please let them both be all right. Oh, God, please let them be together and unhurt.*

'It *is* silly, isn't it?' I said into the darkness. 'Are you hiding? You're doing a super job at it if you are.'

'I'm waiting for Mummy. You go away you Dong.'

'Your mummy sent me to get you,' I said. 'She's waiting for you outside. She wants you to come with me.'

It was a lie, and I hated to use it. They had told me the mother had gone off in another ambulance. I didn't even know if she was still alive.

I shone the torch in the direction of the voice and from the jumble of wood and plaster a small white face squinted into the light. It belonged to a bright-eyed little boy, about three years old, who was hugging a big torch to his chest. I supposed he had turned it off when he heard me approaching. Grey dust coated his hair and the blue striped pyjamas he was wearing; he seemed to be in a cave, until I realised that he was in fact under the kitchen table. It had saved him when the walls came down on top of it, but I wondered how much longer the table would hold with the ton of rubble it bore.

The boy shook his head. 'I'm looking after Emily, our baby. She's asleep.'

Oh, God, please let her not be dead. I had seen too many dead children in the past weeks.

'It's all right, sweetheart, I've come to take you both to Mummy,' I said as I crawled across the rubble towards him.

It wasn't until I was almost at his sanctuary that my torchlight revealed the baby lying on her back on a blanket in front of him. She looked about nine months old and was, just as her brother had said, fast asleep. With a sense of wonder I watched the quick and regular rise and fall of her chest.

'Emily cried and cried,' he said. 'But she's asleep now, you mustn't wake her up.'

I reached out a hand to the infant and the boy immediately tried to push me away. 'Mummy said to wait here. Go away you Dong.'

I backed off a little. 'How are you, old chap,' I asked. 'Are you hurt anywhere?'

He shook his head and shrank back, but said nothing more as I gently felt along Emily's body to see if there were any indications of injury. She woke as I did so, and gave a high mewling cry of surprise. Her little body was firm to the touch, but her eyes were sunken and she seemed lethargic. I assumed she was dehydrated and prayed that was the worst.

I reached into the hiding place and picked her up, tucking the blanket around her. Her arms wrapped around my neck in a tight, trusting grip that brought hot tears to my eyes. I had thought I was hardened after seeing so much horror and I felt oddly happy to know that tears could still come.

'Leave Emily alone.'

The boy's voice was sharp, imperative; he was close to hysteria. He was also confused and probably hungry and thirsty and certainly terrified.

'You've been such a brave boy,' I said. 'And you've looked after Emily so well. Your mummy will be very proud of you.

But it's time for us all to go now. I'll carry Emily. Can you crawl behind me while I carry Emily?'

'Like a baby?' He sounded unenthusiastic. I could not force him to come out, but I could not carry both of them, and neither could I leave him behind.

'No. Like a—' My mind was blank. I hugged Emily closer. She had my neck in a stranglehold, but she was too quiet and it worried me. The creaks and moans of the settling ruins above us worried me more, though. The panic I had kept at bay was threatening to engulf me again and I needed to get out. *Now.*

'Like a train,' I said, sparked by a sudden, ancient memory of the game I had played with my younger brother, Ben. 'Let's play trains. I'm the engine and Emily is the driver, but we need a coal truck. Could you be a coal truck, d'you think? Grab my ankles and we'll set off.'

With my right arm tight around baby Emily and gripping the torch, I cautiously turned myself around to face the way I had come. A loud sob sounded behind me. He was close to losing control; I was taking his sister and he was terrified of being alone in the dark. *We're all frightened of that*, I wanted to tell him, *in a war we're all afraid of the dark.*

I shone my torch down and back towards my feet, dipping Emily as I did so. 'Quick, grab my ankles. The train must leave on time, but it can't run without coal.'

Instead he switched on his own torch.

'Leave your torch,' I said, 'and take hold of my ankles. Mummy will pick it up later.'

He looked very uncertain.

I raised my voice and made a train sound. 'Woo-oo-oo. All aboard that's going aboard. The train to Euston station is ready to go.'

'You should say that it's about to depart,' he whispered in a mournful little voice.

I repeated obediently, 'The train to Euston station is about to depart. All aboard. Where's my coal truck? Unless there's coal for the engine we won't get far. Is there a coal truck around here?'

'I'll be the coal truck,' he said, and I heard the note of excitement in his voice and knew I had him.

Small hands grabbed my ankles. I turned the torch to light our way and slowly, painfully, we began to crawl through the debris of his shattered home, puff, puff, puffing as we went.

'Woo-woo,' I said. The smell of dust and charred wood and soot was almost suffocating and I coughed.

He sneezed.

'My knees hurt,' he said.

'I know,' I said. 'Not much further now.' My knees felt as if they were on fire, and baby Emily was becoming unbearably heavy in the crook of my arm, which was cramping painfully. When I tried to shift her weight a little she whimpered.

'Let's put more coal into the engine, shall we?'

'Engines can't run without coal,' he whispered and held tighter to my ankles, a dragging weight behind me as I crawled.

I felt my heart jump when at last I saw the circle of light ahead of me. It was not daylight yet, of course. They would have set up arc lights and erected a tarpaulin to hide them from the bombers. We crawled towards the light and now I could hear the generator. But as they pulled us out I heard a more ominous sound, the growling roar of planes overhead and the heavy thump of ack-ack guns. The raiders had returned.

CHAPTER TWO

Later that night, searchlights still ripped through the darkness in front of us; the shimmering bars met and crossed and swept apart in seemingly haphazard arcs, covering the sky with a lattice of light. German aeroplanes, tiny as toys, wove in and out of the thin greenish beams. They were Heinkel bombers by the waugh waugh sound of their engines; their dreary throbbing was a different tone entirely to the comforting growl of a Spitfire or the rumble of a Hurricane.

We were returning at last to the Bloomsbury auxiliary ambulance station in Woburn Place at the required sixteen miles an hour. The Monster, by which name my ambulance was affectionately known, did not appreciate such a slow pace, and was in danger of overheating.

Strings of red tracer bullets rose up towards the planes as the anti-aircraft guns thundered out shells in rapid succession. The rhythmic whomp whomp whomp whomp pounded my ears as I peered through the dusty windscreen and watched shells burst far above us, like flashes of summer lightning. For all the terror of an air raid, I was transfixed by the beauty of it.

'Get 'em,' said Levy, entranced in his own way by the show. 'Get the bastards.'

Blinking my tired eyes, I ignored him to squint at the small part of the road illuminated by the narrow band of headlights we were allowed to show, and tried to avoid the fissures and potholes and debris left by this and earlier air raids.

I shifted in my seat, trying to find a more comfortable position. Comfort was not really possible, given that I was perched on a pile of old newspapers in order to see over the wheel. At least the discomfort kept me awake, a good thing, since I needed all my wits about me to drive the Monster. She was an ungainly beast, a 1937 Ford V8 van with a large box body welded on to her chassis. Inside were four standard metal stretchers, empty at present, as we had dropped off our last patients. Stowed beneath the stretchers were a first aid kit, some basins, and piles of blankets.

The moon was almost full and it illuminated a couple of figures on the footpath, gazing upwards to watch the show.

'Look,' I said, 'bombing as entertainment.'

'Silly buggers,' Levy replied. 'It hasn't taken long for Londoners to grow accustomed to all this, has it?'

'Accustomed to what?' I was suddenly angry, contemptuous. 'The very real possibility of instant, violent death?'

'Londoners are a sophisticated lot, Brennan. They need variety. Even air raids acquire a certain monotony after a while.'

'I'd hardly call this one monotonous.'

Whatever reply Levy made was lost in the shriek of falling bombs. The shriek rose to a crescendo that ended in three crumps as the 'stick' of bombs hit the ground in a line of explosions. These had probably landed over a mile away, but the spectators jumped and bolted for shelter. I shook my head to indicate to Levy that I had not heard what he had said, and we exchanged wry smiles.

'I said, deep down, Londoners love the Blitz,' he shouted. 'It's something big. When it's over they'll look back on all this with nostalgia.'

Over to our right the sky was pink and rapidly turning to red. Fires were inevitable during a raid. In early September, on the first night of the blitzkrieg, the docks in the East End had blazed so brightly that all of London was bathed in a red glow that had reminded me of sunset in the desert around Kookynie.

I had a sudden, vivid image of dry red earth dotted with stunted mulga and mallee, of heat shimmering on a far horizon under a sky of intense cloudless blue and sunsets of red fire.

I had been away nearly three years now, and although weeks could go by without my giving it a thought, sometimes I missed home so much it was like a physical pain in my chest.

'What's up, Brennan? You're looking rather gruesome.'

I ventured a look at him. He was scowling, worried about me, although he would never admit it. Even when he scowled, and Levy scowled a great deal, he was ridiculously good looking. I thought he resembled a young Siegfried Sassoon: exotic, intelligent and disturbingly sensual.

I had joined the ambulance service in October 1939, and had been paired with Levy when he arrived at the Bloomsbury station in February 1940. In the eight months we had been working together I had grown to like him very much. Any early tendency I might have had to think about him romantically had soon faded when he had made it clear, although never overtly, that he was simply not interested in me that way. Which simplified matters greatly once the Blitz began, because he was an excellent ambulance attendant and we worked together like a dream. Anyway, a love affair would have been out of place among the horrors we faced each day.

I assumed he had a girlfriend, possibly many girlfriends, as he was handsome and personable when he wanted to be and the war seemed to invite casual flings – but he had never mentioned any. I knew little else about David Levy, other than that he was single, twenty-five, Jewish, had attended Harrow School and then studied English Literature at Oxford. I had no idea what he did when he was not with me in the Monster.

How could I tell him I was feeling homesick? I smiled and took refuge in a lie.

'Indigestion,' I said. 'One of Fripp's scones sits like a rock in my stomach.'

'I suspect Nola Fripp of fifth column activities. No one could be such a terrible cook as that girl. When she brings in her culinary experiments I'm sure it's a ruse to put the entire ambulance station out of action with food poisoning.'

I loved to hear Levy talk. He sounded like a BBC announcer imitating the King.

'And I've got a numb bum,' I said, which was true.

That remark brought a smile from Levy. He had a lovely smile, which he showed too infrequently.

'Poor old Brennan,' he said. 'You need more padding in the seat area. Put on some weight, old girl. I often worry you'll be blown away in a strong wind, like a pint-sized, curly haired Dorothy, heading for Oz.'

'Up among the barrage balloons,' I said, smiling at the image. 'I'll hitch a ride on a Spitfire and let it take me somewhere over the rainbow.'

'I've a friend in the RAF. He's one of Churchill's Few, but he flies a Hurricane, not a Spitfire. Wasn't it a hurricane that whisked Dorothy away?'

'I think you'll find it was a tornado.'

'I'm sure you're right. By the way, *a propos* of our earlier incident, please don't do anything so idiotically heroic again. Makes me look bad when you go off alone like that, saving children willy-nilly.'

'I was press-ganged into it.'

'Nonsense. They just had to mention children in danger and you dove into that rabbit hole like a demented Alice. Shocking exhibitionism in my opinion, Brennan.'

Levy wore a serious expression I knew well. When Levy looked serious it meant he was joking and when he appeared bored it meant he was annoyed. The bored look was most often in evidence at the ambulance station. He was not well-liked there, and some cruel jokes had been played on him. The anti-Semitism in the station, and in London generally, was widespread and that fact was still shocking to me.

We all knew what horrors that sort of blind prejudice could bring. Ever since the Nazis had come to power in Germany eight years before, newspapers had reported their increasingly brutal measures against the Jews, from refusing to allocate ration cards to them in Germany, to confiscating their property, to herding them into a crowded ghetto in Warsaw to starve or die of typhus, and massacring them wholesale in Polish villages. And now there were reports of concentration camps being built, just for Jews.

Looking at Levy, seeing his face drawn and his body drooping with exhaustion, the old anger surfaced at the injustice of those who had never bothered to try to get to know him, but were willing to judge him anyway. It was anathema to me to think of condemning someone for what they were rather than who they were.

Anti-Semitism made no sense to me. The only Jews I had known personally before I met Levy were my family doctor in Kalgoorlie and his family, and I had liked them.

I changed down a gear with a crunch. Beside me Levy flinched dramatically at the noise. He thought it was amusing to do this when I crunched the gears or drove into a pothole or over debris. I wished he could take over for a spell, and see how he liked trying to control the Monster during a night raid with only a one-and-a-half inch slit of headlight beam showing. The Monster was a fair cow to manage, especially wearing rubber boots. I needed to double de-clutch after every gear change and my muscles were developing muscles from pulling at the steering wheel.

But Levy was not allowed to drive. He had been rejected for military service because of epilepsy, and it had been impressed upon me that he was under no circumstances to get behind the wheel of one of our precious ambulances.

And I found his theatrics insulting, because I knew I was a good driver. I had learned to drive in my early teens and I prided myself on being able to handle just about anything with wheels. I'd been put through an interesting test of my driving skills when I volunteered for the Ambulance Service. With a full pail of water in the foot well of a car I had to drive around London in the blackout without spilling a drop. That had been a doddle compared to transporting beer in my father's truck from Kalgoorlie to Kookynie along rough desert tracks.

'The guns seem awfully close,' I said. I could feel their rhythmic pounding vibrating in my chest as I turned onto the Euston Road.

'Probably a mobile unit,' Levy replied.

A minute or so later a spray of shrapnel clattered onto the ambulance roof and the road around us, making a loud tinkly sound, like cutlery tipped onto a table. Shrapnel – the steel and tin fragments of spent anti-aircraft shells – fell everywhere when the guns were firing. It was more than simply a nuisance and a risk to the ambulance tyres. The fragments were red hot as they fell and they could maim or even kill when they hit exposed flesh. I drove over them carefully and the Monster continued on her rumbling journey.

I mused that shrapnel was just one of the many things that could kill or maim civilians in an air raid. They could also be crushed by fallen masonry, choke on brick dust, be gassed, drown when a burst water main flooded a shelter, burn in a firestorm, be torn apart by bomb fragments, be cut to pieces by flying glass, or succumb to the sheer force of the blast itself.

In my weeks of driving the Monster in this Blitz I had become an expert on death; it haunted my waking hours and my dreams. My greatest horror was the thought of encountering a parachute mine. Even the biggest high explosive bomb was as nothing compared to a naval mine designed to blow up ships. They were dropped over London attached to parachutes to float silently, gracefully downwards wherever the wind took them, and they demolished whole city blocks twenty-two seconds after impact.

'Turn left at the next street,' said Levy, and I nodded.

I relied on him for directions, as I had not lived long enough in London to be able to navigate through a blacked-out city in which all street signs had been removed. Before we left the station he always checked the wall map that was kept updated as to closed streets and obstructions, but the map could not be relied upon as the closures were apt to change without warning.

The moon illuminated our way to some extent, but it was a mixed blessing. On such moonlit nights the Thames, with its unmistakable twists and turns, was like a path of molten lead that took the raiders straight to the heart of London. We had copped a thrashing tonight because of the full moon.

'They used to call it a hunter's moon,' I said to Levy, raising my voice to be heard over the noise around us. 'Now we know it as a bombers' moon.'

'It's the same thing, I suppose,' he said. 'Both end in moonlit death.' His voice dropped. 'Look at that!'

We were both silent, watching in awe as scores of bombers flew across the moon. It was a beautiful, chilling sight.

'Turn right here, please, Brennan,' said Levy. He was taking me on a circuitous route to avoid the wreckage of the last few weeks. But soon we encountered fresh damage.

A barrier had been set up across High Holborn, where a pile of rubble towered over a burst water main that spouted inside a huge crater on the road. Dark figures crawled over the debris and I wondered how many had been trapped inside the wreckage.

'That was the Holborn Empire,' he said in a tight voice. 'Vera Lynn was to sing there last night.'

Diversion signs directed me into a narrow street where we bumped over more rubble and debris. I drove carefully, but without warning the ambulance thumped down in a sickening lurch, bouncing up again with a crunch.

My heart thudded and I slowed to a crawl as I tried to determine if there was any damage to the chassis or wheels, if anything was out of whack. The engine sounded as loud and rough as always and I let out a breath I barely knew I'd been holding.

'Damn potholes,' I said. 'They're impossible to see in this blackout.'

'Is the old rust bucket all right?' asked Levy.

'She's apples.' Levy liked it when I spoke 'Aussie' and I would sometimes lay it on thick for him.

'I take it that means all is well.'

'Too right.' I peered out of the windscreen and frowned at the empty sky. 'Do you think the raiders have gone?'

'Probably not,' said Levy. 'Turn right here and pull over, if you'd be so kind, Brennan. I need a cigarette, and I'd rather smoke outside this rattle trap.'

'Don't you get enough smoke at the incidents?'

He threw me a wry smile and said nothing. I pulled over and switched off the engine. We got out and stood together, leaning against the ambulance as Levy smoked his cigarette. There was a ghost of day over to the east. Dawn was very close.

In front of us a tall brick wall had crumbled to dust, revealing an area of lawn and tall trees. Two big craters pitted the grass and several trees had fallen. Behind us were the usual dirty Georgian houses of Bloomsbury. Most of the windows were gone, because the force of a blast sucked out glass, and the footpath and road were littered with shimmering shards. Dust swirled around us, smelling of smoke.

'Gray's Inn Gardens,' said Levy, gesturing with his cigarette towards the garden. 'We're nearly back at Woburn Place.' He pointed upwards, drew my attention to a tangle of squiggly white lines in the lightening sky to the east. Now a schoolboy grin lit his face. 'Our boys have been fighting the buggers. Hope they got some of 'em.' I could hear the excitement in his voice.

We traced together the remnants of the dogfights that had taken place between the RAF and the Luftwaffe not long before.

Levy murmured, 'They shall mount up with wings as eagles.'

'The Bible?' I asked.

'King James Version; it was rammed down our throats at school – perhaps they harboured hopes of my conversion. Isaiah, chapter forty. It's pretty much the same in Hebrew, and it seems apposite. I know a fighter pilot.'

'The one who'll take me over the rainbow in his Hurricane?'

'The very chap.'

In my mind's eye I saw an eager young man, like the ones in the newspaper photographs, a 'Mae West' over his shoulder, cigarette in hand, smiling into the camera as he waited to jump into his plane and give what for to the enemy.

'He says Hurricanes might not be as sexy as Spitfires, but they're more reliable.' Levy was still staring into the sky.

My mental picture shifted to a keen-eyed man, leaning against a Hurricane, unsmiling and determined.

Levy looked down at his hands, clasped in his lap. 'We were at Harrow together; he was another outsider.'

My picture of Levy's friend shifted again. Now he was a thin faced, dark-eyed man, a twin of Levy with the same ferocious intelligence and intensity, the same goofy sense of humour and innate kindness.

The All Clear sounded, that long steady siren note announcing the raiders had departed from our skies, retreating from the Spitfires and Hurricanes, our daylight defenders.

'Come on,' I said. 'Let's get back or they'll send out a search party.'

Levy glanced at his watch. 'It's nearly six and we've just had the All Clear. You worry too much, Brennan.'

Our sixteen-hour night shift ended at nine. We were on a spell of alternate nights, so after this shift we would not be on again until five o'clock the following afternoon. After three night shifts we had a two-day break, then a week of six eight-hour day shifts from nine until five.

I pressed the starter and the engine sputtered into life. We drove in silence for a while, feeling a little rested after our brief moment of peace. The Monster rattled on through London's streets. Rich streets or poor streets, after weeks of this Blitz they all shared an air of dusty desolation, a sort of shabby equality.

More than just buildings had fallen in this Blitz. It seemed to me that Jack was as good as his master in a ruined city, and after thirteen months of war the English system of class had become as shaky as a bombed mansion. I exulted in the thought. Australia was a great deal more egalitarian than Britain, but even there I had suffered at the hands of people who thought themselves better by reason of birth. At the boarding school my mother had sent me to were girls who lived in big houses by the river staffed by servants, and some of these girls had delighted in tormenting the small country girl whose father ran a hotel.

People were on the streets now, and they looked up as we drove past. They were pale and many looked tired, which wasn't surprising after a night in the shelters, but they did not seem miserable or defeated. On the contrary, most appeared cheerful. Some of them waved and smiled at us.

At St Pancras station I was forced into a complicated detour by a large yellow notice, 'DANGER – UNEXPLODED BOMB'. The Old Grey Mare – the grey painted car allocated to bomb reconnaissance – was parked at the corner. I sent up a quick prayer for the disposal squad, who would be racing the clock to disarm the bomb.

'No rest for the wicked,' said Levy, as we drove past.

He found it hard to remain silent, and often tried my patience with such pointless remarks. I ignored him to concentrate on the road. We were nearly at the station.

In Woburn Place, opposite Russell Square, not far from the ruddy Edwardian grandeur of the Hotel Russell and around the corner from the Russell Square Underground Station, was a large mansion block called Russell Court. It rather dominated that part of Bloomsbury. The Bloomsbury auxiliary ambulance station was located there and in the building's basement garage were kept the five ambulances and the six cars used to transport the walking wounded.

By the time we arrived at the station it was an effort for me even to drive down the ramp into the garage, and when I opened my door I nearly fell out of the cabin. The concrete floor seemed to sway as I pulled off my steel hat and, when I removed my eye shield, my eyes were sore and gritty with fatigue. I massaged my scalp with dirty fingers, trying to ease the knots of tension. When I blinked at my watch, the small dial showed six-thirty. I had hoped it was later. Still, if things were quiet now, I could grab some breakfast before helping Levy clean the Monster. We were obliged to leave her spick and span and free of blood for the day shift.

Poor old Monster, the night had added some dents and dings to her body. I saw them as scars of battle and gave her a pat before heading to the women's washroom to clean off some of the grime.

CHAPTER THREE

Maisie Halliday was in the washroom, also trying to wash away the dirt that collected during a hard shift. She was a tall, dark-eyed girl of nineteen with long legs and a calm disposition, who worked at the Trocadero as a dancer when she wasn't driving ambulances. She had joined us only a couple of weeks before and I had not had much chance to speak to her, but from what I had seen I was fairly sure I would like her.

I greeted Maisie and looked in the mirror. My face was not just dirty, it was a varicoloured streaky mess of grime and blood. I groaned, picked up a bar of soap and turned on the tap. A few minutes later my skin was clean, but bright red from scrubbing and the icy water.

Maisie looked at her own reflection and laughed. 'This job is murder on the complexion.'

'You're a dancer, aren't you? I suppose you know how to cover it all up with make-up.'

She nodded. 'I do, but I wonder sometimes if the little nicks we always seem to pick up at the incidents will mark my face for life. I'm terribly afraid it could hamper my chances at Hollywood stardom when this war is over.'

I wondered if she were serious, until I caught sight of the twinkle in her eyes.

We walked together out of the washroom and headed for the canteen to grab breakfast.

'Are you really interested in acting?' I asked, as we tucked into our baked beans and bacon.

Her expression became dreamy. 'No. I'm a dancer. After this is all over my dream is to head back to France. Before the war I had a peachy job in the Riviera as an exhibition dancer at a big hotel. Good tips and I could laze around on the beach all day, working on my tan.' She threw me a wicked smile. 'Lots of rich men, happy to squire me around.' Her smile faded and she finished bitterly, 'But the war put paid to all that.'

'I was in the Riviera for a few months in 1938,' I said, 'working as a governess for a Czech family. That was in the winter season, though.'

'A titled family?' asked Maisie.

'Actually, yes. Count Szrebesky. I looked after his two daughters for a year and a half. The family hovel was in Prague, but they always wintered in the Algarve. Why did you suppose he had a title?'

She grinned and touched her nose. 'All the titled European families winter in the Riviera. I suppose you speak excellent French.'

'I do, actually. And German, but I don't like *that* language much anymore.'

'I met a dreamy Frenchman in Cannes in '38,' she said on a sigh. 'But my French wasn't up to it. We ended up simply smiling and miming, which is no way to further a friendship.'

Now it was my turn to sound bitter. 'You can't trust the dreamy titled men on the Riviera. They may be charming to your face, but they're often rotters.'

'Therein lies a tale, I'll bet. What happened?' she asked sympathetically.

'It's a common story, I suppose. Young woman, romantic setting, handsome man. He pursued me until he discovered that I was travelling with the Szrebesky family only as a governess and not as a friend or relation. All of a sudden, my charms were not so charming. He dropped me cold.' My tone was light, but that was to hide the fact that it still hurt, to have been so abruptly dropped because I wasn't 'one of them'.

'What was the blighter's name?' asked Maisie.

'Henri, Comte de Valhubert. He was extraordinarily handsome and ridiculously charming.'

She laughed. 'Then I expect you're not the first to have been treated badly by him. The stories I heard about those young aristos.' She smiled. 'I'm rarely romantic about such things. Does that make me sound shallow?'

'No. Sensible. He wasn't the only one, but was the most charming and the most offensive. First he let me know that it would be unsuitable, *pas convenable*, as he put it, for us to be seen together in public, given my background. Then he made a pass at me and suggested we go somewhere private instead. For a while I thought I had a sign on my forehead – Australian innocent, open to advances.'

Maisie laughed. 'It wasn't you, Lily. Gosh, you might as well say the fox is open to the advances of the hounds.'

'It hurt me badly at the time,' I admitted, 'but I've taken it as one of those lessons in life we all need to learn. Mind you, I'm very grateful to have got it learned and put it behind me.'

'How did you come to be a governess in Prague in the first place?'

'That's simple. I was a teacher back home in Australia, and I wanted to see the world.'

The answer wasn't nearly so simple really, but how could I explain to Maisie the almost overwhelming compulsion I had to escape my life as a country schoolteacher and come to Europe.

'Did the world live up to your expectations?' she asked. 'Handsome scoundrels excepted.'

I took a sip of tea while I pondered my answer. Throughout my childhood I had been taught that Europe, and especially Britain, was far superior to Australia in every way. I had accepted this without question. I was also a voracious reader and almost every book I read was set in Britain. I lived in the desert and dreamed of bluebell woods, picnics with Nanny in Hyde Park and snowy Christmases. Once I was able to understand French and German well enough, I read books written in those languages too, and it seemed to me that my life would not be complete until I had seen the countries they described.

So I saved every penny I could from my teaching and begged my parents for assistance. They could see that war was brewing and tried to convince me to stay in Australia, but I had no interest in their words of caution.

'At first it seemed that I was living in a fairy tale made up of all the books I'd read,' I said to Maisie. 'Mind you, I had on pretty thick rose-coloured glasses.'

I had arrived in London on a cold February day in 1938 determined to love the city. And so I did, despite the dark winter days and the reeking smoky air. I had seen only a tiny part of the city, however, before I left for the Continent, and it was not until I returned to England and joined the Ambulance Service last October – was it really only a year ago? – that I first saw the East End slums. Now that had been an education. It was then I realised that there was more to London than glittering Mayfair, the bright West End and quaint Bloomsbury. Nothing could ever make me dislike London, but the East End had been a corrective to my innocent delight in the city.

'Lily? Are you wool-gathering?' Maisie had leaned over and tweaked my arm. 'Did the glasses stay rosy?'

'For a while – and I still love London, although I'm well aware now that it's not perfect. I wasn't here long before the Szrebesky family offered me a job as governess. It was when I arrived in Prague that I really thought I was in heaven. I adore Prague.'

'Were the family good to work for?'

'I was very fond of the two girls, Leonor and Karolina, and the countess was always nice to me, but the count was a fascist. Charming, but a fascist. I had very little to do with him, thankfully.'

Maisie pushed aside her empty plate and concentrated on what I was saying. 'So I suppose he would have been happy when Germany made Czechoslovakia a so-called protectorate.'

My surprise that she was interested in this must have shown. She laughed. 'We've all become experts in politics in the last few years. I was in Cannes then, and I thought it was jolly awful of France and Britain to let Hitler take over Czechoslovakia like that.'

'Count Szrebesky was one of the men who signed the invitation to Hitler to "save" the country,' I said. 'And the Germans marched straight in.'

'I've read in the papers that the Nazis don't treat the Czechs very well.'

'No,' I said bitterly, 'they don't. It wasn't long before they were persecuting Jews and murdering protesting students.'

Now Maisie seemed surprised, by my vehemence, and I swallowed back my anger. 'I'm sorry. It's just that I was there when the Nazis marched into Prague. I wasn't able to get out for two weeks, and that was enough time to make me realise what's in store for Britain if Hitler manages to take control.'

'He won't,' said Maisie cheerfully.

I wished I could be so sure, but I put a smile on my face. 'No, he most certainly will not,' I agreed.

We finished our breakfast and moved to the common room where, despite my best intentions, I ended up asleep in an easy chair.

When I awoke, voices around me were spouting nonsense that would have made Hitler proud.

'The Jews run the black market, everybody knows that.'

Sam Sadler was mouthing off, as usual. I lay still in my chair, too tired to open my eyes, pretending still to be asleep. Levy obviously was not in the room and nothing I could say would change views held since childhood, heard from parents and neighbours, now entrenched as Truth.

Jews were Different. Their ways were subtle and unknowable. They did not celebrate the great festivals of Christmas and Easter so beloved in English households. They were Different and therefore to be feared and mistrusted. The Germans might be the Enemy, but they were basically Like Us. The Jews, on the other hand, were Different.

Most of the men and women at the ambulance station were decent people who put up with hardship, long hours and poor pay to help out in this terrible war. We were a wide cross-section of society, ordinary people who had taken on great responsibility in these extraordinary times. I liked most of them very much, but I had grown up in a bush pub and I was well aware that people were not always good and motivations were not always simple.

'The Yids are the only ones making money out of this war. They're making a killing while the rest of us are dying like flies.'

'Ruddy parasites they are, living off of mugs like us.'

Sam Sadler again, now joined by Fred Knaggs. Levy referred to them as spivs, but in Australia we would have called them lairs. They wore cheap, tight suits and scented hair oil and they angled their hats low on their foreheads. Somehow they gave the impression of being both shrewd and stupid, these scrawny men with East London accents, sharp features and nervous energy.

When not at the station, Knaggs was a tic-tac man at a local dog track and Sadler apparently moonlighted as a dance-band leader at a nightclub in Soho. Levy and I were convinced their main occupation was dealing on the black market, which made their comments particularly annoying. Certainly, they always had scarce items available for purchase, such as stockings, watches, perfume and food. Many at Woburn Place used their services, but Levy and I kept clear of them. Levy had earned their undying enmity by telling them once that while he couldn't give a toss about their black-marketeering, if he ever heard they were involved in looting from bombed houses he would report them to the police.

A girlish voice joined the conversation. 'It's the Jews that started the Great War. People don't know that, but it's true. They wanted the brightest and the bravest in Europe to kill each other.'

That was Nola Fripp; her fast, breathless way of talking always made me feel anxious. My jaw tightened at the offensive words.

'They want power and wealth,' she went on, 'and they're getting it through the big companies. It's a conspiracy. The government is too stupid to see it, and anyway, they've infiltrated the government and the City.'

I pictured the silly young woman who was talking. In her early twenties, Fripp was thin to the point of emaciation. She was the ambulance attendant no one wanted because she often became hysterical during air raids. Her father was high up in the War Office and I wondered if she was spouting the unofficial official line.

A man's voice joined the conversation.

'Well, a great many people would agree with you that it's the Jews who really run this country.'

That was Jack Moray. If the spivs were an annoyance, Moray was a thorn that burrowed deep into my side. He had joined us at Woburn Place in January and within a week had become the right-hand man of our station officer, Mrs Coke, and been appointed her deputy. It was basically a desk job, and he rarely went out to incidents. A dark-haired man in his thirties, his teeth were large and not quite even, which gave him a disturbing, almost vulpine look that some women obviously found attractive. It matched his offhand cynical manner and cruelly amusing sense of humour, which he often directed at Levy.

Moray dressed suavely and his accent was cultivated, but anyone with an ear for vowels could sound posh and the old school tie he wore could have been bought in a shop. I knew what my father would have made of him. Dad would have looked Moray up and down and pronounced him 'flash as a rat with a gold tooth'. Such men might be well-dressed and well-groomed and well-spoken, but some instinct told you they were never to be trusted.

I was almost roused to argue the point with Moray and Fripp. Or rather, since intellectual argument was not my forte, to tell them that they were a pair of stupid idiots who were parroting nonsense. But then George Squire spoke and derailed my train of thought.

'Well, I'd never trust a Jew,' he said.

I sat up and glared at him. 'What about Levy?' I asked, because I had always thought Squire liked Levy. 'You trust Levy to go out into the Blitz and risk his life for others, don't you?'

Squire was a former boxer, not a tall man, but he had big hulking shoulders. At present he was hunkered over the oil heater, and when he reached out his hands to the warmth I was struck by how large they were. He turned to face me.

'I don't mean Levy.'

'But Levy *is* a Jew,' I replied, barely remembering to omit *you stupid idiot*.

'Yeah. But Levy's different. I'm speaking in a – a general sense. I don't like Jews in general. Don't trust 'em.'

How could I respond to that? Everyone knew what was happening to the Jews under Nazi rule; the newspapers had been reporting massacres in Poland, the systematic stripping of all their human rights and dignities in Germany and its 'protectorates'. And yet these ordinary Londoners were still willing to trot out the old stereotypes that could result in such inhumanity.

'How can you say such rot when you know what's happening in Europe?' My hands were in tight painful fists. 'You must have read how the Nazis are murdering Jews in Poland. I saw what they did in Prague. I was there when Nazi supporters smashed Jewish shops, trying to whip up enthusiasm for the Nazis before the invasion. I saw an old Jewish shop owner being beaten in front of me. It was terrible, they were vicious thugs. I tried to help him, but—'

'You tried to help him?' Moray seemed surprised.

'Of course I did! Would you have just stood there? Would you? He was old, helpless. They broke his windows and when he came out they broke his body.'

There were six of them. I'd tried to pull them off the old man; I hit them and kicked at them, but they just laughed at me and pushed me aside so that I landed heavily on the footpath. I'd lain there, dazed, until my friends pulled me back into the crowd and then away into the maze of little streets. I had no idea if those friends were still alive.

'Of course we don't condone *that* sort of behaviour,' said Myra Harris, a plump woman of fifty-odd with a mop of wiry black curls speckled with grey. She was sitting in a Lloyd Loom chair, bent over a half-knitted balaclava as her needles clicked comfortably. 'This is England. Things like that don't happen here.'

I stared at her. Didn't she know the Czechs had thought things like that didn't happen there, either?

'Levy can be very sarcastic,' said Stephen Armstrong. He was a pale and spotty boy of seventeen. When I turned to face him, he had flushed a bright red, perhaps in memory of Levy's sarcasm. Levy did not suffer fools, and Armstrong could be remarkably stupid on occasion.

Harris was nodding in agreement.

'And how many Jews do you see in uniform?' asked Fripp.

'Lots,' I snapped. 'Levy has two brothers in the army.'

Moray laughed. 'In the pawnbroker battalion?'

'Don't be offensive,' I snapped. 'One's a doctor in the Medical Corps and the other is in a tank regiment. They're both serving in North Africa.'

'Well, why isn't he with them?' said Fripp.

I forced myself to reply calmly, as though I were talking to a misbehaving child. 'Levy tried to join the army but was rejected on medical grounds.'

'I don't buy the illness story,' replied Moray. 'I've never seen a healthier looking specimen. Don't be naive, Brennan. Levy took this job to avoid military service.'

'That's a damn lie.' I was no longer calm; my whole body thrummed with anger. 'You know it's not true.' I looked around at the smug faces.

Knaggs began to hum the tune to 'Onward Christian Soldiers', clearly referring to the version played by Charlie and his Orchestra in the German propaganda broadcasts each Wednesday and Saturday. I had often thought the government would be horrified to know just how many of us listened to those broadcasts. Yes, we did so in order to laugh at Lord Haw-Haw, but mainly to listen to better music than was played by the BBC.

But the Germans also used the broadcasts to spread their anti-Jewish propaganda, and often played a song the English fascists apparently sang in the 1930s to the tune of 'Onward Christian Soldiers'. The song referred disparagingly to wealthy and influential English Jews but the words were generally anti-Semitic, nasty and slanderous.

As Knaggs hummed, everyone in that room now seemed to be watching me. Sadler was grinning, Fripp had a small, guarded smile and even Harris had ceased knitting and was regarding me with an unblinking gaze that was somehow intimidating. I felt trapped, surrounded by enemies who had judged me and found me wanting. And beneath it all I felt a brooding intent, observing and manipulating. I wanted to speak, but I could find no words, no voice. As if I were under water.

Then Maisie's light, pretty voice interrupted Knaggs's tune. She was standing in the doorway, frowning. 'I think you're all being beastly unfair. And you're being racialist. I hate that.'

'Halliday's right.' The Hon. Celia Ashwin had joined Maisie, surveying the room with her usual sangfroid.

Celia Ashwin was in her early twenties and a thoroughbred, from the auburn hair framing her smoothly oval face in a loose bob to her aristocratically narrow hands and feet. Levy dismissed her as an empty-headed glamour puss; he called her the station's sizzler, because her lop-sided smile and spectacular figure played havoc with the men there. Her response was to treat them all with a mixture of overt boredom and superciliousness.

Knaggs stopped his humming.

'In this station we rely on each other to get the job done.' Celia's voice was clipped and coldly well-bred. 'Levy does his job and as far as I can see, he does it well. That should be enough for all of you, whether or not you like him or his race.'

Celia could use her voice as a weapon, and this time it cut like a lash. Or perhaps it was the ingrained English respect for her class, but the response was immediate. Armstrong's spots became a deeper red. Sadler and Knaggs looked down at the grubby deck of cards in front of them, while Nola Fripp mumbled what might have been an apology and all the others went back to whatever they had been doing. Moray, however, affected to be unperturbed. He smiled at Celia and I thought I saw him wink.

She ignored him and nodded a greeting to me as she entered the room.

Her defence of Levy had surprised me, as her husband was a high-ranking member of the British fascists, who was now incarcerated with Oswald Mosley. Celia had joined the ambulance service in May, not long after he had been arrested as a threat to public safety.

My time at boarding school and my experience at the Riviera had taught me to mistrust those who had been born into luxury, so Celia's upper-crust background and fascist connections made me wary of her. By chance, we had flats in the same building, but had never been more than superficially friendly.

Levy strolled into the common room, and I noticed her cheeks redden. 'I'm ready to call it a night,' he said to me, giving me his special, sweet smile. He turned to Maisie and gave her the same smile, which she returned. But when he looked at Celia, his smile faded into an ironic twist. She ignored it and walked past him to take a seat next to Fripp.

Maisie slipped into the seat beside me. 'Don't let them worry you with their silly comments,' she whispered.

'They don't,' I said.

31

I glanced at my watch and was surprised to see that it was almost nine. Our shift was nearly over. As Levy sauntered towards us, I lifted my arms in a stretch and frowned at him as I remembered. 'We need to clean the Monster,' I said, as he sat down.

But we had already run out of time: I could hear the voices of the day shift as they arrived.

'It's done. You looked whacked, so I let you sleep.'

Around us the conversation had switched to speculation about the German invasion. We expected it any day, so it was a favourite topic at present.

Squire's booming voice declared: 'We're better off without the frogs. Now we can get on with the job, and no more messing about! We're good and ready for whatever that Hitler throws at us.'

I leaned towards Levy. 'Whatever would I do without you?' I whispered.

CHAPTER FOUR

A week later, at the end of an eight-hour day shift, I emerged from the garage into a chilly October evening. Celia Ashwin rode past me on her bicycle and gave me a slight wave. It was five o'clock Saturday, and I had a break now until a week's night shift started at five on Monday afternoon.

I rubbed my eyes, feeling tired and dispirited after completing several mortuary runs during the shift. During the day, we used the ambulances for all manner of things – carting bread to the hospitals, transporting medical supplies, picking up victims of the daylight raids or road accidents – and we also transported bodies and body parts from bomb sites to the morgues.

I found this deeply distressing, especially when the bodies were those of children, or were extremely mutilated. Levy gallantly tackled the more revolting tasks himself, but I still found it difficult to shrug off the terrible things I had seen.

It was a cold afternoon. Scrappy dark clouds raced across the sky and rain was threatening. I began walking briskly to warm myself up and had gone some distance before I realised that in my hurry to leave the station I had left behind my umbrella. I looked at the sky. It could go either way. My flat was only a ten-minute walk away and I decided to risk it.

St Andrew's Court on Gray's Inn Road was a modern serviced apartment building. Because so many young men were away in the forces and anyone who could afford it had fled London when the bombing began, St Andrew's had become a haven for single women such as myself. I enjoyed living there. My one-bedroom flat was cleaned every second day and I could dine when it suited me in the service restaurant on the ground floor. The set-up was similar to a boarding house but with a great deal more autonomy.

That evening, however, I was exhausted and the ten-minute walk home seemed interminable. By the time I turned the corner into Gray's Inn Road my steps were unsteady and I suspected that the woman in the ugly brown hat who brushed past me thought I was under the influence of alcohol. She gave me a most disapproving look down her long and bony nose. I smiled at her but she turned away with a sniff, disdainful of my shabby appearance, no doubt. Or perhaps she took objection to my wearing trousers in public. It had become much more common now we were performing the traditionally male jobs, but it was only really acceptable if trousers were part of a recognisable uniform. This was one of the problems women ambulance drivers faced in not yet having formal attire.

Women were wearing uniforms all over London: the Air Force blue of the WRAF, the khaki tunic and skirt of the ATS, the navy blue of the Wrens, the buff felt hat and green pullover of the Land Army, the navy-blue trouser suits of the River Emergency Service, the bluish-green tweed coat and felt hat of the WVS, and the red cross cap and apron of the Auxiliary Nurses. Londoners were used to women in uniform and liked to see them on the streets.

The Ambulance Service had assured us that uniforms would be provided 'in good time', but until then we had been issued only a shapeless grey cotton coat that some wag had christened the 'flit coat', after the man in the Flit advertisement who dressed like that to kill flies, a gabardine cap with optional ear-flaps – very fetching! – and, of course, our black steel hat, embellished with a white 'A' for ambulance.

So I wore a uniform of my own devising: blue gabardine trousers, white shirt, a Harrow school tie (provided by Levy for a lark), blue pullover and black lace-up shoes. It was not a stylish or flattering ensemble but it was practical in the ambulance and on a bomb site. Unless I was wearing the flit coat and steel hat, however, or someone stood close enough to see the Ambulance Service badge I used as a tiepin, I more nearly resembled a short, badly dressed male impersonator than an ambulance officer.

I felt a drop of rain and when I looked up the sky had clouded over. More raindrops fell as I plodded past the identical dirty porticos of the identical dirty red brick three-storeyed buildings that lined the street. The rain grew heavier and I quickened my pace, dodging other pedestrians who blundered around me, umbrellas up and faces down.

At last St Andrew's Court was in sight, almost aggressively Art Deco in style. It had been built only four years before, so had not yet darkened into the grubby conformity of its Victorian neighbours and my heart lifted to see its clean modern lines. The metal window frames and delicate iron balustrades on each balcony were painted a bright blue that stood in relief against the stark white walls. A decorative tracery was picked out in blue on the entrance doors too, but the tape that was criss-crossed all over them to prevent the glass shattering and the thick blackout blinds that stayed up day and night rather spoiled the effect.

I enjoyed living in a modern flat, where the rooms held no ghosts of the past. I had grown to love London, and it was like a hammer blow to see so many beautiful and ancient buildings now in ruins, but often the sheer age of the city weighed me down. I came from a place where the imprint of human history was no more than a tickle on the landscape – the long occupation of Aboriginal people had left no built relics. Kookynie had been just a patch of red earth in the desert only forty-eight years before.

Sometimes I found it hard to comprehend that London's history was measured in millennia, and that the city was not so much built, as built over. Roman foundations were covered with medieval cobblestones, which were overlaid with Victorian brickwork. Manor estates turned into Rococo pleasure gardens, which in turn became Edwardian hospital grounds. St Andrew's

Court itself had been constructed on the ruins of an old church and it stood in front of the church's burial ground. In the 1860s the graveyard had become a park, Trinity Gardens, and I would sit there on fine days to read a book or contemplate the gravestones.

I ducked across the road at a jog as I tried to outrun the increasingly heavy rain. I had almost made the other side when a car came out of nowhere, blaring its horn as it headed straight for me. I felt suspended in time, like a kangaroo caught in the headlights, transfixed by the knowledge of certain death.

The car stopped with a screech of brakes and curses from the driver and I was shaken out of my stupor. The utter fatigue of a few moments before had disappeared and I ran along the footpath to the doorway to St Andrew's Court, pushed open the door and entered into the eternal twilight of the gloomy blacked-out lobby.

I walked straight into what appeared to be a delegation. The door swung shut behind me as I pushed wet hair out of my eyes and blinked at Celia Ashwin, Pam Beresford, Katherine Carlow and Nancy Parrish, who had a firm hold on a tall RAF pilot. I was keenly aware that my hair was dripping wet, my jumper was sodden and smelled of wet sheep, and my damp trousers clung to my legs, but I gave them my biggest smile.

'No need for a welcoming party,' I said, 'though a dry towel wouldn't go amiss.'

'Enter our resident heroine, dripping, at stage left,' said Katherine, her thin, clever face alight with mischief. She was a few years older than me and had a sharp tongue, but I liked her. She had stood by me through one of the worst periods of my life.

Before the war, Katherine had been a junior couturier at one of the best London fashion houses. When her husband entered the navy, she joined the Auxiliary Ambulance Service. She was now deputy station officer at the big Berkeley Square station in the West End, and she was surely the best-dressed ambulance officer in London, looking stylish in an immaculately tailored brown tweed suit, cream silk blouse and a discreet string of pearls.

I brushed at my damp and filthy clothes. 'Forgot my umbrella,' I said. 'It's a trifle wet out there.'

Nancy tittered and held her captive pilot more tightly. She was not one of my favourites at St Andrew's; I had once overheard her say, 'I really don't know about Australians. They're so gauche. They laugh too much. Make one feel so very awkward.' At present she was laughing at me, and showing a lot of gum as she did so.

Nancy was married to an army man, now stationed in Cairo. Not long after he left England she had moved to St Andrew's from their home in the country, leaving their young son with her mother. Katherine referred to her as 'Nan the man-eater', or, if she was feeling particularly wicked, 'No-pants Nancy', because quite a few of the men she brought home to her flat did not leave until morning. Nancy was generally considered to be a beauty. She was dressed for a night out, in a yellow frock that clung rather alarmingly to her curves.

'Gracious, Lily,' she said, 'you look like a drowned—'

'Kitten,' cut in Pam, a bubbly twenty-year-old who was the daughter of a Tasmanian bishop and worked as a secretary at Australia House. She disapproved of Nancy on principle. I liked Pam. When I could, I would go to the pictures with her, or join her for dancing at one of the Australia House functions. I could let my hair down with Pam.

I smiled at her, but eyed the stairs for a quick escape. I wished everyone would leave and let me get to my flat. Water was dripping out of my jumper to pool on the tiles by my shoes and I was becoming very cold. As I moved towards the stairs Nancy further tightened her hold on the airman – did she think I was going to drag him away with me? The flight lieutenant had veiled grey eyes and a defensive, arms-crossed manner, which I thought was understandable in the circumstances. Without

Deborah Burrows

warning, and despite Nancy's best effort, he slipped out of her clutches with almost Houdini-like adroitness to stand warily beside her, watching me closely.

Katherine swept her hand towards him in a graceful gesture of introduction. 'Miss Lily Brennan, may I introduce Jim Vassy-something? I'm sorry, Jim, but your surname is unpronounceable. Lily here is our resident heroine. She saved a couple of kiddies last week by climbing into the ruins of a bombed building to get to them. In the middle of an air raid, mind you, and not knowing if there was a live bomb in there.' She paused for effect. 'There was, as a matter of fact. It went off soon after she'd got them out.'

'Do shut up, Katherine,' I said. The children's grandparents had sent me a touching letter, care of the station. That was all I needed by way of recognition.

Pam giggled. She did that a lot, to disguise, I think, the fact that she was a smart and competent young woman. She had completed first aid training soon after the Blitz began and now did three twelve-hour night shifts a week as a shelter officer at Gloucester Road Tube station.

Nancy made an impatient movement. 'And you think Jim just sits on his backside in his Spitfire?'

'I fly a Hurricane, Nan,' said Jim Vassy-something. 'You know that.' His voice was calm and deep and drawling, as coolly upper class as Celia's, or Levy's. I liked the sound of it.

Nancy ignored him and went on, 'He's already shot down five enemy planes,' she said. 'So he's an ace.' I could hear annoyance in her school-girlish boasting, not her usual standoffish style at all. So even posh Nancy could get a crush on a pilot, I thought.

'Oh, we're all heroes here,' drawled Katherine. 'Just as Churchill requires. Noses to the wheel, shoulders to the grindstone, blah blah, blood on the beaches, toil, tears and sweat. All defending the home front in our own ways.'

Jim stood easily, watching me with a slight smile.

'I'm delighted to meet you, Miss Brennan,' he said. 'Did I detect an Australian accent? You're a long way from home.'

He was at least a foot taller than my five feet and half an inch, with one of those lean bodies that seem almost gaunt. I guessed he was around my age. He had a pleasant enough face, of the type you imagined in the best gentleman's clubs, or at the Ritz or the Savoy or Claridge's, but his was given some gravitas by a hawkish nose and a surprisingly firm chin. Fine fair hair completed the picture.

I assumed that he was one of the type I had so often met here in London: beautiful manners, little personality and rather a childish sense of humour. He was undoubtedly brave, though, if he had not only survived the recent aerial war between the Luftwaffe and the RAF but was an Ace.

'It looked like you Poms needed some help,' I said. I ran my hand through my damp hair. My head always hurt at the end of a shift.

'Poms?' Nancy voiced her confusion.

'It's what they call the English in Australia,' said Celia, surprising me.

Jim Vassy-something said, 'The Aussies in my squadron use the word.' He addressed me. 'Is it from *pommes*? French for apples.'

It annoyed me that he assumed I could not speak French, especially as I had been told that my accent was excellent. So I replied in that language to tell him that although the origin of the word was not known, perhaps it related to rosy English cheeks.

'*C'est un mot que nous avons utilisé pendant de nombreuses années. Peut-être les Australiens pensent que les Anglais ont les joues rouges comme des pommes.*'

To my amazement, he blushed. Now he looked as young as Pam. His cheeks were two red blotches, just like pippins, and I laughed without thinking.

'*Touché*,' he murmured, and then he addressed me in a language I did not recognise, but I thought might be Russian or Polish.

'I beg your pardon,' I said.

'Just wondering,' he replied. 'Ready, Nan?'

Nancy smiled at him dreamily. 'I'll fetch my coat. Give me a mo, darling.' She flashed what I'd swear was a warning glance at me, then ducked up the stairs to her flat, leaving him facing the four of us.

'Daniel in the lion's den,' murmured Katherine.

Celia's mouth twitched. 'This lion is desperately in need of a nap,' she said. 'It was lovely to see you again, Jim. Please give my regards to your mother the next time you write.'

She headed upstairs.

He seemed to be on good terms with Celia, I thought, and wondered if he was as fascist in his views as her husband. It seemed unlikely, given that he was a pilot and was fighting the Nazis, but who knew what anyone was like, really?

'I've got a couple of Aussies in my squadron,' he said to me. 'I like them.'

Had he, ever so slightly, emphasised 'them'?

'Good-oh,' I replied, and immediately regretted it. Sometimes the Australianisms just slipped out. His smile returned and I felt my jaw tense.

'Fred Harland? Mike Corrs? They're Australians.'

'It's a big country.'

'Where, in that big country, do you hail from?'

'Western Australia. I grew up in the Eastern goldfields. My parents had a hotel near Kalgoorlie, before they moved to the city.'

As his smile broadened, I could imagine how he was seeing me now: categorising me as a barmaid from a rough goldfields town. Barmaid Brennan. That was what the posh girls at school had called me.

'What's your surname?' I asked. 'Katherine didn't really say.'

'Vassilikov. Ivan Vassilikov, actually, but I'm known as Jim.'

The name surprised me, as I had thought he was entirely English. On looking more closely, there was a hint of the Slav in his broad cheekbones and deep-set grey eyes. There had been Slavs working in the goldfields who came to my father's hotel.

Before I could reply, a metallic screech announced the arrival of the lift, and Nancy emerged with an exquisite Persian lamb coat over her arm. I hadn't seen it before, and wondered if it was a recent gift from one of her admirers. She placed it carefully across a chair to pull on her gloves and check her hair in the lobby's mirror.

'Poor Jim,' she said to her reflection. 'He only has a weekend's leave. So I'm helping him to enjoy it.'

He opened the door and Nancy scurried over to join him. They turned to say goodbye, like grand *seigneurs* surveying the peasants: the tall man in the blue-grey uniform of the heroes of our aerial war against the Germans and the pretty blonde girl in the sunshine yellow frock. Nancy smiled, showing white teeth under pink gums. *All the better to eat you with, my dear.*

'We'll be off, then,' said Nancy. 'Don't wait up.'

'As if,' muttered Pam.

Jim nodded in my general direction. I made my face blank as they left the hall.

'Of all the cheek,' Pam exploded once the door had closed. 'Don't wait up indeed. She's such a . . . a . . .'

'Spit it out,' drawled Katherine.

'She's a *b-i-t-c-h*. You know she is. She's a married woman. How can she play around like she does? Going out with all sorts of men and I know they stay the night. And then she has the cheek to show off the expensive gifts they buy her. She's nothing but a common who—'

'Wholly inappropriate language,' substituted Katherine, laughing. 'Aren't you the bishop's daughter? Yes, she is a bitch. But she's our resident bitch and we have to put up with her. As for her being married, well, hubby's away and while he's in Cairo little Nancy mouse will—'

The door opened and we froze as Jim re-entered the foyer.

'Nan forgot her coat.' He went over to the chair by the mirror and picked it up. 'I was at Cambridge with her husband,' he said, to no one in particular, then looked towards me. 'I'm only English by adoption, as you may have gathered from my name. I was born in Russia, and was seven when I came here. Do I qualify as a, er, Pom?'

As I pretended to consider the matter, he said, 'Why are you wearing my old school tie?'

'That settles it,' I said. 'If you attended Harrow, you're most definitely a Pom.'

He smiled and pulled the door shut with a snap as he left.

CHAPTER FIVE

Katherine, Pam and I stared at each other.

'I didn't think so at first, but now I'm sure he's got it – S.A.,' Katherine said. 'Sex appeal, darling,' she explained to Pam, who replied indignantly, 'I know that.'

'Can't see it, myself,' I said.

'Well, I think he's smashing,' said Pam. 'And a pilot to boot . . .' Her voice faded into a sigh.

The door opened again and Jim poked his head through once more. The three of us stood absolutely still, like wax figures in Madame Tussauds – before it was bombed.

'Forgot my gloves,' he said.

He walked over to a chair and picked them up. 'Regulations. We can't wear the greatcoat without the gloves. Madness.' He flicked me a glance. 'Are you fond of music, Miss Brennan?'

'Yes,' I said, surprised. 'And it's Lily.'

He nodded, and returned to the doorway. There he paused, swallowed, took a breath and, almost as an aside, addressed a point somewhere over my left shoulder.

'I hear they're playing Tchaikovsky in Regent's Park tomorrow. It's the last Sunday afternoon concert for the year. It should be a marvellous concert.'

'Glad to hear it,' I said.

'Begins at three o'clock.'

'What's that to do with me?' I added, but the door had already closed.

'We-ell,' said Pam.

'So he's not interested in our Nance,' said Katherine. 'And he just made a date with our Lil.'

'Shut up, Katherine,' I said. 'He didn't ask me out.'

'He certainly wasn't talking to me, or to Pam, when he mentioned a concert tomorrow.'

'Alas,' said Pam. 'I adore pilots.'

'You know perfectly well he was asking you out,' said Katherine.

'He's a friend of Nancy's, for heaven's sake.'

'Of her husband's.'

'If he wanted to meet me tomorrow he should have asked properly.'

He wasn't even all that attractive, I told myself. Far too tall and gangly, and that nose!

Katherine's smile broadened, became taunting. 'I thought he was a sweetie,' she said.

'Oh, he seems likeable enough,' I admitted. 'But it's a peculiar way to invite someone out.'

'Nancy told me about him,' Katherine went on. 'It's a duty visit – looking up the wife of a college friend who's away in the war.'

Pam sniggered. 'She'll still try to get him into bed.'

Katherine gave her a reproving look. 'Mind out of the gutter, please, Pamela. You heard him – it was before you arrived, Lily – he's staying at the home of a friend of his mother's tonight. Nancy looked most put out.' She smiled. 'Apparently he's a prince or count. Duke? Something like that.'

'What?' I laughed. 'Nancy's been spinning you a line and you've fallen for it hook, line and sinker.'

Katherine raised a shoulder. 'But it isn't a line. He really is some sort of Russian nobility. Although that means less than nothing now the Soviets are in power, of course.'

'Of course,' I repeated, sarcastically.

'You will go to Regent's Park, won't you?' Pam was wide-eyed. 'Oh, please do go. He's a fighter pilot.'

'I don't know. I'll think about it.'

'Going out tonight?' Katherine asked Pam, in an obvious change of subject.

'I'm on duty at the shelter. You?'

Katherine smiled. 'Dinner with friends. At Quags.'

Pam whistled. 'I hope they're paying. What about you, Lily?'

'It's been a tough day. The only company I want tonight is a hot bath – then a good book and the wireless. I've got to get out of these wet clothes.' I suddenly realised I was shivering.

'Meet me for supper in the service restaurant then,' said Pam.

I nodded, said goodbye to both of them and entered the lift. As it hauled me up to the third floor I heard Katherine's clear voice calling out, 'Be sure to use the hot-water bottle trick. Damp clothes can only lead to rheumatism.' Her voice became fainter. 'And dream tonight of pilots and grand music.'

Alone in my bathroom I looked at myself in the mirror. Ash and plaster dust flecked my brown hair, which was damp and flat and greasy after a day under a steel hat and exposure to the rain. My eyes were sunken with exhaustion and there were faint blue shadows underneath.

'You look like something the cat dragged in,' I said to my reflection. 'Flight Lieutenant Vassilikov must be the sort of man who feeds strays. Or has very odd taste in females.'

I grinned at my reflection. *Maybe he likes dimples*, I thought, as I popped a shilling in the meter. I brushed my teeth as the trickle of hot water filled the bath.

When I was clean and warm in my dressing gown, I took down my first aid kit from the shelf where it sat next to the tin of Poison Gas Ointment Number 1. We all had those tins, together with our gas masks. A gas attack was the ultimate horror, one we could only pray would not eventuate.

I dabbed antiseptic on the cuts and abrasions that had collected during the shift, wincing as the astringent lotion met broken skin. I always wore thick gloves and tried to cover as much of myself as possible, but gloves had to be removed sometimes. And my face was always exposed, despite my eye shields and steel hat.

In my bedroom I dressed for dinner, which was served in the restaurant on the ground floor. It was one of the advantages of our building that meals were prepared. They weren't particularly well-cooked, but they were no worse than boarding school fodder.

As I combed my damp hair in front of the dressing table mirror I glanced, as I always did, at the framed photograph standing beneath. A studio portrait of a young man in naval uniform, inscribed 'To Lily, love Denys'. It had stood there since he left for Scotland at the start of the war, and there it had remained after his death.

Denys Crawford and I had known each other only three weeks before we became unofficially engaged, in September 1939. Katherine and her husband introduced him to me and we 'clicked' immediately. It had been easy to fall in love. War had just been declared and we were fired up with the romance of it all and our imminent separation. We had parted with tears and promises and one night of madness before Denys sailed to Scapa Flow, in Scotland. He had died there a few weeks later, along with eight hundred other fiancés, husbands, lovers and sons, when the base was destroyed by enemy action. Four days after I heard of his death I resigned from my clerical job at Australia House and joined the Ambulance Service.

Poor Denys. It all seemed like a sweet dream now that a year had passed, now that I was living through a Blitz. The world had changed, and I had changed with it. Only fragmented memories remained of who he was, this man I'd thought I loved enough to marry. He had become a water-colour memory, one that was fading too quickly in the harsh light of wartime life.

Perhaps that was why I was so ambivalent about Flight Lieutenant Vassilikov's invitation. My life was busy and fulfilled. Becoming fond of a serviceman – especially a pilot – was a sure road to misery. Then again, it was only a concert and

I didn't even fancy the man all that much. Should I go and meet him tomorrow? I really could not decide.

Before I left the flat to head downstairs for dinner I used my little gas ring to boil some water for Katherine's hot-water bottle trick. I filled the bottle with boiling water, and hung it on a clothes hanger. Then I placed my wet clothes over it and hung it up. The garments were gently steaming when I left and I knew they would be dry in a few hours.

As I entered the restaurant I glanced at the blackboard, on which was chalked that evening's menu: tomato soup (undoubtedly tinned), boiled mutton, cabbage and potatoes, and chocolate blancmange for dessert. Meat, tea, cheese and other essentials were now rationed, although food was still in reasonable supply. I was entirely in favour of Lord Woolton's motto of 'a fair share for all of us', but meals were already monotonous and it could only get worse as the war dragged on.

Pam was waving to me and I went to join her. I had just sat down when a quiet voice asked if she could join us. It was Betty Wilkinson, whose husband had been killed at Dunkirk. Her frock hung loosely on her thin frame, and her swollen face and red-rimmed eyes announced that she had been weeping for much of the afternoon.

'Of course, please do,' I said, pulling back a chair. I received a vague, hesitant smile in response.

It had been more than four months since her husband's death, but Betty's grief was as raw as it had been in June. I felt achingly sorry for her, but could do nothing in the face of such unrelenting misery. Other tenants had begun to avoid her, making comments about Betty 'letting the side down' or 'laying it on too thick'. Her persistent suffering had become a confronting embarrassment to many of them, and now she gravitated towards Katherine, Pam and me on her infrequent visits to the restaurant, probably because we never asked her how she was, or took umbrage at her despondent silences.

Betty's dark eyes had sparkled with a newlywed's joy when she arrived at St Andrew's in May. Now there was a greenish tint in their depths, like that seen in the bottom of a dirty pond. She murmured a thank you and sat down, keeping her silence as Pam and I chattered over the meal. I noticed that, as usual, she ate very little.

'You're on night shift again next week?' Pam asked me.

I had a mouthful of soup and merely nodded.

'And that means your shift begins at five on Monday?'

I nodded again.

'I'm taking Monday off to do some shopping,' she said. 'What about an early movie? There's a new Robert Taylor at Leicester Square. Afterwards we could have tea at a Lyons before your shift.' She turned to Betty. 'You're very welcome, too, but I expect you are working.'

Betty murmured a polite refusal.

'Boring old Lyons,' I teased. 'I know a cafe in Soho that serves divine European pastries.'

'Even with rationing?'

I touched my nose. 'Ask them no questions . . .'

'Soho? Are you sure it's safe?' asked Pam, the bishop's daughter, rather primly.

'In the daytime, of course it is. All the best cafes are there.'

Pam nodded cheerfully. 'You're on, then. I'll meet you outside the cinema at noon.'

After the meal Pam headed off to the Gloucester Road Tube station. She would spend the night there, one of only two officers dealing with the needs of up to a thousand shelterers a night. Betty tried to slip away, but I urged her to join me for coffee, which was served in another room. There we sat alone in a corner sipping our drinks.

'I know I'm a wet blanket,' she said, breaking a short silence. 'The women here are sick of me. I try to be cheerful, really I do, but nothing means anything to me anymore.'

I put my hand on her arm, tried to say something bracing but she turned her head away and whispered, 'I wish I could die.'

My grip on her arm tightened. 'If you ever really feel like that, come and bang on my door. Or if I'm on duty, bang on Pam's door, or Katherine's. Come and talk to one of us.'

She nodded, still looking away. 'Don't worry, Lily. I'm not going to do it myself.' She sighed. 'Nights are the worst. I lie in bed wishing I could go out into the raid and let the Germans do it, but I'm too much of a coward. So I pray for one of the raiders to pick this building, drop a bomb and blow me to smithereens. It is unforgivable, I know.'

'Not unforgivable,' I said, really concerned now. 'You work for one of the ministries, don't you?'

'War Office. I can't talk about it.'

'If nights are the worst, why don't you join Pam on her evenings in the shelter? They are always looking for volunteers. I could speak to her about it. May I do that?'

She turned her head to look at me. 'Yes.' Her voice strengthened. 'Yes, that might be a good idea. If I can keep myself busy then perhaps . . .' Again she sighed.

The light was swiftly fading when I reached the sanctuary of my flat. I put up the blackout blinds before switching on the lamp and the gas heater and the wireless. The cool music of Benny Goodman and His Orchestra filled the room, and I settled down on the sofa to think things through about Jim Vassilikov.

Levy had mentioned a pilot friend, who flew a Hurricane and who had been with him at Harrow. Like Levy, he had been an outsider there. It was likely that a White Russian would be considered an outsider at Harrow, so it was odds-on that this was Levy's pilot friend. That made it a bit better prospect to meet him at Regent's Park.

I was still considering the question when the wailing notes of the Warning drowned Benny Goodman out. I let my head fall back as I debated whether to walk down to the cellar which the occupants of St Andrew's Court used as an air raid shelter or remain where I was. I decided I would take my chances in the flat. St Andrew's was a new building and solid, unlike the shaky eighteenth and nineteenth century structures that tumbled into bricks at the first shudder of a bomb blast. And I had seen too many people dug out of basement shelters – and too many of those had not been dug out alive.

The nine o'clock news began, as usual, with the chimes of Big Ben.

'Here is the news and this is Alvar Lidell reading it.'

I loved to hear his voice, but Alvar had no good news to report. The war dragged on. Two Italian destroyers had shelled a British convoy in the Red Sea; there had been damage sustained in raids over London and an unnamed 'coastal city' but few casualties; the RAF had engaged with the enemy and brought down several German planes with the loss of no British planes.

I was inclined to take comments like 'material damage is slight and casualties few' with a grain of salt. I knew how many bodies we delivered to the mortuaries. The BBC always dramatically understated the casualties. I wondered if they equally overstated the number of enemy aircraft shot down.

The news finished and the delicate notes of a piano piece played by Myra Hess trickled out of the wireless. Usually I would have listened with delight, but tonight it was unsatisfying somehow. I told myself it was because I was keyed up by the impending air raid and worried about Betty; it had nothing to do with Flight Lieutenant Vassilikov.

So I turned off the radio, picked out a poetry book from the bookshelf and flicked through to the poems of Lord Byron. He had been mad, bad and dangerous to know, and in my mind's eye he looked exactly like Levy.

'I defy you all,' I said, to no one, as the nightly noises began.

The distant drum-fire of the outer batteries. The crum-crum of the Regent's Park guns. Then the sharp notes of some nearer batteries. In the middle distance the rocket sound of the heavy guns in Hyde Park. And always, above the noise of the guns, was the dentist's drill of the German aeroplanes, circling round and round, waiting to drop their sticks of three bombs. I waited.

Then . . .

Crump, crump, crump.

CHAPTER SIX

I woke to a cold morning. Damp white mist swirled around the gardens and the sun was like a great orange ball. It was nearly winter, I realised disconsolately. It would be my second winter in England, and I was not looking forward to it at all. It was the darkness that had affected me the most last year. I expected that I would find it as miserable this year also, with the added bonus of nightly air raids. I couldn't help sighing. It was springtime in Perth now and my mother's roses would be in full bloom in our small garden.

On the table in the lobby, next to the cubicle that housed the building's telephone, were the letters that had been delivered for the occupants of St Andrew's in yesterday's second post. There were three letters for me, all from Australia. The flimsy aerograms were creased and a little grubby after their long journey. One was my mother's weekly epistle. I recognised Uncle Charles's scrawl on the second, and when I turned the third letter over, it was from a school friend. I was delighted at this tangible connection to home, but I sighed as I tucked the letters carefully into the pocket of my jacket; I would read them once I had breakfasted.

I had been away from Australia now for nearly three years, and I missed my family terribly. After so many letters, I knew what my mother's would contain: she would tell me that my father and my brother Ben were well, give me a small anecdote about each, and then concentrate on her 'war work'. Mum had formed a local Red Cross branch as soon as war was declared and now spent most of her time rolling bandages, packing parcels for

Australian prisoners of war and helping to run funding drives for Blitz victims, in between knitting scarves and jumpers for servicemen. From her letters, it seemed my mother was the same tiny ball of energy as she had been when she waved goodbye to me at Fremantle Dock on that hot January morning in 1938.

My father hated writing letters, but I knew he would have scrawled a message of love at the bottom of my mother's epistle, telling me that he missed me and longed to see my beautiful smiling face. He always wrote the same message, and it always made me cry. If I were lucky, my brother Ben, now fifteen and about as fond of letter writing as Dad was, would also have written me a short note.

I was well aware that my parents were desperate for me to return home, but they never pushed. Sometimes I wished I could leave London and sail back to Australia, but I knew the work I did in London was worthwhile and essential, and I had made up my mind not to leave until the war was over, no matter how many cold, dark winters I had to endure.

Breakfast in the service cafe was the usual porridge, followed by a small rasher of bacon set upon a generous pile of watery scrambled dehydrated egg. As I chewed I pondered the mystery of how Americans managed to make the dehydrated eggs taste exactly like chalk and what they did to manufacture that peculiarly dry yet slimy texture.

Somewhere in the course of the meal I made up my mind to take a walk around London. I thought I would clear my head and also see what damage last night's raid had caused. The newspapers were not allowed to publish detailed information about the bombings, in case it aided the enemy and hurt morale. We were all interested, of course, and Londoners wandered around the city streets, inspecting the damage and swapping gossip about the numbers of casualties.

If my walk took me in the direction of Regent's Park, I thought, so what? Jim Vassilikov was not bad looking, despite the nose. He was an RAF hero, most probably a friend of Levy's and, anyway, I enjoyed classical music concerts on fine autumn afternoons.

In my bedroom I stood in front of my wardrobe, gazing at its contents. I pulled out a pale green afternoon dress in lightweight wool that had been made for me in Prague before the war. I loved the dress, which was trimmed with green velvet on the collar and cuffs. Although clothing was not rationed, material was in short supply and it was becoming difficult to find pretty outfits. I wished I had spent more of my money on clothes when I lived in Prague, where women's fashion was as stylish as it was in Paris and the tailoring was excellent.

Silk stockings were also in short supply – we had been warned that there were to be no more available after 1 December – and rather than risk my last silk pair I made do with rayon. I slid my feet into a pair of low-heeled shoes – the dusty, shattered pavements and London's Blitz-blighted roads destroyed pretty shoes.

Should I wear gloves? Before the war, a lady would never be seen on the street without them, but the old rules were falling away as the war dragged on. I picked up a pair of soft dove-grey gloves and popped them into my handbag. If I did end up meeting Jim Vassilikov and if he took me somewhere nice for tea after the concert, I would slip them on then.

I patted on powder and rouge, swept mascara onto my lashes and pouted to apply the bright lipstick that brought out the golden highlights in my brown hair. There was a definite sparkle of excitement in my light-brown eyes – it had been a while since I had been out with an eligible male. I grimaced at my reflection in the mirror.

'He may not even turn up, you silly chump,' I said, and grimaced again. I wondered if he would recognise me, clean and all dolled up.

My precious bottle of Je Reviens was on my dressing table. I picked it up and stared at it for a moment, before replacing it, unopened.

'Not yet,' I murmured. 'No need to overdo it.'

Finally, I fluffed up my curls and placed my green felt hat at a rakish angle, then shrugged on my raincoat, which I firmly buttoned and belted for protection against not only rain but also the brick dust that had whirled constantly in London's air since the raids began. I slung my gas mask over my shoulder and headed for the door.

When I stepped down onto the footpath, the familiar smell, sour and chill, of bomb-blasted ruins assailed me. A block of flats along the street had been hit and the sight was a shock. Yesterday a sturdy building had stood there. Now it was a jumble of wood and bricks and plaster. The road outside the building was roped off and red warning lights flashed. Clean-up crews were at work. Their job, once the dead and wounded had been recovered, was to clear the road and footpath and make the site safe. They would engage in primary demolition and use wooden props to shore up the walls and doors and windows that remained.

It constantly amazed me how quickly repairs were carried out after a raid. A railway line might be wrecked by a bomb in the morning and be in use again in the evening. Our electricity had been restored earlier that morning, as had the gas supply. Every day lorries rumbled through the streets, carting away tons of bomb debris from damaged buildings.

I asked a lorry driver once where all of the rubble ended up and he told me, 'We're off to the 'Ackney Marshes. And if 'Itler keeps this up, it won't be long before there won't be any 'ouses in between.'

I had to ask Katherine what he meant and she sang the old music hall song for me with gusto, and in a Cockney accent.

Although they worked quickly, the crews did their job with an ear to the ruins. They were always listening, always hoping to find someone still alive. Of course, finding a live person after the rescue crews had been through the ruins was rare. It was the bodies that remained and these had to be recovered and removed for transfer to the mortuary in our ambulances.

The crew in front of me obviously had been working hard. Their shouted conversations and whistles competed with the thud and splatter of falling masonry. A couple of the men there knew me from my work and called out a greeting. I waved in reply.

The sun soon burned away the morning's mist and it shone brightly as I walked down Gray's Inn Road. I thought, not for the first time, that it was a terrible irony of this Blitz that it began in a golden autumn, when London should have been a delight. Now fallen leaves shared the streets with a sunlit shimmer of broken glass, sometimes inches deep. The air stank of cordite. Clear skies of cloudless blue, in peacetime so delightful, were deplored for making London an easy target for raiders. We were all waiting for a dose of really bad weather, hoping it would bring some respite.

Hundreds of people milled around on this sunny morning, like tourists in a strange, devastated land. In Lamb's Conduit Street the little shops and businesses seemed oddly vulnerable with their fronts in pieces on the pavement and the interiors exposed to casual onlookers. Brick and plaster dust caught in my throat as I walked past the shamble of shattered windows and breached walls.

A policeman stood in front of the shattered windows of a draper's shop, guarding the contents and keeping an eye on the rest of the street. I smiled at him and walked on, dodging barricades to get through the maze of diversions but giving a wide clearance to a roped-off area where a notice said 'Danger: Gas Leak'.

The extent of the damage of the past weeks became more apparent as I headed towards Oxford Circus. Great gaps had been blasted in rows of shops and houses and the glassless windows were like empty eye sockets with only darkness behind them. From Holborn to New Oxford Street, heavy and light rescue crews scrabbled around in piles of rubble and tangles of beams and metal. The devastation reminded me of photographs

I had seen of Ypres in the Great War. At High Holborn, an ARP officer in a steel hat directed operations from a desk that stood in the middle of the road among fallen masonry and glass shards, ignoring the couple of inches of water from the snaking hosepipes that swirled around him.

Tottenham Court Road seemed derelict at first glance, but the Lyons' Oxford Corner House was still open for business. In Oxford Street, Peter Robinson's stood, gaunt and spare, like a ruined cathedral, but across the battered front an enormous banner had been hung, declaring it to be 'OPEN'. Strings of Union Jacks had been draped over the ruins of Bourne & Hollingsworth, which also was declared to be open for business. John Lewis had been devastated by blast and fire and water. Selfridge's windows were all gone. I had seen enough for the moment, and doubled back to the Lyons for an early lunch.

There I picked up a *Dispatch* that someone had left on the table. The French columnist, Madame Tabouis, said ominously that things would only get darker for Britain; the Nazis would soon dominate the Mediterranean. I put it aside and concentrated on my grilled chop, boiled potatoes and carrots.

I had just left the Lyons when the banshee wail of the Warning sounded. Hitler's lunch break, people called those raids in the early afternoon. The streets were crowded, but there was no panic. Londoners now tended to ignore daylight raids, possibly because they somehow felt braver than they did in the hours of darkness. I knew all too well that mutilations due to shattered glass were far worse in the daylight raids because people had not taken cover, and I looked around for a shelter as the siren sputtered out in a few strangled notes and the roar of bombers came closer. The pavement shook with the thunder of the guns.

'There they go.' An elderly man in a suit was standing beside me, staring upwards at curls of smoke in the sky. Far above us aircraft were dodging each other in an aerial dance we'd all seen before, a dance that Jim Vassilikov would know well.

'They've just turned 'em. Spits, God bless 'em.'

'And Hurricanes,' I said. He nodded.

An ARP warden appeared and told us all to get to shelter, repeating in a kind of helpless resignation: 'Nah then, show a little common sense, can't you? It's no good standing there like one o'clock half struck.'

'Are you going to take shelter?' I asked the old man. I nodded towards a handwritten sign that had been propped up in the window of the tailor's shop nearby, 'Public Air Raid Shelter 10 yards', and underneath was an arrow, pointing to my left. The roar of planes, allied to the thunder of the guns, now was almost deafening and shrapnel had begun to fall around us.

'No, miss. I reckon I'll keep watching.' He pointed to the shop awning above him. 'I'm safe enough under here. Daylight raids aren't usually all that bad. Mebbe I'll see a real dogfight.'

A thin, sad-faced man standing beside him said, 'I saw one last week. A mass of German bombers were suddenly set upon by RAF fighters. They were smaller, of course, but they sailed into the middle of the pack and performed the most amazing antics in and around the bombers.'

The old man suddenly pointed upwards. 'Did you see—'

'R*ather.*' His companion nodded enthusiastically as he, too, stared into the sky.

I left them to it as I marched towards the public shelter and ducked down the stairs. The room was empty. I picked up a discarded *Observer* and read. After about twenty minutes the door opened and the shelter caretaker clumped down the stairs. He was balding, middle-aged, and had short, rather bandy legs.

'Afternoon, miss,' he said. 'Sitting in solitary splendour are you?'

I laughed. 'I wish people would take these daylight raids more seriously.'

'And I, miss. Madness to stay up top with the shrapnel flying.'

'Any bombs in the area?'

'None have fallen yet. But who's to say they won't.'

He sat beside me on the bench and took off his steel hat to wipe his forehead. 'You know, I reckon Holborn has caught it worse than anywhere else in London – barring the East End, of course.'

'Do people use this shelter at night?'

'Of course they do. About fifteen or so arrive in the late afternoon and stay all night.' He grinned. 'All sorts. Old, young and in between. More comfortable here than the Underground.'

I looked around at the small room with its cement floor and the wooden benches set around the sides and thought he was laying it on a bit thick.

He saw my glance, and added, a trifle defensively, 'They bring bedding, cards, board games and even a phonograph. It's really quite cosy.'

The All Clear sounded twenty minutes later. When I emerged it was evident that no bombs had fallen in the immediate area, and I wondered if the old man and his companion had been treated to a good show.

A bus drew up next to me, and I hopped on. It took a roundabout route to Regent's Park because of bomb crater diversions, but I still arrived early for the concert.

Part of the park had been requisitioned by the RAF and a barbed wire fence cut off the area to the north, but the lake and rose gardens were open and apparently as yet undamaged by bombs. I spent the time wandering around the garden beds, wondering what I thought I was doing. I had half a mind to cut and run. Perhaps Jim would not turn up – it had not actually been an invitation, no matter what Katherine thought. What if he turned up with another girl? What if he turned up with Nancy and they laughed at me? I realised then I was quite fearful because of Henri Valhubert's dismissal of me in the Algarve. That decided me – I would stay, consequences be damned.

Regent's Park was crowded with Londoners determined not to let the Luftwaffe ruin what might be the last fine Sunday of the year. Barrage balloons floated listlessly above us, like shoals of silver fish. They were tethered to the balloon unit in the palatial Winfield House beyond the lake. Gnats rose and fell in shimmering waves above the massed roses. The light warm breeze was only slightly marred by the smell of smoke and cordite. It was a beautiful afternoon, as beautiful as that Saturday six weeks before, when wave after wave of German planes appeared, dropping death and despair from the sky. I shivered. The sun might be shining but there was a chilly wind and little warmth to be found in the sunshine.

I wandered aimlessly. The brilliant green of the turf was as astonishing to me now as it had been when I first arrived in England. My childhood had been spent on dry, red earth and this abundance of green was almost hurtful to my Australian eyes. When I reached out to touch the petals of a rose, the sublime softness was somehow profoundly moving and I suddenly wanted to cry. I did not try to analyse the emotion and let my hand fall away.

Before the war, if you walked in Regent's Park you could sometimes hear the lions in the zoo roaring and the sounds of elephants and other animals. Not now. The dangerous animals had been slaughtered or evacuated when it all began, in case they were to escape during a bombardment. The week before, several bombs had fallen on the zoo, but I had heard that no animals were hurt. The big anti-aircraft guns were positioned on Primrose Hill, and I spared a thought for the terror of the trapped creatures surrounded by the unearthly noise of an air raid.

When I checked my watch it showed ten minutes to three. I took a breath, straightened my shoulders and walked towards the area where the concerts took place.

The open-air theatre was in a natural depression, almost encircled by thickets and tall trees. Rows of chairs had been set up, facing the orchestra. Jim Vassilikov who was really Ivan was waiting by the entrance, so he scored points for politeness. He was alone. I took a breath and tried not to look as if my heart was thumping. Ambulance work was a doddle compared with this.

A Russian nobleman? I found it hard to believe as I walked across the grass towards him. He looked so ordinary, until I realised that no man wearing an RAF uniform in London could look ordinary. The admiring glances he was getting from the people around him showed that. I tried to consider him dispassionately. Apart from the uniform, he did not appear different from any other reasonably good-looking Englishman.

'Handsome is as handsome does,' my grannie used to say. It was one of those old-fashioned aphorisms that she adored, although I was less partial to another of her favourites: 'Be good, sweet maid, and let who will be clever.'

As I walked up to Jim I wondered whatever he and I would talk about. The music would require our full attention, though, which left only intermission and the goodbye at the gate. He would learn quickly that this Aussie was not to be easily charmed into bed. Not even by one of Churchill's 'Few', and one with a title to boot. If indeed getting me into bed was his intention, because I still had no real idea why he had asked me out.

'Good afternoon, Australia.'

'G'day, Pom.'

He'd bought the tickets, so we went straight in. As we walked to our seats I realised that this would have to be our one and only date, because he was just too tall for me. I felt like a midget walking beside him.

'I'm so glad that you came,' he said.

'How could I refuse such a charmingly obscure invitation?'

'Oh, I excel in obscure invitations. After the concert I'll allude to the English custom of taking tea in the afternoon, and make a vague gesture towards the exit.'

'And I may or may not reply that I'd be delighted,' I said, wondering where he had in mind for tea.

He smiled.

Once we were seated in our astonishingly uncomfortable chairs I looked up beyond the tall trees surrounding us, to the tops of the Regency terraces in the Outer Circle of the park. The pale blue autumn sky showed through a lattice of empty windows and shattered walls. I shivered, wondering when the night's raid would begin. The planes usually arrived at eight or so, but sometimes there was a short raid around five o'clock.

'Cold?' Jim's whisper made me start.

'Always, ever since I got to this country.'

'Want my coat?' He stood, in an ungainly mess of knees and elbows, and began to shrug off his greatcoat.

'Why don't we share it,' I said.

He moved his chair closer to mine and draped the thick woollen coat over both of us. It was warm from his body. The wind had picked up and a few autumn leaves drifted past as the St Marylebone clock began to strike three and the orchestra tuned up. His shoulder was hard against mine. I debated moving away from the contact, but decided it was better not to make a point of it.

The man sitting in front of us was leaning forward, elbows planted on his thighs, grimly intent. The woman beside me was asleep, her head to one side, peaceful after a night I supposed had been spent in a shelter. I suspected that everyone was hoping to lose themselves in the music that afternoon, so they did not have to think about the night to come.

The orchestra played first the *Serenade for Strings* by Tchaikovsky. I cannot listen to music without being affected, and that music in that place was deeply affecting. It was more than the music; it was the setting and the atmosphere of only partially subdued fear in the audience around us.

As the music ebbed and swelled I thought of Jim, now safely beside me, who tomorrow would be up in the sky I could see through the ruined terraces, his tall body tucked into a thin shell of paper and wood, playing chasey with death. For the second time that afternoon tears threatened and I was annoyed with myself; there was simply no room for sentimentality in a war.

I pulled my hankie from my sleeve and dabbed my eyes, sneaking a look at Jim, hoping he had not noticed. He was staring – almost glaring – at the orchestra, his face set and intense. I found myself watching him rather than the orchestra, his hair as fair and soft as a child's, framing a pale face with broad cheekbones and those deep-set eyes. Strongly arched eyebrows, a long mobile mouth, firm chin, large beaky nose. He had the young-old look of men who had been given too much responsibility too early, and there were lines of stress etched around his eyes and his mouth. His face was not as insipid as I had originally thought. It was an interesting face, and surprisingly attractive.

He did not move until the music stopped. When the last notes played, he shook his head, seemingly bewildered to find himself sitting in the park. He joined in the applause and turned to me with a contrite expression.

'Sorry. I become engrossed in music. Especially the Russians, I'm embarrassed to admit. Cliché, I know. Tchaikovsky and Rachmaninoff are favourites.'

He laughed self-consciously. His gaze drifted down and I realised my hankie was in my hand and my eyes were still moist.

'It's a beautiful piece,' I said.

He smiled.

'Shh,' I said, although he had not spoken. 'They're starting again.'

CHAPTER SEVEN

When the concert ended he turned to me.

'Time for tea,' he said. 'Sorry to be so appallingly direct, but what about the Dorchester?'

I smiled assent, pleased I had brought my gloves. I imagined the Dorchester was the sort of place that would expect gloves.

We walked past the beautiful, ruined terraces along the way to Marylebone Road, where Jim had parked his car.

'So you go out in all this?' he asked, waving at the desolation around us. 'In the middle of a raid?'

I stumbled on some rubble, and he grabbed my arm, holding me steady. He did not let it go when we began to walk again.

'When the Blitz first began we were supposed to wait for the All Clear before we set out,' I said, 'but that's not very much help for injured people. So now we whizz around picking up casualties no matter what's going on.'

'You and Celia.'

I had a moment of blankness. Celia? Then I realised he meant Celia Ashwin. 'She picks up the walking wounded in a saloon car. I drive an ambulance with an attendant.' I decided to see if he was Levy's friend. 'I'm always paired with a man called David Levy.'

'David Levy?' Jim's voice was amused. 'I know a David Levy. Around my age, dark-haired and devilishly handsome?'

'That's the one.'

'So that's why you wear a Harrow tie.'

'He gave it to me as a joke. I suppose I shouldn't wear it.'

Jim laughed and tightened his grip on my arm as we negotiated some broken pavement.

'I'll give you mine if you like, to make a pair. It looks much nicer on you than it ever did on me or David.'

'Levy told me he had a friend from Harrow who was a pilot. I'd been wondering if that was you.'

'Probably. We were great friends at school, then caught up a few months ago and discovered we were still friends. Here's the car.' He gestured in front of us, at a sports car parked by the roadside. It was a sleek and beautiful machine, although ash and brick dust obscured what must have been a shiny blue bonnet.

'She needs a wash,' I said, 'but she's gorgeous.'

His face shone. 'My pride and joy. A thirty-seven Alfa Romeo Touring Spider. Fairly eats up the road when she's given her head.'

'Not much chance of that these days.' I gestured at the debris on the road.

'I'll take you for a drive in the country, then we can put her through her paces.'

'I'm told there's the odd sheep in the country.'

'The horn's good and loud. They'll just have to get out of our way.'

'Oh, what dust clouds I shall make! What carts I shall fling into the ditch!' I was quoting Mr Toad; I had loved *The Wind in the Willows* as a child.

'What are you saying? I'm a toad?'

'Not *a* toad,' I said, laughing, '*the* toad.'

'Well, Toadie and I share a love of the poetry of motion.' Jim had met my quote with another. 'Are you game for a country outing?'

'You're on. But only if I can have a drive of her.'

'We'll see.'

He opened the door for me and when I saw how low the passenger seat was, I tried to picture how the elegant Celia Ashwin would seat herself as I squeezed in. I landed with a thump.

'Do all pilots have a weakness for fast cars?' I asked, as he eased himself into the driver's seat.

'One becomes rather addicted to speed up there.'

But few would be able to afford this little beauty, I thought. He pushed the starter. It roared into life and took off with a burst of power, juddering a little as it ran over the inevitable potholes.

As we drove through the ruined streets towards Mayfair, I reached discreetly into my handbag for my gloves and pulled them on.

Jim parked the car in a narrow street and we walked along Park Lane towards the Dorchester, passing houses that had been scarred and shattered by bombs. Shredded curtains fluttered from empty windows. The entire front of one house had been torn away, revealing a grand staircase covered in broken glass that lay like drifts of brittle snow.

The Dorchester Hotel, however, seemed to be untouched. Not one of the glittering mirrors in the hall was even cracked.

'It's as if they don't know there's a war on,' I said.

'Oh, they know there's a war on,' he said. 'They've set up the basement with artificial sunlight and put in Vichy baths, gymnasiums and all the fittings of the Continental spas. Dorchester Hotel guests are able to see out the Blitz in an ersatz holiday resort.'

'While London has to damn well take it,' I said quietly. We all knew the hotel was a fortress made of concrete and steel, and that was why the guest list was so eminent. It was a fortress propped up with moneybags.

I excused myself to visit the ladies' room to remove my raincoat and freshen up. The decor was opalescent pink and the attendant was a slender girl of around sixteen, dressed in severe black.

'Oh, you do have lovely curls, miss. Are they natural?' A pink enamelled tag told me her name was Doris. I admitted that my hair was naturally curly.

'Please let me help you with it.' Her tone was gently insistent. I hadn't realised that it Just Wouldn't Do as it was.

Doris ruthlessly brushed my hair and spritzed it with something, before expertly wielding a comb. When she stepped back, I looked as if I had just left the hairdresser. She brushed a soft cloth over my hat to remove any dust and replaced it carefully, tilting her head to make sure the angle was sufficiently chic. Her nod of approval made me happy, until she said, 'Shame no one can get nice hats in this war.'

A practised eye was cast over my outfit.

'Paris, miss?'

It was a measure of how much this slight young thing had intimidated me that I actually nodded, and then felt cheapened by the pointless lie.

'Actually, it was made in Prague to a Parisian design.'

Her look was sympathetic. 'It's still a lovely frock.' She pulled open a drawer and extracted a clothes brush. 'Oh, that brick dust. It gets everywhere.'

Once my dress was brushed free of air-raid grit, Doris used cleaning fluid to sponge away a few almost invisible spots on the fabric.

'Stand up straight, miss. It's not hanging right.' She reached down and gave a couple of tugs at the hem, which improved the line immeasurably.

As I was about to leave she picked up a perfume bottle and sprayed it in my direction.

'Thanks so much, Doris. You've done a fabulous job. I'm really grateful.' I smiled and tipped her a good proportion of what was in my purse.

'Oh, miss, it's no bother really.'

Most tables in the restaurant were occupied, but as soon as we appeared a sloe-eyed waitress pounced upon us, addressing Jim in French as if he were an old friend. She threw me one glance of exquisite contempt before assuring him that of course they could find a table for him.

As she led us to a table Jim asked, also in French, after her mother. She replied that *maman* was as well as they could expect during such terrible times and that so far they had been spared any damage from the bombs of the filthy Nazis. Once we were seated, the waitress took our order, seemed almost to curtsy and turned around with a graceful flick of her black-clad *derrière*. We both watched her walk away. I wondered if managing to walk in a straight line despite that sinuously swaying bottom was a learned or an innate skill.

Jim turned to me. 'Natasha's mother was a famous ballerina in Imperial Russia and is a great friend of my mother's. Unfortunately, what she saw and experienced in the Revolution affected her mind, so it's been hard on Natasha, who has to care for her.'

'Why did she speak to you in French, if she is Russian?'

'We St Petersburg émigrés speak French to each other as a rule,' he went on. 'And how does an Australian girl come to speak French so beautifully?'

'In 1938, soon after I arrived in England, I took a position as governess to the daughters of a Czech family. I taught the girls how to speak English with an Australian accent and they perfected my French and German. And I went with the family to the Riviera for several months, which probably also helped my accent.'

'The Riviera?' He smiled. 'Plush job.'

'Count Szrebesky was my employer. I looked after his daughters and I stayed a year with the family. Mainly in Prague. It was before the German invasion of Czechoslovakia, of course.' With a laugh, I added, *'Levy dit que mon accent était australien, mais d'autres ont dit qu'il est très bon. Que pensez-vous?'*

'I think David's standards are too high. You sound slightly foreign, but I'd not pick you as Australian.'

'That's good to know. Leonor and Karolina – my charges – took pride in my French accent. Once I arrived in Europe I lost interest in perfecting my German. But what about you? I suppose you speak a few languages.'

'Russian, French, German, Italian, Spanish, some Polish.' He shrugged, then smiled. 'Oh, and English.'

Natasha arrived with a tray of wafer-thin sandwiches, tiny cakes, scones and a pot of tea. Food rationing did not apply if you ate out, and I was determined to eat all I could of such luxuries.

Jim poured the tea into a pair of terrifyingly delicate cups. My hands were unsteady and the cup rattled in its saucer as I took it from him. Embarrassed, I remarked teasingly that he had poured like an expert.

'When we arrived here my mother insisted on becoming more English than the English,' he said, settling back in his chair and picking up his cup and saucer with the effortless grace that I assumed was taught by nannies and governesses and tutors. 'That included the English tea ceremony. It was tea at five every day, and not a samovar in sight.'

'But you love Russian music?'

He placed the cup back into its saucer and picked up a sandwich. 'Yes. It's odd. I don't really see myself as Russian.' He took a neat bite, and seemed to consider the matter. 'Actually, my bloodline is as German as it is Russian, and there is a fair dollop of French as well, on my father's side, though I was born in St Petersburg. I speak the language, of course, but I dislike most of the food, detest ballet, never managed more than a few pages of Tolstoy. Don't like vodka, either.' The sandwich was polished off. 'And yet, I adore Russian music. Must be in the blood. Who knows?' He gave a soft bark of laughter.

'Well, I like Russian music too, and I doubt there's a drop of Russian blood in me. But who knows?'

'Brennan's an Irish name.'

'Oh, Dad's people were from there but I'm all Australian.'

'A Botany Bay sort of Australian? I must say, I've always found your convict history fascinating.'

I settled for an enigmatic look.

69

An eyebrow rose, the corner of his mouth hooked up into the slight ironic smile that seemed habitual and he changed the subject.

'So you spent some time in Prague, how did you like it?'

'I loved it. It's such a beautiful city. I met some very fine people there, mainly students, people I think of as friends. We solved all the problems of the world in those little cafes in the Old Town. It was a very happy time for a while.' I stared at the tablecloth. 'I was in Prague during the betrayal of Czechoslovakia by the Allies and during the Nazi invasion in May 1939. I had an English passport, and so they let me travel to London.'

There was a pause as we both took another sandwich and sipped our tea. My thoughts were stuck in that terrible time when the Germans invaded and my friends were swept away in the storm. Dita, Bedřich, Stela, Nikol, Tomas. Tomas escaped to Poland in the first few hectic days after the invasion. He came to Britain with thirty other battle-ready Czech airmen in June and was now with the RAF. We met not long after he arrived, but his news had not been good. Bedřich was dead, shot in the street after he had been caught posting anti-Nazi material. Nikol had been interned in October 1939 along with more than over a thousand other student protesters. He had no news of Stela and Dita.

Jim's voice brought me back to the present with a jolt.

'Was it difficult to get out of the country? I know that Britain wasn't at war with Germany then, but the Germans can be very officious.'

'It was all very orderly, really.' I could hear the bitterness in my voice, but there was nothing I could do about that; my heart ached for poor Czechoslovakia. 'No one cared about one Australian governess who wanted to go to London – they were too busy arresting Jews and communists and student protestors and building the new concentration camps to house them.'

'And after you returned to London?'

I pushed aside my memories of those awful days and managed a smile. 'I got a clerical job at Australia House. After war was declared I joined the Ambulance Service, but at first I wondered what I'd got myself into. After all those uneventful months of the phoney war, people began to say, "It won't happen." They laughed at us when we were doing exercises in the streets.'

My smile became wry. 'So when the raids started we were all rather thrilled and excited. Little did we know.' I looked up at him. 'They're a grand bunch, on the whole, my colleagues.'

'So you work with old David Levy,' said Jim. 'I headed off to Cambridge after Harrow, and he went to the other place. We've not seen each other much in the past few years.' His smile became teasing. 'A few months ago he told me he was in the Ambulance Service and that his driver was a doll.'

I picked up a scone, and pondered whether it was really a compliment to be described as a doll. I knew that was probably the intention, dolls were pretty, but they were also rather vapid-looking, surely? And they were inanimate. I had never liked dolls much as a girl. For playmates I had preferred Minnie, the hotel cat, and my mongrel dog, Prince.

'I suppose David's a conscientious objector?'

Again I came back to the conversation with a start. 'No. He was rejected for service on medical grounds. Why would you think he was a conchie?'

'Because he's a communist.'

'What?' Levy and I had never discussed politics. Flustered, I took a little cake and bit into it, savouring the delicate sweetness.

'I really don't think so,' I said.

'Well, he used to spout communist nonsense at school. We came to blows over it on one occasion.'

'Who won?'

A smile tugged at his mouth. 'I did. Gave him a black eye. Then I told him that the Bolsheviks murdered my father and after that he stopped trying to shove Marx down my throat.'

'*Did* the Bolsheviks murder your father?'

'Yes.'

I didn't know how to respond to that. In the end I said, 'I'm so sorry.'

'Why apologise?' His voice was brusque. 'You didn't drag him out of his house in front of his wife and five-year-old child, take him to the Peter and Paul Fortress and shoot him without trial.' Anger flashed in those deep-set eyes.

He did not want my sympathy, that was clear. I played with the fingers of my gloves, which I had placed neatly on the table. I said, to my gloves, 'Levy never mentioned communism to me.'

'Maybe he's seen the light.'

His tone was curt, almost unpleasant. I was out of my depth. It was my turn to change the conversation.

'So you went to school with Levy and to university with Nancy's husband. How do you know Ashw— I mean Celia?'

'I had rather a thing for Celia's sister when I was up at Cambridge and I hung around with her set for a while.'

So Jim might be a closet fascist after all.

Suddenly my delicious cake was far too sweet, and I finished it with difficulty. I wondered how long this tea would continue, how long before I could excuse myself and go home.

'Celia's husband was part of our group,' he went on. 'It was before they were married, of course. I never liked him much. He's rather a cad, and Celia's far too good for him.' He grimaced. 'It all leaves rather a bad taste in one's mouth, don't you agree? Communism, fascism – whatever they call it, it's simply about imposing someone's will on the powerless.'

I nodded and took another little cake. I was wrong before, I decided. They really weren't bad at all.

'Nancy said you had a weekend's leave,' I remarked. 'Does that mean you're back on duty tomorrow?'

'No rest for the wicked.'

'Levy says that.'

'I suppose you've fallen in love with him.' He reached for a scone, avoiding my eyes.

'With Levy? Love among the ruins?' I laughed at the thought of it. 'No. Levy and I are friends. Colleagues. Mates. We rely on each other. Or rather, I rely on him.'

'You looked absolutely done in yesterday,' he said.

'It had been a tough day, at the end of a tough week of day shift. I honestly don't know how I could do it without Levy. He's a wonderful ambulance attendant, and makes it all much easier than it could be.' I smiled at Jim. 'He's great company, always making me laugh. Tomorrow we're back on night shift together.'

'Night shift must be ghastly.'

'Oh, I prefer it to day shift.'

'More exciting?'

'More satisfying. Levy and I whizz around picking up casualties and taking them to hospital.' I took a sip of tea. 'The worst part of day shift is the mortuary runs.'

'It does sound rather unpleasant, taking bodies to the morgue,' he said.

I had the feeling that he was having to work at keeping the conversation going, as if he wasn't all that interested any more. I wondered if I'd said anything wrong and regretted the bitter way I'd referred to the Nazis in Czechoslovakia. He didn't want to discuss politics on his day away from the airfield. I should be trying for light, amusing conversation. Flustered, I spoke without thinking.

'Oh, I can cope with that side of it. It's just – well, the bodies are not always intact. Sometimes we have to wander around the bombsites to help find the bits and pieces and put them in buckets and sacks. I find that rather dire,' I finished in a light tone.

He turned away slightly, so his eyes were hidden. 'I see,' he said, in an expressionless voice. When he turned to look at me again his eyes were shadowed. Although his face gave nothing away, I supposed that I must have horrified him with my insouciance.

'That sounded dreadfully blasé,' I said, looking down at my plate. I didn't know how to regain the lightness we had begun with. 'But – as Levy says – you need – well, you need to grow a protective shell. Otherwise you simply couldn't do the job. Although, without Levy I don't think I could—'

Jim was silent, twisting his cup around in its saucer, regarding it thoughtfully as he did so.

I said, hurriedly, 'When I started with the Ambulance Service I'd never seen a dead body, I was even squeamish about handling dead animals. I've had to learn how to deal with things I'd never dreamed of. Levy – I'm lucky that Levy – he's—' My cheeks burned as I remembered how in the early days Levy had always dealt with the horrors I could not face, picking up body parts, everything.

Jim sat back in his seat and regarded me, unsmiling, as if attempting to puzzle me out.

I blundered on. 'At my first incident we found a baby. It had been thrown through a window by the blast and it was—' I sucked in a breath, remembering the poor little broken body. 'Levy found a bit of curtain to wrap it in and I—'

And I had howled like a dog when I returned to my flat.

Eventually I looked up at him. 'You really can cope with anything if you have to. Levy – he's very kind.' I knew what would happen next: Jim would take me back to St Andrew's, drop me off and forget about me because I was boring and common, talking about my job in such an offhand, callous manner and blathering on about politics.

He nodded, not unsympathetically. Then he sat up, drained his tea and replaced the cup in its saucer. 'If you don't mind, I'll drop you off home now,' he said. 'I have to drive back to the airfield tonight as we're expected to be at readiness at first light.'

'Readiness?' I felt deflated, unready for such an abrupt end to our afternoon, even though I'd seen it coming.

'That's when we sit in the dispersal hut, togged up in our Mae Wests with our aeroplanes ready, waiting for the order to scramble.'

'And "scramble" is when . . .?'

'That's when we run for the planes and take off. Speaking of which, I'm awfully sorry, but we do need to get going.' He stood and came round to draw my chair out. As we walked to the car we continued the conversation in a rather desultory fashion. It seemed clear that we were both just waiting for the day to be over.

'It must be a terrible strain on the nerves, one sortie after another,' I said.

'Things have quietened down for us now. At least we have time to sit in the dispersal hut. When they were hitting the airfields – before they started this Blitz on London – we were sleeping in the cockpits in between scrambles.'

The ironic twist returned to his smile. 'The worst part is waiting for the scramble telephone to ring.' There was a mirthless laugh. 'Once I've made my first interception I'm usually too busy to think.'

'Interception?'

'When we engage with the enemy.'

It was like that at Woburn Place, when the Warning went and we knew the raiders were on their way. We would sit there, wondering what lay ahead. All of us preferred to be on the road, dealing with problems as they arose, no matter how bad the raid.

And yet, I well knew that driving around in an ambulance was nothing compared to jumping into a plane and doing battle with German fighters, high up in the sky.

'Do you think the air battle Churchill referred to in his wonderful speech – the one where he referred to you pilots as "the Few" – do you think that's over now?' I asked. 'From what I can gather, Churchill seems to think the Blitz is a different thing entirely.'

'Things are certainly less hectic for us now, although much worse for you.'

We had reached the car, and he opened my door. As he got in and sat beside me, he said, 'It's difficult to know when a battle of that kind ends. We're still having trouble with Messer one-o-nines during the day. Their high-flying capacities can make things pretty dicey, especially if one flies a Hurricane, as I do.' He stopped talking abruptly and looked at me as he turned on the ignition. 'And I shouldn't be mentioning such things when I'm with a lovely girl.'

Jim was like Henri Valhubert, I decided, as the car roared into life and we set off down the road. Like that Frenchman, Jim Vassilikov was a titled and somewhat pompous ass, who was arrogant enough to judge me and find me wanting. I wondered what it was that men of his class so despised about me, what I had said to make Jim so sure that I Just Wouldn't Do. And yet, I couldn't help a feeling of misery because I had really liked him to begin with, had delighted in our repartee and his sense of humour.

We drove home through the shattered landscape of London. At the door to St Andrew's he thanked me for a delightful afternoon and gave me a smile as dazzling as sunlight on water. Yet it did not reach his eyes. Although I knew it was a dismissal, my heart raced and my cheeks burned as I automatically smiled in response. I remembered Katherine's remarks and thought I would have to tell her that she was right about the S.A.

'I hope we can meet again soon,' he said, but without much enthusiasm. 'Perhaps we could dine at the Ritz one evening. In the Ritz, one can forget about all this.' He waved his hand towards the ruins across the street.

'That would be lovely.'

He returned to his car and disappeared in a cloud of exhaust smoke down Gray's Inn Road.

'Well, Lily,' I murmured, 'that's that, then.'

CHAPTER EIGHT

'So, how did the concert go yesterday? Tell me *everything*.'

Pam was waiting for me outside the Empire laden with two string bags stuffed with brown paper parcels. Her hair had been freshly set and she was wearing a blue woollen dress and an eager expression.

'I doubt I'll see him again,' I said, as we entered the lobby. 'I was boring and he was bored. Actually, he was a bit boring too.'

'But—'

'No buts. I don't want to discuss it.'

Pam could take a hint. We went into the movie to see her idol, Robert Taylor, who was as woodenly handsome as ever. I was more impressed by his co-star, Hedy Lamarr, playing a woman desperately and unsuccessfully trying to fit into a world that would not accept her. It ended in tragedy, which I suspect would have been my lot if Jim really had taken a shine to me.

'And now for some delicious pastries,' I said, when we emerged. I grabbed her arm and pulled her towards the narrow streets of Soho.

'This is the dark centre of vice in London, isn't it?' Pam asked, as we stepped gingerly around bomb debris to enter Greek Street. Her face was alight with a kind of horrified glee.

'It's also the bright cosmopolitan centre of London. I like it,' I replied.

'D'you think she is a – you know?' Pam whispered, after a well-dressed woman sauntered by.

I laughed. 'How should I know? By the way, I suggested that Betty see you about volunteering in your shelter at night. I think she's worse, if anything. She talked about wanting to die.'

'She did seem to be in a bad way on Saturday, poor thing. Of course she can come to the shelter with me. We could certainly use her.'

'Good. Will you tell her?'

'I'd be happy to. My father says that feeling needed is the panacea for loneliness and misery.'

I said, in a teasing tone, 'I wonder how your father the bishop would feel about you wandering the vice-ridden streets of Soho.'

'I haven't seen anything in the slightest bit vice-ridden,' she responded glumly. 'Ooh, unless that man is heading to a . . .?'

I looked up to see someone I knew striding ahead of us.

'That's Jack Moray,' I said, feeling the confusion of seeing someone you know in an unexpected place. 'He's a deputy station officer at Bloomsbury.'

'And do you think he's going to a – a you-know-what?' asked Pam again. She was making a bad job of trying to hide a smirk.

'A what?' I asked, wondering myself what he was doing in Soho, and slightly embarrassed that I should be so curious.

She lowered her voice and hissed, 'A brothel.'

'Katherine is absolutely right, you know. For a bishop's daughter you have a very low mind, Pamela Beresford.'

Pam giggled. 'Is he the one you don't like very much?'

'He's horrid to Levy.'

'Then come on, let's see whether he is of questionable morals as well as a horrid disposition.'

Moray had by now disappeared behind a surface shelter on the corner. The government had built hundreds of these square brick structures when the Blitz began, but people disliked using them, preferring the Underground. Pam tugged at my arm until I followed her to the shelter. Sheepishly, I peeped around the corner to see that Moray had halted in front of what had once been a stylish residence facing Soho Square. As we watched he turned into the shadows of the deeply recessed entrance and disappeared.

'I bet it's a you-know-what,' said Pam. 'Let's check.'

With some trepidation I allowed her to pull me to the building's portico. Two well-worn steps led up to a magnificently carved and pillared doorway – now chipped and scratched and worse for wear – above which was an ornate fanlight that had been painted over for blackout purposes. The list of names pencilled into holders by the door indicated that the building had been converted into flats. Pam chortled as she read out the names of the tenants – in many cases only their first names appeared.

'Carmen, Cherry, Mindy, Aimée, Coco, Lola. They're an exotic-sounding bunch.' She turned her eyes to me in fascinated horror. 'I was right, wasn't I? Golly. It really is one of those places? I can't believe I was right.'

Beside the portico, stone steps led down to a basement.

'I think he must have gone down there,' I said. 'He didn't go through the front door.'

Pam peered at the list of names. 'There's no name listed for the basement flat.'

'Perhaps Moray lives there?' I ventured.

Pam rolled her eyes. Her mouth quivered, and I knew that any moment she would be in a fit of giggles.

I grabbed her arm and we set off down the street at a brisk walk, almost a trot. My face was flaming. A brothel! And Moray had marched up to the place as if he was on his way to a garden party at Buckingham Palace.

On my way to work that afternoon I wondered whether I would tell Levy about seeing Moray in Soho. We usually did share gossip, but this was salacious gossip, and Pam and I might well have jumped to the wrong conclusion. In the end I decided that, even if he was visiting a brothel, it was his business. Telling on him would be a nasty thing to do.

My route to the ambulance station took me past the Guildford Arms, a cheerful old pub in peacetime. Now, its windows were covered with thin boarding and this gave the building a blank, unwelcoming aspect, so that it seemed to crouch blindly on its corner behind piles of sandbags. Mr Richie, who was the publican as well as my local ARP warden, was wiping tables inside.

I liked Mr Richie. He reminded me of my father. Not in looks, because Mr Richie was a small, squat man and my father was big, but in the force of character apparent in his no-nonsense attitude to life and the knowing expression in his eyes. His thick body was all bone and muscle rather than fat, and he kept his hair very short, like a fighter.

Mr Richie had an uncanny instinct about timed bombs. Sometimes bombs did not explode immediately because the Germans had attached a timer, hoping they would explode as the rescue parties were digging for survivors. In such cases the special bomb disposal squad had to be called to make them safe and everyone had to keep their distance until the fuses were removed.

Somehow Mr Richie always knew when one of the timed bombs on his 'patch' was going to explode. Pam and Katherine had laughed when I had told them and said I was pulling their legs. But Levy and I knew how many lives he had saved because of his strange faculty.

He waved me over and when I joined him in the doorway he looked grim.

'It was bad here in Bloomsbury last night,' he said, shaking his head. 'A couple of hundred-pounders smashed two houses in Roger Street and fire took out another. A young feller bought it when they hit Long Yard in Lamb's Conduit Street. Only eighteen, poor lad.'

He gave a table near the door a quick rub with his towel. 'We Do Not Recognise The Possibility Of Defeat' announced a sign that hung over the bar behind him.

'You know a hundred-pounder fell in Calthorpe Street, early Friday morning?' he went on.

I nodded. I had not attended the incident, but I'd heard about it.

'One dead, I was told,' I said.

'Killed a mother and injured three kiddies.'

I made a sympathetic noise. To my surprise, his response was to pull tight the cloth he was holding with a sudden jerk and twist his mouth into a scowl.

'Saw one of your ambulance attendants take a bottle of whisky out of the house. Saw him tuck it under that grey coat you lot all wear. Then he scurried away like the rat he was, 'fore I could get a name. Might'a taken more, 'cos the house's back door stood open when I went back there in daylight and things looked like they'd been gone through. I telephoned your Mrs Coke about it yesterday, but she didn't seem interested. Sounded annoyed that I'd phoned.'

It did not surprise me that Mrs Coke had done nothing. She had done as little as she could since taking over as the station officer.

'Did you get a look at the man?' I asked.

'Scrawny little feller. Couldn't see his face. He had on one of them grey coats and a steel hat. Thought it looked like that Fred Knaggs what's always at the dog track, but I couldn't swear to it.'

'I'm so sorry, Mr Richie.' It appalled me to think of ambulance officers looting from bombed houses, but from what I knew of Knaggs he would have to be a likely suspect.

'Not your fault, love. There's always bad apples. Next time I sees anything, though, it'll be reported to the police, not to your Mrs Coke.' He scratched his head. 'Keep yer eyes open, will you? If you notice anything suspicious when you're on duty, let me know?'

'Of course I will.'

I thought about what Mr Richie had said as I walked down Gray's Inn Road. Most looters were regular criminals, but there were plenty of rumours about the heavy rescue workers and demolition men who mixed business with pleasure by helping themselves to objects in the houses they were working on. And there were stories of ambulance officers and even firefighters stealing bottles of spirits, valuable knick-knacks, money, clothes and jewellery from bombsites. Wallets disappeared from the injured, never to be found again; women awoke in hospital without rings or brooches or earrings, without the fur coat they had slipped on to wear in the shelter, without their precious handbag containing personal papers, cash and valuables.

Levy had nursed a bee in his bonnet about looting since the Blitz started. If he had any suspicion that Knaggs was looting houses he would take matters further. And yet, if anyone had to catch Knaggs, I hoped it would not be Levy. His life was hard enough at the station without complicating things further.

CHAPTER NINE

Four days later, on Friday afternoon, I arrived early at Woburn Place to start the last night shift for the week. As driver, it was my responsibility to check the oil, water and petrol before each shift, but I also wanted to make sure that no unpleasant little 'jokes' had been left for Levy to find. Although Levy brushed off such anti-Semitism with a shrug, I hated him to be bothered with it.

Sure enough, I found a pair of pig's ears and a tail arranged on top of a pile of blankets in the back of the ambulance, together with a rather artfully conceived pamphlet entitled 'This is a Jews' War!' On cursory inspection, it asserted that it was the Jews who had planned this war in order to achieve their aim of world domination. On another pile of blankets were two books, Douglas Reed's *Disgrace Abounding*, which had a sealed, blank envelope tucked inside, and *Dachau the Nazi Hell*, which appeared to be an account of a Jewish prisoner's terrible suffering in a German concentration camp. This last was puzzling, unless whoever had put it there wanted to scare Levy with what might happen to him if the Nazis invaded Britain.

I had been lent Reed's *Insanity Fair* last year, and had found his descriptions of Hitler's Germany to be fascinating. He had an easy journalistic style that was persuasive, but his anti-Semitism was a nasty feature of the book.

I had some pleasure in tearing the pamphlet into bits as I walked past the line of ambulances and cars to the bin. There I threw in the remains of the pig and pamphlet but I was not sure what to do with the books or the envelope. I had a strong aversion to destroying a book. Hitler destroyed books.

'More presents left for me?'

Levy was standing behind me.

'Pig's ears,' I said. 'A pamphlet about how you lot are going to take over the world. And these.' I handed him the books.

He smiled slightly, which surprised me, and held up the book on Dachau. 'This one's mine, actually. I lent it to a friend. A distressing book, but needs to be read. I borrowed the other one. It's good to know what the intelligentsia – if you can call Reed that – is writing about us.'

'It has an envelope inside.'

He found the sealed envelope, smiled and tucked it into his breast pocket before closing the book with a snap.

'I can fight my own battles, Brennan. Whoever is doing this is targeting me, not you. Leave it for me to deal with.'

I began to remonstrate, but he cut me off and I could hear real anger in his voice. 'I mean it. Leave any little gifts for me to deal with in future. And don't bother defending my honour against the morons in the common room.'

'But how can you bear it?' I blurted out the words without thinking and wished immediately that I could take them back.

Levy stiffened, sucked in a breath and sighed it out.

'I survived boarding school. This is nothing compared with what I went through at Harrow.'

'But it's so unfair.'

He shrugged. 'It's so common that I hardly notice it now. It's like people whispering in the cinema or coughing at a concert. You don't really hear it because you're concentrating on the music or the film. One would only need to deal with such things if they greatly interfered with one's enjoyment.'

'Have you ever *dealt* with it?'

'On occasion.' He looked up, into my eyes. 'But I've found that it never really helps. Not me or my tormentors.'

He looked away and shivered a little. 'Of course I hate it, but it's so pervasive, Brennan. The slight reluctance before a handshake, the muttered comment, the look of polite contempt. I can't change centuries of hatred. I just have to live with it.'

We walked together back to the Monster. 'I grew up hearing how lucky I was to live in a country without pogroms,' he said. 'My mother's family fled Russia in the last century and ended up in Germany. They thought Germany was a haven. "The most civilised country in Europe," my grandparents would tell me whenever they came to visit when I was a boy.' His hands clenched. 'Only, we've not heard from them, or any of my mother's family, for some time now.'

'Oh, Levy . . .'

I shut up. When I thought about what I had seen in Prague, I shivered.

Levy turned to me, shrugged and tried to smile. 'I was born in this country, as was my father and his father. My brothers wear its uniform and they fight for it, as my father fought for it in the last war. I went to Repton, then Harrow and Oxford. My passport says I'm British, but to most in this nation I'll never be an Englishman.'

'But—'

Levy touched my cheek, very softly. 'You can't fight my battles, Brennan. Hanging on to anger is like drinking poison and expecting the other person to die. There's no point. Now, scram, there's a good girl, and have a nice cup of tea. I'll check my supplies and join you in the common room.'

As Levy walked away from me, I wondered how it must feel always to be the 'outsider', always to face unreasoning discrimination. It was annoying for me in London to be constantly judged by my accent, but it had never been anything more than annoying.

Of course I knew something about being bullied as the outsider at school. It all came to a head near the end of my first year when I returned to the dormitory to find a pack of giggling girls – all from 'good families' who delighted in tormenting me – standing around my bed.

'Oh just look at this,' their leader, Phyllis Gregory, had announced, bending to sniff the urine-coloured stain on the mattress. 'Barmaid Brennan has wet the bed. Smells of beer. Barmaids wee beer apparently.'

When I got closer I could smell that it was indeed beer, no doubt poured on my bed by one of her lackeys.

I had dressed myself in silence and left the dormitory accompanied by laughter. I had walked past the dining room, down the main drive and out of the front gate of the school to end up at my uncle's house, a mile or so away. I found him in his front garden, choosing a rose for his buttonhole.

'I've run away from school. I won't go back, so don't think that you can make me. I'm going home to Kookynie.'

Uncle Charles placed the rosebud carefully in his buttonhole before looking up at me.

'Tell me about it over breakfast.'

He took me to a small tearoom near his law chambers where, over bacon and eggs and tomato and sausages and toast and jam – a veritable feast to a boarding school girl – the story was told. When I had finished, Uncle Charles sighed.

'It's a very good school, Lily. Your mother and father would be most upset if you allowed yourself to be driven out by some badly behaved girls.'

'But it's—'

'Yes, it's awful. I know the Gregory girl's father, and he spoils her terribly. Do you hate everything about the school? Lessons, the teachers, the routine?'

'I don't mind any of that. But I don't have any friends and the girls are so awful to me. I want to go home.'

'Who would you like to be friends with?'

'I like Rose Pellew. She plays violin in the orchestra.'

I had rather a crush on willowy Rose, who cultivated a dreamy expression and dealt with Phyllis by steadfastly ignoring her.

Uncle Charles had considered the matter for a minute or so, before stating, 'Join the orchestra. You play the piano well enough.'

The thought had never occurred to me. 'I do, but they don't need—'

'Well what *do* they need?' Uncle Charles didn't waste words.

'They've been asking for a percussionist, but I couldn't do that. Phyllis would tear me to pieces.'

He smiled. 'Don't over-dramatise. Phyllis may tease you, but I'm sure the girls in the orchestra will be happy to have you.' There was a decided nod. 'Yes. That will solve the problem nicely, and you will learn a new skill.' He gestured at the empty plate. 'Eaten enough?'

'Yes, but—'

'I was called Stinky at school,' he said, which made me laugh. 'I think it was to do with my tennis shoes. My old schoolmates call me Stinky even now.'

He had carefully brushed away some crumbs from his jacket and grimaced. 'I was bullied as well, for a while. But it's easier to deal with such things in a boys' school.'

'Why?'

'We tend to resolve our problems with our fists, and I'm a pretty good fighter.'

My uncle was a fastidious man, and the idea that he had ever been a smelly little boy was very amusing. But it was frankly amazing to think of him as a fighter, even though I knew he had been away to war when he was a young man.

I agreed to stay at school. Uncle Charles was proved right to some extent, because I became good friends with Rose and the other girls in the orchestra. Once I had friends, no spiteful remark ever cut so deeply.

But it was something else Uncle Charles said, but never intended me to act upon, that really improved matters for me. I dared Phyllis Gregory to meet me behind the big gum tree.

'Barmaids have to know how to deal with nasty customers,' I told her in front of witnesses, with my fists clenched and my head high. 'I'll show you how they do it.'

She knew I was serious, and I saw the spark of fear in her eyes. More importantly, she knew that I knew she was afraid of me.

Of course she refused my challenge point blank, which I thought was rather cowardly given she was more than a year older than me and much taller. The next day her father arrived at school and raged at the headmistress, demanding my expulsion, but Dad and Uncle Charles somehow managed to talk her around. After that Phyllis and the posh girls of her set left me alone. I was happy enough at school, but my real revenge was trouncing the lot of them in the final exams, and winning state exhibitions in French and German.

After my abortive challenge to Phyllis, I found my nickname Barmaid had been shortened to Barmy. Letters from school friends were still addressed 'Dear Barmy'. I had heard recently from one of them that Phyllis was engaged to a very handsome, very wealthy war hero.

Life is so often unfair.

I was in a low mood by the time I reached the common room. What I had suffered was almost nothing compared to what Levy had to put up with, simply because he was Jewish. He had asked me not to take the matter any further, but it was the third time I had found pig parts and pamphlets in the ambulance and I was sick of it.

I was in a fighting mood as I knocked on the door of Mrs Coke's office. Levy would never raise with her the subject of the nasty 'surprises' that I had been finding in our ambulance. So it was up to me.

She was seated at her desk, surrounded by raffle ticket butts, cheques and letters. Mrs Coke ran the Ambulance Benevolent Fund, which raised money to buy ambulances. The main money-making venture for the fund was a raffle, where the prize was

War Bonds, but she also actively encouraged donations. Levy maintained that the only person to really benefit from it all was Mrs Coke, because she made important contacts and it gave her a reputation as a 'good woman'.

For my part, nothing about Mrs Coke seemed real. It was as if she had read a description in a book of the type of woman she wanted to be and had spent the rest of her life imitating, but never actually becoming, the phantom she so admired. She was large-bodied and tall, neither good-looking nor plain, with no outstanding characteristics beyond her faded blue eyes that protruded slightly. By moving quickly and decisively she somehow gave the impression that she had just come in from a bracing walk and was managing everything splendidly.

Mrs Coke had told all of us, at one time or another, 'in absolute confidence', that she was the daughter of an Irish earl whose name she would never reveal. She said her father had cast her off when she married Mr Coke for love. I don't think any of us really believed the story, but only Levy had drawn her anger by replying to this confidence with a snort of laughter, followed by the comment that he had seen the play at the Shaftesbury, and it ended badly.

'High-jinks, Brennan,' she said, cutting me off before I had even finished my story. 'We all need to keep up our spirits in a war and Levy is perfectly capable of dealing with such things himself.'

'But—'

'Oh, "but me no buts," as the Bard said.' Mrs Coke was all smiles and false teeth as she misquoted Shakespeare. 'Levy's a big boy. Let him stand up for himself.'

It was a disappointing response, but what had I expected? Mrs Coke never put herself out for anyone but herself. I conceded defeat.

'Yes, Mrs Coke.'

Her smile became sly. 'He's a handsome man, I grant you. But, honestly, Brennan, be realistic. And Halliday should stop making sheep's eyes at him as well. Jews marry their own and they treat girls like you with contempt.'

'Girls like me?' I kept my tone polite, but I wanted to shriek at the silly woman.

She wagged a finger. 'The Jews have a name for Christian girls who chase Jewish boys.'

'Really?'

'Oh yes, they certainly do.' Her voice sharpened. 'And there's no need to look at me like that. You may go now, Brennan.'

CHAPTER TEN

I returned to the common room, where the conversation had settled into the usual war gossip and rumours. While people never discussed war-related matters such as troop movements, it had proved impossible to stop people from chattering, gossiping and speculating about the war. I took most of it with a large grain of salt.

Last month the chat had been all about the invasion: where it would happen, when it would happen, how it would happen. Now we were well into autumn it was generally accepted that there would be no German invasion this year.

Maisie smiled at me as I sat down.

'Oh, I hate all this nonsense about the invasion,' she said. 'We all know Hitler has put it off until next year.' She glanced at the door to the kitchen. 'Is Levy in there?'

'I think so. We've finished preparing the Monster.'

'Want a cuppa? I need a cup of tea.'

'Love one,' I said.

As she walked to the kitchen, I wondered if Maisie was Levy's book borrowing friend. She was a lovely girl, and friendly with Levy, but they had never seemed all that close. I suppressed a sigh. Levy's love affairs were his business, but I hoped he wouldn't break the girl's heart. Or vice versa.

'It's the God's own truth,' said Doris Powell. She was a driver, aged around forty, with frizzy hair and a high girlish voice.

I realised that the discussion had moved on to a perennial favourite: spies and fifth columnists.

'It happened to a friend of a friend of my Aunt Glad. She'd been shopping in town and was on the bus back home to Swiss Cottage. Sitting next to her was a nun, all in black and covered right up, like they are. She thought she looked a bit hefty, but thought nothing of it until the – shall we say – the person reached to get something out of her bag. Then she saw how muscly and hairy the arms were. So she got up, very casually you understand, and went to tell the conductor, who told the driver, who detoured to the nearest police station. The police carted her off quick smart.'

Who did the police cart off, I mused, *Aunt Glad's friend's nosy friend or the hairy nun?* Powell's pronouns were confusing. I had heard the story before and it always was a 'friend of a friend' who discovered the German paratrooper or spy in nun's robes. I thought that life must have become extraordinarily difficult for hirsute or athletic nuns if they were to be mistaken for the enemy whenever they went out of doors.

'It's the looters I hate,' said Maisie, entering the room with Levy. 'A friend of mine was bombed out the other day, and when she was allowed to return to her flat it had been cleaned out. Her jewellery, her winter coat, even some of her underwear. She suspects it was the heavy rescue team, but the police say there's no evidence of that. It was devastating on top of the bomb damage.'

A few hours later, Levy and I were at a major incident close to the station in Bloomsbury. Two ambulances and two saloon cars from our station had been sent there. Light rescue were inside, trying to extract the injured from a cellar. I had accepted a cup of tea from the mobile refreshment van and was sitting with it in the darkness when I heard a yelp.

Levy appeared with Knaggs in a firm grip, followed by Mr Richie.

'Let me go, you bastard,' Knaggs panted, trying unsuccessfully to break away.

'What happened?' I asked.

'He tucked a bottle of something inside his coat,' said Levy. 'Maybe other items also. It was hard to make out what, he was very quick.'

'Constable!' Mr Richie's voice rang out across the bombsite. 'Police. Over here!'

A long minute of Knaggs's bluster passed before a policeman came up to us.

'What's all this, then?'

'I ain't done nothing wrong. He planted the stuff on me,' whined Knaggs.

'No he didn't,' I said, shocked.

'Let's have a look inside your coat, then.'

The policeman was gruffly officious as he opened Knaggs's coat and found a bottle of whisky tucked into an inside pocket.

'Look in the other pockets,' said Mr Richie.

A quick search revealed silver spoons and bits of jewellery.

'I've never seen these before,' said Knaggs in an aggrieved tone. 'He planted the stuff on me. He's always had it in for me.'

'That's enough,' said the constable. 'You're nicked.'

I glanced at Levy, who also appeared to be amused at the dialogue, which seemed to have come straight from a Punch and Judy show.

The policeman blew his whistle and another constable arrived at a run. 'Looter,' said our policeman, and the constable's lip curled.

They walked off with Knaggs between them, but before they turned the corner he twisted around to shout at Levy, 'I'll get you for this, you kike bastard.'

On our way to hospital, dodging bombs and bomb debris, I heard Levy's calm voice reassuring the patients, talking loudly to counter the deafness caused by blast. Helping, encouraging, sympathising, sometimes flirting.

'I'm sure they'll be able to fix the scarring. They're doing wonderful things now with scarring.'

'Pretty girl like you will be up and out dancing quick as a wink. I'll see you at the Café de Paris yet – be sure to save me a dance.'

'Don't fall asleep on me. Wake up! Wake up now. That's the ticket. Stay awake. Talk to me. I get terribly lonely back here you know. The driver's a stand-offish creature, won't chat with me at all.'

'Of course you won't die. I won't let you die.'

The air raid warden was standing in the middle of the road, pointing his torch towards the ground, where it made a small puddle of light, but the white letters 'ARP' on his steel hat showed clearly enough. The Monster jerked to a halt, and as I pushed open the door another ambulance raced past on its way to hospital with its load of injured.

The road was crunchy under my shoes and the surface was uneven, so that I lurched rather drunkenly towards the warden. What had been a row of houses lay in front of me. One was now a pile of rubble and another three were barely standing, but the rest of the row was seemingly untouched.

Several dark figures moved about in the gloom and there was the occasional flash of a torch. The raiders were retreating and the guns had become spasmodic, but when they sounded they lit up the whole scene, silhouetting the rescue party on the heaps of debris. As always, in the background was the steady swish of running water; water mains always ruptured in a blast.

'Quiet!' someone yelled.

Everything stopped as three figures crouched over the ruin in front of us. There could be no silence in such a scene, but they listened intently. Someone shook his head, and the slow work of searching the ruins recommenced.

I coughed a little in the bombsite fug of soot and dust and that indefinable 'air raid' smell of cordite and something I had not yet identified. The air seemed electric; it always did after a raid, as if the normal atmosphere had been sucked away and we were left with staler, thinner air to breathe.

The warden had a soldierly, erect carriage. When I got closer I saw the neat black moustache on his upper lip.

'It was a couple of tip and run raiders,' he said, and I thought I heard traces of a Welsh lilt. 'The latest thing.'

He meant that a couple of planes had flown over and dropped strings of bombs. Somehow it seemed worse when it was only one or two planes, as if actual spite were involved.

'Flew off half an hour ago,' he added.

He flicked a glance behind me and I turned to see Levy walking towards us, his gait unsteady as mine on the shifting rubble. He was carrying a couple of blankets from the ambulance.

'Right-oh,' I said, ignoring Levy's smile at the Australianism, 'where are our casualties?'

The warden removed his helmet to swipe at his forehead with a handkerchief. He gestured to the ruined houses behind him.

'The other ambulance took away four survivors. Your two wounded are over there.' He sounded tired. 'Elderly couple. He's been cut about by flying glass. She's worse off, looks like a badly broken arm. We're still searching for others, but no need for you to wait. I don't think we'll find anyone else alive.'

He let out a sigh. 'A family – mother, grandmother and two kids – were in an Anderson shelter behind that one,' he said, nodding towards one of the houses on the right that seemed to be undamaged. 'There was a direct hit on the shelter and not one of them survived.' He ran the handkerchief over his face again.

'How awful,' I said. It was totally inadequate, but what else could I say?

'We didn't find much of them.'

I hardly supposed that they would. We had found the Anderson shelters remarkably effective at protecting people, but nothing and nobody could survive a direct hit.

'We've put all that we found of them . . .' He began to shake, and I wondered if it would all crack and crumble away, this calm demeanour that was his only defence against the night's horror. He took a breath, paused, straightened his shoulders and continued, nodding towards the house, 'in a biscuit box.'

I shuddered involuntarily. A family of four whose remains could fit in a biscuit box. I had heard that in many cases the authorities were weighting coffins with rubble to sustain the pretence for relatives that there was something worth burying.

'There may be more to find, though,' he said. 'So I'm supposing we'll wait until the morning to hand it over.'

'Yes,' said Levy. 'We want all the remains together. Light rescue will deal with it.'

Light rescue searched the bombsites, trying to find the injured. If they did they would prepare them for removal by ambulance. Light rescue also found the bodies of the dead, which included digging into the earth around such sites, looking for the smallest bits of human remains. Sometimes they used sieves. It was a job that needed daylight.

'I knew them,' said the warden, in a strained voice. 'They were a nice family. Follow me. I'll take you to Mr and Mrs Nicholls.'

Stumbling as we negotiated the debris, we followed the warden to our patients. His thin strip of torchlight illuminated a pair of ghosts sitting on a pile of rubble. The old couple were coated with plaster dust and were holding hands like lost children waiting for their mother.

Levy and I tucked blankets around thin shoulders, then checked their injuries. In the past weeks we had found that blankets were more important than anything else. The force of the blast stripped away clothing, which meant that bomb victims were often chilled. We had learned that if a patient was not kept warm, death could come from no other reason than shock.

The old lady's right arm was at an unnatural angle.

'Compound fracture, humerus,' said Levy, unnecessarily. He looked around, flashed his torch on the ground and picked up a piece of wood to use as a temporary splint. We were both trained in first aid, but our job was to make only a quick appraisal of the injuries, prevent further damage and take the patients to hospital immediately. There was no time to dress superficial wounds or apply elaborate bandages.

'I'm the ambulance driver,' I said to the old man, flashing my torch at his face. It was like a modernist canvas: chalky white from plaster dust and overlaid with crazy streaks of black dirt and bright red blood that oozed from innumerable little lacerations caused by flying glass. 'I'll give you a quick once over, and we'll get you to the ambulance.'

He peered up at me suspiciously, holding a hand to his ear.

'What? What'd you say?'

It was likely he had been deafened by the blast, but he may have been deaf anyway. I repeated the words more loudly as I checked him over. His face and scalp were slick with blood and I was worried about a spongy patch on his head. Such injuries were always worrying, but he batted away my hands, preventing further examination.

'You're a bit young for this lark, aren't you?' he bellowed. 'You can't be more than sixteen.'

My mother always said that one day I would be pleased to be taken to be younger than I really was. This was not that day.

'No,' I replied loudly, in my schoolteacher voice. 'I am much older than sixteen. Please keep still and let me get on with it.'

The old man shook his head to show that he hadn't heard a word. Then he laughed, although his face looked like raw meat and the pain must have been almost unbearable. He turned to his wife, who was sitting rigidly, submitting to Levy's ministrations. 'Oi, mother. This little girl's taking liberties.'

Levy had pulled out a roll of bandages from his bag and was splinting the old lady's arm with the piece of wood he had picked up from the site and wrapped in a bandage for padding. She held her lips in a tight grimace, and made no sound at all as he did it, but the rigidity of her body and her quick shallow breaths were an indicator of the pain she was suffering.

'What? What d'ye say?' he bellowed at me.

I gave up any further attempt at examination. 'I'll bandage your head and then we will take you into the ambulance,' I said, speaking louder still, and more slowly. 'Mr Levy will be looking after you on the way to hospital.'

The old man looked up at Levy. 'Does she know what she's doing, this kid?' he yelled.

'Speak louder,' I muttered. 'They might not have heard you in Liverpool.'

Levy raised his torch to shine at his mouth and he said, loudly and distinctly, in his beautiful accent, 'She's bloody brilliant. Best driver in the service. Now won't you shut up and let us work.'

And with that, everything seemed to calm down and the old man lifted his head so that I could bandage the worst of the wounds.

I had seen it time and again when we attended at a bomb site. It was more than just Levy's clear upper class voice, although that always made an impression when it could be heard. I had decided it was his air of being completely in control. He spoke and acted as if he expected people to listen to what he was saying and to do what he asked them to do. And people usually listened and obeyed.

'Honest to God, miss, it was like the end of the world had come,' the old lady whispered, shivering under her blanket as Levy finished wrapping the bandage around her thin arm. 'Is the house going to be all right? Was anyone else hurt? They've not told us anything.'

I gave a false, reassuring smile. How could I tell her that the house behind them was listing badly and I suspected it could not be saved? How could I tell her that the family next door had all been killed?

As we took the couple to the ambulance I heard Levy humming something. I listened closely and realised it was the music hall song, 'Is 'e an Aussie, Lizzie, is 'e?'

'Shut up, Levy,' I said.

'Right-oh.'

CHAPTER ELEVEN

It was close to dawn when we headed back to Woburn Place. Our patients had been dropped off at hospital and the drone of the raiders was becoming fainter.

A thought struck me.

'Levy, do you think Goering gives the pilots specific instructions about where to drop their bombs?'

He laughed. 'We're talking about Germany. I suspect they're given specific instructions about when and how to scratch their backsides.'

'Be serious, how can trashing the West End or the City or the outer London suburbs help the German war machine?'

'Maximum terror, Brennan. You know that. They want to destroy our morale so we'll be a crushed people when they invade.' He lowered his voice to imitate a German accent. 'Then you English pigs vill be taken *en masse* to Poland and work as slave labourers under ze lash.'

'Fat chance of that!'

He laughed.

I thought about what Levy had said, and said slowly, 'I really don't think this bombing will achieve what Hitler thinks. It seems to me that, in the middle of such suffering and hardship, the heroic side of human nature takes over. Haven't you noticed how friendly and helpful people are being to each other?'

'Yes, we have very friendly looters.'

'Speaking of looters, do you think Knaggs will go to jail?'

He shook his head. 'More likely a fine. Knaggs was lucky. Didn't have much on him when he was caught. Doubt he'll return to the station though.'

'He was very upset when you caught him. Someone like that has friends, nasty friends who might—'

'You worry too much, Brennan.' He was peering out of his window. 'Do you know where we are, right now?'

Levy asked me that often when we were driving around in the dark. He adored London with a passion matching that of Dr Johnson, who had declared that to be tired of the city was to be tired of life. Levy knew its history and often told me stories about the places we visited. I was well aware what misery this constant bombardment was causing him, as he saw so much of what he loved being destroyed.

'Soho,' I replied. 'Vice and crime. The Windmill and its naked girls. Lots of foreigners and probably lots of spies. The only place in London where you can get decent coffee and *koláč*.'

Levy shifted in his seat beside me. The passenger's seat was probably as uncomfortable as the driver's, I thought.

'And looters, black marketeers, thieves, pickpockets and extortionists,' he declared in a sombre voice. 'All here in Soho, our Latin Quarter.'

Then, in a brighter tone. 'D'you know where the name Soho comes from?'

'No.' I knew he'd delight in enlightening me.

'It was a hunting cry, from the time when all this was woodland and the king and his knights hunted deer and wild boar here.'

'So *ho*!' I said, with spirit, over the rumble of the engine.

'So ho, indeed. Only nowadays it's we Londoners who are the prey.'

Levy pulled himself up straight and peered out of the window again. 'Do you know where we are now, Brennan?'

'Haven't a clue, Levy. Somewhere near Soho?'

In the gloom I could feel, rather than see, his smile.

'Turn right at the next corner, please.'

I followed Levy's directions through the darkened streets, as he took us back by a circuitous route. He did that sometimes, guided me into areas of London he particularly liked or that he wanted to tell me about. We had been in trouble more than a few times for not returning directly to base.

'Where are we going?'

'Not much further. Right here and then sharp left.'

We emerged on to what even I recognised as the Embankment. In front of us the Thames was an opalescent shimmer in the moonlight.

'Mrs Coke will be sending out a search party,' I said. It would be one more black mark against us, one we really did not need. My fear was that she would assign Levy to another driver, separate us, just as I used to separate the troublemakers in the class when I was teaching. Levy made a gesture that indicated his view of the importance of Mrs Coke.

'Pull over, if you'd be so kind, Brennan,' he said.

'Levy, we can't stop here. We should go back to Woburn Place.'

'I need a cigarette. And I'm not about to let that upstart fraudster dictate my movements.'

I pulled over and switched off the engine.

'Whatever do you mean?'

'I'll tell you about it outside.'

We got out and stood together, leaning against the ambulance.

'What did you mean about Mrs Coke?'

He gave a short laugh. 'You'll be annoyed.'

'What have you done, Levy?'

'Let's not spoil the moment, Brennan.'

He refused to say more, and so I put away my worries and simply enjoyed the quiet time as Levy smoked his cigarette and the sky lightened around us.

'The ladies' bridge is coming along nicely,' said Levy.

The new Waterloo Bridge, still in the process of being built, stood starkly incomplete over the river. Londoners called it the 'ladies' bridge' because, in the absence of the men who had been called up or were being used for war work, it was mainly women who were constructing it.

I turned to look at the river. In the hour before dawn it was wide and quiet and beautiful. It had been flowing through London since the city was merely a few huts on a muddy bank, I mused, and it would probably continue to flow when all around us was dust. Sometimes bombs fell into the river and it swallowed them whole. The Thames would survive whatever the Luftwaffe threw at it. Would London?

'I used to tell my students back in Australia that London was the biggest city the world has ever known,' I said. 'To give them some idea of its size I'd say that if we took all the people in Perth, and all the people in Sydney, Melbourne, Adelaide, Brisbane and Hobart, and then every other resident of Australia and added to that lot the whole population of New Zealand, still you would not have totalled the inhabitants of Greater London.'

'Were they impressed?'

'Mightily. But they were country children in a tiny town in the middle of nowhere. How could they comprehend the enormity of London?'

'I think Hitler and Goering are only now beginning to realise the enormity of the task they set themselves with this Blitz.'

'What did you mean about Mrs Coke?' I asked.

He gave a short laugh. 'You're like a terrier aren't you. Won't let things go.'

'You're always saying Mrs Coke isn't on the up and up. Have you found something to prove it?'

'I've discovered some interesting information about the way she runs that charity fund of hers.'

'The Ambulance Benevolent Fund?'

'Yes. There's a decided whiff of corruption about it all. The registered address is our ambulance station, which means that Ma Coke receives all cheques for the fund there. She's been paying them directly into her personal bank account.'

'How do you know that?'

'She's asked McIver to deposit a few of them.'

Beryl McIver was one of the deputy station officers, a Scotswoman. I liked her. She was not the sort of woman to exaggerate or make up tales.

'Into Mrs Coke's personal account? Not into a specific account for the fund?'

'There is no bank account for the fund, apparently. McIver asked her about it and was told to mind her own business.'

I frowned at the river.

'That is odd, I agree. And McIver told you this?'

He seemed flustered. 'She told someone who told me. But there's more.'

'What do you mean?'

'Mrs Coke has been using the letterhead of an exclusive London club to write letters seeking a generous monetary donation for Lady Mary, Mrs Coke.'

'That stupid fake title again. Why would people give money to Lady Mary?'

'She's signed the letters as Lord Castledown.'

'I repeat – why would anyone give fake Lady Mary money, even if fake Lord Castledown asks them to?'

'The money is sought,' said Levy, barely able to contain his mirth, 'to fund Lady Mary in forming a secret force to go behind enemy lines in France and sabotage the German invasion.'

'What?' I gave a short bark of laughter. 'The woman doesn't even speak French. I tried her out once and she was hopeless. This is a fantasy. I can't believe anyone would fall for it.'

'She's pulling on their patriotic heartstrings, Brennan. And if only a small percentage respond, she's got her profit.'

I no longer felt like laughing. It was unforgivable to prey on people's patriotic goodwill in such a calculated manner.

'The evidence will be passed on to the proper authorities in the Ambulance Service. She'll be gone by the end of the month, I suspect.'

I was confused. 'Who told you all of this? Who gave you the evidence? Was it in that envelope, the one in the book?'

He turned away to stare at the river and did not reply.

'Levy, be careful,' I said. 'If Mrs Coke gets any hint of what you're doing she'll have you transferred to another station straight away.'

'I'm always careful,' he replied, smiling.

The All Clear sounded, that long steady siren note announcing that the raiders had departed our skies.

'They're heading back to France,' said Levy, looking up at the empty sky. 'Racing the dawn and the RAF.'

I thought of Jim, up there, chasing them. I had not told Levy about my date with Jim, who had not contacted me again in the past week. If he had been at all interested in me, he would have sent me a note or flowers or called me after two days. Not that I was surprised. I was simply not a Dorchester type. If that was the sort of woman he wanted, I was better off without him. And yet, I'd really liked him at first. I thought again of Henri Valhubert. Perhaps I was simply a bad judge of men's character.

As if he could read my mind, Levy remarked, in a teasing tone, 'Speaking of the RAF, I hear you met Jim Vassilikov the other day.'

'However did you find that out?' I said lightly. 'We went to an afternoon concert on Sunday and then tea afterwards. It was all very dull, I'm afraid, and he's not contacted me since.'

'He's a fast worker,' Levy replied, obviously surprised. 'Anyway, you shouldn't take it personally that he's not contacted you. He was shot down earlier this week.'

It was as if I was in some other place, one where I was bitterly cold and the air was thin.

'Shot down?'

'Don't look like that, Brennan. God – you only met him once. He's fine – well, I'm told he'll live.' His voice softened. 'Apologies for breaking it to you so flippantly. I didn't realise . . . Do you want me to find out what hospital he's in?'

I nodded, then shook my head vigorously. 'He won't want to see me. We obviously didn't "click" because he didn't seriously suggest another meeting.'

Levy laughed. 'What is it with girls and pilots? At least write to the poor chap. Maybe you intimidated him – you intimidate me.'

'Ha. I doubt that. Isn't he some sort of Russian duke or something?'

'Would it make a difference if he was?'

'Probably,' I admitted. 'I'm more a Lyons girl than a Dorchester lady.'

'Snob,' he replied. 'That's prejudice, pure and simple. If you like him, forget about all that rot.'

'What is his title?'

'Old Harrovian. Decent chap despite it. That's all you'll get from me. Except . . .'

'Except what?'

'He's shy, you know.'

'Shy?' I laughed. 'He's a Russian duke or something. I doubt he's shy. He didn't seem shy to me.'

'He was shy at Harrow. Maybe you're right, people change. Maybe he simply found you to be dull and your company tedious.'

I decided to ignore that. 'You really think I should write to him in hospital?'

'Common politeness to write, Brennan. Or send grapes or something.'

'Who can get grapes nowadays?'

'Anyone with a deep enough pocket.'

'How deep?'

'Twenty-five shillings a bunch I believe.'

'I'm hardly going to waste two weeks' pay on a bunch of grapes. You're sure he's going to be all right?'

'Yes, I heard he'd pull though.'

We climbed into the ambulance to begin our journey back to Woburn Place. In one of those dramatic English weather shifts, a soft drizzle had set in, the sort that could last all day. It matched my mood. I needed all my concentration to negotiate the hazards on the road and I tried to push my worries about Jim out of my head. But I felt a little shaky after hearing the news that he'd been shot down, and I realised just how disappointed I had been over not receiving a note, or flowers or anything to show that he really did want to see me again.

'Going out tonight, Brennan? It's Saturday night, after all.'

When I glanced at him, Levy was resting his head on the back of the seat and his eyes were closed.

Going out was the last thing on my mind.

'I think I'll spend a quiet night in – if Jerry lets me.'

'I thought you Aussie girls were out every night.'

'Enjoying the bright lights of London?' I laughed. 'I'll let you in on a secret, cobber. There's a thing called the Blitz and it means there are no bright lights now. It interferes with our social life something dreadful.'

He laughed. 'Cobber.'

'It means friend.'

'I know; I like the way it sounds,' he said and repeated the word. 'Cobber.'

'Maybe something will crop up to tempt me.' Or maybe I'd spend the evening writing a get-well letter to Jim. 'Do you have plans?'

He took a breath and let it out slowly. Nodded.

'You don't seem too happy about them,' I said. 'What are they?'

'Madness most discreet,' he murmured, twisting his head away from me to stare out of the window.

'Whatever are you on about, Levy?'

'Never mind.'

CHAPTER TWELVE

The caretaker banged on my door that afternoon with the news that I had a telephone call. I raced downstairs to the lobby, expecting the worst, to find it was Levy who was on the line. Apparently Jim was recuperating in the Princess Mary Hospital, near the Halton RAF Base in Buckinghamshire.

'How is he?'

Levy's voice was flat and tinny through the phone line. 'Took a couple of bullets but managed to get the plane to ground.'

'For heaven's sake, Levy. That doesn't tell me anything about how he is. *How is he?*'

'All I know is that he's expected to recover. Won't be flying for a while, though.'

'Good.' I breathed the word.

I heard him laugh. 'Pilots. It's as if they become magically attractive to women once they pin on those bloody wings. Here we have Brennan, an otherwise sensible young woman, who goes out once with old Vassy and falls head—'

'Shut up, Levy.'

'I was at school with him. I feel obliged to inform you that his feet smell and he's—'

'I'm hanging up now. Thanks for the news.'

'Wait. If you want, I'll go with you to Halton.'

I stood holding the receiver, unsure. 'Levy, we can't just lob into the hospital and expect to see him. Anyway, it's miles away, right out in the country.'

'Couple of hours by train.'

I said, cautiously, 'When would you go?'

'Tomorrow's our day off.'

'He may not be up to seeing visitors so soon.'

'I'll find out. Stay by the phone.'

I sat by the lobby telephone glaring at anyone who looked as if they wanted to use the machine. Levy telephoned back a quarter of an hour later.

'Vassy told the nurse he'd be delighted to see his old school chum David Levy and Miss Lily Brennan. So, are you in?'

I was not sure if I believed him. I was not sure it was the right thing to do. I suspected it would all end in tears.

'All right.'

I hated the hospital smell, that first sharp carbolic whiff as we entered the vestibule. I hated the officious white-garbed nurse at the desk. I hated the neat rows of beds that held a world of suffering. I hated seeing Jim Vassilikov lying there, white-faced and sunken-eyed, wincing with each breath and trying to smile.

'I say, Vassy, damned clumsy to let Jerry get you. Waste of an aeroplane.' Levy had turned into Bertie Wooster. I knew it was a protective mechanism. He hated hospitals as much as I did.

'Sight for sore eyes,' said Jim, looking at me.

'Steady on, old man,' replied Levy. 'Like you, of course, but—'

'Not you, silly ass. Lily.' Jim's voice seemed very strained.

'Don't try to talk,' I said, as I perched awkwardly on one of the chairs beside the bed. Levy sat next to me. There was silence for a moment.

'I'll talk for everyone, then,' said Levy, and he began to chatter about people I had never heard of while Jim and I shot nervous glances at each other.

'Shut up, David,' said Jim, finally looking at him. 'Don't people usually bring grapes?'

Levy stood. 'You know, I forgot the grapes. I'll just pop out and get them. I'll leave Lily with you, shall I?' He gave Jim a look, got up and left the ward.

'We both hate hospitals,' I said.

Jim tried to laugh, which clearly pained him. 'I'm not partial to them myself.' He took a breath and said, haltingly, 'It's marvellous to see you. I meant to write, thank you for Sunday, but in the event . . .'

'It's fine. Don't worry about it. How . . .?'

There was a movement that could have been a shrug, but ended in a grunt of pain. 'A one-ten came out of the clouds ahead of me. As I dived after it the rear gunner started up, and bullets came through into my cockpit.'

My hands were tingling and I realised it was because I was holding them in tight fists. 'And you were hit.'

'Bit of a mess inside, they tell me. But I'll be fine.'

'That's good to hear.'

He smiled. 'Never play poker, Lily. Honestly, I'll be fine. Won't fly for a while, maybe never again if my lungs . . .' His smile had disappeared and he sounded bitter. 'There's a desk job already lined up for me once I'm out of here.'

I looked down, to brush some invisible lint off my jacket and hide from him my joy to hear that he could no longer fly. Desk jobs were safer than flying; if anywhere could be said to be safe at the moment.

'I'm a bit of a linguist, you see,' he said. 'The RAF can still use me. Even if I can't fly.' He stopped after each short sentence to take a breath.

'Will you be based in London?'

'Mainly in London.'

I had run out of conversational gambits and we lapsed into silence.

When Jim spoke next he made little sense. 'Lily – when I'm – it would be – I mean, I'd like – if you're not – but I suppose you're—'

'I love concerts,' I said. 'The ones at the National Gallery are usually—'

'That sounds marvellous.'

Levy returned in a clamour of chattering energy. 'You've got other guests, my lad. Had no idea you were so popular, otherwise wouldn't have bothered to bring little Lily all this way to see you.'

I looked up to see Celia Ashwin and another woman entering the ward behind him. Her hair was auburn and she had the same thin straight nose as Celia, so I assumed the other woman was Celia's sister, the one Jim had 'had a thing for' at Cambridge. She did not catch the eye the way Celia did, because there was a liveliness and grace about Celia that was striking. Still, she was an attractive woman, and dressed up to the nines in an elegant bottle-green suit and a tartan blouse.

Jim puffed out the introductions. He was tiring fast, and I felt embarrassed to have exhausted him. Celia's sister was Mrs Helen Markham, a fact which gave me some comfort. I assumed she had not been married when Jim knew her at Cambridge.

There was a slight shudder when Helen Markham heard Levy's name, and a bare nod in reply to his polite 'How do you do?' She flicked a glance at me.

'Australian? You're a long way from home. Whatever are you doing over here?'

'Miss Brennan works with me at the ambulance station,' Celia explained, in her cool way. 'As does Mr Levy.'

'So we are all involved in the war effort,' said Helen. 'I help to run a small charity – Comforts for the Bombed. We provide blankets and clothing for those who've been bombed out.'

And I bet you do it with an immaculately gloved iron fist, I thought. My instant dislike of her air of self-congratulation had nothing to do with her past involvement with Jim. She was the sort of woman I detested.

'There's a great deal of work to be done,' she went on. 'A great deal. Often we are working far into the night.'

I murmured something appropriate in response and wondered if she knew anything about the long hours her sister, Levy and

I worked. I glanced at Celia, who seemed to be uncomfortable with the exchange: she was examining something over to her right with a fixed, wooden expression.

'And how do you know Jim?' Helen asked me, because, apparently, Levy had become invisible.

'I work with Mr Levy, who was at school with him,' I said.

Helen addressed Jim, seeking confirmation. 'Goodness. At *Harrow*? Really?'

Jim's ironic smile appeared, although his face was now chalky white and he winced as he took a breath to reply.

'Yes, at Harrow. David was my best friend at that godawful place.'

'Young Ivan was as Jonathan,' said Levy, in his most irritating drawl and putting a hand to his chest, 'to David.' He raised his voice, and declaimed theatrically, 'Oh, Jonathan. How are the mighty fallen in the midst of the battle. They were swifter than eagles, They were stronger than lions.' He added, in his normal voice, smiling radiantly at Helen, 'My people know how to string a word or two together.'

Jim's smile widened, but as soon faded. His jaw was tight and his lips stretched flat against his teeth.

'Do you need morphine?' I asked.

'Wouldn't mind a dash,' he grunted.

'I'll find a nurse,' said Helen imperiously. As she turned to leave she muttered, 'Your people did *not* write the King James Bible. The English did.'

Celia and Levy locked glances for a second, but her gaze swiftly slid away from him to rest on me. 'How on earth did you get here?' she asked.

'Train,' I replied. 'Though there was an hour's delay because of damage to the line just out of London.'

If Celia and her sister had come by car from London, the obvious thing to do would be to offer us a lift home. Nearly everybody who had private cars offered lifts nowadays. Drivers would stop at bus stops to offer rides to complete strangers.

Many kept a notice on their windscreen, 'Hail me if you want a lift.'

Celia seemed about to say something, thought better of it, then turned her attention to Jim.

'We should be going,' I murmured when Helen returned with a nurse. As Levy and I made our farewells, Helen was leaning over Jim making soft, cooing noises. I assumed there were words, but I could only hear the coo.

As we neared the doorway I slowed, wanting to look back and not daring. I looked back finally and met Jim's eyes as Levy hustled me out of the door.

On our way to the bus stop I took pleasure in muttering every nasty name I knew and applying them all to Helen Markham under cover of the din of planes taking off and landing somewhere nearby.

A queue had formed along the footpath and we joined it. Behind us was a small copse that smelled of damp earth and growing things. Across the road were open fields. Normally I would have been delighted to be out of the city, breathing air that was fresh and not tinged with brick dust and cordite, but the walk had not dulled my rage.

'Helen Markham is a nasty witch,' I whispered to Levy.

He smiled. 'She was polite, at least.'

The bus for the railway station arrived and the queue began to shuffle slowly forwards.

'Only just,' I said. 'And Ashwin should have offered us a lift back to London. She's as bad as her ghastly sister.'

He shrugged as he ushered me into the bus. 'Ashwin's not that bad,' he said when we had sat down. 'I can't see Helen Markham squatting in the dirt beside a dying old man, holding his hand with raiders dead overhead and strings of bombs falling nearby.'

'No,' I admitted. 'Mrs Helen bloody Markham wouldn't do that.' My rage boiled over. 'He used to be in love with her.'

'Who?'

'Jim. He was in love with Ashwin's wretched sister when he was at Cambridge. He told me so. I've lost all respect for him now.'

'Cambridge was years ago, Brennan. Gallons of water under the bridge since then.'

I wasn't so sure. He had told me he was part of her set at Cambridge. Levy might have been his friend at school, but that fact alone did not mean Jim was not anti-Semitic in general. It was easy to like Levy once you got to know him. Jim, like Squire, might simply consider Levy to be 'different' from the rest of his people. I detested such prejudice. When I was seventeen there had been race riots in the Eastern Goldfields, near to Kookynie. Angry mobs set fire to the homes of Italians and Slavs who had done absolutely nothing to harm anyone, and a man had died. The violence I had seen in Prague was far worse, but it all sprang from the same source: ignorant prejudice fanned by unscrupulous people.

'Jim was frightfully embarrassed at Mrs Markham's behaviour, as was Ashwin, I think,' said Levy.

'You've not been close to Jim for years. How do you know that? How do you know what he believes in?'

'He's no fascist, Brennan. I'm quite sure of that.'

I sucked in a breath and let it out slowly. 'I bet Helen Markham's husband is a fascist, just like Ashwin's ghastly husband and Oswald Mosley.'

Levy shook his head. 'You'd lose that bet. Major Markham, who is a fair deal older than his wife, is a friend of Churchill's. He's high up in the War Office.' Levy's smile was bitter. 'He probably does loathe Jews, though. Anti-Semitism is a fact of life in their class.'

'I hate it. Hate them all.'

'Don't hate Ashwin for not offering a lift. She did us a favour. Just imagine the horror of a couple of hours trapped in a car with Helen Markham.'

'Too true.' I laughed. 'Thank you Ashwin.'

'And don't hate Vassy,' he said. 'No matter how he felt about the woman when he was a lad of eighteen or so, he's not in love with her any more.'

I snorted my disbelief.

'Jim's eyes did not light up when he saw Helen bloody Markham. They most certainly did when he saw Lily Brennan.'

CHAPTER THIRTEEN

November came in a flurry of crackling leaves, thick and golden-brown on the pavements, blowing in crisp eddies, shushing under my feet. And for the first days of the new month daylight raids ceased entirely; the night raids seemed to have become lighter and they brought far less damage. We all began to hope.

There was no air raid on the night of the third of November. At half-past five in the evening the sirens sounded their monotonous prelude, but an hour later we heard the All Clear. I waited. Nothing happened. After fifty-seven consecutive nights of warnings and bombings, the darkness brought no German planes over London. In the morning there was talk on the streets. Had the English weather become too bad even for the Nazis? Could this be the finish of the Blitz?

The next night dashed our hope. The raiders returned, and the following morning the street sweepers again swept up glass with the leaves. Every night thereafter the raiders came. They attacked us in all weather, through gusty autumn showers and nights of great moonlit beauty, through black soaking rain and through thick clouds and fog, their deluge of bombs falling equally on the just and the unjust. Squire reported at the station one morning that he had been bombed out for the third time. The following day Mrs Coke's 'charming little place in Kensington' was a pile of rubble.

In the West End, a dogged crowd of revellers and working girls defied the danger, but otherwise the darkness of blacked-out London was now almost entirely the haunt of wardens and police and rescue workers. Levy and I were among the few who saw the beauty of a London under siege, lit by the dusty bluish glow of 'star-lighting', as we called the hazy shimmer of the filtered street-lamps, and by the thin crosses of red, green and yellow that shone through masked traffic lights. Passing buses glimmered blue inside their curtained windows, and in the early evening sharp flashes of torchlight on the footpaths illuminated the quick-stepping feet of the few pedestrians.

On clear nights the stars blazed overhead in a glittering curtain that was invisible in the neon lights of peacetime. We saw the city's austere beauty under a bombers' moon that bleached the grand buildings to bone-white skeletons. By moonlight even the most overdone Victorian monstrosity assumed a remote and classic magnificence.

Each evening the city seemed to hold its breath. Then the wailing notes of the Warning siren would sound. The drone of approaching bombers would become louder, until at last the world fragmented into colour and light: sharp flashes of gunfire, whitish-green and hissing incendiaries, the blazing brightness of exploding bombs. Tall yellow flares of burning gas mains raged at the sky and the inevitable fires saturated everything in a fierce orange-red glow.

With daylight, the raiders retreated and Londoners emerged to see what destruction they had wrought in the night. Each morning we would be reminded anew that we lived now in a wartime landscape, one that shifted and changed overnight. Anything – buildings, people, a lifetime of memories – could disappear without warning into the maelstrom known as the Blitz.

And still, as far as was possible, it was 'business as usual'. We became used to the new timetable of life, with all its discomforts and uncertainties. Life went on. Unsafe buildings were flattened by demolition charges, paths were pushed through to re-open streets, bridges were rebuilt, gas and water mains re-laid, telephones reconnected. When the main sewer was damaged, sewage was diverted into Levy's beloved Thames.

Everyday life continued, despite the destruction that came every night, and some of the changes were welcome ones. English men and women of different classes, localities, sets and tastes talked to each other now without constraint. We smiled at strangers in the street, swapped Blitz stories and lived with the unimaginable. Children played among the rubble on the bomb sites, looters continued their dirty business, babies were born – one in our ambulance on the way to hospital – people died, and people fell in love.

I arrived back at St Andrew's two weeks after our visit to the RAF hospital to find in my letterbox a postcard from Jim Vassilikov, asking me to join him at the National Gallery for a concert the following week. He left a number for me to call and added, 'I think it is your week on nights, so you choose the day.'

I was impressed that he knew my schedule, and supposed he had asked Levy.

Katherine entered the lobby as I stood looking at the postcard, which was a rather garishly coloured photograph of Trafalgar Square.

'Bad news?' she asked.

I laughed. 'No. Surprising.' I handed her the postcard and she too laughed.

'Not the most romantic of men,' she said. 'First an invitation to a concert that wasn't really an invitation. Now an offhand, "If you're free, would you care to attend another concert?"' She turned it over to look at the picture. 'It's always music with him. Are you going?'

'Yes, I will. Friday, I think. He was shot down a few weeks ago and is just out of hospital.'

'Hmm. A Mayfair number. What will you wear?'

'It's not always about clothes, you know.' I smiled at her. 'Not *always*.'

'Heresy.' Katherine smiled and handed back the postcard.

*   *   *

I slept badly on the Thursday night. We had been expecting a heavy raid, because the moon was full and it was a fairly clear night, but the Warning had not sounded by the time I went to bed. I was so used to the air raid din that silence was uncanny; it kept me edgy and wakeful. In the early hours I was woken by a couple of planes that came in low over St Andrew's. I held my breath, wondering if we were the target, and cringed at the whistle of falling bombs. It sounded as if they had fallen very near because the building shook alarmingly a second or so later. There were no further disturbances that night.

It was when I turned on the wireless the following morning that the reason for the quiet night over London became clear. While I had tossed and turned, expecting aeroplanes that did not arrive, Coventry had been just about annihilated. The medieval centre of the city was gone, Coventry Cathedral had been practically destroyed, and there were around a thousand casualties.

At breakfast, everyone in the restaurant was sombre and upset. We Londoners knew that other towns were being bombed, some very badly, but London was bearing the brunt of German attacks and London could take it. It seemed 'unsporting' to so devastate a small town such as Coventry.

'And the news from the Balkans is bad too,' said Katherine. 'The Germans have virtually occupied Romania. It won't be long before Herr Hitler adds another country to his list.'

'I shall never bother with Germans or any other foreigners ever again,' said Pam. 'Never. Even after we win this war.'

'Yes you will,' said Katherine. 'British are bad at hating.' She picked at her breakfast. 'I think I'd sell my firstborn child for a real egg.'

Pam sniffed. 'I'm Australian, and you don't have any children.'

'What about the Greeks?' I said. 'They've supported us throughout.'

'I like the Greeks,' admitted Pam.

'Czechs?' I asked. 'And the Free French forces? You were saying what wonderful dancers they were.'

'I don't mind Czechs. Or the Free French. Except when they recite Verlaine at me, with soulful expressions. My French isn't good enough.'

'The Dutch?' asked Katherine, obviously teasing. 'Belgians? You must like Norwegians and Danes.'

'The gallant Finns?' I put in.

'Albanians?' said Katherine. 'How can you dislike a people whose king is named Zog?'

'And what about the poor Poles? Their pilots are wonderful, I hear.'

'So, Lily, you're meeting your flight lieutenant again today,' said Pam, changing the subject in a very determined voice.

I admitted I was. Pam glanced at Katherine, who nodded.

'What?' I asked.

'Katherine and I have decided we will make you presentable.'

I laughed. 'What do you mean? I'm fine as I am.'

Pam shook her head. 'Your hair is a mess, and your nails – well, Lily – frankly, they're a disgrace.'

'I'm an ambulance driver. I don't have time—'

'Pam's right,' said Katherine, pushing her plate away. 'If Celia Ashwin's sister was his best girl at Cambridge then he has an eye for a well-turned out woman.' She gave a decided nod. 'So we're going to assist you. We will brook no argument.'

They put in a good two hours that morning to make me 'presentable'. My hair was coiffed, my nails manicured and my eyebrows plucked. Katherine went through my closet and picked out a navy blue coat dress with embroidery on the neckline and cuffs.

'It'll do as well for a Lyons as for the Ritz,' she said, as she tied a sash of scarlet ribbon at the waist.

When I left the building they were smiling like a pair of fairy godmothers sending their charge off to the ball.

It was a rainy, blustery morning and my umbrella was constantly blown inside out. My rain bonnet kept my hair dry but my face was dripping wet when I found Jim at the Gallery. The doors opened at twelve-thirty, half an hour before the concert began, but long queues always formed in Trafalgar Square well before then, so we had arranged to meet at noon.

He was already in the line, close to the front of the queue, sheltered under the enormous portico, his greatcoat firmly buttoned against the weather. I had forgotten how tall he was. When I first saw him he had a grave expression, but his smile was sweet and rather boyish when he caught sight of me.

I wiped my face with my handkerchief. It was so wet there was no point worrying about my lipstick, or the face powder so carefully applied an hour before. I wrung out the dripping hankie, tucked it in my handbag and looked up at him with a smile. 'How long have you been waiting?'

'About half an hour. I didn't want us to miss out. They're using the basement shelter because of the possibility of daylight bombing, and there's room for only three or four hundred people down there.'

I undid the rain bonnet and fluffed up my hair. 'I picked a bad day for this. Sorry to make you queue in the rain.'

'No need to apologise for the rain, not if it might keep Jerry away. And it's a marvellous programme. The Griller Quartet playing Dvořák and Sibelius. Worth a bit of water.'

Before the programme began, Myra Hess said a few words about Coventry and how music, at such a time, was surely an assertion of eternal values. Then the quartet began to play. We sat, gently steaming, in the crowded basement and were entranced. In common with half the audience I found myself in tears. As I gave myself up to the joy of the performance I thought that wars were undoubtedly barbaric, but if human beings could also conceive, perform and appreciate such music then there was some hope for us.

Afterwards, we walked through the largely empty galleries to the exit. The art had been shipped out to God knew where at the start of the war and they had put up exhibitions of sketches and paintings done by the official war painters.

In the basement Jim had appeared to be fully recovered from his injuries; in better light he had the pinched look of men who have suffered great pain. Deep lines furrowed his forehead and his uniform hung loosely. Despite his calm demeanour I sensed an agitation that was being held firmly in check.

'How long do I have you for?' he asked.

'I beg your pardon?'

'When do you start your night shift?'

'Oh. I should be back at the flat by four-fifteen at the latest, to change and get to the station by five.'

He glanced at his watch. 'Two hours, then. Are you hungry?'

'Starving.'

He laughed. 'What about the Lyons on the Strand for lunch?'

I wondered if Levy had reported my comment about being more a Lyons girl than a Dorchester lady. The Lyons on the Strand was a Corner House. It was grander than a teashop, which had a cafeteria counter, but nowhere near as grand as the Dorchester.

'I'd like that,' I said.

An elderly nippy showed us to our table. She wore the black dress, white apron and little lace cap of all the J. Lyons & Co. waitresses. She did not speak Russian or French to Jim, although she was obviously impressed by his uniform. Nor was there a wiggle in her walk as she left to deliver our order.

On our way to the Corner House we had spoken of innocuous things – the weather, the raid on Coventry, how prices had skyrocketed with the war, what we thought the government would put under the ration next – but now we seemed to have run out of conversation.

Jim sat back in his chair. On his face was the grave, rather melancholy expression that seemed habitual when he was not smiling. The long fingers of his right hand slowly tapped on the table, as if he were playing a piano.

'Do you play?' I asked.

He seemed surprised at my question, and I nodded at his hand, still tapping the table. He laughed.

'Just adequately, but with great enthusiasm. Or so my piano teacher always said. You?'

'Piano. Also only adequately. And percussion in my school orchestra.'

Jim laughed.

'People always laugh when I tell them that,' I said, with some dignity.

His smile was remorseful. 'I suppose because you're so small, and percussion is loud,' he said.

'It's not always loud. Sometimes it's very soft and subtle. What about the celesta?'

Jim bowed his head in apology. 'I give you the angelic celesta,' he said. 'Beloved by Tchaikovsky and all sugar plum fairies.'

'Sometimes, I admit, I could be very loud,' I conceded, smiling at him. 'Especially with the cymbals.'

'Is that why you chose it? To make a noise? To stand out?'

I shrugged. 'They needed a percussionist and no one else volunteered, so I said I'd give it a go.'

'Fair enough,' said Jim. 'Isn't that what you Aussies say?'

'Too right.'

Our glances met, slid away. He straightened his knife, then his spoon. Looking at him now I thought that Levy might well be right, that Jim was shy.

'So,' I said, 'had you always wanted to be a pilot?'

He looked up at me. 'I joined the Cambridge University air squadron when I first arrived at university. That meant I went straight into the RAF as a pilot officer.'

'You must love flying.'

'I do love flying.' A spasm of what might have been pain twisted his face. 'Only now I'm now a ground wallah.'

I gave him a quizzical look.

'An RAF officer who does not fly,' he explained.

'You'll never fly again?'

'Not for a while, at least.'

'Your mother must be pleased,' I said.

His smile became sardonic. 'She doesn't know. My mother resides in Paris. She's been there since 1937.'

'How is she coping with the German occupation?'

'My mother survived the Bolsheviks; she doesn't fear the Nazis. I don't hear from her much. But then, I didn't hear from her much before the war either. She's not the doting kind of mother.'

The note in his voice led me to change the subject.

'You said they'd found you another job. Here in London?'

'Yes, in London. I start next week.'

'Anything exciting?'

'I'm going to be sitting behind a desk.'

'Just sitting?'

'Occasionally I'll get up and walk around.' He was obviously not going to tell me what he would be doing.

'My uncle was here in the last war,' I said. 'He told me that he spent his time sitting behind a desk, not doing much. He was an intelligence officer, of course, doing top secret stuff.' I meant it as a joke.

There was no reply. When I turned to look at him, Jim was staring at a point over my shoulder. Two red blushes stained his cheeks and I caught the wry smile. I realised that I'd guessed correctly and began to mumble something – anything – when he gave a laugh.

'Look, Lily, they've put me into a rather boring job. It's probably exactly what your uncle was doing in the last war. Reading reports, filling in forms and basically being terrifically bored while my chums are risking it all up there.' He pointed upwards. 'What I'll be doing is not exciting and it's not dangerous and it's not that important.'

I nodded dutifully. 'Of course. I understand.'

That was exactly what Uncle Charles would have said. Jim was intelligent, could speak several languages and was posh.

He had to be in counter-intelligence and it was probably very important indeed.

'What did you read at Cambridge?' I asked, to change the subject again.

'Law. I was called to the bar just before the war, at the Middle Temple.'

I made a groaning sound. It was inadvertent, and he threw me a quick look of surprise.

'Sorry,' I said. 'My uncle's a judge.'

Jim seemed amused. 'I take it he's not your favourite uncle.'

In fact I loved my Uncle Charles dearly, but he was able to annoy me more than just about anyone I knew, for two reasons. First, he rarely lost his temper, no matter what provocation I gave him; secondly, he never gave an opinion unless he had thought it through from every angle. This meant, annoyingly, that he was almost always right.

'He's my only uncle and I love him. It's just that he's so very . . . sure of himself.'

'A professional failing, I suspect,' he said, with a laugh. 'I'm told I can be insufferably smug at times.'

I had a sinking feeling that Jim Vassilikov would turn out rather similar to my Uncle Charles.

CHAPTER FOURTEEN

Our lunch arrived and we applied ourselves to the food.

'You were born in Western Australia, yes? I must admit to a frightful degree of ignorance about the place.'

So I told him about my home and myself. He drew me out, led me to speak of my parents, and how my mother had been a respectable schoolteacher heading towards spinsterhood when she fell irrevocably in love with the most unsuitable man.

'My father. A big red-headed Irish-Australian who had just bought the Kookynie pub with money he'd won at the races, or so he said.'

'How did your uncle the judge take it?'

'The whole family was horrified. My mother is very determined, however, and they grew to accept the match. Uncle Charles – he wasn't a judge then – is very fond of my father now. They're complete opposites, but they seem to understand each other. It helps that my father has a head for business. He's done well for himself, despite the Depression. He moved my mother back to Perth a few years ago, to her delight.'

'And the marriage worked?'

'They've been happily married now for thirty years. My mother is very soft-spoken, but her word is law to Dad.'

'I'm not surprised by that,' he said, giving me a speaking look.

I made a face at him and then laughed. 'Mum is much tougher than I am, if that's what you're getting at. But she's also sweet. She says stupidity is the eighth deadly sin, but she values kindness above all virtues.'

'I'm inclined to agree with her there. My mother is . . . formidable. I don't think anyone would describe her as kind, or sweet, but she is truly admirable in her way.'

When I asked him to elaborate, he refused, and changed the subject to my age. 'Just how old are you, if that's not too impertinent a question?'

'Older than I look. I'm twenty-five, nearly twenty-six because I was born in January.'

'What date in January?'

'The twelfth,' I replied. '1915.'

His boyish smile appeared. 'Morning or evening?'

I shook my head. 'Don't tell me you're a follower of astrology.'

'Australia is a few hours ahead in time from Russia, isn't it?'

I thought about it. 'Yes, but I don't know how many hours. I was born near dawn on the twelfth of January.'

He actually grinned.

'What?' I said, laughing. 'What's so special about that?'

'I was born in St Petersburg, close to midnight on the eleventh of January, 1915. Perhaps we're cosmic twins, born at the same time, half a world apart.'

'If so, we've nothing else in common. According to my mother it hit one hundred and six in the shade on the day of my birth.'

'It would have been well below freezing in St Petersburg. Always is, in January.'

'Don't you have some sort of title? I should warn you that my great-grandfather was transported to Western Australia as a convict, and my father is suspiciously reticent about his misspent youth.'

'We have more than one of those in my family.'

'Titles?'

'Criminals.'

'It's all very mysterious, this title of yours. Levy wouldn't tell me anything about it.'

His mouth became a hard line. 'My father was murdered because of his title. I hate it and I don't use it.'

I was embarrassed for bringing up another subject that so obviously upset him and I tried – clumsily – to lighten the mood. 'Just tell me you're not related to the late Tsar.'

'Oh.' He seemed to relax, and the ironic smile appeared. 'You must know that every White Russian émigré is the unacknowledged heir to the Romanov throne.'

'You're not? Are you?'

'I'm definitely not the heir, acknowledged or otherwise, to the Romanov throne.'

I laughed. 'Glad to hear it.'

'Anyway, none of our Russian titles is worth tuppence now the Bolsheviks run the show.'

'Do you remember much about Russia?'

He settled back in his chair. 'Not much. I was only five when my father was killed and my mother fled the country. We drifted around Europe for a while before ending up here. I became a naturalised citizen once I turned twenty-one. My mother preferred France and eventually settled there.'

'I'm thinking your mother must have smuggled out the family jewels, if she could afford to send you to Harrow.'

A smile touched the corner of his mouth. 'We left Russia without any money at all, and just a few of my mother's jewels,' he said. 'My mother worked in Paris as a dressmaker. All we have, we've earned ourselves, except that a family friend paid my fees at school and at Cambridge. I was an outsider at Harrow because I was a foreigner, and a poor one at that.'

'Levy said you were both outsiders. I thought that meant you were Jewish, too. But you're not, are you?'

'Jewish? Good God, no. I'm Russian Orthodox.'

He gave a soft laugh. 'I didn't mind Harrow, after the first year or so, which was hellish. David hated the place to the end, but I enjoyed the sports and liked some of the masters. The boys could be difficult, but David was his own worst enemy in many ways, arguing with boys, masters, anyone he thought wrong, or stupid. Not following rules, often behaving badly. And often with good reason, I must admit.'

'I like that about him,' I said, 'but it makes his life difficult at the station as well. And there's also the anti-Semitism – the nasty comments, practical jokes.'

'He got that at school, pretty hard.' Jim shook his head. 'You know, one thing they really drummed into us there was the Old Testament. They do that at all the public schools. "I must be a gent," we'd say, "for I know who begat Zerubbabel."'

'Who did?' I asked.

'Shealtiel.'

'And I could have sworn it was Zeruprattle.'

He grimaced to acknowledge the weak joke. 'It used to infuriate David that they never really acknowledged that Jehu son of Nimshi and Zerubbabel son of Shealtiel and all the others we had to learn off by heart were actually Jews. Or that Jesus was born a Jew.'

The conversation drifted to where we were living.

'I'm living in a flat in Half Moon Street, in Mayfair.'

'Half Moon Street? Jeeves and Wooster?' I thought it had to be a joke, but he nodded.

'The flat belongs to a friend of my mother's who has gone into the country to escape the bombs. She allows me use it when I'm in town.'

When we had finished our lunch we stood uncertainly in the doorway to the cafe. 'It's stopped raining,' he said, glancing at his watch. 'If you'd like, we could walk for a while, before I take you home.' He gestured towards the Strand.

I said in a sing-song voice, 'Let's all go down the Strand?'

'Have a banana!' chimed Jim softly, finishing the title of the old Music Hall song. 'I wonder what we'll find.'

I laughed. 'A lot of bomb damage I suspect. But, by all means, let's go down the Strand.'

So we wandered along, past damaged buildings and sandbags and shelter notices. Past Charing Cross station and the Eleanor

Cross, both sandbagged for protection, but looking somewhat battered. Outside the Savoy was a large water tank for fighting the inevitable fires. All the little shops were sandbagged, their windows boarded over.

'Not exactly a cheery stroll,' remarked Jim.

'I like to see what damage they've done. The papers tell us nothing.'

We passed the entrance to Aldwych, curving away like a boomerang, and then Somerset House was spread out alongside us. The site reached all the way to the Embankment, where I had stood with Levy on a still morning just a couple of weeks before and watched the Thames. Like all the buildings we had seen, the facade was pitted with shrapnel scars and its windows had been shattered. We peeped through the entrance. The central courtyard was a mess of rubble. Both the south and west wings had been badly hit, quite recently. We turned away and continued our walk.

The church of St Mary le Strand loomed up in the middle of the street, like a medieval island set about with rusty rails. Amazingly, it seemed to be untouched, although the buildings around it were badly damaged and there was a bomb crater in the road not ten yards from the church's doors.

Further on along was Australia House, where Pam worked. It held pride of position at the farther end of the sweeping Aldwych curve and rather resembled a massive, snub-nosed flat-iron. Pam had warned me that it had been battered by bombs, but I thought the damage did not seem too severe.

It was when I looked across the open space in front of its main doorway to another medieval island in the Strand that my heart seemed to stop. The area around St Clement Danes Church had been hit. The church itself was a shambles and its stained glass lay in pieces on the ground. Some of the walls were still standing, though, and the spire still reached for the sky.

'I was here in April for the Anzac Day service,' I said. 'They draped Australian and New Zealand flags over the chancel.'

Its loss hit me harder than I would have thought. Because the church was so close to Australia House, it had been regarded almost as a sanctuary for Australians during the Great War. It had become traditional for services associated with any Australian anniversary or event to be held there.

'At least St Paul's Cathedral is still standing,' said Jim. 'The High Altar was hit the other day, but that's all.'

'At least we still have St Paul's,' I agreed.

St Paul's had had a narrow escape in September when a massive time bomb – weighing a ton – had landed in front of the steps. The bomb had penetrated deep into the earth but failed to explode, and the Royal Engineers disposal squad spent three days working to remove it. According to the newspapers, when it was finally carted away to the Hackney Marshes and deliberately exploded, the crater it made was a hundred feet deep and houses miles away had rattled.

I could not think of any loss that would more devastate Londoners than the loss of St Paul's, other than that of Big Ben, which had not yet missed striking an hour. St Paul's and Big Ben: they were London's two talismans. But I hated to see St Clement's like this.

We turned away from the damaged church and continued down the Strand. We passed the studded doors of the mock gothic Royal Courts of Justice, now pitted with shrapnel scars, to reach the fiery-looking dragon that marked the beginning of Fleet Street. And so we entered the City, where medieval London linked fingers with the present.

I loved the City, with its laneways and narrow streets and smoke-grimed walls of huddled buildings. When I first arrived in London I would often wander there, trying to feel the presence of those that had walked the City in the centuries before me.

Sometimes, in my solitary rambles, I felt that I had almost caught a glimpse of the City's ghosts. The feeling intensified when black-gowned lawyers brushed past me, arguing the meaning of those strange terms in legal French that my uncle could rattle off at whim. I would walk the narrow lanes and imagine leather-jerkined apprentices from the medieval guilds, Elizabethan gallants with ruffs and short swords, footpads hiding in the dark alleys, rough Jacobean sailors up from the docks and looking for a female or a fight, Regency dandies, Victorian lamp-lighters and grubby little chimney-sweeps.

I had no such fantasies that afternoon. The Luftwaffe had hit the City hard in the past weeks. The old places were open to the sky now and the ghosts of my imagination had fled the carnage.

Jim turned into a narrow laneway to the right.

'I heard that they hit the Temple a few weeks ago, both my Middle Temple and the Inner Temple,' he said. 'If we've time, I'd like to take a look.'

I agreed and we wandered down a narrow, winding laneway in which a touch of past centuries still remained, despite plaster dust swirling around and a curious feeling of lightness, which hinted at damage to the buildings behind the dark walls.

'Your uncle the judge would have come here in the last war,' said Jim. 'The Temple Church is a wonder. It was built by the Knights Templar, and like all their churches, it's round.'

We had reached a set of serious iron gates guarded by a porter, diminutive and wizened, who looked as if he had stepped straight out of one of Dickens' novels.

'Mr Vassy,' he said. 'How nice to see you, and in uniform, too. Come to see the damage?'

'How bad was it, Cartwright?'

'Bad enough. In September a big one fell near the Middle Temple Hall and blew a large hole in the eastern wall. Then, on 15 October, we had a parachute bomb. It wrecked Elm Court and blew the masonry through the east end of the Hall.'

'How bad was the damage?'

The porter grimaced. 'Bad enough, I'm sorry to say. The minstrels' gallery was smashed to pieces and the lovely screen was shattered.'

'Can it be repaired?'

'Course it can, sir,' said the porter brightly. 'They gathered up all the pieces and put them into sacks. And it will be made good as new, once we've given Hitler his marching orders.'

Jim frowned. 'The windows?'

'Bless you, sir, they were removed for safety at the outbreak of war. The Inner Temple copped it, too. A bomb tore through the oak ceiling of the Hall. Knocked about them bronze statues and the wood panelling. But the main damage was to the clock tower: one side was ripped out.'

Rain began to fall as we walked into the gardens and we put up our umbrellas. The clean-up crews were long gone, leaving behind them a flat sea of mud that lapped at the walls of a gothic-looking building of grubby brown and white stone. Some of its windows were covered in boards and a big hole in one wall was shored up with wood. The acrid smell of soot hung heavily in the air, despite the rain. Other buildings had been damaged also, and a fountain in the paved square was smashed, but not irretrievably.

Jim gestured towards the fountain.

'Reputedly the oldest permanent fountain in London. It dates from the 1680s. Do you know your Dickens? In *Martin Chuzzlewit*, it was here that Ruth Pinch meets John Westlock.

Jim stared at the Hall.

'That is probably the finest example of an Elizabethan Hall in London,' he said. 'Shakespeare played *Twelfth Night* there. It survived the Great Fire of London. The carved screen was so beautiful, Lily. I wish you could have seen it. I hate all this.'

He grabbed hold of my arm, and said urgently, 'London is being swept away in the night. We need to *look* at the city, try to remember how it was – before all this.'

I felt a little giddy, wondered how to respond. 'I never saw the Temple before the bombing. I can't remember London the way you and Levy do.'

Jim released me abruptly and stood still, gazing again at the broken Hall. The only sounds were the steady beat of rain on my umbrella, on the gravel path and the muddy ground. Water pooled and ran in dirty rivulets through the soil.

'Ships, towers, domes, theatres, and temples lie, Open unto the fields, and to the sky,' I murmured, thinking of all the ruins I'd seen in the last months. Then, more loudly, 'I'm as sure as the porter at the gate that once this war is over they'll rebuild and reconstruct and all this will be beautiful again.'

'It won't be the same.'

'It will still be London. And there will still be places of great beauty and grandeur. Including the Inns of Court.'

He didn't answer for a moment. Watching him, I saw again the melancholy that lingered just beneath his skin, imprinted on the bone, perhaps, when the five-year-old boy saw his father being dragged away to death.

'It is quite a tradition here,' he said, 'that nearly every passageway and building is associated with a more or less tragic story. This is just one more, I suppose.'

'I wonder what has happened to the Temple ghosts?' I said, lightly.

I saw the glimmer of a smile as he replied. 'I expect they're hiding, and terrifically annoyed at the Germans.'

'They'll come back.' I looked around. 'Didn't Shakespeare put that scene about the start of the Wars of the Roses in the Temple garden?'

Jim did smile then, for the first time since we had entered the gardens. 'Henry VI Part I. These gardens were famous for centuries for their roses.' He paused, looked again at the devastation around him. 'Actually, the roses haven't bloomed for decades, because the smoke and grime of London chokes them. So I can't mourn the Temple roses, I've never seen them.'

I looked at the wet rubble by our feet, edged in the grime of centuries. 'It's right to mourn the desecration of your legal Temple,' I said. 'It grieves me too, as does the loss of Coventry Cathedral last night, although I never saw it whole.' I smiled at him. 'But I'll bet you anything you like that the roses bloom again one day in these gardens and that you'll see them.'

He reached out an arm, put it around my shoulders and gathered me close under the shelter of his umbrella, resting his head gently on mine as I nestled under his arm. We stayed like that for a while, viewing the ruined gardens through a curtain of falling rain.

Jim left me on my doorstep, with an annoyingly chaste kiss on my cheek. We parted on the promise that we'd meet up the following evening for dinner and dancing.

I closed the door behind him and stood for a few seconds in the foyer, thinking about my afternoon. I wanted time to consider it all, to work out what it had all meant. But a quick glance at my watch told me that I was going to be late if I didn't hurry. So I pushed thoughts of Jim Vassilikov out of my head and raced up the stairs to my flat, changed into my work clothes and headed off to Woburn Place under heavy, low clouds that hung over London like a shroud.

CHAPTER FIFTEEN

Mr Richie was wiping tables inside as I approached his hotel on my way to Woburn Place. He came to the doorway to greet me and I stopped to have a few words.

'Jerry's been busy lately, eh, Lily?' he said, shaking his head. 'Poor old Coventry. I wondered why it weren't so bad here last night.'

'There was a bombers' moon,' I said. 'They didn't even need to use flares to do their dirty work.'

'They didn't leave London out altogether. A couple of tip and run raiders came over Bloomsbury. Three houses were hit in Caroline Place, opposite the Foundling Hospital.'

'I heard them,' I said. 'Two planes – they flew in low over St Andrew's at around midnight.'

'There's a UXB still in the ruins, but it won't go off for a while yet. The team is working on it now.'

He glanced up at the dark clouds. 'Hope the rain keeps Jerry away tonight.'

'I hope so, too,' I said. 'Send 'er down, Hughie.' I smiled at his look of astonishment. 'That's what we say in Australia, when we want rain. I think it's an invocation to the rain god.'

Mr Richie laughed, as I knew he would, and muttered something about barmy Australians. I doubted anything would keep the Germans away, but it was good to hope.

'I see that Knaggs feller only got a fine for looting,' he said. 'They're too soft by far.'

'I know, I was disappointed too. Mrs Coke told us he had been dismissed from the Ambulance Service, though. I only hope he doesn't cause trouble for Levy.'

Mr Richie frowned. 'Looters like Knaggs are vermin. Need to be got rid of quickly. Mr Levy might'a seen him first, but if he hadn't then someone else would have caught the blighter in the act. I'd asked a few good men to look out for him.'

'And me,' I said.

Mr Richie smiled. 'You're a good man, Lily. And so's Mr Levy. I didn't like him much at first, thought he was too proud and prickly. I know better now.' He gave a quick bark of laughter. 'I like his sense of humour. It's very dry. Yes, he's a good man, Mr Levy. You'd never think he was a Jew.'

I said my goodbye on a sigh before continuing along the road. Fat, shining barrage balloons drifted comfortably above me in the increasing gloom of the November evening. They were tethered at the station in Coram's Fields, which older Londoners such as Mr Richie still referred to as the Foundling Hospital, and they were a reminder of the night raid to come.

The wind picked up and brought the rain with it. When I paused to open my umbrella, I suffered bumps and apologies from passing Londoners. They were hurrying home, no doubt anxious to get to the shelters before the raids began. There was no panic, it was Churchill's 'business as usual'.

Guildford Street was roped off and the ominous yellow sign had been hung on the rope: 'No Entry, Unexploded Bomb.' Caroline Place, where the bombs had fallen, was the next street down. It had once been a pretty street of Regency houses facing Coram's Fields, but now at least three of the houses were in ruins.

I could not linger. My watch showed it was nearly five o'clock, so I set off for Woburn Place along the back streets at a rattling pace, fighting a stiff wind all the way.

As always, I went first to the garage to make sure that the Monster was ready for the night's mayhem. By the time I arrived at the common room most of the day shift had already left the station. Those that remained were making noisy good-natured jibes as they collected coats and belongings.

Over the fourteen months of the war, our common room had acquired a few comforts. There were rugs on the concrete floor, a card table, a bookcase and books and even a piano, but the room was always chilly, despite the oil heater. One end had been partitioned off into two rooms, a small storeroom and the station's office, which contained a table, three chairs, the safe and the vital telephone.

The office was where 'reports of incidents requiring assistance' would be telephoned through from Central Control. A window with sliding panes had been set into the wall between the office and the common room. Through this window the officer in charge for the shift would shout out instructions or hand over the chits detailing the incidents to the drivers and attendants.

Mrs Coke was in the office when I arrived, engrossed in paperwork. She always worked the day shift, from nine to five Monday to Saturday, so she would be off duty soon.

The roster board informed me that I was paired with Levy, no surprise there, and Jack Moray was to relieve Mrs Coke. I could not see Levy.

Maisie approached the board, unbuttoning her raincoat as she did so. 'It's pelting down outside,' she said. 'The raiders won't be able to tell if they're over London or the ocean. Hope it keeps up and keeps them away. Isn't it awful about Coventry? They say the centre is utterly destroyed and the casualties are horrendous.'

'Truly awful,' I agreed. 'A quiet night here in London would be just the ticket – so long as they don't hit Oxford or Cambridge or some other medieval town instead – but I don't know that we'll be that lucky.'

'I don't want any church crypts with shattered wood flying about like needles. St-Martin-in-the-Fields was hellish. Or any bombed shelters, like Balham underground.' She shuddered, and turned away to call out a general greeting.

Balham Underground Station had been sheltering hundreds of people when it suffered a direct hit in mid-October. There had been many casualties. The water and gas mains had been broken, as well as the sewage pipes, and the flooding and leaking gas had hampered rescue efforts. One rumour was that scores of Balham victims had drowned, crying out in the darkness when the water mains broke. I had transported some of the bodies and I knew the victims had all died of blast or the effects of flying debris, but the story persisted.

'I don't want any heavy lumps of patients to carry,' I said. 'And no injured children.'

'Amen to that.' Maisie reached her arms above her head in a leisurely stretch. 'Care for a cuppa? I'm about to make one for myself.'

'Thanks. And if Levy's in there, tell him I want a word,' I called out to her. She nodded, and disappeared into the kitchen.

'He's not in the kitchen,' said Harris, looking up from her seemingly interminable knitting. 'He's not come in yet.'

The door to the office opened and Mrs Coke stood there, glaring at me.

'Is Levy here?' Her voice was a hissing whisper.

'No, not yet.'

'Come into my office, Brennan.'

As I followed her into the small office I was surprised to see that her stocking seams were askew. There was fury in each of her tight little steps.

'Sit,' she said.

The whites of her rather prominent blue eyes were red-veined and her face was flushed. She looked like an angry lobster.

'You can tell Levy from me that sneaking little stool-pigeons always get their wings cut,' she said.

'What do you mean?' I was shocked at her blatant threat, and worried what it might mean for Levy.

'Just give him that message when he arrives. If he arrives. He may be too scared to face me. And you just tell him I've got friends – good friends – influential friends.' She dashed a shaking hand across her eyes. 'Go.' She almost spat the word at me. 'You can go now.'

I returned to the common room feeling bewildered and apprehensive. I could only suppose she had discovered Levy knew about her schemes. He had told me the information would be given to the proper authorities. That must have happened and she must have found out that it was Levy who had reported her. I was worried that Levy had earned the woman's hatred and could only pray that she would be sacked as station officer before she could have him transferred. I really didn't know if I could do my job if Levy was sent to another station.

As I turned to leave the office Jack Moray appeared in the doorway. I must have looked upset, because he gave me a puzzled look as he entered. Mrs Coke left the station immediately afterwards.

Maisie returned with the tea and glanced around the room. 'Levy will be very late if he's not careful.'

She handed me a cup and saucer and I took a sip of hot, sweet tea.

'Have you any perfume for sale?' she asked Sadler. 'And I desperately need stockings. Silk if possible.'

He looked up. 'Nah. Supply is temporarily suspended due to circumstances beyond my control.'

Maisie tried to suppress a smile. 'How is Knaggs?'

Sadler assumed a look of injured innocence. 'Knaggs has nothing to do with the shortage. It's all above board, our little supply business, but we are experiencing some distribution problems at present.'

'Do the problems wear blue helmets and stern expressions? Let me know when supplies are available again.'

Ten minutes later Sally Calder bustled in, looking windswept and flustered. 'Sorry I'm late. I was bombed out last night.'

There was a flood of shocked sympathy and horror. She managed a wan smile. 'My mother is staying with friends tonight,' she said, in a high, fast voice, 'and I spent all day going from agency to agency, trying to find out what to do. Thank goodness the kids were evacuated to Devon last year and Sam's away with the navy, so it's only us to worry about. We'll find somewhere to stay tomorrow.'

'You were in the Anderson when the bomb hit?' asked Harris.

'Yes, we were in the shelter. Worth its weight in gold, that thing. Only, there's nothing left of the house. All our furniture, clothes, wedding presents. All my mother's linen that she'd had from her mother and hers before that. All gone.' Her voice broke a little, but she sniffed back the tears and smiled again. 'Oh well,' she said, in a trembling voice, 'worse things happen at sea.'

CHAPTER SIXTEEN

By six o'clock Levy still had not arrived. He had never been late before and fear for him was like a niggling pain that might be the forerunner of something much worse.

'Perhaps he's taking the night off,' said Fripp, glancing at the clock. She returned to the book she was reading with a tight, self-satisfied smile.

'He wouldn't do that,' I said. 'Not without letting us know.'

Celia was sitting next to Fripp, leafing through a magazine, but turning the pages too quickly to be reading them. Her mouth tightened.

'Maybe someone bashed 'im,' said Sadler. He was sitting crouched over a table near the oil stove playing one of his endless games of patience.

'Why would anyone do that?' I asked.

Sadler's face took on a nasty expression and he shrugged. 'Wouldn't need much provocation, not with Levy. But it could be because he's a commie. A fellow looks like Levy's been handing out those leaflets in the shelters.'

'What are you talking about?'

'This bloke's been handing out those leaflets – you know, saying we should lobby Churchill to bargain for peace. The ones that say this war is . . .' He paused, trying to remember the words. 'They say it's a conflict between imperialist powers and the working class has a duty to oppose it. And my mate said it was Levy that was handing them out.'

'That's utter bulldust,' I said. 'Levy is no communist.'

My voice was as certain and self-righteous as I could manage, although I was feeling slightly ill. The communists had at first supported the war against Germany, but when Stalin signed his non-aggression pact with Hitler, they adopted the line dictated by the Comintern, which was exactly what Sadler had said. Jim had told me that Levy had spouted communist nonsense at school, but Levy had never mentioned communism to me. Surely he was not a communist any more.

'Many Jews are,' said Harris. 'They invented communism after all. They were the ones behind the Russian revolution and they want to see the same thing happen here.'

'Not Levy.'

'You're wrong, Brennan,' said Sadler. 'My mate saw him in the Holborn Tube station handing out those leaflets.'

'Your friend wouldn't know Levy from a bar of soap.'

'He would. We was walking along the road together and my mate pointed him out to me, saying that he was the one who'd been handing out leaflets. And I said, "That's Levy, from my station. You know, the bastard what shopped Knaggs to the police." And my mate said he'd bash 'im next time he caught 'im with those pamphlets.' He smiled. 'Levy'd better be careful. My mate carries a knife.'

'Your friend got it wrong and it wasn't Levy he saw in the Tube, or you mistook the man he pointed out. Levy wouldn't do that. He's a Jew, for heaven's sake. He hates Hitler. He's desperate for us to win this war.'

'I only know what my mate said. And it was Levy he pointed out to me.'

I couldn't believe that I was, yet again, in a futile argument with one of the spivs about Levy. I sipped my tea and shut up.

'I'm spare tonight,' said Fripp, in her high, breathy voice. 'If Levy doesn't turn up you'll have to take me instead.' She seemed unenthusiastic about the idea. I was not pleased about it myself.

'Lucky Brennan.' It was Sadler again and his tone was heavy with sarcasm. 'She gets the kike or an attendant who screams when she hears a bomb.'

Fripp's face coloured bright red, but before she could respond Moray appeared in the office doorway.

'What's the matter, lovely Lily?' Moray asked, looking at me. 'Lost a shilling and found sixpence?'

'She's moping because Levy's late,' said Sadler. 'And she may have to go out with Fripp, who screams at bombs. I'd prefer the kike myself.'

Fripp flushed again and threw Sadler a look of poison. She seemed on the verge of tears.

'Shut up, Sadler,' said Moray. His yellowish-green eyes were cold and his mouth tight and hard. Sadler glared at him and seemed about to speak, but thought better of it.

Fripp looked down and wet her lips with the tip of her tongue. She stole a look at Moray a moment later. Levy had said once that Fripp was the sort of woman who would throw herself into passion and see redemption in a man. I'd never been able to imagine her in any circumstance that involved any sort of passion, but from the way she was looking at Moray, I wondered if Levy was right.

Sadler gave Moray a cool look, and then he turned to me.

'Levy might'a been bashed by my mate, like I said, but I think it's more likely that your boyfriend's been Blitzed.'

'He's not my boyfriend,' I said. 'And he'll be here.'

'Nah.' Again he looked at Moray. 'He was Blitzed in Soho. I was there last night with the band, we was playing at the Red Room.' There was a nasty eagerness that I'd heard in the voices of schoolyard bullies. 'If you keeps your eyes open you see all sorts of things in Soho.'

Fripp squeaked 'Soho?' at the same time as I said, 'What?' I knew he was only trying to upset me, but it was working.

Sadler's smile broadened, and I rounded on him. 'You're making this all up. There were no raids last night.' As I spoke

I remembered the two raiders over Bloomsbury. Single planes could show up anywhere.

'There was no raid in Soho—' began Fripp, but Celia's cool voice cut in.

'Just shut up, Sadler,' she said. 'You're not in the least amusing.' She stood up. 'I'm surprised to see you here on night shift. What's in it for you, I wonder?'

Sadler's face was livid.

'What d'ya mean by that? Knaggs was set up.'

Celia was walking to the door. She gave him an almost theatrical look of contempt. 'Knaggs was indiscreet, dishonest and stupid. It was only a matter of time before he was caught. It just happened to be Levy who caught him.'

She left the room and for a moment there was silence.

'We'd have heard by now if Levy had been caught up in an incident,' said Moray.

'He's never missed a shift or been late before,' said Maisie.

Moray shrugged and went into the office.

I had fallen into bleak despair. Levy was more than an hour late, which had never happened before. My imagination was running riot, fuelled by Sadler's comments. I saw Levy in an accident, as an injured Blitz victim, or worse.

In the office the telephone rang and we all jerked with surprise. It was abruptly silenced as Moray picked it up. The mood seemed to sharpen into a fixed awareness of Moray on the telephone and what it meant for us during the shift ahead. Levy always said that he inhaled more smoke in the common room than on the bomb sites, as he lit cigarette after cigarette, trying to settle his nerves. Once you were out in the Blitz there was little time for fear.

'I suspect we're in for another rough shift,' Harris said, still knitting. 'Moon's full, and London's wide open to them.'

'Moon's no use to them if there's a solid layer of cloud over the city,' growled Sadler.

'They say the Italians are bombing us too now,' said Armstrong. 'They'll dump their bombs anywhere.'

The sliding window into the office opened and Moray poked his head through.

'A car is needed in Tavistock Gardens – a car accident, not a war injury. Armstrong?'

The boy collected the chit and disappeared.

I picked a tattered novel out of the small bookcase, a murder mystery set in an Oxford college. Levy had gone to Trinity College in Oxford, I recalled. I tried to lose myself in the book, but I kept reading the same passages over and over.

At seven o'clock the silence was broken by a long sustained scream, rising and falling like banshee wail. It was the Warning siren, announcing that raiders had been sighted on their way to London. Celia returned to her seat and began to leaf through her magazine.

'Listen to moaning Minnie,' said Sadler.

Maisie rushed out of the room, heading for the ladies' washroom to throw up. She was always physically ill at the sound of the siren, but she never missed a callout.

The first rumble of distant explosions began half an hour later, followed by the thumping percussion of the guns. Then the swish and crump of falling bombs, still some distance away. The guns' thunder became constant and as the crumps came closer, the building shook. I gave up any attempt to read a book that jerked in my hands.

The telephone rang and was silenced as Moray picked it up. We all exchanged glances, united by the knowledge of what probably lay ahead of us that night. I felt the usual anxiety, like a cold ribbon of fear snaking through my gut. At this time I usually shared a look with Levy, who would calm me with a whispered joke or a smile.

Moray poked his head through the window. In his hands were paper chits, on which he had written the addresses and some details of incidents that Central Command had assigned to us.

'Prepare for a bad shift,' he said. 'Hundreds of planes are coming over, they tell me, just like Coventry last night. We've an incident in Doughty Street. I need a car and an ambulance. Is Armstrong back yet? No? Harris, you and Sadler take it. Ashwin, you take a car.' Harris and Celia rose and went to the window to collect the chits.

Moray caught my eye.

'Levy still not turned up?'

'No.'

'Then you've got Fripp.' He waved another piece of paper. 'Incident in Judd Street. Needs two ambulances. Halliday and Squire, you're on that one as well.'

Fripp went over to collect the chit. I put down my book and got to my feet. The night's work was beginning, and I was going out into that chaos without Levy.

CHAPTER SEVENTEEN

Nola Fripp's eyes were pale green, like a gooseberry. Her father was something big in the War Office and her mother ran all sorts of war-related committees. Fripp spoke well and dressed well, wore lipstick, rouge and mascara every day, and had her hair regularly and expensively set, but somehow none of it worked. She always, I suspected, would look nondescript.

She was undoubtedly intelligent and had passed the first aid course easily, but her fear of loud noises made her a liability during an air raid. This night was no different. When we drove to our first incident she cringed back in her seat, and as the raid thundered around us and fire lit up the night, she screeched at me to, 'Pull over so we can find a shelter.'

I ignored her and continued driving.

At another incident the stretcher-bearers were busy and the warden asked us to go into a bombed house to collect our patient.

Fripp refused point blank. 'You know that's the job of the stretcher-bearers, Brennan.'

In theory, it was the task of stretcher squads to find the injured and remove them from a bomb site into the ambulances. In practice, the stretcher squads often had such heavy calls on them that drivers and attendants did the stretcher work as well. Tonight was one of the worst raids I had yet experienced, and the stretcher squads were too busy to help us.

'The stretcher squads are flat out.'

'It's not our job,' she repeated.

'We can't leave the poor chap inside the ruins. Come on, Fripp. We must get him out.'

She shook her head. 'The whole building is about to topple.'

'All the more reason to get him out now.'

Eventually one of the firemen went in with me and helped me carry the patient to the ambulance.

It was a long, difficult shift and throughout it Fripp was panicky and critical.

Towards dawn we were at last heading back to Woburn Place in driving rain, taking a roundabout route because of diversions. I turned into a street of Georgian terraces. There was a gap in the row where a house had taken a direct hit that reminded me of the gap-toothed smiles in my infants' class. Fripp gave a loud sniff.

'You think you're so special, Brennan. So heroic. You and that Jew boyfriend of yours.'

'He's not my boyfriend. You know I had a—'

'Yes, yes. We all know you had a boyfriend who died at Scapa Flow. You soon forgot him when you met Levy, didn't you?'

'David Levy is not my boyfriend,' I repeated firmly. 'But he is my friend, so just be quiet, will you. I'm worried about him.'

Fripp made a soft snorting sound.

'Why do you hate Levy so much?' I asked, genuinely curious.

'He's a nasty stinking Jew,' was Fripp's reply.

'That's no answer,' I snapped.

'It's the only one you're—'

She broke off with a little scream and cowered in her seat at the loud roaring sound directly overhead. A plane was coming in low. I ducked down as far as I could behind the wheel, knowing we might well be strafed, despite the red cross on our roof. I twisted the wheel and increased speed, trying to make us harder to hit. Fripp screeched more loudly as the road lit up in another sudden flash of white light. Bullets hit the road in front of us. I jammed on the brake and there was a sharp hammering on the ambulance roof, as if someone had uploaded a tray full of tin cans on us.

For a moment I was sure we had been hit. Then I saw the small cylindrical missiles that were falling around us, each hitting the roadway with a sharp crack before beginning to hiss and spit and ignite in a white-green flash. The plane roared away, up into the sky.

'Damn,' I said. My heart was thumping wildly and I took a deep breath to steady myself. 'Incendiaries. They'll bring the raiders back.'

Incendiary bombs were dropped in batches and each bomb contained thirty-six small canisters of phosphorus. I parked the ambulance, waiting for the thumping of my heart to subside and watched the dark figures that had appeared from the buildings around us and were running around dumping sandbags on to the devices. Incendiary bombs could do little damage on the road; the ones that fell through roofs or windows were the real danger. Unless the fire wardens could get to them they would spit and hiss until the phosphorus inside them exploded into flames.

'There's no need to swear,' said Fripp, in such a prissy voice I was tempted to let fly with every expletive I knew. I stayed silent. Eventually I stopped shaking.

'Let's get out of here,' said Fripp, her voice high and terrified. 'Let's get out now.'

It was clear that she was close to hysteria, so I pressed the starter and then the accelerator. As the Monster picked up speed we experienced a series of small jolts.

'What is it?' shrieked Fripp.

'The incendiary devices,' I shrieked back at her. 'I can't avoid running over them.'

On Barnsbury Road we were diverted into smaller streets because of a gas leak, but even these were pitted and strewn with debris. The narrow beam of my louvred headlights picked up bricks, tiles and fragments of furniture on the road and the crunch of broken glass was loud under my wheels. Dark figures were crawling over mounds of wreckage in a desperate search for survivors, but moving lightly, carefully, so as not to disturb further the silting plaster and drown those beneath with dust.

Above us, the raiders still circled in a ceaseless roar. The noise of the guns was almost deafening.

I stopped the ambulance at the direction of a warden. He came up to us and shouted into my window.

'You from Dolphin Square?'

'No. Bloomsbury.' We could not pick up injured who were not on our chit. There were strict instructions about that.

'Then get out of here. This way's blocked. Turn around and go down the street to your left.'

A bright column of yellow fire roared into the darkness a block away, bathing the scene in a sickly greenish glow. The sound of fire bells grew louder until they ceased in a screech of brakes. We heard men shouting, followed by the hiss of water.

'Gosh,' I said as we slowly drove away. 'They really copped it. This raid is the worst yet.'

Fripp was quiet for a while, until she sat up straighter and electrified me by saying, 'None of this would be happening if we'd just agree terms with Germany.'

The ambulance lurched as I pulled too sharply on the wheel. I corrected, slowed and twisted to look at her face; it was a ghoulish grey in the pre-dawn light.

'Agree terms with Hitler? Are you insane?' I thought about what Sadler had said. 'Are you a communist?'

She pursed her lips. 'Of course I'm not a communist. And you want to know what's insane? Making London put up with this night after night. Churchill's got a special shelter with all the conveniences. It's the poor old ordinary Londoners who are bearing the brunt of it, just like those we picked up tonight. Britain can't withstand Germany on its own. Not now France has capitulated. The rest of Europe knows it. Why don't we?'

'We'll never give in to the Nazis,' I said. My voice was shaking in my outrage. 'How can you even think it?'

'You're not even English, Brennan. It's not your country that's going to lose everything because Churchill's too stubborn to see sense.'

'Australians are British citizens, you ninny. More importantly, I care about freedom.'

'What? The freedom to die? Germany is just too powerful. They might not have invaded this year, but we'll see paratroopers and barges come spring. This Blitz is designed to soften us up. We'd be better off negotiating terms now, from a position of strength.'

I was so angry that I didn't trust myself to talk, and drove back to the station in a furious silence.

'I know you're all fired up with this idea of freedom,' she said, as we cleaned the Monster at the end of our shift. 'Whatever that word actually means. But Germany's just too powerful. We can't win.'

'The RAF has decimated the Luftwaffe,' I said, scrubbing furiously and not looking at her. The water from the garage tap was freezing and my hands were nearly numb with cold. 'And we will win this war, because the alternative is barbarism.'

She gave a high-pitched giggle. 'You are silly, Brennan. The government is lying to us about the air war. The RAF isn't doing nearly as well as the propaganda makes out. That's what my father says, and he should know. Moray knows, too. The anti-aircraft guns are practically useless. I think it's a scandal that we're not being told the truth.' She put down the rag she was using and turned to look me straight in the eye. 'Britain is going to lose, and if we don't realise it soon we'll throw away any chance to negotiate favourable terms with Germany.'

It occurred to me that this was not something Fripp would think up on her own. I wondered if I should report her for spreading defeatism. And report her chatty War Office father! But I knew I would not do it. I hated the idea of informing. That was what they did in Nazi Germany. And while I hated her stupid ideas about politics, underneath the bluster I could sense her fear. She was scared of an uncertain future. I was scared, too.

'You don't know just how terrible the Nazis are,' I said. 'I saw what they did in Czechoslovakia.'

'The Germans like the British. They'd treat us differently.'

I made a soft snorting sound. 'Oh, yes,' I said, 'they like us so much they're trying to bomb us to smithereens.'

And as to what 'terms' they'd insist upon – the thought was terrifying. I knew how the Nazis would treat Levy and his family, and that was just one reason we had to keep fighting. Anyway, Britain wasn't alone in her fight against the Axis powers. She had the Empire. She had Australia!

'They will treat us differently if we just see sense,' she insisted.

'You are being very naive,' I said.

'We'll see who's naive.'

There was no point arguing. I finished cleaning the Monster and dashed to the office without bothering to wash off the grime of the night. I was desperate to know if there was any word from Levy, or about him.

I knocked quickly and entered without bothering to hear Moray's response. He was sitting behind the desk, which was covered with incident reports and maps and pamphlets and other paraphernalia.

'Any news about Levy?'

Moray looked up from a pile of papers and frowned.

'No. Nothing.'

'Have you telephoned anyone? Bothered to ask?' My voice was shrill, and his frown deepened.

'I've been busy, Brennan. Almost every one of London's boroughs was bombed during the night. Westminster Abbey and School, the National Portrait Gallery, Euston station, Wellington Barracks and four hospitals were hit. A dozen factories, hundreds of houses. They've been using a new type of delayed action bomb – and it's already been nicknamed Satan. It's the most intense raid we've had yet, and one missing man isn't high on my list of priorities.'

I turned away from him, my hands clenched into tight fists, fighting back the tears.

'Brennan.' His voice was softer and I looked up. 'When the All Clear sounded – twenty minutes ago – I rang the number Levy gave for his next of kin.'

'Did you—', I began to ask, but he shook his head.

'I didn't even get the number unobtainable sound. So I rang the exchange and the operator tried the number. She said the line is out of order. You know what that means.'

He ran a hand across his stubbled chin. Moray had been on duty all night taking calls and his face had a pinched, exhausted look.

'I asked Sadler about his Soho story and he admitted that he made it up. But I think Levy's family have been bombed out. If he was in the house when it was hit, then . . .'

I shrugged, refusing to give him the pleasure of showing my misery. He stood and walked around the desk to stand beside me. To my astonishment he put a hand on my shoulder. I was too tired to shake it off.

'I'll ring around the hospitals, see if anyone of his description has been brought in.'

I shrugged his hand away. 'It's the end of my shift and I'm going home. I'll find him.'

Moray continued to stand beside me for a few seconds of uncomfortable silence. When he returned to his desk I turned to walk out of the office.

Fripp pushed by me to enter the room. The door didn't quite shut behind her and I heard her high rather whiny voice complaining about me.

'Brennan is impossible. She never takes cover during a raid. I hate going out with her. And she's so high and mighty. Tried to lecture me about freedom.'

Moray sniggered.

I walked away.

*　　*　　*

By now I was so tired that coherent thought was difficult. I had to know if Levy was hurt – I wouldn't consider the alternative – and it seemed that the only way to find out was to contact his parents. They were rich and probably on the phone, but I did not want to ask Moray for their address and telephone number because it upset me just to speak to him.

Jim would know their number, and I wanted to see Jim. I desperately wanted to see Jim. He was Levy's friend. He knew Levy's family, where they lived. We could go there together.

Only I did not know Jim's actual address. All I knew was that he was living in a flat in Half Moon Street, Mayfair.

I tried to work out what to do. It was likely that his mother's friend was on the phone, but Jim's name would not be in the directory because the flat belonged to his mother's friend. I did not know her name. *Think, Lily.* Celia knew Jim, well enough to visit him in hospital. She might know his address. If she did not, I would simply have to ring the bell of every house in Half Moon Street, because I would not go back into that office to ask Moray for the Levys' address.

The common room was filling with people rostered for the day shift. 'Anyone seen Ashwin?' I called out.

Someone said, 'She headed off a couple of minutes ago.'

I ran out of the room into the garage. Celia was standing beside her bicycle, bending down to place clips on her trousers. I ran across to her, spoke without a greeting.

'Do you know Jim Vassilikov's address?' My voice sounded sharp, a staccato bark. 'He told me he was living in a flat in Half Moon Street, but not the number. All I know is that it belongs to a friend of his mother's.'

Celia did not look up, or even acknowledge me. She continued to carefully adjust the clip on her leg. Perhaps I had sounded rude. I took a breath and when I tried again, I heard a wheedling tone in my voice.

'Please Ashwin, I need to see Jim, but I'm not sure of his address. I'm hoping that he will . . .'

She twisted slightly toward her other leg to place the second clip, and still did not look up. Her movements were deliberate and unhurried. Exasperated, I tried again.

'Levy is missing. We – Moray, I mean – he couldn't raise Levy's parents. He thinks they may have been bombed out. Jim might—'

'Jim's staying in Lady Anne Gresham's flat. Half Moon Street, number 26.'

'Thank you.'

It was after I had whirled around to return to the common room that she said, 'I hope you find him.'

I was not sure if she was referring to Jim or to Levy.

On the common room wall was the large map of London marked up to show current detours, blocked streets, UXBs, bomb craters and other hazards. I ran my finger past Soho into Mayfair, stopping at Half Moon Street. Green Park station was three blocks along from Jim's street, and Green Park and Russell Square stations were both on the Piccadilly Line, which meant I could be there in less than thirty minutes.

Jim would know what to do.

CHAPTER EIGHTEEN

I emerged from the ambulance station into a chilly November morning. My eyes felt heavy and my entire body ached, and for a few seconds dizziness almost overwhelmed me, but I pressed on until I reached the corrugated metal arch piled about with sandbags that was the entrance to the Russell Square Underground Station.

Although it was after nine o'clock, some people who had spent the night on the platform were just emerging, clutching their bundles of bedding and blinking at the morning light. The children were still in their dressing gowns and pyjamas, the adults had winter coats or raincoats belted over night attire. It was then I remembered that it was Saturday morning and I had promised to meet Jim for dinner that night.

A sailor in Royal Navy uniform walked out of the station, singing the haunting folk song 'Siuil a Ruin' in a fine tenor voice.

A man walking by said, 'Shut up, will you. Irish scum.'

The singing stopped and the sailor threw a curse into the wind before walking away with a hard, angry tread.

I wondered why people were so harsh to strangers. Was the sailor Irish? I had no idea. The song was a Scottish one, and perhaps he was from there. In any event, he was in uniform. You would think, in a war, that such prejudices would be forgotten, but although the bonhomie was there, prejudices remained and if anything, were magnified. Perhaps, I thought, people simply needed a scapegoat that was near at hand and not in Berlin.

I sat in a crowded carriage as the train hurtled through dark tunnels, pinching my arm to keep myself awake, yawning constantly. When I emerged on to Piccadilly, exhaustion made my steps unsteady and I had a few puzzled looks from passers-by when I stood leaning against the sandbags to blink at the daylight.

The traffic along Piccadilly was heavy. A Daimler passed slowly by me, its front and back seats full. A man and a woman were sitting in the luggage boot chatting together most composedly with their feet sticking out. As the car drove away the woman pulled out an umbrella and opened it.

A drop of rain hit my forehead and I looked up to see the sky dark with low ragged clouds. It did not look real; it was a watercolour painting of a sky, by Turner. More raindrops fell as I plodded past the buildings that faced Green Park.

I wiped my hand over my wet face and it came away grimy. It was then I remembered that I had not washed after my shift. No wonder I was getting suspicious looks, I thought. If Jim's apartment block had a doorman he might refuse to admit such a grubby ragamuffin as I must seem to be. If Jim was even in his apartment. I had a moment of grim fear. What if he had gone to work, or spent the night elsewhere?

Suddenly dizzy, I leaned heavily on the wall of the building behind me, gaining strength from the solidity of the stone at my back. My eyes were sore and gritty. When I closed them I began to slide slowly down the wall and I felt myself tumble into comforting velvet darkness.

'Steady on,' someone said, and a hard, painful grip pulled me upright. 'It's all right, I have you.'

I forced my eyes open and squinted at my arm. My sleeve was in the firm hold of a long, fine-boned hand, scattered with light freckles. The world was spinning and everything seemed blurry, so I caught impressions only of the face that belonged to the hand. Looks like Jim, I thought. Then I gave up trying to think at all.

*   *   *

I was searching for a lost child in a bombed house, crawling through unstable ruins, only I was clumsy and kept catching my limbs on wood and plaster. All the while I was terrified that the whole edifice would collapse and bury me alive. In that strangely logical way of dreams, the child I was searching for became Levy and I knew that if I managed to shrug my way into a small, dark hole in front of me, I would find him. I wanted to go in after him, but it was such a small hole and the house was creaking so alarmingly that I was paralysed. I could hear Levy laughing, just beyond my reach. 'I'm not lost,' he called to me. 'I've been here all along. You never look in the right place, Brennan.'

I felt myself take a gasping, snorting breath and my head jerked. The patter of rain was loud above me, but I was dry and sitting in a slightly inclined seat that was firm but comfortable. The heavy softness of a blanket or rug lay over my body. I stretched out my hand and felt metal, and I opened my eyes to realise I was in the passenger seat of a low-slung motor car. The windows were wound up and slightly fogged and outside it was raining heavily.

'Good afternoon, sleepyhead,' said a familiar voice.

I sat upright, realised I had been drooling and put up a hand to wipe my mouth.

Jim Vassilikov was sitting next to me. We were in his car. I stared at him, uncomprehending, embarrassed.

'You were asleep on your feet,' he said. 'I've seen it before – after a tough few days the boys in my squadron would be the same. I'd be talking to one of them and when there was no reply I'd realise he'd fallen asleep where he stood.' He smiled. 'Just like the dormouse in Alice.'

'I fell asleep?' It seemed incredible. 'On the footpath?'

He nodded.

I was now fully awake. 'Where am I? How did I get here?' We were in a street of elegantly proportioned Georgian houses.

'You're in Half Moon Street, outside my flat. Around the corner from where you collapsed. I saw you in the street and was coming over when you started to topple.'

'But how did I get here?' I repeated.

He shrugged and ducked his head a little. 'I carried you. You hardly weigh anything, and you really were out for the count.'

'You carried me to your car?'

His boyish smile appeared. 'I considered carrying you up to my flat, but thought it was probably inadvisable. Not least because you're not *that* light and I'm not completely recovered. And I had visions of long, difficult explanations to the doorman. So I put you in the car. I thought I'd let you sleep. It's a quiet street when the planes aren't overhead.'

'What's the time now? You said afternoon.' I was suddenly, painfully aware of my bladder.

He glanced at his watch. 'It's nearly one o'clock.'

'What!' I had been asleep for over three hours.

He gave a short, soft bark of laughter. 'Long night? It was a bad raid. Pitts Head Mews over near Park Lane was destroyed. Blast took out all my windows and shook the place up badly. It's lovely to see you, but why are you here?'

I had forgotten Levy in the shock of my awakening.

'Oh, Jim, Levy's missing. He didn't report for work yesterday and his parents seem to have been bombed out. I have to find him. I need your help.'

He gestured behind me. 'My flat is just there. We can talk about it after you've had a cup of tea. And then I'll take you to lunch.' There was a quick, embarrassed smile, almost a grimace. 'If you'd care to bathe, the gas was put back on this morning. The flat's a trifle chilly because I haven't had time to cover the windows, but at least the water will be hot.'

I opened my mouth to say more about Levy, but closed it again. First things first. I had to make myself presentable, and I needed to use his facilities.

'I'd love cup of tea. And a bath. Thanks.'

159

He touched my arm lightly. 'It doesn't mean much, Lily. He simply didn't turn up for work. I survived being shot at twenty thousand feet, and David's much tougher than I am. Anyway, you can tell me about it when you've freshened up.'

He got out and came around to open my door. It was raining heavily so we ran to the shelter of his building's portico where I stood for a moment to look at his street, because I loved the Wodehouse books and it was Bertie Wooster's street. At one end was the spire of a large church, at the other was Green Park. It was a place of obvious wealth, but not of grandeur or even pretension. I liked the look of it. The houses seemed eighteenth century and were a pleasant mish-mash of styles. The blast had blown out most of the glass in their windows but they seemed otherwise untouched. It saddened me to think that they would all fall like sticks at the first hint of a serious bomb, and that when they fell not even Jeeves would be able to put them together again.

Jim pushed open the door and ushered me into the lobby. I had the impression of cool checked tiles, a wide staircase, elegant mouldings and general opulence. An elderly uniformed porter came out to greet us.

'Good afternoon, Greenfield,' said Jim. 'This is Miss Lily Brennan. She's an ambulance driver and has just come off duty after a very hard night. I've offered her a bath.'

Greenfield was a little bull of a man, whose wide smile revealed two rows of glistening false teeth. He did not seem in the least surprised that Jim had offered me a bath. The gas was off so often these days that baths were at a premium and were a very acceptable form of hospitality.

'Bless you, miss,' he said. 'You're such a tiny scrap of a thing to be driving one of those ambulances in an air raid. It surely was a bad one last night.'

'It's much easier to be out in the fuss, than sitting home listening to it,' I said.

'I know what you mean, miss. It's why I like to get up onto the roof each night to do my bit of fire watching.'

Jim waved towards the staircase. 'I'm on the first floor, and there's no lift,' he said. 'Can you make it?'

'Yes, I'll make it.'

We climbed the stairs slowly. At first I thought it was out of consideration for me, but it soon became clear that it was Jim who needed to take it easy and I wondered how he had managed to carry me to his car if he was so weak. When we reached the first floor landing he drew in a ragged breath and gave me an apologetic smile.

'I'm much improved, but I find stairs still somewhat challenging.'

He opened a door into a tiny hall, where we hung up our dripping raincoats. This led into a large living room. Several excellent engravings in narrow pearwood frames hung on the whitewashed walls. Crimson brocade curtains framed long, glassless windows and I shivered a little in the chilly air. A delicate writing desk stood between the windows and on it was a bronze of Diana the huntress with the crescent moon on her forehead. The floor was covered with a faded Turkey carpet. Alabaster lamps sat on low tables. A pair of chintz-covered armchairs by the fireplace looked soft and welcoming, and a more formal brocade-covered sofa was heaped at each end with cushions. In a corner was a glossy piano with sheet music scattered over the top. The overriding impression was one of irreproachable taste, and of old wealth.

He waved towards the passage. 'Bathroom's through there. I'll get you a towel. If you leave your shoes outside I'll clean them for you. When you're finished, sing out and I'll put on the kettle for tea. Then we can talk about David.'

Once I was in the bathroom I gave a tentative glance into the mirror and grimaced at my dirty, bloody face and flat, greasy hair. A huddle of bath salts in fancy jars was on the shelf by the bath and I sniffed a few, chose the one that smelled the most delicious and tipped a generous amount into the water that was filling the bath. I picked up a bottle of scented shampoo and decided that Jim's mother's friend could spare a dollop for a tired ambulance officer to scrub her hair free of the grime of a long night shift.

After a lengthy soak in the hot water I smelled of roses and felt pampered and drowsy. I was imagining Jim's long fingers trailing over the piano keys, playing Debussy, when a sharp rap on the door jolted me awake.

'Don't fall asleep in there. One of our boys nearly drowned that way. Tea's made.'

'I'm awake,' I yelled. 'Just a minute and I'll be out.'

Although I was now clean, there was little I could do about my clothes. My blue cotton coat had protected them to some extent, but they showed all the signs of a hard night's work. I took the flannel I had used in the bath, wrung it out and wiped away as much grime as I could from my jumper and trousers. When I rinsed the flannel in the bathwater it remained stubbornly streaked with a medley of brown and grey stains. I wrung it out and guiltily set it to dry on the side of the bath, before pulling the plug.

The bathwater swirled and disappeared with a nasty shriek that echoed my state of fractured, sleep-deprived uncertainty. I opened the door and prepared to face Jim.

CHAPTER NINETEEN

My shoes were outside the door, cleaned and polished to RAF standards. As I put them on I heard the rattling of cups and I followed the sounds to a kitchen that was so tiny it was really a kitchenette.

Jim filled the small room, so I stood in the doorway and watched as he poured water into the teapot and placed it on a tray together with the cups and saucers, sugar bowl, milk jug and a plate of digestive biscuits. He carried it into the living room and we sat facing each other in the two big armchairs with the tray on a low table between us.

'You look much improved,' he said, then gave a slight, embarrassed start, possibly at my grimace in response. 'I mean that in the nicest possible way. You looked quite done in before.'

'I looked like a Morlock.'

'And now you look like an Eloi.'

I had read *The Time Machine*, and I wasn't sure that being compared to those small, childlike creatures was my preferred compliment, although as Wells had described the Eloi as having a Dresden china-like prettiness, I gave a brief smile in response.

'Actually I simply feel human again,' I said. Then I blurted out, 'I don't know where to look for Levy.'

Jim glanced away from me. 'Would you care for a spot of Lady Anne's fine French brandy?'

Now I was confused. 'Lady Anne?'

'The owner of this place. My mother swears by brandy when the nerves are shot.'

I dithered, which he obviously took for assent, because he rose and went over to a table on which were various bottles. He came back with one and poured a large tot into my teacup and another into his. He raised the cup and said something that sounded like, 'a *fstrye-tchoo*'. A Russian toast, I assumed.

I raised my cup in similar fashion and took a sip. The alcohol burned in my throat. I took another sip and enjoyed the sensation.

'You'll have me tipsy,' I said, and put the cup down with a more decided thump than I had intended. As I did so my stomach gave a gurgle. I snatched up a digestive biscuit and took a quick bite.

'When did you last eat?' he asked.

'Um . . .' I tried to remember. I had been so worried about Levy the night before that I'd not had my usual supper and breakfast at the station. 'With you? Yesterday lunchtime?' I finished the biscuit.

He took another sip of his brandy-laced tea and for politeness's sake I did also. I was used to the burning sensation now and the alcohol was dissolving my tense fear for Levy. Each sip caused a delightful warmth in my stomach and a jittery happiness.

'Drink up,' he said. 'It'll do you good. Then we'll adjourn to a nearby tearoom for a spot of lunch.'

'We have no time. Levy's—'

'What's all this about David?' he asked.

My words tumbled out. 'I don't know if Levy was in his parents' house when – if – it was hit, or if he was actually in Soho like Sadler said. But Fripp said there was no raid there.' I paused, confused. 'How would Fripp know anyway? She lives in Kensington.' I stared at Jim and shook my head slightly to regain my train of thought. 'Or Levy may have been the man from Holborn Underground and if he was then he may have been attacked, not bombed. But I think that's the most unlikely scenario. I must sound like a lunatic, do I?'

Jim shook his head, as if he hadn't understood a word.

'Soho?'

'Sadler – he works at the ambulance station – said that Levy had been caught in a raid in Soho on Thursday night, but I think he was just teasing me. Moray said he was, and Fripp said there was no raid in Soho on Thursday, but I still can't see how—'

'Holborn?'

'Sadler said his friend said Levy was a communist, handing out anti-Churchill propaganda in Holborn station and he – Sadler's friend – was going to attack him.'

I took another hurried sip of tea, savouring the warmth of the alcohol as it slid down my throat.

'He was going to attack Levy, not Churchill,' I added quickly. 'But I don't think it was Levy he saw. Because Levy likes Churchill and hates Hitler and he wants total victory at all costs. So, it's all terribly confusing, I know. We just have to find Levy.'

Jim was watching me with a quizzical look.

'What it all means,' I explained carefully and slowly, 'is that Levy did not turn up for duty yesterday. Moray tried telephoning his parents this morning but there was no answer and the operator thought the line was out of order. It may be that the line is just down, but they may have been bombed out. I'm so worried, Jim, because of the nasty things Sadler was saying. I don't know what is true. I thought I'd come over here to see if you knew where his parents lived, so we could go there together. Even if they have been bombed out, maybe someone can tell us how to contact them, to see what they know about Levy.'

Jim reached across to take the teacup out of my hand. 'Let's get some real food into you,' he said. 'And then we'll see about David.'

The rain had stopped but the pavement was slick and wet. As always after rain, there was a deceptive freshness to the air. Jim took my arm in his and I walked carefully, lightheaded from lack of food and too much brandy. He tightened his grip on my arm as we negotiated some broken pavement and we turned together into a street off Piccadilly to stop in front of a small tearoom.

The boards over its glassless windows made it dark inside, especially as the walls were covered with crimson flock wallpaper. It was furnished with bentwood chairs and a dozen or so small tables draped with oilcloths, upon which stood small vases of flowers. In a corner was an enormous smoking, spluttering samovar of fluted brass. Most of the tables were occupied, but as soon as we appeared a waitress, as sloe-eyed and exotic as Natasha from the Dorchester, pounced upon us and led us through the cafe to a table in a corner. Jim requested a good, plain lunch.

'Pirozhki? Soup, stroganoff, tea?' she said.

'Perfect,' said Jim.

She flounced off.

'Another White Russian émigré?' I asked.

'Yes, this place is a favourite. Irina – that's the waitress – her parents own it. Her mother cooks and her father – who used to be an Imperial Guard under the Tsar – is sure to be over to talk to us in a moment or two.'

'You White Russians are everywhere.'

He laughed. 'We scattered when the Bolsheviks came to power. It's ironic to think that I could have just as easily ended up living in Germany as Britain. I've got cousins all over Europe. And also in China, where they are now at the mercy of the Japanese.'

'Australia?'

He smiled. 'Even there, I'm fairly sure.'

A big man with a waxed moustache appeared, shook Jim's hand vigorously and made a formal bow. He introduced himself to me as Monsieur Denisov and smiled. 'How charming you are, mademoiselle. Like a *feya*. A fairy, you know?'

I smiled at him in return, though I was not too enamoured with the compliment.

'We have for you today soup and stroganoff,' he said. 'No caviar. It is this war, you know. But first I will bring you pirozhki, straight from oven.'

'Any tyanuchki?' asked Jim.

M. Denisov lowered his voice, and glanced around. 'For you, tyanuchki. But be discreet, others have been told there is none left.'

He wandered off to talk to another table.

'Tyanuchki?' I ventured, trying not to make too much a hash of the pronunciation.

He smiled. 'The speciality of the house. It's a sublime caramel. You'll love it.' He met my eyes. 'Let's not discuss David until after you've eaten.'

I nodded.

Mercifully, Irina soon arrived with a dish of pastries. I pounced on them, trying not to embarrass myself by eating too quickly. Some were stuffed with seasoned meat, others with cheese. They were delicious.

When the plate was empty Irina returned with black rye bread and a pale, thick soup that smelled wonderful.

Once the soup had disappeared I felt much better. Jim finished his and sat back. His fingers began to tap out the notes of an invisible piano.

Before we could speak, Irina arrived to replace our soup bowls with plates of a meat casserole, its sauce pink in colour, and spicy and sour at the same time. I could only hope that they had not used horse meat, because I ate it all with relish.

When we had finished the waitress delivered lemon tea, served Russian style, in glasses. It was accompanied by the tyanuchki, which was squares of thick caramel-coloured fudge, as smooth and sleek as marble, and as sublime as Jim had promised.

'Feeling better?' Jim asked.

'You have no idea. I really was dead on my feet. And that brandy made it worse, not better.'

'My mother swears by it.'

I concentrated on making the tyanuchki last as long as possible in my mouth.

'So,' said Jim, 'if I have this right, David didn't turn up for work, which is unusual. You've had no word from him as to why he didn't turn up. Someone telephoned his parents' number and was told that the line was out of order. A man who works with you at your ambulance station teased you by saying that David was killed in a raid on Thursday night in Soho, or alternatively that he had been identified as a man handing out defeatist propaganda in Holborn Underground Station and he was assaulted because of this.'

It could have been my Uncle Charles speaking. I nodded.

'It seems to me,' said Jim, 'that the only fact I can glean from the story is that one of the men you work with has a doubtful sense of humour.'

I toyed with the carnation in the vase on the table, reluctant to agree with him, and suddenly started in fright. How on earth could I have forgotten? Knaggs had a serious grudge against Levy. He had threatened him. Mr Richie was a witness to that. And Mrs Coke had also made threats, just last night.

I tried to explain this to Jim. Again, it was hard to know where to start, because the roots of both stories seemed to go back such a long way. I managed to make some sense, but Jim pointed out in his coolly logical manner the flaw in my fear.

'Mrs Coke wouldn't have been making a threat if she had already arranged for him to be hurt, would she? And that man Knaggs sounds like a petty criminal – such men are ready to loot for easy money but draw the line at actual violence. They know how much trouble it is. I've met many of them in my time in the criminal courts.'

I could only retreat into the one salient fact.

'But Levy is missing.'

'Lily, all we know is that David didn't turn up for work. There may be a perfectly good reason. His parents may have been bombed out and needed immediate rehousing.'

'He would have telephoned the station if he wasn't going to turn up. I need to know for sure that he's safe.'

'Then we'll visit his parents' house and see what's what.'

* * *

Jim drove through the usual maze of detours until we arrived outside the Levys' house, which was in Bayswater, near Hyde Park. The facade was white with an elaborate portico, like all the other houses around it. There was no sign of damage to the structure, but it was roped off with a 'No Entry' sign.

We stopped an elderly man, tall and thin with a slight stoop, who was walking a yappy little terrier.

'Did this house get it?' asked Jim.

'Not last night, the one before.'

'Anybody hurt?'

The man nodded. 'I was on duty that night – I'm a local warden. Injuries, but nothing fatal.'

My heart seemed to thud and for the first time since Levy had not turned up for work I felt happy. *Nothing fatal*. He may be injured, but it was nothing fatal.

'We know the people – do you know where they went?' asked Jim.

'You know the Levys?'

'Yes.'

'Mr Levy was cut about a bit. Mrs Levy . . .' He paused, gave us a long, considering look.

'I was at school with one their sons,' said Jim.

The man looked him over, obviously taking note of the uniform and the cut glass accent.

'We had to dig her out.' He gestured behind us. 'It was all at the back of the house. You wouldn't think there was a jot of damage from out here, but it's rather a wreck inside.'

'And David?' I cut in. 'Their son?'

'They said there was no one else in the house when it happened.'

We thanked him and he wandered off along the street, turning into the portico of a house a few doors down.

'We're back to square one,' I said.

'Not at all. We know that David's parents were bombed out and that he wasn't with them at the time. Which makes it more likely that he is with them now and that he simply forgot to telephone your station.'

'He wouldn't do that,' I repeated stubbornly.

'If your parents had been bombed out and your mother badly injured, would you telephone work to say you'd not be in that evening?'

I grimaced. 'Fair enough. I'd probably forget about everything except them.'

'I'm sure he'll turn up at the ambulance station for his next shift. When is that?'

'Monday morning. We're on days next week.'

'You'll see him then, I'm sure. Or he'll have telephoned your station officer.' He gave me a level look. 'Do you want to ring around in the meantime, find out what hospital his parents were taken to, see if he is with them?'

'Please, Jim. If you could. I'm nearly out of my mind with worry.'

'I'll make enquiries, I promise.'

Jim drove slowly back to my flat, threading his way through detour after detour, past wreckage and ruins and mud and misery. It was like one of those endless mazes pursued in dreams and I remembered my own dream of earlier that day.

'I was so worried I even dreamed about Levy. When I was asleep in your car I dreamed that I was looking for him and he told me I was looking in the wrong place.' I laughed. 'I wondered if it had been a sign.'

He turned down a small street at the direction of a notice marked 'Detour – Gas Leak'. As we rounded the corner he nodded at the notice. 'That's a sign. Your dream was a simply a manifestation of your concern.'

Yep, just like my Uncle Charles. That thought made me laugh out loud, and Jim turned to look at me.

'You're such a lawyer,' I said.

He smiled, then sighed. 'That sounded damnably pompous,' he said. 'Sorry. I find it difficult . . .'

'What?'

'To find the right words around you.'

'I'm not so scary,' I said.

'No. But you're in love with someone I count as a close friend, which makes it—'

'I'm not in love with Levy.'

He made no reply.

'I'm not in love with Levy,' I repeated, more loudly. 'He looks after me, and I've been worried sick about him. I hate the way people treat him, just because he was born a Jew, but I'm not in love with him. We're mates. Why do people assume that I'm in love with him?'

'Perhaps because you never shut up about him.'

'That's ridiculous.'

Jim pulled over to the side of the road and switched off the engine.

'The first time, when we met in Regent's Park, you talked incessantly about Levy. So naturally I understood that you and he—'

'But I told you we weren't.'

'I didn't believe you. Only, David brought you to the hospital and he let me know that the path was clear for me. So I—'

'He what?'

'David wrote to me and said you were simply friends. He left us alone together at the hospital.' Jim smiled briefly at my expression. 'That's why I asked you out again, and I thought it went well yesterday. Only, this morning you turn up out of the blue, and it's all about David again.'

'I'm worried about him. But believe me, I'm not in love with him. Our friendship is purely platonic.'

Jim shrugged. It was getting late and the light was fading fast, despite the continued summer time. I had a sudden need for familiar surroundings.

'Come to dinner at my service restaurant,' I said. 'My treat.' I thought about it. 'Not that it will be exactly a treat, because the food is rather dire, but it'll be hot and more or less nourishing.'

The eyebrow rose. 'How could a chap refuse such an invitation?'

It was tomato soup (tinned), mutton with cabbage and potatoes and bread pudding. Jim ate it all manfully, and ignored the curious looks of the other diners.

We took our coffee upstairs to my flat. I put the blackout blinds in place and turned on the lights.

Jim looked around with unabashed curiosity.

People are judged by their surroundings and I wondered how Jim saw mine. I had furnished my flat somewhat eccentrically with cheap and second-hand furniture and objects that appealed to me. The low oval mahogany table was crowned with a lustre bowl of iridescent blue that I had picked up cheaply because it was chipped, and it was filled with late autumn roses; their scent permeated the room. The bookcases on either side of the fireplace were crammed with books I had bought second hand on Charing Cross Road. An old but comfortable sofa lay beneath the double windows that overlooked my narrow balcony. Its brocade cover was heavily stained, so I had thrown a dark green velvet curtain over it, hoping it added a sumptuous note to the room. I loved to lie on the velvet to read.

'I like your flat,' he said. 'Do you get to the balcony from the bedroom?'

'Yes.'

I wondered if he would ask to see the bedroom, where French doors, framed in steel like the windows, led to the tiled balcony.

'There's not much of a view,' I said, 'but it faces east so I have morning sunshine and I overlook the gardens. I love having a balcony.'

I left him gazing at my bookshelf while I slipped into the bedroom to draw down the blackout curtains. I was about to return when I saw Denys's photograph on my dressing table.

The man I had loved, or thought I loved. Now it was time to move on. I picked up the photograph and tucked it inside my dressing table drawer.

As I returned to Jim the Warning sounded.

'Do you usually take shelter?' he asked.

'No. I'd prefer to travel down to earth with the ruins rather than be trapped in the cellar.'

'Suits me,' he said. 'I hate sheltering underground. I never go into the basement at Half Moon Street, no matter how bad the raid.'

As Jim sipped his coffee I wondered how I could explain my friendship with Levy.

'I know I talk about Levy a lot,' I said, 'but you must understand that he's been an important part of my life over the past months. I think I only survived the early days of the Blitz because of Levy.'

Levy was so handsome that I'd had a few daydreams when we first began working together, but those feelings had changed, and not only because of Levy's lack of interest in me in that way. Working through the Blitz forced us to confront together the horrors of aerial warfare on civilians. As I kept facing those horrors, day after day, night after night, what Levy came to mean to me was more than an emotional attachment to a handsome face. Our friendship was now solidly based on comradeship in harsh times, on mutual respect and the knowledge that we would look after each no matter how hard the shift might be.

Jim sat quietly on my couch, watching me carefully as I tried to explain. And while I spoke I observed him as well. It really was too soon to know how I felt about Jim Vassilikov, other than that I liked him and I was attracted to him. Our characters and our backgrounds were very different, and yet we seemed to get on well together and to share interests and views. On the other hand, his ease with the Dorchester life presented a real obstacle for me.

I needed time to work out what I felt, but I well knew that in a war, when emotions were stretched tight and life itself was so tenuous, time was what we did not have.

I put down my coffee cup and walked across to where he was sitting. When I sat beside him I was intensely aware of him, of the blood moving under his skin and flushing his pale face, pulsing in rapid beats in his neck. I could feel the air moving as he breathed in and out.

'The question is,' I said, 'what to do?'

He put down the coffee cup. 'We could play cards. Penny a pop?'

Obviously, I was not a born vamp. I tried again. 'What I mean is, what can I do to convince you I'm not in love with David Levy?'

When he began to pull me close, I resisted a little, saying, 'I should tell you that I became engaged last year. He died at Scapa Flow.'

'David mentioned that. Are you still—'

'No. He was a good man, and I . . . No, not any more. Not now.'

The nightly thunder of the guns began and the throbbing roar of planes was overhead. Jim pulled me close again and this time I yielded. The room began to shake and we clung to each other as if the world was ending.

CHAPTER TWENTY

Gently disengaging himself from my embrace, Jim stood up. His face was flushed and his eyes unfocused and there was no irony in his smile, but real regret. He took a deep, ragged breath. I made a soft, annoyed sound.

'Lily, you fell asleep on your feet this morning. Your nerves are shot and you need a good night's sleep, if that's possible in this racket. And we both need time.'

'Time?'

'To work things out, work out what you want, where we should go with this. Especially with David . . .'

The local All Clear sounded and he smiled again.

'Fate,' he said. 'Telling me to get out before my resistance is entirely swept away or you fall asleep. Or both.'

'But—'

'Stay there. I'll see myself out.'

'Will you come back tomorrow? It's Sunday, are you free?' I hated sounding so feeble.

'Yes, of course, and yes I'm free. I'll telephone you once I'm back at my flat, to let you know I've arrived in one piece.'

He turned to leave, but then he was in front of me again, leaning down to brush his lips across mine. As he straightened he murmured something in Russian. And he was gone.

I waited fifteen minutes and raced downstairs to the pay telephone in the foyer, standing guard over the machine, already longing to hear his voice again. After another long fifteen minutes the telephone rang.

'I'm home and all's well.'

'Tell me something lovely.'

'Your kisses are like the first soft fall of snow.' His voice was dry, unsentimental. 'Is that romantic enough?'

I laughed. 'Brute. Is there no romance in you?'

'I'm a barrister. I'll kiss you again tomorrow and find a suitable metaphor then, but you sleep now.'

I hung up. 'First fall of snow,' I murmured, and laughed to myself as I climbed the stairs to the flat. Once I was inside I tidied up, unwilling to go to bed, wanting to remember the evening.

But what about Levy? I sat down on the couch with a thump. Surely Jim was right, and Levy was with his parents. Surely he was fine. And there was nothing I could do, not at this hour of night. I didn't want to think of Levy, not at this moment. I would worry about Levy tomorrow.

I felt absurdly happy. Jim was entirely different to Denys, who had been my first serious lover. My only lover. He had been persuasive on the night before he left for Scapa Flow.

'I may die up there. We're getting married. Everybody is jumping into bed. There's no point in waiting. Please, Lily. I need you so much. Don't let me go away like this.'

Katherine had known the moment she saw me the following day.

'It's Russian roulette with your life, Lily, not to have taken the proper precautions,' she had told me firmly.

'It will be fine. I love him. We're getting married.'

Three weeks later, Denys died. In my grief I forgot to count the weeks. One month, two months went by. I turned to Katherine, terrified I was facing an unwanted pregnancy. I had no money, I was far from home and unmarried. Society judged very harshly the women who were seen to defy its rules.

'You'll need to decide what you want to do,' she had said.

'I don't know what to do. I can't think.'

She made an appointment for me to see the doctor who 'made arrangements' for all the society women. It was probably the most embarrassing experience of my life, visiting that ugly little doctor in Knightsbridge, and I had no idea what I would do if he confirmed my fears. But after he examined me he told me that I was not pregnant. He recommended contraception and said he could arrange it.

Katherine was a firm follower of Marie Stopes. 'No child that is unwanted should ever be conceived, and women should be free to love without fear,' was her motto. 'Please do Lily, you can't go through this again.'

In the bittersweet joy of knowing I was not carrying Denys's child, and at Katherine's urging, I let the little doctor fit the device. In the past year it had remained in its box, unused. I had not found or sought another love affair. At first it was because I was mourning Denys, later the Blitz drained my energy and left too little time for dalliance.

Now, I would see what happened.

Jim arrived the following day just before lunch and swept me into a kiss that was entirely and satisfyingly passionate.

'First fall of snow?' I asked dryly, when he released me.

He looked at me until my gaze fell away, overwhelmed by the burning intensity in his eyes. He said something in Russian and kissed me again.

'Before you ask,' he said, 'I've not been able to find out yet which hospital Mrs Levy was admitted to, but I've made enquiries and left messages. I don't really want to spend the day by the telephone waiting for news, so could we try to put David out of our minds, just for a while. I'm sure that he's with his parents and has forgotten about everything else. If he's not at your station tomorrow morning I'll pull out all the stops and find him for you.'

It wasn't difficult to believe that he was right about Levy; I so wanted it to be true.

'All right. What do you have in mind for today?'

'What about some fresh air? Hampstead Heath?'

It was a day of sunshine and unexpected showers. He drove to Hampstead and we lunched in a little tearoom on the High Street. We walked on the Heath until the light began to fade, discussing those inconsequential matters – favourite songs, colours, books, childhood memories, likes and dislikes – that new couples find so fascinating, and in the evening we dined in a small restaurant near his flat in Mayfair. As the day progressed I began to get the measure of this stranger I had allowed into my life.

Levy had been right. Jim was shy. He hid it behind a grave courtesy and dry humour that I suspected could all too easily be mistaken for pomposity or condescension. That was unfortunate, as I felt sure he was no snob. His courtesy extended to everyone we met. He was quiet, unembarrassed by silence, but when we discussed a topic that interested him, such as flying, he would talk eagerly. The breadth of his reading was astonishing, but he wore his learning lightly, and we were able to talk easily together.

After dinner he drove me home, and although we kissed in my small hallway, he soon put me at arm's length.

'It's my first day in my new duties tomorrow,' he said, 'and you've another tough shift ahead of you. Be sure to give my regards to David when you see him.' He smiled. 'Would you care to meet me for dinner tomorrow evening?'

'I would.'

Another quick kiss, and he was gone.

Levy was not at the station when I arrived at nine o'clock the next morning, and had still not arrived ten minutes later. If I had been anxious before, now I was filled with dread.

'What's wrong, Brennan? And wherever is Levy?' Maisie asked with a sympathetic smile.

'I don't know. I'm worried sick about him.'

'Mrs Coke hasn't come in yet, either,' she said. 'What's going on around here?'

Through the window I could see Moray talking to Fripp in the office.

'I'll see if Moray's heard anything,' I said, rising.

The door to the office was slightly open. I raised my hand to knock, when I heard Fripp say, 'And I nearly fainted when Sadler mentioned Soho.'

'That's enough.' Moray's voice was sharply imperative. 'He's got nothing to do with this.'

'Sorry.' Fripp sounded contrite. 'When are we meeting next?'

'Usual day, time and place.'

'I don't like the usual place.'

'It's private.'

'Will Mr Mitchell be there?' Fripp sounded almost girlish.

'You're rather partial to him, aren't you?'

'He's a very nice man.' Now she sounded prim. 'Did you know that he's read . . . the book . . . in the original German?'

'Bully for him,' said Moray. 'Now back to work with you. You're accompanying Brennan again.'

'I don't like Brennan.'

'You'll work well enough with her if you keep away from politics. She'll never agree, so there's no point in talking to her about it. Especially now Levy's disappeared.'

'Where is he anyway? Did you—'

'There's no news about Levy. Now, back to work. And remember, no discussing politics when you're out with Brennan.'

I whirled away from the door. When Fripp reappeared I was sitting in the common room pondering what I had just overheard. It sounded terribly suspicious, her remark about the German book. Was she speaking of Hitler's *Mein Kampf*? Yet surely even Fripp wouldn't be so stupid as to mention that, here in the station. More disturbing to me, however, was hearing that there was no news of Levy.

Fripp came waving a chit at me. 'I'm to be assisting you again,' she said. 'It's a mortuary run. Come along.'

'Just a moment. I want a word with Moray.'

I knocked briskly on the door and entered at Moray's command.

'Is there any information about Levy?'

He frowned at the desk and shuffled some papers before looking up at me.

'I've heard nothing. I'll make some enquiries when you're out this morning.'

I was about to leave him when Mrs Coke arrived. She seemed agitated as she pushed past me into the office. I closed the door behind her, but could not help myself from watching the pair of them through the window. Mrs Coke was in tears in front of Moray's desk.

'Come on,' said Fripp.

'Just a minute,' I replied, transfixed by the scene in the office. I exchanged looks with Maisie, who shrugged.

Mrs Coke dabbed at her wet eyes with a handkerchief as Moray rose from the desk, came to the door, poked his head out and asked Harris to come into the office. She put her knitting to one side and went in.

'We should go,' said Fripp, now impatient.

'Just a minute.'

Harris, Moray and Mrs Coke engaged in an animated conversation, then all three of them came into the common room.

'I have to tell you,' said Mrs Coke, in a faltering voice and quite unlike her usual decisive manner, 'that for the next few weeks at least, I will be taking sick leave.'

The news was greeted with a stunned silence.

'I did not want to bother you with my concerns,' she went on, 'and although I have attempted to continue in these strenuous duties, I have been instructed to rest. Mr Moray will be acting station officer until I am well enough to return, and he will be assisted by McIver and by Harris, who will be acting as deputy.'

Moray said some words about how much we would miss her and there was some desultory clapping. Mrs Coke strode out of the common room with her back straight and head high. It was a grand exit.

'What was that all about?' asked Fripp, as we drove to the incident site.

'I haven't a clue.'

That was a lie. I was fairly sure it had something to do with Levy's evidence that Mrs Coke had engaged in fraud, and I had to wonder whether it had any bearing on Levy's disappearance. Mrs Coke had made threats against him on Friday evening, after all.

I wondered if Jim had been able to find out the hospital where Levy's mother had been taken. If he had then I'd go there as soon as I could, but there was nothing I could do now except drive the Monster and do my job.

As I went about my duties with Fripp I was surprised to discover that she was less squeamish than I was about dealing with body parts. I could only assume that her fears centred upon injury to herself, and thus she could deal with the horror of death or injury to others without fuss. Consequently we managed fairly well together, despite the gruesome condition of some of the bodies that had been removed after some days in a caved-in cellar.

'Kensington was hit badly last night,' she said, as we headed back to Woburn Place that afternoon. 'Especially Campden Hill. There was a lot of damage as I cycled to work this morning.'

I made a non-committal sound and stared doggedly out of the windscreen.

'Mummy, Daddy and I spent the night in the backyard shelter, and it rocked like a cradle. I heard that Marble Arch and the City were hit badly. The old Dutch Church – the Church of Austin Friars in the City – that's been completely demolished.'

I murmured something about it being a terrible shame.

'Do you think Mrs Coke is really ill?'

'I have no idea.'

'I think she's been involved in questionable activities. She was always with Knaggs and Sadler, who are obviously connected with the black market, and Knaggs was caught looting, after all.'

'Who knows?'

'It's interesting that Levy was the one to catch Knaggs in the act.'

'Hmmm.'

'How did he know when to go after him? I think Levy was spying on them. Was he?'

'I don't think so.'

'So, what do you think? Is he dead?' Fripp sounded unconcerned, but curious. I flinched to hear the words. The woman had the sensitivity of a brick.

'If you mean Levy, I really don't know.'

'I thought you two were thick as thieves.'

'We're friends, I told you that. And that's why I'm worried about him.'

I edged the Monster past a dray filled with beer barrels, pulled by a large horse that clopped along placidly, ignoring the traffic.

'Those bodies we just delivered had been buried for days,' she said. 'I wonder sometimes how hard they really do look for bodies in the ruins. Levy may have been blown to smithereens. Or he's lying in the cellar of a bombed building somewhere and is food for rats. Just like the ones we picked up this morning.'

I pulled the ambulance over to the side of the road with a sudden jerk, pushed open the door and ran to the curb, where I emptied my stomach of whatever was in there. Even when my stomach was empty, I was still retching.

CHAPTER TWENTY-ONE

Jim telephoned me that evening, not long after I arrived home.

When I told him that Levy had not turned up at work, he was not surprised.

'I thought that might be the case.' His voice was husky and he seemed to have some trouble catching his breath. 'I've had word that David's parents haven't heard from him for the past four days. He came home from the ambulance station on Thursday morning as usual. He had a shower, slept until around three and then went out. He never returned home.'

'Have they checked the hospitals?'

'They're checking everywhere, Lily. They are frantic with worry.'

I was, too.

'Jim, Mrs Coke, the station officer – she went off on sick leave today. I'm sure it's because Levy reported her for fraud. She was making threats against him on Friday night. What if she—'

'Are you suggesting that she has done something to David? That he met with foul play?'

'It's not just her. When he caught Knaggs looting Knaggs made threats against him, too.'

'Honestly Lily, it's a great deal more likely that he's a victim of the Blitz.' He paused and seemed to catch his breath. 'I've made all the enquiries I can.'

'But—'

'I'm so sorry, Lily. I just don't know what else I can do. It's very concerning that it's been four days without word from him.'

He sounded exhausted, and I wondered if he was going to tell me, very politely, that he no longer wanted to meet me for dinner. I was too worried about Levy to worry about fine dining, but I wanted to discuss it all with Jim, make him realise that Levy had enemies at the station.

'Look,' Jim said at last, 'I'm longing to see you, but—' He gave a short, bitter laugh. 'I hate to admit it, but I'm shattered after just one day of my new duties. Perhaps I'm not as fit as I'd thought. Would you be terribly upset if I put you off? I'd be poor company tonight.'

I forced myself to swallow my disappointment. 'It's understandable. You're only just out of hospital. When do you want to—'

'And there's something else. They're sending me to a place in the country for some training. I'm off tomorrow and I won't be returning to London until the Friday after next.'

'Oh.'

'I'm so sorry, Lily, believe me.' I believed him, he sounded terribly sorry. 'I'll telephone you every night. Nine o'clock on the dot. Will you be there if I call?'

'Of course.'

'And we'll go to dinner as soon as I return.'

'I'll look forward to it.'

'What about the Ritz?'

'Dinner at the Ritz? I saw the movie – it didn't end well for the titled suitor.'

'We'll make our own ending.'

On Tuesday morning, Moray came into the conference room with a letter he had received from Levy's father. When he read it to us, it confirmed what I had heard from Jim the evening before, namely that Levy had left home on Thursday afternoon without informing his parents where he was going and he had not been seen since.

Maisie's eyes became wide as Moray finished reading the letter. 'Oh, that's terrible news,' she whispered. 'Perhaps he's got amnesia. He might be in a hospital with no identification and nobody knows who he is.'

Sadler made a snorting noise and I glared at him.

'If Levy's not reported for duty by the end of the week I'll have to arrange a replacement,' said Moray. 'In the meantime, Brennan you're paired with Fripp.'

From the look on Fripp's face, she felt as happy about that arrangement as I did.

The general consensus in the common room, once Moray had returned to the office, was that Levy was an unidentified air raid victim. I was not so sure.

'He disappeared on the night they bombed Coventry,' I said. 'There were only a few attacks on London that night.'

'Only takes one bomb,' said Sadler.

I turned to the man and regarded him coldly. 'You told me Levy had been Blitzed in Soho. Why did you say that? Just what do you know about it all?'

His eyes seemed to flicker slightly and he quickly looked down at the cards he was holding, before looking up again.

'I made it up about Soho, Brennan. There were no raids in Soho that night – I was there with the band in the Red Room like I said, but no bombs fell in the area. I was teasing you, because you was so hysterical about Levy not being here. It was cruel and I'm sorry about it now he's really gone.'

I couldn't believe a word the man said, and I decided to find out for myself if any bombs had fallen in Soho that night.

'And what about your friend,' I went on, 'the one in Holborn? You thought he might have hurt Levy.'

He met my gaze steadily this time. 'Turned out it wasn't Levy after all. The blighter was there again on Sunday, handing out his bloody pamphlets. He looks like Levy, but it's not him.'

Something wasn't right about Sadler's story, but apart from asking about the Soho bombs, I wasn't sure how I could take the matter any further.

As the week progressed and there was no word about Levy my fears for him were like a niggling pain that sometimes receded but never entirely disappeared. It grew more difficult each day to keep any hope that he was still alive. In one regard, though, my luck held. The weather was poor. This meant that few raiders appeared over London in the daylight hours, and Fripp and I were rarely in any personal danger as we carried out our duties. In such circumstances Fripp was a competent attendant and I noted with a dull sort of apathy as the days went by that I was becoming used to her. It was nothing like the camaraderie I had shared with Levy, but if we kept our conversation to innocuous subjects, Fripp and I were able to work together comfortably enough.

And, to my surprise, Jim kept his promise and telephoned me each evening at nine. I ignored the smiles from other occupants as I waited outside the small cubicle that housed the building's telephone, ready to pounce on the receiver at the first ring, because my conversations with Jim had become the high points of my days. Although he couldn't tell me anything about his duties, he was always interested in hearing about mine and he seemed especially to enjoy the station gossip.

'Any more interesting rumours from Powell?' he asked during Friday night's call.

'The usual. She is now convinced that German paratroopers have been landing here disguised as parsons.'

'That one's been around since September last year. She needs to find a new rumour to panic herself with.'

'There's an interesting twist to this one. It seems that her Aunt Minnie —'

'What happened to Aunt Glad?'

'Still looking for hairy nuns, I expect. Anyway, Powell's Aunt Minnie is reliably informed that the fake parsons are coming here in order to kidnap healthy English girls and force them into German baby farms. Hitler likes the English bloodstock, you see.'

Jim laughed. 'I wouldn't have thought we were pure enough for the Nazis. Britain is made up of a bit of everything. Anyway, don't she and Aunt Minnie know that Nazis disguised as English clergymen invariably give themselves away when they stub their toe and swear loudly in German?'

'Well, we all know that! But Powell is safe from the fate worse than death even in the absence of toe stubbing. She can identify a Nazi just by looking at him.'

'Oh?'

'Apparently, a German's eyes are so cold that it is like death is staring straight at you.'

'Er, by blood my mother is three-quarters German.'

I thought of Jim's steady grey eyes and smiled to myself.

'I'll have to introduce you to Powell. If she shrieks and runs away, we'll know you've inherited the death stare. I swear one day I'll jump up and shout "tittle tattle lost the battle" at the woman.'

Our conversation inevitably arrived at Levy.

'His parents have made enquiries at every hospital, in the hope that he was admitted without identification. And they contacted all the rest centres, in case he had amnesia.'

'And nothing?'

'No one of his description has turned up anywhere in London.'

'Jim,' I said hesitantly, 'I'd like to visit Mr and Mrs Levy. But only if you think it would be appropriate. I don't want to upset them any further . . .'

'I'm sure they'd appreciate a visit from you. Can it wait until I return?'

'Of course. I'd prefer to go there with you.'

'Lily, I think we all accept now that he must be dead.'

And that was that.

* * *

I lay in bed that night, wakeful and unhappy as the raiders droned overhead, and I imagined all the gruesome fates that might have befallen Levy in an air raid. And I brooded on what could have happened if he was not a Blitz victim. Both Knaggs and Mrs Coke had threatened him. What if one of them had followed through on those threats? And Sadler disliked him and made up tales about him. I thought I owed it to my friend to at least make some enquiries about these people.

Bloomsbury was spared a major attack that night, but two aircraft passed low over St Andrew's at around midnight. The swish of their falling bombs was loud and from the way the building shook, I knew they had dropped their load nearby.

On my way to work on Saturday morning I discovered that the remaining houses in Caroline Place had taken another hit and most of the street was a pitiful heap of mud and rubble.

I was gazing at the scene of desolation when I heard a squeak of bicycle brakes and turned to see that Fripp had pulled up next to me.

'What an utter shambles,' she said, nodding at the ruins. 'London nowadays is like the last days of Pompeii or something. I doubt they'll find much to salvage here. Better to pull it all down and start again.'

'It's sad, though,' I said. 'To lose the history, I mean.'

'I hate old buildings,' said Fripp. 'I'd be happy to see the end of most of this city. Start again. Modern buildings. Fresh slate.'

Fripp wheeled her bicycle beside me as we walked to Woburn Place, neither of us talking much. As we passed the rosy magnificence of the Hotel Russell I saw how its elaborate wedding cake exterior was chipped and battered after weeks of attacks. I couldn't help smiling, though, at one of the carved putti holding a garland in its chubby hand. Levy had called the building a mishmash of Art Nouveau Gothic, and had chaffed me when I said I liked the hotel's Edwardian magnificence.

'Any news about Levy?' asked Fripp.

I shook my head briefly.

'I think he's another Blitz casualty, poor chap,' she said cheerfully.

'I thought you hated him.'

'Hate is a harsh word, Brennan. I'm better than that.'

Most of the day shift was already in the common room when we arrived. Everyone looked exhausted. It was the seeming interminability of the Blitz; it consumed our energy and dulled our wits. It destroyed our homes and it killed our friends.

Armstrong was chalky white under the galaxy of spots on his face; the area under his eyes was purplish, so that he seemed to have been punched. Maisie darned a pair of socks with shaky hands and seemed near tears. Celia had lost weight, I thought. There were fine blue shadows under her eyes and the bones of her face were sharply fragile under her skin. Squire was turned away from me, hugging the heater, as usual, but he held his shoulders bent, like an old man. Sadler played one of his solitary card games with dogged intensity.

'Any news of Levy?' Maisie asked me, looking up from her stitching.

As I shook my head Moray joined us. He had heard Maisie's question. 'No news at all,' he said. 'It's been over a week now. After all this time there's really no hope. We'll be sent a replacement officer on Monday.'

Maisie's eyes were wide and her mouth trembled. She hid it with a shaking hand.

Moray caught my eye. 'Lily, I'm very sorry . . .' His glance slid past me like a shiver and landed on a spot near my ear. 'It's best to keep busy,' he said.

He turned to Fripp and held up a chit.

'You and Brennan take this. It's a delivery of supplies to Great Ormond Street.'

I spent the rest of the day with Fripp, driving back and forth between warehouses and Great Ormond Street Hospital, delivering medicines, food, bandages and other necessities.

We returned to Woburn Place just before five. The night shift were arriving and what was left of the day shift were preparing to leave. Muttered conversations in the common room ceased as soon as I entered, and I deduced they had been talking about Levy.

I decided to begin my enquiries.

'Does anyone know what Mrs Coke is doing?' I asked the room. 'How long is she to be on sick leave?'

Sadler looked up. 'She's already left the service. Personal reasons. I heard she'd got a job as a clerk for one of the ministries. More money, less stress, lucky bi—. I mean, she's landed on her feet.'

'Which ministry?'

'Food. She'll be one of Woolton's pets. *She* won't go hungry on three pounds five and six a week.'

Mrs Coke had certainly landed on her feet. It seemed she had benefitted from being reported by Levy. In the circumstances it was unlikely that she would want to extract revenge and risk losing her cushy new position.

But what of Knaggs? I opened my mouth to ask Sadler about him when the Warning sounded. Moray appeared in the doorway, rubbing his eyes. 'I've been told it's only a couple of German surveillance planes. It's probably safe to leave.'

I walked home in a haze of misery about Levy, wondering why I was still in England. Australia was heading into spring; the wildflowers would be putting on their brilliant display and the weather would be warming up for summer. My parents were desperate for me to return and I could be home for Christmas. If I returned home to Perth the ambulance station would soon find another driver to replace me, just as it had replaced Levy so quickly, and I could spend a lazy summer in the sunshine. I imagined lying on white sand with the clear blue Indian Ocean in front of me, and for a moment I could almost taste the salt spray on the wind.

But I knew it was only a dream. I would not leave London so long as the Blitz raged. If I did then Hitler would have defeated me, and I could not live with that. And I needed to know what had happened to Levy.

The All Clear went as I crossed the road to St Andrew's. I felt a few sprinkles of rain on my face and I sighed as I pushed open the door into the lobby.

Jim was standing by the lift, I realised with surprise. *The RAF uniform suits him*, I thought, *but he's too tall and out of my league*. I sighed to myself. *There's no point in continuing this.* Then I remembered our easy conversations when he had rung me each evening that week.

'I managed to snaffle some weekend leave,' he said, 'and I dashed down here before they could change their minds. Are you free for dinner?'

My spirits lifted. Levy had thought I should give him a fair go. If Levy thought Jim and I were suited, then we must be. But I had no desire to go to the Ritz that night.

'Of course, but nowhere fancy. I'm really tired. It's been a horrid week.'

'I know just the place. No dance band, just good simple food.'

'Perfect.'

He seemed to hesitate, then said quickly, 'Look, if you feel up to it, Mr and Mrs Levy have said they would like to see you tomorrow afternoon.'

I felt my stomach tighten.

'Of course I'm up to it.'

CHAPTER TWENTY-TWO

David Levy's good looks had come from his mother. Mrs Levy was a darkly elegant woman. She was lying on a chaise longue when we were shown into their suite at the Dorchester, where they had moved until they could find new accommodation. Her skin was flawless and she had given David her high cheekbones and heavy-lidded dark eyes. Those eyes were reddened at present and puffy with weeping. Her hands plucked constantly at the soft woollen rug that hid her legs.

She made a vague gesture towards the rug. 'I am very sorry not to rise, but the bomb . . .'

Her accent was European. I would not have been able to pick from which country she had come originally if Levy had not told me it was Germany. She responded to Jim's introductions with a smile that reminded me so much of Levy I felt tears flood hotly into my own eyes.

The chairs she gestured towards looked too fragile to hold even my weight, but were sturdy enough when we sat down on them.

'David spoke of you often, Lily. I may call you Lily?'

'Yes, of course. I wanted to tell you how very – how much David meant, means—' I swallowed and began again. 'I wanted to tell you what a marvellous ambulance attendant David was, and what a good friend he was to me.'

Mr Levy came into the room, a middle-aged man, dark-haired and soft-eyed, and as charming as his wife. His accent was English, as entirely English as his son's had been. His sorrow showed itself in restless energy. He seemed unable to sit still and spent much of our visit stalking the room, adjusting the curtains, touching various small ornaments.

I told them what I had wanted to say, about how good Levy had been to me throughout our time working together, his kindness to patients and his dedication to our work.

'Thank you, Lily.' Mrs Levy put out her hands and I rose to take hold of them. They were cold. I looked into her eyes and saw her haunted despair. 'Thank you for coming. David told us so little about his work, but he spoke often of his driver, Miss Brennan. He told us that you were the bravest woman he had ever met.'

I felt my cheeks flame. 'He exaggerated, I'm afraid.'

She smiled. 'David could be – what is the English word? – ah, yes, prickly. He admired very few people, but he thought the world of Lily Brennan.'

Hot tears filled my eyes. 'Lily Brennan thought the world of him also,' I said.

We talked for a while longer about Levy, and I told them some amusing stories about him at work. The Levys told me that they now accepted that David was dead; Mrs Levy in particular mourned the fact that there was no body to bury.

'We don't know where he went after he left the house that day,' said Mr Levy. 'If we had some idea where he went then we would know where to look for his – for him.' He glanced at his wife.

'I have nightmares,' she explained. 'I dream that David is out there, calling to me, expecting me to find him.' She began to cry, silently, unashamedly. Mr Levy came across to her and put his hand on her shoulder.

'Should I ring for a pot of tea?' I asked, unsure of what else I could do.

Mrs Levy touched her wet eyes with a lacy white handkerchief and waved her hand in a gesture I had seen Levy use many times, one of dismissal and contempt.

'Tea. It is always tea with you English. You are a nation of tea drinkers.' I flinched at the pain in her eyes.

'I do not want tea,' she said. 'I want to hear the Mourners' Kaddish sung for my David. I want the chazan to say "Kel maleh rachamim". I want my boy back. I want to tell him I love him and tell him goodbye.'

I ached with sympathy for her, and there was nothing I could say.

'We are holding a memorial service for him,' said Mr Levy. 'It will be in the Hallam Street Synagogue on the Friday after next. You and Jim are welcome to attend, as are any of his friends at the station.'

'Maisie Halliday and George Squire were friendly towards him,' I said, 'I'll make sure they know.'

'Let them all know. All who wish to attend will be welcome.'

Jim and I left the Levys and the sophisticated glamour of the Dorchester and walked for a while in Mayfair's bomb-damaged streets as the afternoon shadows lengthened into evening. The large houses sat smugly as ever behind their impressive porticos, despite the broken windows and the dust and debris that choked the elegant thoroughfares. Jim seemed very at home in this world – and I found myself feeling increasingly like a mere tourist.

At the top of Curzon Street, we turned left towards Berkeley Square and Jim gestured towards the mansion beside us. Shrapnel and blast and fire had damaged but not destroyed the building. Chunks of the white Portland stone facade had been torn away and in its glassless windows hung the tattered remains of what had been delicate pink satin curtains, now flapping mournfully in the chilly breeze.

'Lansdowne House,' Jim said. 'One of the last big private houses in London. It became a private club in 1935. The gardens were sold, but the house remains, thankfully.'

'Eighteenth century?' I asked, admiring the clean lines of the building.

'Yes, and there's a lot of Art Deco in there as well. It was decorated by the firm who fitted out the great Cunard ocean liners, the *Queen Mary* and the *Queen Elizabeth*.'

'And the *Titanic*?'

He laughed and shook his head.

'What sort of club is it?' I asked. All I knew about London's private clubs I had gleaned from P.G. Wodehouse, where they appeared to be the haunts of wealthy old men who wanted to escape their wives to drink port and read newspapers, or wealthy young men who wanted to act like idiots.

Jim shrugged. 'Oh, it's social, athletic and residential. The only private members club in London where women have equal standing with men.'

'Oh, I suppose I had assumed they were all gentlemen's clubs. Are there many women members?'

He seemed surprised at the question. 'I suppose so. Always seem to be a fair few when I go there.'

'So you are a member?' I thought he might have been, because he seemed to know a great deal about it and spoke with some pride.

He nodded. 'Since I came up from Cambridge. I'm very keen on foil and épée and the club has an excellent fencing master.'

As we continued our walk my footsteps seemed to tap out a refrain: *Too posh for me, too posh for me. Jim, my lad, you're too posh for me.*

In Berkeley Square, branches had been ripped from the splendid trees and leaves were strewn over the road. Many of the exclusive little Mayfair shops in the streets around the square had been reduced to piles of dust-covered wreckage, jagged with splinters. At the furrier's shop, furs sprawled in the dust and grime like the carcasses of slaughtered animals, and in the milliner's establishment next door all the pretty little hats perched, dusty and battered as bombed budgerigars. Behind glassless windows the plum-coloured carpet was so deep in grey dust that it looked like a lava flow.

'At least Mayfair can look the East End in the eye,' said Jim, as we walked past the devastation, echoing the words of the Queen after Buckingham Palace was bombed.

Jim suggested that we dine early at Mirabelle, a restaurant in Curzon Street. I was wearing a suit of black lightweight wool that was one of my Prague outfits. It was perfectly acceptable for an afternoon visit, but Mirabelle was very smart. I gestured at my outfit.

'I'm not really dressed for a place like that.'

'You look gorgeous,' Jim said. 'Look, it's close and I know the food will be very good. No one cares about that sort of thing nowadays.'

With some trepidation I agreed.

Mirabelle had been one of the most exclusive restaurants in London before the war and many celebrities had dined there: Vivien Leigh, Orson Welles and even Winston Churchill. Now, after months of Blitzkrieg, the canopy over the doorway was cracked and those windows that still had glass were criss-crossed with tape while the rest had been covered with board.

The Warning sounded as we pushed through the heavy blackout curtain and handed over our coats, before descending the stairs to a restaurant that, despite the war-damaged exterior, still maintained an air of classic luxury.

There were no more than five couples in the entire restaurant, but the dance band was playing with verve for a single pair – both in khaki – who twirled around on the pocket-handkerchief dance floor.

As we perused our menus I noticed that a dapper little man was greeting the diners at their tables and holding up an ugly looking piece of shrapnel for their inspection. He came over to us eventually, introduced himself as the manager, Mr Ratazzini, and displayed the shrapnel piece to us with some pride.

'It came down – whack! – just beyond the glass canopy last night,' he said. He grimaced expressively and waved his hand around the restaurant. 'It is no wonder we have so few diners here. This Blitz is terrible for business.'

'I suppose people worry that they won't be able to get home,' said Jim.

Mr Ratazzini smiled. 'I have camp beds available for my customers. There is no need to hurry your meal.'

The nightly raid began just as the soup was set before us. Jim looked at me and raised an eyebrow. I shrugged.

'Nothing to say they'll hit Mayfair tonight.'

'We're probably safer here than in Bloomsbury.'

'Very likely.'

'He has camp beds available.'

'And I'm starving.'

We ate to the accompaniment of aeroplanes roaring overhead and the thunder of the guns on Primrose Hill. The food was beautifully cooked and delicious. We toasted each other as our cutlery rattled on the table and the bottles in the bar clinked together alarmingly. We lingered over our coffee, hoping for the All Clear; the idea of camping out in the restaurant was not one that really appealed to me.

Jim ordered brandy and when it came I held the glass under my nose, inhaling the warmth of the fumes. If scents had colours, I thought, this would be golden with a hint of fiery red. Like the flames of burning buildings in a Blitz. And yet, not all the buildings burned, no matter how bad the raid.

'Because London is just so damn big,' I mused.

'Biggest city in the world,' agreed Jim. 'But I'm not sure I follow you.'

'That's Hitler's problem.'

'What is?'

'He can't wipe London off the map, no matter what he throws against it. Look how hard he's been hitting the City. A lot of it is destroyed, but most of it remains. And that's only a tiny part of Greater London. We're just too big.'

'Unlike Coventry. Or Southampton. Or Bristol.'

I nodded glumly. 'I hate it when he hits the smaller towns and cities. It's unsportsmanlike.'

'Just not cricket?'

I made a face at him. 'Yes, I'm a little tipsy. But I'm very happy.'

'Good.'

I looked at Jim over my glass.

'I feel so terribly sorry for Mrs Levy, being unable to hold a proper funeral. Don't you think it's suspicious? That we can't find Levy's body, I mean?'

He seemed troubled. 'I doubt it. Some bodies are too damaged ever to be properly identified. Some will have disintegrated entirely.'

I shook my head in disagreement. 'Very few bodies are not claimed.'

It was remarkable to me that so few persons were missing, given the scale of the Blitz. The authorities made great efforts to identify everyone who was killed in the bombing, by scraps of clothing, effects and witness accounts. In most cases it was known that someone had been in a particular place when it was bombed and it could be assumed that they died there, even if there was nothing recognisable left. I knew that an Australian ambulance officer had been recently identified only by the cufflinks her husband had given her.

I took another sip of brandy. 'What if his body has been hidden? I can't stop thinking that Levy made quite a few enemies in the last few weeks.'

'You know I think that's fanciful, Lily. Look, I asked some questions about your former station officer, Mrs Coke. The upshot is that the Ambulance service accepts she has engaged in fraudulent activities but it didn't want to charge her.'

'I heard today that she's already taken a job with the Ministry of Food,' I said. 'She'll just do the same there. I don't understand why she wasn't prosecuted.'

'Morale, I expect,' replied Jim. 'The authorities would not want people to know that crooks are running our ambulance stations during a Blitz.'

'They should have prosecuted her,' I said, annoyed. 'What about Knaggs, then? "I'll get you for this," he said to Levy, in front of the ARP warden.'

I was talking too fast and could feel my face getting flushed, but it was all coming up and I couldn't stop it.

'And Knaggs was in the black market with Sadler, and Levy reported them,' I went on. 'Sadler was very odd on the night Levy didn't turn up for work. Remember – I told you he said that Levy had been killed in an air raid in Soho, or assaulted at Holborn. Now he says he was just teasing me, but what if there's more to it than that?'

Jim gave me a look such as one might give to a child telling a particularly unlikely story.

'And now there's Moray and Fripp.'

'What about them?'

I told Jim about the conversation I had overheard, and about Fripp's reference to meetings and the German book. As I had expected, he was unimpressed.

'There are several possible explanations, all of which are more likely than there being a nest of fifth columnists at your ambulance station. This Fripp woman and Moray may meet to discuss Goethe or Hegel or other German philosophers. Or they could be communists. Marx's *Communist Manifesto* was first published in German, remember.'

'They're not communists,' I said, annoyed at his tone.

'How can you be sure of that?'

'Fripp's a fascist, not a communist,' I said. 'She spouts defeatist views, saying we should parley with Hitler to stop the bombing and she thinks that he would treat the British differently because he likes us.'

'She may have lied to you about her political views.'

'I've just spent all week with her. Fripp is not a communist.'

His fingers began to tap out a tune on an imaginary piano, so I knew he was troubled.

'Lily, Military Intelligence has people all over London watching and listening for traitors. Let them do their job and you do yours.'

'So I should simply ignore signs of fifth column activity?'

He did not respond. I picked up my cup and took a sip of the really excellent coffee and looked around the room. The tiny dance floor was empty, but the band continued to play. The thumping of the guns and the roar of the planes had faded and I hoped we would soon hear the All Clear. I wanted to go home. Alone.

We were silent for a while, listening to the band, and my attention wandered. Something was bothering me about Fripp and Moray. Something one of them had said some time ago, and I could not remember what it was. I was jolted back to the present by Jim's voice.

'Look,' he said, in a conciliatory voice, 'I'll mention what you overheard to my superior officer, see if he thinks it should be discreetly investigated. Don't let's quarrel about it. And please, Lily, don't go turning the tragedy of David's death into a murder mystery.'

The All Clear sounded and I let the matter drop, pleased that he was going to at least tell his superior about Moray and Fripp. He left me at my door with a promise to take me to dinner the following Saturday, after his return from the country.

'This week I'm on night shifts with Fripp,' I said. 'I'm sure I'll need some comfort, material and emotional, by Saturday.'

'Happy to oblige.'

I thought about it all in bed that night. It was most unusual for people to disappear entirely. Levy had been my mate and that brought obligations, especially if he had met with foul play. Despite what Jim said, I knew it was suspicious that his body had not been found. Jim had said he would follow up on my concerns about Moray and Fripp. I now thought it unlikely that Mrs Coke was involved, given her plush new job. That left the spivs.

The question was, how could I even begin to investigate them?

CHAPTER TWENTY-THREE

The final week of November brought strong south-westerly weather that was impartial to both sides. The nights alternated between brilliant pro-German skies and pro-British clouds and heavy rain. Daylight air raids seemed to have ceased, apart from incendiary drops around dusk, but night raids continued unabated and they were fierce.

We were all thrilled to finally receive our uniforms from the Ambulance Service. That morning we also welcomed Levy's replacement. He was Rupert Purvis, a young artist with dark hair brushed back from a high forehead and clear blue eyes behind round glasses. Purvis was a conscientious objector, and Sadler immediately began referring to him sarcastically as 'the conchie'.

Maisie was interested though. 'What did you tell the tribunal?' she asked Purvis. All conscientious objectors had to have their case determined by a special tribunal.

'I said that as every individual human being was the holder of values such as beauty, truth and goodness, to destroy another human being was to destroy those ultimate values too. I said I was not prepared to put myself into a situation where I might have to take another's life.'

'And they really bought that?' Maisie sounded frankly amazed.

He shrugged. 'I meant it sincerely. I'm not a coward. The tribunal gave me an exemption from military service on the condition that I undertake civilian war service. So I joined the Ambulance Service and here I am.'

Moray partnered Purvis with Maisie. That meant I still had to go out with Fripp, and she was as difficult as ever. I mentioned this to Jim in our telephone conversation the next evening.

'She calls me insane, screams at me when I'm trying to drive through a raid. We need to reach the injured. Does she really think I'm not just as scared as she is?'

'Probably. David told me he'd never seen you look the least bit afraid when you were attending an incident.'

'Well, that's just silly. I'm always terrified, but when I'm busy I forget. It's later, once we've arrived back at the station, that I remember and then I start shaking like a leaf.'

'It was like that for me, when I was flying.' He paused. 'What is courage anyway? If it is doing something despite your fears, then in a way, it's admirable really that your Miss Fripp forces herself to go out and do her job.'

'She's not my Miss Fripp and it's all very well to say that, but she makes it bloody hard for me to do *my* job.'

On Wednesday night the German planes came in waves. There were several local All Clears during the night, followed by Warnings and raids of varying intensity. We were sent out during one of the lulls to a serious incident near Euston station.

Not long after we were on the road a local Warning siren sounded and soon the roar of enemy aircraft was loud overhead. The anti-aircraft guns started up, firing non-stop. Their thunder competed with the cacophony of thuds and shrieks and whistles and crumps as bombs and shells landed too close for comfort, and a menacing red glow in the sky in front of us indicated that we were heading towards large conflagrations.

I ignored Fripp's rising hysteria to concentrate on driving the Monster on a road that shook with each explosion. I had skirted a large pothole when, without warning, she shrieked into my ear. I was startled and the Monster swerved alarmingly. Then I understood.

'Crikey!' I whispered.

The ambulance and all around it was lit up in the sudden, shocking illumination of a flare. My heart seemed to stop. There was safety in darkness. In this day-bright radiance the Monster was clearly visible to any passing German who felt the inclination to annihilate us. And yet, it was beautiful. The bright chandelier dripped stars as it slowly descended.

'There's a shelter,' Fripp shrieked. 'Over there. Pull over, Brennan. Pull over.' She tugged at my arm, trying to force me to the side of the road. In response I elbowed her savagely.

'We're far better off if we keep moving,' I yelled. 'Makes us a harder target to hit.'

Four bombs fell close by in quick succession and sparks and debris shot up into the air.

Fripp slumped down against her door, repeating a shrill mantra of fear: 'I can't bear it. I can't bear it. I can't bear it,' punctuated by sad little hiccupping sobs that made me actually sorry for her.

As soon as we arrived at the incident, Fripp wrenched open her door and ran to a nearby wall, to crouch there with some of the other rescue workers. We had been taught that keeping low was a protection against blast, but I thought she had picked a daft place to shelter as walls were liable to collapse without warning.

The whole sky was now ablaze with light; a vast tent of searchlight beams were waving and weaving around what looked like three or four small silver flies that turned and twisted in the lights. Anti-aircraft guns kept up a tremendous barrage, but the shell bursts fell far short of their targets.

Bits of shrapnel were falling, drifting almost like snowflakes through the air in an aimless, leisurely way. They clinked as they landed on the Monster's roof and the road beside me. I jumped down from the cabin and ran over to the warden, slipping a little on the wet and muddy ground. The air was smoky and I could taste brick dust. Bombs were still falling and the ground shook under my feet with each explosion. Fires burned fiercely nearby and the air was hot as a Kookynie summer; I could hear the hiss of fire hoses whenever there was a lull in the gun barrage.

The warden glanced over at Fripp. 'Bit of a 'fraidy cat, that one,' he said, shouting over the noise.

'It's a bad raid,' I shrugged.

Once I had helped the stretcher-bearers to load the wounded into the Monster, I called out to Fripp, who was still huddled against her wall.

'Are you coming?'

Great tongues of flames licked the building behind me, illuminating the scene, and I could see the fear and indecision in her face as clearly as if it were day.

I climbed into the cab and started the engine. Fripp jumped up and scurried over to the back of the ambulance. I heard her high voice trying to reassure the wounded and assumed that she had decided it would be more terrifying to be left behind than to drive with me through the mayhem. I pressed down on the accelerator and the Monster rattled away over the rubble, shrapnel and debris.

Fripp said nothing to me when she climbed back into the cab after our wounded had been unloaded at the hospital, and we drove back to Woburn Place in an ominous silence. As soon as I had parked, Fripp pushed open her door, jumped down from the ambulance and almost ran out of the garage. At the door she turned around to shriek at me that I was a suicidal idiot and she never wanted to ride with me again.

I muttered, 'Good,' and stepped down from the cabin. I felt a little dizzy and leaned against the Monster until the garage stopped spinning and I had forced away the tears.

When I entered the common room I could see Fripp remonstrating with McIver, who was duty officer that night. McIver looked up and saw me, and motioned me into the office.

'We are supposed to take cover during an air raid,' said Fripp to me when I entered. 'You know that, Brennan.' She turned to McIver. 'I've told her time and again and she won't listen. I will not sacrifice my life because Brennan's a suicidal lunatic.'

'We can't just park the ambulance and run off to a shelter until the local All Clear.' I tried to sound reasonable. 'If we don't get to the incidents quickly then people might die.'

Fripp opened her mouth, but McIver forestalled her. 'You can drive, can't you, Fripp?'

'Yes, but I can't drive an ambulance, and I won't drive during an air raid. It's suicidally dangerous and—'

'Quite,' said McIver. 'I think it would be best if you take over Ashwin's duties, driving the saloon to pick up walking wounded. There's not so much urgency with them and you can wait out the raid in safety.' She turned to me. 'Ashwin will act as your assistant until further notice.'

I was happy with that. I would prefer Celia Ashwin, who was cool under fire and as dedicated as I was to helping save lives.

Celia said she had no objection to swapping duties with Fripp, throwing the girl a look of barely disguised contempt as she did so.

Fripp flushed an angry red, saying, 'I'm not going to get myself killed just so people think I'm brave.'

Celia looked at me. 'Do your worst, Brennan,' she said with a smile. 'I quite like being out in the maelstrom.'

CHAPTER TWENTY-FOUR

Friday night was my first shift with Celia Ashwin as attendant and it was entirely different from being on duty with Fripp. Celia seemed almost to glory in the danger, and I wondered what risks she had taken when she was on her own in the saloon car. And yet, she was also a competent and caring assistant. Like Levy, her cool upper-class voice and manner struck a note of calm into a frenzied scene, and habits of deference that seemed ingrained meant that wardens, rescue workers and patients alike took note of what she said and followed her orders without question.

With one exception. We had crawled into a shattered house to collect an old woman, who was partially paralysed after a stroke. When we found her she was grubbing around in what was left of her bedroom.

'Come along,' said Celia, taking hold of her arm. 'The house is going to collapse at any moment.'

The old woman shook off Celia's hand. 'I'm not going out without me corsets on,' she replied with some asperity. 'I never 'ave and that beastly 'Itler won't make me.' Once Celia and I had found her corset and helped her into it, she went with us like a lamb.

I had never really got to know Celia, mainly because of her fascist husband, but also, I was embarrassed to realise, because of my feelings against her class in general. We would be spending a great deal of time together in future, so I decided to try to break down my self-imposed barrier.

'Did you grow up in London?' I asked her, after we had dropped the old lady off in hospital.

'Good heavens, no. I mean, I had to come here for the season and to be presented to the King, but my family has a mouldy old pile in the country and I grew up there.'

'Whereabouts in the country?'

'In Kent. It's a big old place, on the Greensand Ridge overlooking the Weald. The coldest house imaginable. Nobody would come to stay with us in the winter.'

'I thought you lot all lived in luxury,' I said, surprised.

'We weren't rich. Not really.'

'But you had servants?'

'Oh, yes.' Her tone was offhand. 'Nine servants inside. Butler, housekeeper, two pantry, three kitchen, two upstairs. But the staff were my friends. They never told on me to my parents, no matter what mischief I got up to as a child. The servants were more like family than my parents in many ways.'

I raised an eyebrow and she smiled.

'Helen, my brother John and I lived a life entirely separate from our parents when we were children. They were away nearly every weekend in summer and went off shooting in winter. When they were at home we'd only see them for formal half-hour visits after tea. Which I used to hate.'

'Hate seeing your parents?' I must have sounded scandalised, because she threw back her head and gave a gurgle of laughter.

'Well, I was only allowed into the drawing room once I'd been primped and starched and brushed and combed to within an inch of my life by Nanny, which was ghastly for a tomboy like me. I had to be shoved through the drawing room door, as I never really wanted to go in. The grown-ups would usually be playing bridge or mah-jong or discussing grown-up things and it was terrifically boring, as I was supposed to simply sit quietly and look decorative. I was so terrified of my father that I never said a word. It was easier for Helen, who was five years older and Father's favourite. And for John, who spent most of his time at school.'

'It's not at all as I imagined your childhood to be,' I admitted. Talking to her was also not at all as I'd imagined. She was far warmer and more open than I'd supposed.

'How did you envision it?'

'Oh, I don't know. Lots of toys and pretty clothes, ponies and governesses, or a posh boarding school.'

'Helen and I weren't allowed to go to school, although I'd have given anything to do so. I so envied my brother, John, who regularly swanned off to Eton. My father thought girls' schools were frightfully common, and couldn't see the need for paying anything much to educate girls. He insisted only that we should be able to write in a fair hand, be fluent in French and able to dance properly. So we had a succession of poorly educated governesses who tried to instil some modicum of learning in us and we went to dancing classes once a week.'

I thought of my happy childhood, with my close and loving parents. And although I'd not enjoyed my boarding school experience, the teachers had been excellent and had instilled in me a love of learning.

Celia was smiling. 'I suppose you're feeling sorry for me, having had a delightful childhood, out there in the colonies.'

'Actually – I did have a wonderful childhood.'

'Mine wasn't too bad, you know. Nobody really bothered about me and I ran wild in the countryside most of the time. Wish I was there now. London isn't really my cup of tea at all.'

'Because of the Blitz?'

'Oh, the Blitz isn't the problem. As I said, I quite like being out in the mayhem. It's the frivolous life my set insist upon leading. It bores me to death.'

Celia gave me her crooked grin and I wondered if we might become friends. Then I remembered her fascist husband and decided I would not rush into friendship. I would see where the wind took us.

Towards the end of our shift we were sent to an incident in one of the winding little streets near the British Museum, just behind New Oxford Street. The planes were still overhead, but they were dropping their bombs a mile or so away and we felt safe enough.

It was a major incident and the teams attending it were well-organised. By the time we arrived, light rescue had got out all the wounded they could find and the mobile first aid crew were sorting them into groups: those who should go by ambulance, those who would be transported by car, and those who could be sent off without the need for further treatment. A refreshment van was at the scene, handing out cups of tea. I took one, grimaced at the taste of chlorinated water and looked up to see an Aussie digger.

Standing near the Mobile First Aid post was an Australian soldier, a corporal, in a khaki uniform that was coated in plaster dust. He was watching another Australian soldier, a private, being patched up by the nurse. He was not the first digger I'd seen in London, as they came here for R & R and usually ended up in Australia House. But I'd never seen one at an incident before.

I walked over to him. 'G'day dig,' I said.

His face was a mess of blood and white dust, which made his wide grin seem rather surreal.

'An Aussie girl?' He called out to his mate. 'There's an Aussie sheila here.' Then he turned back to me. 'G'day yerself. Where're you from?'

It was always the first question when two Australians met. I assumed it was the same with all nationalities when they come together in a strange land.

'Kalgoorlie, then Perth. What about you?'

'Melbourne, Elwood. Jack Wallace.' He nodded towards his mate. 'Charlie's a Queenslander, from Toowoomba. Charlie Proctor.'

'How did you get involved in this?' I waved at the destruction around me.

Leaning against what remained of the wall behind him, he rolled a cigarette one-handed and squinted at me. Plaster dust coated his eyelashes, like white mascara.

'Well, it's like this. Me and Charlie are here on leave.' He lit the cigarette and took a deep drag, oblivious or indifferent to the possibility of a gas leak. 'We'd just had some tucker and were heading back to our lodgings. Next thing we knew, hell seemed to be coming down in lumps. So we thought we'd lend a hand.'

'Good on you, how was it?'

He shook his head. 'There was a terrace of houses there and I saw it vanish. It just lifted at the roots, rose up in the air and fell flat.' He took another deep drag. 'You know, that building,' he waved his cigarette at a pile of rubble behind me, 'isn't where the bomb hit. I think it was simply cracked to pieces by the force of the explosion nearby.'

'All these buildings are so old that the floor shakes when you sneeze.'

'I could hear a girl in there, crying, hysterical. So we ran inside. She said she couldn't move. Charlie took hold of her shoulders and I lifted her feet. Just then the staircase fell in, but we all made it out in one piece and we got the girl to a shelter. I think she was just paralysed with shock. Charlie hurt his arm – that's why he's over there – and my foot got bruised a bit.' When I made a move to look at it he waved me away. 'No fear. She'll be right.'

He took another drag and threw the cigarette on the ground; when he stamped it out under his boot he winced a little. Then he gave me a wide smile. 'Wouldn't have missed it for quids.'

Celia's voice came out of the gloom. 'Are you quite ready, Brennan? We should be off.'

After we had delivered our patients to hospital we headed back to Woburn Place. I was quiet in the ambulance, thinking how much I had enjoyed meeting another Aussie and hearing the lingo, as Levy put it. Levy would have loved to meet Jack.

'What's up, Brennan? You seem down in the dumps.'

I laughed a little, embarrassed. 'There was an Australian soldier back there. He and his mate had helped to get people out of the ruins.'

'Why would that make you sad? Are you homesick?'

'No. Not really. A little, maybe. It's just that Levy liked it when I used the Aussie slang. He would have enjoyed meeting the man.'

She was quiet for a while. The Monster kept on rattling along the deserted, bomb-blasted streets. It was a misty morning and although the world was lightening around us it was difficult to see my way. I was completely reliant on Celia for navigation.

'You were very close to Levy, weren't you?' Her voice was so soft I could hardly hear her over the noise of the engine.

'Yes, I was. But no matter what people say, I was never in love with him. We were mates – in the Australian sense of the word, which is something more than friends. It means someone you'd risk anything for and who'd do the same for you.'

'I heard there's to be a memorial service for him.'

'That's right. At the Hallam Street Synagogue, next Friday.'

I watched swirls of white mist squirming in front of the narrow beam of headlight, and I thought what a terrible situation it was for his parents.

'Mrs Levy is positive he's out there,' I said. 'She thinks he's waiting to be found. It's so sad. Mr and Mrs Levy are such lovely people . . .'

'Whatever do you mean?'

Her tone was cool and mocking and hot anger flooded through me. I wrenched the wheel to the left and parked by the roadside. When I turned towards her I almost spat out the words.

'How can you, Ashwin? How can you be such a – a bitch?' I shook my head, unable to believe her crass stupidity. 'Of course the Levys are lovely people. Levy was a lovely man and they are his parents. More than that, I've met them and they are – are . . .' I couldn't think of another word to describe them. 'They are lovely. I know you lot don't see Jews as human beings—'

Celia visibly flinched, which surprised me so much that I shut up. I could make out her face, despite the gloom. She wouldn't meet my eyes.

211

'I didn't mean that,' she said, in a tightly controlled voice. 'I'm sure that the Levys are very nice people, and I'm well aware that Jews are human beings. That is not what I meant at all.' She took a deep breath and let it out slowly. 'God, Brennan, do you honestly think I'm that bad?'

She looked at me then, held my gaze.

'No,' I admitted, remembering how she had spoken in Levy's defence in the common room. 'I don't think you are that bad. I'm sorry if I misunderstood. What did you mean?'

'What I meant was, what do you mean about Mrs Levy thinking that he is waiting to be found. Doesn't she accept that he is dead?'

'She accepts that he's dead, but she's convinced herself that David is out there, dead, calling to her to find his body. It's so sad.'

'David?' Celia's voice was shaky.

'Didn't you know? His name was David.'

She shook her head, recovered her poise. 'Of course I knew. It sounded odd to hear you say it. What a horrible story, but I suppose a mother might have such morbid fancies.'

'That's why they're holding a memorial service for him. Halliday and Squire are going.'

'Is everyone at the station invited?'

'Yes.'

'I'm not surprised Halliday would want to be there,' she said. 'She adored . . . David. Moray may feel it's his duty as station officer as well. Oh, I don't know, Brennan. We all worked closely with him. Wouldn't it be the proper thing to go to his memorial service?'

'The Levys told me that all would be welcome.'

I turned into the Euston Road. It was still not properly light, and the mist was rapidly becoming fog so I was finding driving difficult.

When Celia spoke again her voice was surprisingly hesitant. 'Levy's father is in finance, isn't he?'

I frowned at the windscreen. 'You're not going to go on about the Jewish conspiracy, are you?'

'Have you ever heard me do so?'

'No,' I admitted, 'but your hus—'

'I'm not Cedric. I do not believe that Mr Levy is plotting world domination. I simply asked a question.' Her voice was as sharp, clear and cold as an icicle. Celia was formidable in this sort of mood and I decided to placate.

'I'm sorry,' I said, 'that was wrong of me to assume. Yes. He's in finance, and apparently his opinion is highly regarded. Jim tells me he has been advising the government. Mrs Levy is involved in supporting Jewish refugees from Nazi-occupied Europe, especially the children – what do they call it? The *Kindertransport.*'

'Bloomsbury House?'

'Yes, I think so. She's a—'

'Quite. A lovely woman. You said so before.'

Her ice cube voice indicated to me that she was still seething, so I shut up. We arrived back at Woburn Place as the All Clear sounded, a little before seven o'clock.

'You and Jim Vassilikov have been seeing rather a lot of each other,' Celia remarked, as we scrubbed the Monster clean.

'We've been to a couple of concerts and out to dinner a few times.'

She dipped a rag into the soapy water and scrubbed the bonnet. 'I know you won't like me saying this, and please don't think that I'm prying or trying to make trouble for you, but I think it would be as well if you didn't become too serious about Jim Vassilikov.'

My jaw tightened. 'I'm afraid I do think that you are prying and I'd rather not discuss it.'

'I'm only saying that England is not like Australia. These sort of things can end in misery.'

'What sort of things?'

'It's easy to – to become attached to someone as personable as Jim. But, honestly Lily, you must see that there can be no future with him. You are too different.'

I was so angry I could not reply and we finished cleaning the ambulance in silence. While I had my own reservations about the differences between Jim and me, I would not be dictated to by her ladyship. Any hopes of friendship with the woman had evaporated. I had to be civil to her as we would be spending a great deal of time together, but that was it.

We found most of the night shift in the canteen, scoffing the tasteless scrambled eggs, bacon and sausages that were served for breakfast.

At nine o'clock, I was about to leave when Moray sauntered through the door, having just come on duty. Now that he was acting station officer, he always worked the day shift. It meant I saw him less, which pleased me.

'For those of you who haven't yet heard, David Levy's parents are holding a memorial service for him next Friday,' he announced to the canteen at large. 'If anyone wants to go, please let me know so I can arrange cover.'

'What do the Jews do for a service if there's no body?' Fripp asked. I had given up expecting tact from her, but this was an outstanding lack of sensitivity. I sat rigidly and glared at the table, but had to accept that I, also, had wondered.

Unexpectedly, it was Moray who replied. 'It would be a problem, because burial is supposed to take place within three days of death.' He seemed pensive. 'And there are certain rituals that should be performed. None of that can happen now.'

'It's tough on his family not to be able to do what their faith requires for the poor devil,' said Squire.

Celia was looking at Moray, frowning. 'How do you know all this?' she said.

'Is it a case of "know your enemy"?' said Sadler, sniggering.

Moray gave an easy laugh. 'It's no secret, how the Jews deal with their dead.' He shrugged, and held up his hands. 'Look, I don't like Jews very much, but I'm sorry Levy's dead. He was a fine ambulance attendant.'

I got up and walked out of the room feeling as if I were propelled by something other than my own muscles and sinews. As if I were a marionette, kept upright by invisible wires, dancing to the will of an invisible puppet master. I walked back to St Andrew's fighting a cold breeze and hot tears all the way.

By the time I reached my flat I was so weary that I was bumping into furniture, so after a quick bath I went straight to bed. My sleep was fitful and I found myself in a familiar nightmare, where I was five years old in Kookynie and my father had killed the white rooster. In my nightmare, as in real life, the headless bird ran towards me, its claws raising red dust. It was a bloodstained, mutilated thing, dead but still somehow alive. I was paralysed with fear and I screamed for my father to save me, but this time he didn't come. Someone else grabbed my arm and pulled me away from the horror. Someone tall and dressed in air force blue. 'Steady on,' he said. 'It's all right. I have you.'

I opened my eyes to the sound of rain pattering on the windows. My bedside clock told me that it was one o'clock in the afternoon. I lay for a while staring at the ceiling, trying to will myself back to sleep, wondering why I had woken and if the Warning had sounded.

Eventually I pushed aside the bedclothes and got up, shrugging on my dressing gown. My stomach growled as I shuffled into the kitchen to find something to eat. I could go downstairs to the service restaurant, but I would need to dress and I simply could not be bothered. My own larder, when closely examined, contained a tin of dehydrated egg, a tin of pilchards and one rasher of bacon. I sighed.

In the bread bin I found the remains of a stale loaf of bread. After cutting mould off the edges of a slice I put it under the grill to toast while I fried the bacon and made a cup of tea.

On the bench was one of the many leaflets that had been distributed since the beginning of the war. This one told us what to do 'If the Invader Comes'. It concluded: 'Think before you act. But always think of your country before you think of yourself.'

'Put that in your pipe and smoke it, Fripp,' I muttered.

I put the toast on a plate and tipped the hot bacon onto it. Then I went out on to my tiny balcony, munching as I looked out over St Andrew's Gardens. Old tombstones were dotted about in the grass, a reminder of the church that once had stood on the site of the flats. The air smelled of damp vegetation and decay and the gardens were dreary in the rain. On a sunny day the graves presented a delightful whimsy, but on a wet afternoon that was edging towards darkness and the inevitable German attack, they were bleak reminders of mortality.

'The dolorous day grew drearier toward twilight falling,' I quoted softly. I liked Tennyson.

The wet afternoon was making me morbid, I decided. What I needed was some light-hearted company. Jim was to take me to dinner that night, but really I would have preferred to see a movie with Pam. I sighed. I did not like to admit it, but I knew Celia was right. Jim really was far too posh for me, and it would surely be better to end things now, before either of us was hurt. I was certain that he was no snob, but it was telling that he was yet to introduce me to any of his friends. It was easy to conclude that he might be ashamed of me – or were my own fears the problem?

Barmaid Brennan. Barmy Brennan. The bullying I had faced at school had come from the sort of girls who would be at home in the restaurants Jim took me to, or in his club. The sort of girls Celia, and Jim's formidable mother, would actually approve of.

The noise of someone knocking loudly on the door to my flat shattered my thoughts. Strangely reluctant, I walked to the door. The banging began again before I had reached it.

When I opened the door, Jim stood there, his face flushed. My heart began to thump against my chest and when I spoke my voice was high and shrill.

'What is it?'

'Someone has . . .' He paused and took a breath. 'We may have found David's body.'

CHAPTER TWENTY-FIVE

It had been more than two weeks since Levy had disappeared. I backed into my living room and sat down with a thump, pressed my hand to my mouth, forced myself not to be sick. My skin felt clammy to my touch. My stomach swirled with bacon and toast and tea and bile and horror.

Jim followed me in and stood above me, frowning ferociously.

'Are you all right? I shouldn't have blurted it out like that, Lily. I'm so sorry, please forgive me.'

'I'll be fine. Tell me.'

'Someone telephoned the police this morning to say that David's body could be found in the ruins of a house in Caroline Place.'

'Caroline Place? By Coram's Fields? That's just around the corner from here.'

'Let me get you some water.' He disappeared into the kitchen and returned with a glass of water. I took a gulping sip.

'It's been more than two weeks,' I said, in a voice I scarcely recognised. 'And Caroline Place was hit again last week. Oh, God.'

'It could be a hoax. Drink some more.' Jim's voice was cool and reasonable and all at once I was furious with him.

'Was it a man or woman who called?' My voice was terse.

'I don't know.'

I took another sip of water, and felt better for it, so I drained the glass.

'The police will be attending the site with a rescue crew to comb the ruins this afternoon. Mr Levy asked if I could be there to perform the initial identification if they find anything. Marcus and Simon, David's brothers, are overseas on active service, and the Levys trust me.'

'I'm off duty,' I said. 'Do you suppose the Levys would mind if I went there with you?'

'I don't know that it's a good idea for you to be there.'

'I've seen worse than a two-week-old body,' I snapped. 'He was my mate. I owe it to him.'

Jim turned away and I couldn't see his face.

'I'll be at Caroline Place this afternoon whether you like it or not.'

'I gathered that.' His voice was dry. 'We'll go together.'

The scent of smoke and cordite still hung in the air, although it was raining heavily when Jim and I stood together outside what we thought was number 25. We had counted down from the corner, but it was difficult to tell whether this was the right one because so many of the houses were now rubble.

I was cold and wet and miserable, huddled under my pretty tartan umbrella. It gave little protection from the sheeting rain that beat against us, driven by an icy wind. My raincoat kept most of me dry, but my legs and stockings were sopping wet from the knees down and my shoes were soaked.

I wished I could have a tot of Lady Anne's brandy.

'What if the rescue crew insist on waiting until this downpour is over?' I asked, clutching at Jim's arm.

'They'll search for him, Lily. The police will make them search for him. Or I will. Trust me.' There was a feverish look in his eyes although his hair was sodden and had clumped palely on his forehead. Water was dripping down his face.

'Heavy rescue made the ruins safe last week,' I said. 'Why didn't they find Levy's body then?'

'I don't know, Lily.'

'Maybe it's been placed here since, for us to find.'

'I think that's unlikely.'

I looked at my watch. 'They're late. It's past three o'clock.'

As I spoke, a black police sedan pulled up across the road, closely followed by a van towing a trailer and an ambulance. Doors opened and slammed shut and men spilled out: a constable and two men in dark suits whom I assumed were detectives, and four men in overalls and steel helmets who were obviously the heavy rescue crew. The ambulance belonged to light rescue and I didn't know the driver or his assistant.

The crew began to unload lamps and ropes and tarpaulins and heavy lifting equipment from the trailer attached to the van, while the detectives put up their umbrellas and squelched across the road towards us. The constable was wearing an oilskin cape. He walked to the corner and stood on guard under a large blue umbrella.

I looked curiously at the detectives. The older of the two was a massive man with a thoughtful face and an unassuming manner that conveyed an air of quiet authority. He introduced himself as Detective Chief Inspector Wayland.

He shook Jim's hand. 'You knew David Levy well, I understand.'

'We were at Harrow together.' Jim gestured to me. 'Miss Lily Brennan. She worked at Bloomsbury auxiliary ambulance station with Mr Levy. They were close friends.'

I shook Wayland's hand. 'I am so very glad to meet you, Miss Brennan,' he said. I was surprised at the warmth of his greeting, and of his handshake.

Wayland's companion, Detective Sergeant Norris, was his opposite, a wiry man of average build, whose quick dark eyes summed me up with a glance. They moved on to Jim and lingered as Jim spoke to Wayland, before darting away to scan the site. When they returned to me, he smiled and held out his hand for me to shake.

'It's very nice indeed to meet you, Miss Brennan,' he said. 'You're a bit of a legend around our bit of the Yard, I must say.'

Wayland quelled him with a look as I gasped in surprise.

'But that's mad,' I said to Norris. 'I don't know anyone at Scotland Yard. Why would Scotland Yard be interested in me?'

Wayland cleared his throat gently. When I looked at him he ducked his big head and gave me an embarrassed smile.

'I'm the reason for your notoriety, Miss Brennan.' He had a nice smile, and I found myself returning it, despite having no idea what he was talking about. 'I owe you an enormous debt, you see.' His smile was even wider.

I shook my head. 'Why? I don't understand.'

'You saved my grandchildren, Miss Brennan. You crawled into a bombed house to bring them out. You're known as "the train lady" in our house.'

I laughed, forgetting Levy in my delight. 'The little boy and Emily? You sent me a letter. How are they? And how is their mother?'

'They're both right as rain. Young Ted still talks about you a great deal. My daughter? Well, she's had a tough time, but we think she's on the mend now.'

'I'm so glad to hear that.'

His smile faded. 'I wish we were meeting under better circumstances.'

I nodded and looked away.

'What's the plan?' Jim asked Wayland.

The detective became all business. 'The crew will dig into the basement flat and see if Mr Levy's body is there. If it is, it will be taken to the morgue and the forensic pathologist will examine it to see if there are any obvious suspicious circumstances. The family have said they won't give permission for an autopsy without good reason.'

'What do you know about the person who telephoned?'

'Covered the phone with a handkerchief, we think. East London accent, but the constable who took the call couldn't even tell if it was a man's voice or a woman's, let alone whether the accent was put on.'

221

There was a shouted command from the ARP warden who was in charge of the heavy rescue unit. We turned to watch as the men put up tarpaulins to protect themselves from the rain as they dug into the site.

'Wasn't the site checked for survivors or bodies the day after the raid?' asked Jim.

'According to the warden, they were told that all the residents of the street had been accounted for, so a cursory check only was done – they called out and had a quick look around when they were making the site safe the morning after the first raid, and again after the second. The roof caved in on the basement flat during the first air raid and they didn't see the need to look further.'

The tarpaulin was up, and the men began to dig into the rubble. The warden held what seemed to be a blueprint and referred to it as he shouted directions to the crew. When a sufficiently large hole had been dug, a rope was tied around one of the men. He switched on his torch and crawled inside.

We waited. The rain eventually ceased, but the arctic wind remained. I furled my umbrella and stood close to Jim, shivering in the cold air. He put an arm around me and the wet wool scent of his greatcoat competed with the smell of bombed ruins and old smoke.

There was a shout. The searcher had reappeared at the top of the hole. He exchanged words with the warden, who walked over to us.

'He's found a hand poking out of a mess of rubble.'

I had a vivid image of Levy's hands resting on the forehead of a patient, unfolding blankets, helping me to clean the Monster. The scene seemed to sway as nausea roiled in my stomach. Jim pulled me closer, but I pushed away from him and forced myself to stand firm, to wait as the team enlarged the hole and several other men went into the ruins. Eventually there were other shouts, and a large hessian sack, similar to those we used to collect bodies, was lowered into the hole. When it was hoisted up a short while later it clearly contained the weight of a man.

Wayland turned to me. 'It's only if Flight Lieutenant Vassi . . . vassil—'

'Vassilikov,' I said.

Wayland nodded an apology to Jim. 'It's only if he identifies the body as Mr Levy that we'll need further identification by his parents.'

I was unable to speak. He turned to Jim.

'Ready, son?'

At Jim's curt nod, the two men walked over to the hessian bundle, which had been laid on the ground under the tarpaulin. Wayland pulled back the material to reveal what lay beneath, and I saw Jim's head jerk back. He pulled away, before turning back to the body, and looking at it for what seemed a long moment. He nodded and then, to my surprise, raised his right hand and made the sign of the cross. He remained there as Wayland replaced the material and the attendant tucked it in more securely.

As the stretcher-bearers carried Levy's body to the waiting ambulance, I felt a strange sense of confusion. How could that bundle wrapped in canvas encompass Levy's humour, intelligence, kindness, arrogance, and his delight in life? It made no sense.

The rain began to fall again, dripping heavily on my umbrella, pattering onto the muddy ground in front of me. *It is all too normal*, I thought. That is Levy's body. My friend is gone from the world and yet the rain still falls. The world has changed and nothing has changed.

I had seen many dead bodies in the past year, but none had been the body of someone I loved. Denys had died on his ship and his body was never found. Even before his death he had vanished from my life, become merely a signature on a letter, a photograph in a frame. Denys had never been a canvas wrapped bundle carried past in the rain.

Jim and Wayland walked towards me with heavy, sombre steps. As they drew nearer Jim looked straight at me, and again he nodded. There was a bleak look in his eyes.

'Flight Lieutenant Vassilikov has identified the body as that of Mr Levy.' Wayland pronounced Jim's name slowly and correctly. His voice was coolly professional, but his face was sympathetic. 'The team will have another look around and then close the site. Do you want us to take you anywhere? Where would you like to go, Miss Brennan?'

'Home,' I said. It sounded like a whimper. I meant Australia, but they assumed I was referring to St Andrew's Court.

'I'll take her,' said Jim.

The ambulance drove away. The heavy rescue crew were packing up. Wayland and Norris walked back to their car. Jim stood still, staring at nothing with eyes devoid of expression as rain ran down his face. What had he seen when he looked at Levy?

The needle sharp thread of pain I had been pushing away all day became suddenly intolerable. I made a small moan, and Jim was beside me, holding me close, keeping me upright. And then the tears came, but I was not sure if they were for Levy or for Jim or for myself.

'Come,' said Jim. 'I'll take you home.'

But how could he do that? My home was ten thousand miles away.

CHAPTER TWENTY-SIX

When my sobs had become whimpering little gulps and I was at last empty of tears I felt lightheaded, empty somehow, dazed. I became aware of the sound of rain on the window and the wind soughing through the tall trees outside. I realised I was sitting on my couch and Jim's arms were tightly around me. We were in the warm shelter of my flat, but I had only a vague recollection as to how we had got there.

Jim pushed away slightly and reached around to the table beside the couch. He poured brandy from a bottle into a glass.

'Drink this,' he said, handing it to me.

He must have brought Lady Anne's brandy with him, I thought, just like a St Bernard brings brandy to travellers lost in the mountains. I gave a hiccupping laugh and Jim looked at me with concern.

'I'm fine,' I said, and took a sip. It was like fire in my throat and it burned all the way into my stomach. 'Thank you.'

He poured himself a drink and swallowed it in one gulp. He poured himself another and when he turned to me his eyes were haunted. 'One shouldn't have friends in wartime. They die. Seeing David like that . . .'

I reached an arm around his back and we held one another fast. His heart was thumping in hard, quick beats. After a minute or so he let go, to sit stiffly beside me on the couch, bending forward to rest his arms on his knees and frown at the carpet.

'Nearly all the men I trained with have died since June.' He made an impatient movement with his hand. 'At twenty-five I was the oldest in my squadron. They called me Dad, thought I knew what I was doing.'

He raised his head and when he looked at me his face seemed distorted, altered somehow.

'I'm not brave, Lily. Not like you.'

'I'm not—'

'We were all frightened, I think,' he said, 'but we couldn't let anyone see it. So we put a bold front on it as our mess-mates bought it, one after another. Shot down in flames or drowned or shockingly disfigured.'

He wrapped his arms around his stomach and crouched over, as if he were in pain. 'We were running out of trained pilots, so they began to send us boys with a few hours' flying experience, who said, "ra*ther*", "wizard" and "gosh", or "I'm such a dim", just before a one-oh-nine came out of the clouds behind them with its guns blazing.'

He took a noisy breath before continuing. 'If they were lucky the poor little sods lasted a week. And do you know what the rest of us did?' He raised his head to stare at me. I forced myself to hold his gaze. 'We shared jokes, laughed it all off, kept that British upper lip stiff, and pretended not to care as name after name was rubbed off the board and new names of new boys who were destined to die were chalked into the empty places.'

He sat up and reached into his jacket, presumably for his cigarettes. But his hand was shaking and he couldn't find the packet.

'This is stupid,' he said. 'I don't know why I'm telling you this. It's just that . . .' He took a gulping breath. 'What was it all for? We didn't stop the Germans. We might have forced them to postpone the invasion, but look at what they're doing now to London and to the other cities. What was the point of all those boys dying if we couldn't stop the Nazis from killing people like David? He – Oh, God, Lily, his face . . .'

I leaned across and pulled him against me, held him as he sobbed.

When his shoulders had stopped shaking and it seemed that, like me, he was empty of tears, Jim pushed away from me and refused to meet my eyes.

'I'll wash my face,' I said, rising. I thought he probably needed some time alone.

The bathroom mirror showed me a blotchy face with red, puffy eyes. I bathed it in cold water and dried it carefully. I looked again. Now I could be mistaken for a fifteen-year-old with conjunctivitis. I paused before opening the door, wondering if Jim would still be waiting for me out there. A lot of Australian men would have fled, embarrassed to have shown such raw emotion, ashamed to have cried.

So I made sure to open the bathroom door noisily, to give him some warning that I was coming back into the room. He was still sitting on the couch, elbows on his knees, his head downcast as if he were examining the carpet. He seemed calm, however.

'I am truly sorry about that,' he said, without lifting his head. 'It won't happen again. Look, if you don't mind, I'd best be off.' Then, carefully avoiding my eyes, he began to look around the room. I assumed he wanted to find his hat and then he would leave.

'Please don't go. Would you like something to eat?' I mentally ran through the little food in my pantry. 'I have some dried egg and – er, pilchards and some bread.' I decided to be honest. 'Actually, the bread's a bit stale and mouldy but,' I finished brightly, 'we can cut off the mould and toast it.'

He shook his head and made to get up.

'Jim, please don't go. I think you need to eat. We both do.'

'You sound like my nyanya,' he said, sitting down again. 'My Russian nursemaid. "Eat, Vanya," she'd say. That was her panacea for any problem.'

'So – I assume she was a large lady, your nyanya?'

He laughed at that, and finally looked at me. 'Actually, yes. Nyanya was large and loud and very loving. I adored her. When we left her behind in Russia I wept for months, until my mother lost patience.'

'What did she do?'

'She bought me a dog. I called it Nyanya, to her disgust. I really think I loved it as much as its namesake.'

I walked across to sit beside him on the couch. When I took hold of his hand he did not pull away.

'My parents had a lot of trouble having children,' I said. 'They were all born too early. I was the first to live past a few days, and two more died after me. It wasn't until Ben came when I was eleven that I had a sibling.' I was silent for a moment, thinking of my poor mother and the five little graves in the red earth of the Kalgoorlie cemetery. 'We lived in the middle of nowhere and I was terribly lonely, so when I was six I was given a puppy. I called him Prince, because I loved fairy tales.'

'Prince?' Jim's laugh was more like a sob. 'So you call your dogs Prince in Australia. What do you call princes?'

'Mate,' I replied. 'Or "you bastard". We don't much go in for princes, or anything like that, at home.' Which was an oversimplification and perhaps a lie. 'Except for the British royal family, of course. We adore them.'

Jim leaned across and kissed me. It was a gentle kiss, hesitant, improvised, and in it I tasted the salt of his tears. When I responded, he put his arms around me and drew me closer, so that his body was hard against mine, warm and so very alive. And as his kiss deepened I felt the familiar sweet pain, the ache deep inside me, the yearning for more. I pressed myself against him and gave up trying to think.

He spent the night in my flat, in my bed. He held me close until I slept, lying quietly beside me. When the All Clear sounded at five-thirty the next morning we were already awake, lounging in bed, in each other's arms. I felt jittery, anxious, wondering what we had started and how it would end. Jim, by contrast, seemed for the moment entirely at ease, playing with my hair, teasing my curls through his fingers.

'I like that sound,' I said, as the long sustained note sounded. 'The All Clear always makes my spirits rise.'

'I hate sirens.'

He pushed aside the bedclothes and went to pull across the heavy curtains and open first the blackout blind and then the French doors, to stand on the balcony. He was dressed in his trousers and vest and the red glow in the sky was bright enough to give a rosy cast to the milky skin of his arms and shoulders.

'Fires in the City,' he said. 'As usual.'

'Come back to bed,' I said. 'You'll freeze.'

He turned his head; his face was an indistinct blotch but I saw the white teeth as he smiled.

'It takes more than this to freeze me.' But when he slid into bed beside me his skin was cold as iron. I snuggled in closer, warming his body with mine, as the red glow of the burning City lit the early morning darkness.

We talked of Levy as we lay together, warm and sleepy, but it made me too sad to think of my friend in the past tense. And so our discussion drifted.

'Tell me about Helen Markham,' I said.

I was snuggled against him, pushing aside the ornate gold cross he always wore, to put my ear to his chest and feel the rise and fall of each breath and listen to his heart beating through the thin cotton of his vest. My voice was calm, although I was pleased about the darkness because Levy always said I gave too much away in my face. I had to know more about this. She was a hateful woman and it unnerved me that Jim had ever been in love with her.

'She was Helen Palmer-Thomas then. I met her when I first arrived at Cambridge. She was visiting her brother and was a couple of years older, beautiful and sophisticated. What we in the RAF call "lush".'

It was as if my own heart had twisted, it was such a sharp, strange pain. I knew I would never be described as lush.

'She quite literally picked me up. I never thought to marry her,' he went on, 'although I think that's probably what she expected. I just wanted to laze about in bed with her, reciting good poetry and writing bad. She wanted my title, I think. Is it all right to be telling you this?' He said, but rushed on, giving me no chance to respond, 'I probably sound like a bit of a cad. I had little experience of girls before Cambridge, no idea what to expect, really. And there it was, on a plate . . .' He trailed off, as though he didn't know how to finish.

Was this a way to tell me he didn't want to marry me, either? That if he didn't want to marry the daughter of a lord, he certainly wouldn't consider marrying the daughter of an Australian publican. Was that why he had not wanted to take matters further the other night? Was he afraid that might lead me into false assumptions?

Well, I don't want to marry you either, I thought. *There's no need to humiliate me.*

'What ended it?' I asked.

'With Helen? It took me a while, but I grew up.'

'Got bored with her?' Would he tire of me so easily? Just what was he trying to tell me?

'No. Yes. In a way, I suppose. When we met I was very young, I didn't really know . . .' His heart was racing, beating fast in his chest where my cheek lay against it. I wondered what he was gearing himself up to say and my own heart began to thump.

'I went a little mad for a while,' he said.

'Mad about her?'

'I think I went a bit mad in general.' His voice drifted away, and then he said, tersely, as if he wanted to get it over with, 'There's something you should know, Lily. I joined Helen's set for a while.'

'What do you mean, joined her set?'

'The ones she ran around with all belonged to the January Club and the National League of Airmen. She wanted me to join them. I'm ashamed to say I did.'

'So? What were they all about?'

'The League was a pressure group through which Lord Rothermere and Oswald Mosley promoted the expansion of British air power.' He laughed, dismissively, as if he had been a fool. 'It was 1935. Sounds reasonable enough, doesn't it?'

I nodded, rubbing my head up and down against his chest.

'Only the purpose of the League was to join forces with Germany and America to attack, as they put it, "the enemies of the White race, human sub-species".'

'Jews?'

'Jews, communists, homosexuals, gypsies, slavs – you name it, they were agin it.'

I felt the thudding of his heart, the tension in his body and I began to feel a prickle of apprehension.

'And the January Club?' I asked.

'That was a group set up to encourage support for the British Union of Fascists. I hated communism so much, I—'

'You became a bloody fascist?' I tried to pull away, but he held me close, forced me to listen.

'I'm not a fascist, Lily. I hate what Hitler and Mussolini and Franco and Mosley stand for. *Hate it.* I love this country and I'll fight to keep it safe from Hitler, and that's because Britain follows a rule of law I believe in – one that at least tries to protect the weak and deal fairly with all its citizens. I'm no fascist.'

'But you did follow Mosley and the British fascists for a while.'

He drew in a breath. 'I did. I'm not proud of it.'

'Why? How could you do that, Jim?'

'Look, I was nineteen, in love, trying to work out what I really believed in. Mosley is a charismatic man and, like me, he loves to fly. But I mistrust anyone who thinks they have all the answers and after a while – too long, maybe – I understood what he really was.'

'What changed your mind?' My voice came out cold, suspicious.

He laughed, but without any mirth. 'Cambridge did. I read a lot. What I was reading made more sense than what I was hearing from Mosley and from Helen's crowd. Eventually I found the Club uncongenial and the League ludicrous, so I bowed out, as graciously as I could. Helen and I had some terrific rows about it because she'd fallen hard for all their blather. The scales, as they say, fell away from my eyes. We agreed to go our separate ways. That's the story.'

I cut to the chase. 'Why tell me all this?'

He seemed surprised. 'I needed you to know the truth about me. That despite a dubious beginning, I loathe all that fascist tripe as much as I loathe the communist claptrap.'

'Do you still have feelings for Helen?'

'No. And nor for anyone else, for that matter.' His heartbeat had quickened again. 'Just you.'

'Oh.' I hesitated, then rushed in as usual, addressing the faint outline of his head, lit by the fiery glow from the windows. 'We're very different, Jim. Our backgrounds—'

'I don't care about that.' He reached out and pulled me close so we were each on our side, looking one another in the eyes.

'Do you remember the first time we met?' he said. 'You'd come off duty after a hard day.'

'Yes.'

'You took my breath away.'

'I don't recall that you looked particularly overwhelmed.'

'You came through that door like a whirlwind, drenched and dirty and bloody and exhausted, yet unbowed. And then you smiled.' His chest rose and fell in a sigh.

'Hah. I must have looked like something the cat had dragged in. Through a hedge, and across the barnyard.'

'You looked magnificent. You terrified me.' He began to play with my hair again, twisting it around his long fingers.

'You hid it well.'

'You put me in my place when you spoke French.'

'You still managed to ask me out.'

'It terrified me more to think that I might never see you again.'

'Come to think of it, you didn't ask me out. You vaguely suggested that you might perhaps be at a concert the following day.'

'I spent a sleepless night, wondering if you would turn up. I'm not usually so gauche.'

'You'd already bought the tickets when I arrived. What if I hadn't turned up? Would you have picked up a passing stray female?'

'I would have gone to the concert alone and spent the time working out a way to meet you again.'

'Now that's a good answer, flight lieutenant,' I murmured, kissing him. He responded warmly, then he stopped and pulled his head back to look at me again.

'Lily, I'm – I can't be casual about love. Not any more.'

I became very still. My mind was whirling, trying to work out what he meant. It was far too soon to talk of marriage. There was only the sound of our quiet breathing to disturb the silence in the room.

'What does that mean?' I asked.

He breathed a laugh. 'I suppose it means . . . tread softly.'

I knew the poem by Yeats, and I loved it. I reached up to kiss him. This time he responded without hesitation, and when we moved together I forgot about my concerns, forgot the sound of bombers overhead, forgot the war and even Levy.

I woke again at seven-thirty and watched the fire-red sky become pearly dawn and lighten into a bright morning. I lay still, listening to Jim's soft breathing, until I propped myself up on an elbow to watch him sleep. He lay sprawled beside me, utterly abandoned to sleep in the manner of a small child. His face was relaxed and peaceful. He had thrown off some of the blankets and I studied the rise and fall of his chest as he breathed, watched the flutter of a pulse at the base of his throat, under the Adam's apple.

His body was lean and rangy, and he would have been gaunt but for the subtle ridge of muscle under the milky-white skin. A scattering of pale caramel-coloured freckles on his shoulders matched those across the bridge of his nose. He seemed young and terrifyingly fragile. I flinched as he shifted slightly, murmured something, frowned, nearly woke and drifted again into oblivion.

I had known him for such a short time, and now here he was, in bed beside me on a cold November morning. I could hardly contain all these big feelings, the exquisitely painful tugs of protectiveness, delight and fear. It was the war, I thought. It stripped away the usual defences, forced quick decisions. It made you act without really thinking. But surely all lovers needed a touch of blindness before they could jump across the abyss in front of them. If anybody really thought about falling in love – considered the consequences – they would never, ever do it.

What did we really want from each other? Marriage? I thought not. We were too different, and I wanted to go home to Australia and to my family after the war. This was a wartime romance, and if I saw it as such I might be able to leave England with my heart intact.

The timbre of his breathing had changed. He opened one eye, then the other and looked at me. Smiled.

'Good morning, sleepyhead,' I said.

He reached out for me and pulled me close.

He said he was worried about my reputation. Questions would be asked if he breakfasted with me in the service cafe, and my reputation would suffer. Questions also would be asked if I failed to turn up for breakfast. It was a valid point. I did not want to fall victim to society's double standards.

Temptation abounded in a London that thronged with the remains of the shattered continental armies and troops from all parts of the Empire. When life seemed so very fragile many women found it easy simply to give and accept pleasure, found it easy to fall in love.

Married women, to whom the wartime separation from their husbands had become unendurable, were shocked to discover themselves so vulnerable to temptation. Young brides who had only known their husbands for a few weeks of marriage were desperately lonely and willing to take solace where they could find it. Unmarried girls facing death every night wanted to experience all that life could offer, rather than die in unfulfilled ignorance.

The stakes in these games of love were far higher for women than for the men they slept with. A woman with a ruined reputation not only faced terrible guilt but also risked being shunned by friends and family, while the consequences of unwanted pregnancy might be utter disaster. I had taken precautions, but the worry was always there, and it was, inevitably, the woman's worry.

I knew all that. And right now I had an attractive man in my flat and I lived in a hotbed of gossip.

'No one could expect me to ask you to leave during an air raid,' I said.

'But they may wonder why we didn't go down to the basement.'

That was true. If we had spent the night in the basement shelter then no one would have thought anything of it. But to spend a night in my flat . . . Nancy was the talk of the building. I did not want to face the censure that she did, but surely it was my business who stayed in my flat.

'I don't care about my reputation,' I said, trying to force myself to believe it, 'not in London anyway. And no one really cares about that sort of thing any more. At least we're both single. For goodness, sake, Nan—'

I broke off, horrified that I had been about to tell on her. We in St Andrew's all knew about Nancy's escapades, but Jim knew her husband, who obviously did not.

I jumped up and pulled on my dressing gown. 'Cup of tea? You have first bath.'

He came into the kitchen a little while later, dressed in his uniform, flushed from his bath; he leaned against the doorjamb and watched me fuss about.

'Nan used to be a mousy little thing,' he said. 'The sort of woman who lived for her family, always put them first. Quiet, home-loving. Married at twenty, then the doting mother to their honeymoon baby. Happy with her life in a Hampshire village.'

'Nancy?' I squeaked. 'Our Nancy Parrish?' I had always seen her as shallow, grasping and venial, interested only in fashionable people and fashionable clothes. When she referred to her husband she gave the impression that he was an inconvenience who was conveniently out of the picture. She talked about her son as if he was an absent pet, not a small child who was undoubtedly missing his mother. I had assumed that she had always been such a woman.

'Yes, Nancy Parrish. Bob adores Nan, but he's heard things. He's worried. It was out of character for her to dump Teddy on her mother and come up to London to work. She could get a job closer to home, but she's stayed here despite the Blitz.'

I handed him a cup of tea and took a sip of my own.

'Bob wrote and asked me to see her, to report back on what I found.'

'And did you?'

'I gave him a version, not too specific. Living in London has changed her. She loves the excitement of it all. Loves the anonymity. Loves her new life.'

I had to know. 'Did she . . .?'

'Ask me to stay the night? Yes.'

'Were you tempted?'

Jim looked down at his tea, intently, as one would do to read the leaves, plan an action, think up a lie. When he looked up, though, he held my gaze steadily.

'No. Bob is an old friend and a fine man and he does not deserve that.' He smiled a little. 'And I kept thinking about an Australian ambulance driver I'd just met and was hoping to meet again.'

Who had ended up giving him exactly what Nancy had offered. Did he assume then that we would end up in bed? Girls all over London were sleeping with pilots. Could I trust his fine words said in the dark?

We finished our tea in silence. I rinsed the cups. Watched the water swirl around and disappear like dreams into the darkness beneath.

'Anything wrong?' he asked.

'No,' I lied.

'Lily,' he said, 'I'm not seeing anyone else and don't intend to if you are willing to put up with me.' He ducked his head, rather boyishly. 'As I told you last night, I've never been much of a lothario, actually.'

I smiled at that. 'And I've never been whatever the female equivalent is.'

'You have breakfast downstairs. You do need to eat. And something more appetising than mouldy bread, dried egg and pilchards.'

I laughed. 'All right.'

'I'll breakfast nearby. I have an errand this morning, so I'll pick you up at twelve? I want to drop into my flat and then we can spend a lazy Sunday afternoon together.'

'An errand? On Sunday morning?'

He seemed strangely embarrassed, and then a little defiant. 'I usually attend church on Sunday morning if I'm in London. There's a Russian Orthodox church in Buckingham Palace Road.'

'Do you go every Sunday?' I wondered why I was so surprised, given the antique cross he always wore, and I'd seen him cross himself at Levy's body.

'When I can. Orthodox churches are not that common in England. I'd drifted away from it all, but then I took to the skies and began to do battle with Jerry, and . . .' He looked at me. 'Is it a problem?'

'No. Not at all.'

'I find the service restful. It brings me peace.'

I knew nothing about the Russian Orthodox Church. I was Church of England, baptised and confirmed, but had never been a regular communicant except when I was teaching at Duranillin, because it was expected in that small community that the local teacher attend the local church. My church attendance schedule was otherwise Christmas, Easter, Anzac Day and whenever I needed comfort and was not too exhausted. It was yet another difference between us.

I kissed him goodbye and he crept down the hallway to the fire escape.

CHAPTER TWENTY-SEVEN

I joined Katherine for breakfast and began to stagger through a lie about when Jim had left the night before, until she stopped me with a look.

'Never explain without being asked,' she said. 'It always smacks of a lie, even if it's the truth. And Lily . . .'

'Yes?'

'You're a shocking liar.'

I applied myself to the porridge.

'Promise me you'll be careful, though.' I looked up in surprise, and she winked. 'Did you use—'

'Of course,' I said, face flaming.

'And I don't just mean careful about the mechanics of stopping babies. It's easy to break your heart in wartime.'

'He's not flying any more. He has a desk job.'

'They don't have to die to break your heart. London's a smorgasbord for men nowadays, especially if they're wearing a pilot's uniform. He may be playing the field.'

'He's not like that. He won't break my heart. Not intentionally anyway.'

Katherine smiled and sipped her coffee. 'To tell you the truth, Lily, if Jim was the sort of man who simply wanted an affair, he would be unlikely to choose you.'

'Why not?'

'Don't look like that. You're adorable, just like a little doll.'

'I am *not* like a doll,' I said. 'I wish people wouldn't compare me to a doll. Veronica Lake is shorter than I am. Norma Shearer is my height. They're both sexy as anything.'

'And Shirley Temple?' said Katherine, laughing.

She had me there. Of all the Hollywood stars, it was twelve-year-old Shirley Temple I was most often compared with, mainly due to my curly hair and ridiculous dimples.

'As I said,' Katherine went on, 'you're adorable, and of course any man would be interested in you, but if Jim wanted a fleeting affair, then a married woman like Nancy, or even me, would be a much better bet. The knowledge that there's a husband floating around in the background makes a man feel safe. A married woman is unlikely to want to tie him up, demand a ring, get pregnant to ensure a marriage. He can have fun without responsibility.'

'It sounds as if you've put a lot of thought into this.'

She laughed again. 'In a way, I have. I'm not saying it's a good thing to fool around the way Nancy does, or for a married woman to fool around at all really. I'm just saying – oh, I don't know what I'm saying.'

'You're saying you won't judge me for an affair with Jim.'

She smiled. 'Darling, I'll applaud it. I'm neither straight-laced nor narrow-minded. You're both single and he's an attractive man who obviously is very taken with you. But do try to ensure he doesn't break your heart or give you an unwanted baby.'

I looked at Katherine's shrewd, clever face. 'Are you ever tempted?'

She gave me a guarded smile. 'Harry was posted overseas in late 1939, so it's been a year since I last saw him. I'm in an odd situation, married but not married.' She began to play with her table napkin. 'I sometimes wonder if Harry has been faithful.'

'I'm sure he is.' I tried to make my voice certain.

She looked up at me. 'Are you? Actually, I'd forgive him a couple of transient infidelities. Because, if this war drags on and I don't see Harry for another year, or two or three years – well, I suspect it's inevitable that I'll drift into an affair. Danger is so erotic, don't you think?'

I stared at my empty bowl.

'That's why I don't judge Nancy,' she said. 'I'm not made to be celibate, either.'

I remembered what Jim had said about Nancy.

'But what if your husband found out?' I felt my cheeks heat up again. 'Jim said Nancy's husband had heard about Nan's goings on.'

'So Jim was spying on her?'

'Sort of.'

'Will he tell Nancy's husband what she's been doing?'

'He said he'll be discreet. But I think that discretion may just confirm Nancy's husband's worst fears.'

'If I go down that path I'll be a great deal more discreet than our Nancy.' She put down her knife and fork and looked away, out into the room. 'Falling in love,' she said, with a sigh. 'That's the real danger for married women like Nancy and me. Whatever do you do if you fall in love with the man?'

Jim arrived to pick me up on the dot of twelve. I sank into the low seat of his car fairly gracefully now I had had some practice. He pressed the starter. The little car roared into life and we set off down Gray's Inn Road.

'I met your station officer when I was having breakfast around the corner,' he said, as we turned into Guildford Street. 'There were no spare seats in the cafe, so I shared a table with him.'

'Jack Moray? How do you know him?'

'I don't. He mentioned he was the acting station officer at Bloomsbury auxiliary ambulance station and I said I knew you and Celia and I had known David.'

'I don't like Moray. He might appear friendly enough, but he's pretty ruthless at the core, I should think.'

'He seemed all right to me. He was most upset about David's death.'

'Moray? I doubt it. He's as anti-Semitic as they come.'

'Well, he told me that David had been a fine ambulance attendant and he was sorry that he'd died like that.'

'Like what?'

'Lily, I don't know. In an air raid, I suppose. He was very complimentary about you.'

'Oh? But he really is an anti-Semitic bigot. I work with him, remember?'

'Well, he's a bigot who thinks you do a wonderful job and that David will be hard to replace. He seemed sincere to me.'

At Shaftesbury Avenue we were forced to halt as a heavy rescue unit moved debris off the road in front of us.

'What did you say to Moray about me?' I asked Jim.

I caught a slight smile. 'I told him I was a very close friend of Lily Brennan.'

'What did he say?'

'That Miss Brennan is a lovely young woman and I am a lucky fellow.'

'Hmm,' I said, 'he's the sort of man who would try to get on the good side of an RAF officer, especially one who knows Ashwin. He's a frightful snob.'

Jim gave a roar of laughter. 'I think he meant it, Lily.'

We arrived at Piccadilly Circus to find the Lyons' Corner House there had been devastated by blast and fire and water. The whole area looked desolate and damaged, but people milled around on the street quite cheerfully. Eros was not flying high above us, as the statue had been stored away for safety at the start of the war and wooden boards had been put up to protect its base. These had been decorated with a frieze of flower sellers and London bobbies, which was now obscured by dust and soot and pitted by shrapnel.

'Looks like the West End copped it last night as well as the City,' I said.

He frowned at the destruction around us. 'Hope they didn't get Half Moon Street.'

Jim turned the car on to Piccadilly, driving slowly to avoid glass and debris. Half Moon Street was roped off. Jim parked the car on Piccadilly and we stepped onto a footpath that was ankle-deep in glass.

'It's from that shop,' I said, taking Jim's arm to steady myself. The heavy plate glass windows of the antique furniture store on the corner lay shattered on the footpath and great pieces of shrapnel were embedded in the gilt and ivory painted wood panelling inside. The blast had played its usual trick of leaving one fragile thing intact, as an elegant porcelain vase stood untouched on its stand amid the chaos.

Carefully, apprehensively, we stepped over the rope and into Half Moon Street. Bricks and plaster and splintered wood were strewn on the narrow roadway and the smell of smoke hung around us. Clean-up crews were at work amid the sound of machinery and falling masonry. We walked past them until we stood in front of what had been Jim's apartment building. The elegant staircase was open to the sky, with no roof above it and no walls around it.

Jim took my hand and his fingers closed around mine in a hard, painful grip. We stepped gingerly across the lumpy piles of mud and rubble and paper and charred wood. The staircase itself seemed solid and stable to the first floor, although beyond that the stairs stepped into space. We climbed slowly and carefully to where Jim's flat had been, and stood in the doorway. The door had been ripped away by the blast and his living room was a sodden mess of charred beams, splinters, chunks of masonry and broken glass. There were no rooms beyond.

'It's all gone,' said Jim, walking into the ruined room and staring around.

His face was white and he had a tense, puzzled expression. I had seen that reaction before. Now he knew what I had come to accept, that nowhere was safe in this Blitz.

'I hope to God that Greenfield – he's the doorman, you met him – I hope he's all right. He would insist on spending his evenings fire-watching on the roof.'

'Gosh, I hope so.'

Jim turned to look at me. 'I would have been here,' he said. 'If I'd not stayed with you last night I would have been here.'

I remembered that he had told me he never went to the basement in an air raid, no matter how bad the raid. My hands were suddenly moist inside their gloves and I felt a little dizzy. Jim would have been here, and his broken body would have been lying alongside the dirty rubble and the bits of clothing and books, wet and blackened, that were visible among the bricks. I would have lost Jim, as well as Levy.

'Pepys,' he said.

I looked at him, surprised out of my morbid fancies. He was gazing at the sodden pages by his feet. 'Is that ironic? His London was almost destroyed, too.'

'The Nazis burn books in Germany and bomb them to bits in London,' I said. 'I don't know if that's ironic.'

We both started at a harsh voice behind us.

'Oi! You two. Wotcha doing up here? It's dangerous. The crew's not finished making it safe.' A steel-hatted warden stood at the top of the stairs.

Jim turned and said to him, 'Cotton? It's me, Flight Lieutenant Vassilikov.'

The warden nodded sympathetically. 'Flight Lieutenant Vassy, of course. I apologise, sir, for not recognising you. I'll find out if they'll let you fossick about to see what can be salvaged.' He looked at the mess and grimaced.

'Is Greenfield all right?' asked Jim.

The warden shook his head. 'He was on the roof when it hit. Shame.'

I left Jim alone with his thoughts until the warden returned with permission for us to stay and gather what we could. Not much had survived the blast, the fire that followed and the drenching water of the fire hoses.

We drove back to my flat with a few books (water damaged), one alabaster lamp base (chipped), a well-executed engraving of

Florence (water damaged) in a narrow pearwood frame (edges charred), and the bronze statue of Diana the huntress with a dented crescent moon on her forehead.

We carted the remains of Jim's mother's friend's flat inside to find Nancy in the foyer, dressed to go out.

'I've been bombed out,' he told her. 'Lily has offered to keep this stuff for me.'

'Will you be dossing down here until you do?' she asked sweetly, but with a knowing air.

'No. I'll be in the Air Force Club or the Lansdowne until I find a more permanent place to live.'

It wouldn't be hard for him to find somewhere to rent. Throughout London 'To Let' notices were proliferating, as so many former inhabitants were fleeing to the countryside.

'Jacques Decasse is leaving his place in Riding House Street tomorrow,' Nancy said. 'It's just around the corner from Portland Place. He was saying he wanted someone to look after the flat.'

'You know Jacques?' Jim seemed surprised.

'Oh, yes. We're close friends.' I heard a hint of desperation in her voice. She stroked the fine ermine stole she was wearing and briefly rested her cheek on the fur.

'I'll give him a call,' said Jim.

'You do that, darling,' she said as she slipped away outside. 'Bye Lily.'

'Jacques Decasse?' I asked when she was gone.

'One of de Gaulle's Forces françaises libres officers. He's been waiting for his embarkation orders; they must have come. I like him, but he has a bad reputation as far as women are concerned.' He flicked me a look. 'Let's dump this stuff, and I'll take you somewhere for lunch.'

The lift arrived with its juddering shriek and we carried our small bundles of damaged items inside the cage. As we were hauled up through the floors I said, hesitantly, 'You could stay here tonight.'

Jim glanced at me from over the alabaster lamp and shook his head in a quick, decisive movement. 'Not with Nan floating around, prying.'

'Of course,' I said quickly, and shifted the books and picture to hold them more securely.

'I don't want to sneak around, Lily. It's our business, not Nan's or any of the other people in this building.'

The lift shuddered to a stop. Jim pulled the cage door across, revealing an empty hallway, and bent down to kiss me.

CHAPTER TWENTY-EIGHT

At a quarter to six the following evening Celia and I were sitting beside each other in the common room, waiting for our first call-out. I was trying to read and she was smoking cigarette after cigarette, much as Levy used to do when we were waiting for a raid to begin.

The Warning sounded, the wailing notes rising and falling in a sobbing rhythm that made my heart pound. Celia lit another cigarette.

McIver was on duty that night. She appeared in the doorway and her expression was grave.

'They're dropping flares and incendiaries over the City,' she said, in her soft Scottish accent. 'Lighting up the raid. I've been told to expect a bad night.'

Forty minutes later the main event began. The City and the government offices in Whitehall were bearing the brunt of it, as usual. Or so McIver informed us at nine o'clock, when she began to hand out the chits.

'We're on diversion tonight,' she said. 'You're all off to the City. It's fearfully bad there.'

We set off in a lull in the action, rumbling south-east in a small convoy, towards the City.

Celia and I were silent for a while, as the Monster rumbled on, then she said, 'God, what a bore. Another bloody raid.'

'A bore?' I responded. 'Are you trying to be irritating? I'd suggest terrifying as a more appropriate word.'

'What's the matter, Brennan?' asked Celia. 'You seem a trifle blue-devilled tonight. Not the little Aussie ray of sunshine we've come to know and love.' Her tone was coolly mocking.

I was tired and miserable with all the loss – Levy, brave Greenfield, even Jim's flat – and in no mood for Celia's comments.

'Go to hell, Ashwin.'

'It was a compliment, you silly girl. That was uncalled for.'

We were forced to halt while they cleared the road in front of us and I turned to look at her. Outside, the searchlights gave a day-bright radiance and the fires in front of us reddened her face.

'We're driving through an air raid to a bomb site,' I said, 'hoping to help people who've lost just about everything they care about, not to mention that they've been injured as well. I certainly don't find it boring.' My voice rose. 'At least Fripp has the sense to be afraid. Fake world-weariness annoys me, Ashwin. So go to hell.'

'You are abominably middle class.' Celia's voice was coolly contemptuous. 'I was taught that emotions were rarely discussed and were secondary always to manners.'

'What does that even mean?'

Celia regarded me with a steady, but rather wooden, gaze. 'That it is regrettably gauche to be annoyed at anything, and particularly so to *show* annoyance to anyone. I wish you'd learn that.'

I was well aware that, as usual, my face was giving me away. Middle-class Lily Brennan was obviously – regrettably – annoyed at the toff, Celia Ashwin.

'So you think it's gauche to be afraid? Or miserable?'

'It's gauche to show it,' she said.

'Or happy?'

She shrugged and stared out the window.

'You think I'm not good enough for Jim because I show my emotions?'

She gave a short laugh. 'I suspect you're far too good for him. That's not the problem at all.'

'*I'm* too good for *him*? Make up your mind Ashwin.'

'You're not suitable for him, and he's not suitable for you. Fish and fowl, Brennan. They don't mix.'

Suitable. The French word – the word Henri Valhubert had used when he had told me what amounted to the same thing – was *convenable*. He had said I was not suitable for a French count, and now Celia was saying I was not suitable for Jim. My face flamed and my grip on the wheel tightened.

'So Jim must choose a *suitable* woman,' I said, through gritted teeth. 'One who's trapped by her social obligations in a no-man's-land where nothing and nobody can reach her.'

Celia now looked bored, which inflamed me even further.

'What about love? Are your lot not allowed to show that either? Sounds like it would be a bit tough on your lover.'

She took a long slow breath before turning to stare at me in silence. Her eyes had narrowed and I had the feeling that I had made a hit, that I had pierced her armour.

My hands were clenching the wheel so tightly that they hurt. I released them and, as Celia had done, I drew in a deep breath, and instantly felt calmer. I could not imagine anything more horrible than to be always hiding what you felt beneath a veneer of civility. Because I knew that Celia's cool poise was only a veneer; the emotions she was holding in check so masterfully swirled around us. *They must be choking her*, I thought.

On the road in front of us, the air raid warden waved us forward. We set off, and the world pitched alarmingly as the Monster dipped into a pothole and up again. Through the windscreen, the sky glowed with a fierce redness and tiny, momentary flashes, like a faraway Guy Fawkes celebration, followed by the faint crump of explosions.

'I suppose it's a defence,' I said, once we were on less bumpy ground. 'It makes sense not to show emotions when you're always surrounded by servants.'

She laughed. It was a brittle sound. Unconvincing.

'That's not why we live that way,' she said, her voice again competing with the sound of the engine and now also the roar of aircraft above us and the crump of falling bombs. 'We prefer it. It simplifies things. And there is nothing quite so elegant as discretion.'

'It sounds horrendous to me,' I said. The Monster was forced to halt again, this time to allow a fire truck access to a bomb site in one of the streets to our left. I turned to look at Celia, who was regarding me with a slight smile.

'It's how polite society works, Brennan. Ask Jim how we do things.'

'*You* tell me.'

She addressed her words to her clasped hands lying on her lap. 'One simply pretends that any unpleasantness is not occurring and conceals all untoward emotions behind – oh I suppose you'd describe it as a manner of fey brilliance. Silliness – of the juvenile kind – is perfectly acceptable, even welcomed, but one must at all costs avoid intimacy in important dealings, social *and* personal.'

'It must involve a lot of lying,' I said.

Her head jerked up and she looked at me, unblinking, for a moment. 'That's one word for it.'

We were waved on again and the Monster bumped off towards the City.

'I know I'm too forthright,' I said. 'Maybe it is regrettably gauche, the way I show my emotions. But I hate lying. And anyway, I simply don't care what any of you lot think of me.'

'Stupid girl. It matters.'

'I'm sorry if I was rude,' I said, to the road ahead. 'I'm upset because – because they found Levy's body on Saturday.'

'Oh?' Celia sounded merely politely interested. 'Where?'

'In Caroline Place.'

'I wonder what was he doing there. It's been more than two weeks. He must have been in a terrible state. I've always suspected that rescue crews don't properly search the ruins.'

Again I was furious with her, at her insensitive dismissal of something that was so dreadful to me. We finished the journey in silence.

At the incident site the raid was in full swing and the warden in charge refused to allow us to drive through it to the hospital, so we ended up huddled in a surface shelter with other emergency workers and our four injured patients. Outside, a seemingly constant rain of bombs was falling.

The noise of it all was appalling and I prayed it would end soon. To my horror, Celia suddenly stood up and walked out of the shelter into the fury of the raid.

'She's barking mad,' shouted the ARP warden next to me. I agreed with him. He must have supposed that I was mad, too, when a moment later I rose and ran after her.

Celia was standing just outside the shelter, her face turned up to the sky, backlit by a multitude of explosions. I grabbed her arm and tried to drag her back, but she resisted.

'Look,' she cried out. 'Just look at it. It's perfectly marvellous.'

Clusters of bombs screamed down and exploded with a thunderous roar, throwing up spectacular displays of flashes and sparks as they set their targets ablaze. The inevitable pieces of shrapnel, red hot and lethal, fell like tinkling rain around us. She was right, of course, it was indeed beautiful. It was also terrifying.

'I've looked,' I cried. 'It's *Götterdämmerung*. Come back inside. Or at least lie down for protection from blast.'

She let me drag her down so that we ended up crouched on the ground by the shelter. It gave us some protection from shrapnel and from blast, but not from the noise, which was incredible. The guttural galumph of an oil bomb travelling drunkenly through the air, the staccato bolero of incendiaries and the earth-shattering explosions of nearby guns were rounded off by the drone of massed aeroplanes that seemed only a few hundred feet above us.

Gradually the bombers retreated and the clamour began to die down. The guns became intermittent and then stopped completely. We stood up as the rescue workers came out of the shelter, eyeing Celia warily, as if she were an unpredictable animal. She froze them with a look.

'Come on then,' she said to me, 'let's get our patients to hospital.' She smiled then, and her face blazed with vitality. And yet, it was also a little frightening, that smile, because it seemed so removed from real feeling.

Celia really was a superb creature, I thought, slim and straight, beautiful and fearless. Impetuous, confident and yet so very vulnerable. For the first time, I pitied her.

The coroner's jury sat on Tuesday to consider Levy's death. Jim attended the inquest and had promised to tell me about it when we had dinner that night at a restaurant near his new flat.

We walked together in the blacked-out streets of Fitzrovia on our way to the restaurant. Jim shone the slim light of his pencil torch on the broken pavement just ahead of our feet, so we could navigate its obstacles. He made a small sound of triumph as the torch lit up a doorway set between the usual boarded-up windows.

'Here it is.'

Over dinner, Jim told me that the verdict of the coroner's jury was that Levy's death was due to 'misadventure caused by enemy action'.

'The police pathologist said most of the injuries to David's body occurred post-mortem.'

'They were caused by the air raid?'

'Yes, probably when the building was bombed and the ceiling came down on him.'

'If most of the injuries were post-mortem, what actually caused his death? Could the pathologist say?'

'A blow to the back of his head. The pathologist suspects he was struck by a falling beam when the place was bombed, or he tried to escape, but fell and hit his head. He died then or soon after and suffered further injury as the raid continued.'

'The pathologist suspects! How could they give a verdict of misadventure when so much is unknown?'

'The evidence supported the verdict, Lily. The fatal injury was consistent with David falling or being struck when the ceiling caved in.'

'That's all very well, but why was Levy in the flat in the first place? That's still a mystery.'

'Yes, it's a mystery, but nothing was found to indicate that it is sinister.'

'Did they say who owned or leased the flat?'

'It belongs to a woman who left England for Canada when war was declared. She was contacted and she telegraphed to say she has no idea why David would have been there. The place had been left empty.' He gave me a stern look. 'Don't go thinking you'll be doing any investigating, Lily. It's over.'

I made my voice light, the intonation as flippant as Celia's. 'But what about the anonymous telephone call to the police about where to find his body? That's unusual, isn't it?'

Jim's chest rose and fell in a sigh. 'Let David rest in peace, Lily. There's nothing to indicate foul play. You've been reading too many books by Agatha Christie.'

'I just want the truth. There are too many people who hated him, or had a grudge against him, to let it go so easily.'

'Lily, the coroner has handed down his finding. The evidence supported it. There is nothing whatsoever to indicate that David's death wasn't due to the raid. The flat was bombed, beams fell, and one hit David. Or, as David was trying to get out, he fell and struck his head and was trapped. End of story.'

We glared at each other. I put my glass down on the table in a jerky movement and some wine spilled on to the white linen. It was as if drops of blood lay between us.

'At least Mrs Levy has a body to bury now,' said Jim, in a placating tone.

'Yes, there is that.' I wished I could let that be an end to it, but I couldn't. I said, quietly, 'I'm sorry to harp on this, but I just can't see why Levy was in the flat in the first place. It makes no sense.'

Jim sighed. 'Use your brain, Lily. Why would a man go to an empty, furnished apartment? To meet a girl. The raid started, she ran off in fear and David stayed. The ceiling fell on him and he died. That's it.'

I had been an idiot; of course that was the likeliest explanation, except . . .

'Then why didn't she tell the authorities?'

'Scared? Married? Perhaps she thought his body would be found by the rescue crews and there was no need to be involved. Perhaps she simply didn't care. Very likely she felt remorseful when weeks went by without his body being found, and it was she who telephoned the police. Lily, there's no mystery here.'

What he said made sense, and I acknowledged that. But I wondered why he was unable to see the logic of my fears. They felt very real and reasonable to me.

We went to Jim's flat after dinner. He had moved in the day before and it was the first time I had seen it. It was in a rather grand building in Riding House Street, just around the corner from Portland Place and Broadcasting House. The curtains were a rich burgundy velvet, the carpet thick, the armchairs deep and the bed enormous. It was a very comfortable flat. I was anticipating I would spend the night with him and had brought a discreet holdall with me.

He turned on the phonograph, placed the needle on a record and we settled down on his couch to listen to music. Jim leaned back and held me close. I felt his body relax as a trickle of Mozart's golden notes filled the flat, but I scarcely heard the music because my thoughts were still feverishly considering the possibilities of Levy's death. What if his head wound was not an accident, but had been intentionally inflicted? Caroline Place was only a short walk away from the ambulance station, where he had enemies, or at the very least, where some people intensely disliked him.

Anyone could have sent Levy a letter, purporting to come from Maisie or from me, asking him to meet us in the deserted flat. Levy had been investigating Mrs Coke's fraudulent activities. Perhaps she had lured him to the flat in that way and hit him over the head, or arranged for someone to do it for her. She had always been awfully pally with the spivs.

And yet, although Mrs Coke was venial and annoying, I could not see her as a murderer; she had too fine a sense of self-preservation to risk being caught out, and she had landed on her feet after being dismissed from the service. As I'd concluded before, she was unlikely to jeopardise her new job to get revenge.

The spivs? Knaggs had sworn vengeance on Levy for assisting in his arrest. He and Sadler easily could have overpowered Levy. They might only have wanted to teach him a lesson, but things got out of hand. Sadler had behaved so oddly on the first evening Levy failed to turn up for work, as if he knew something about it all. Why had Sadler mentioned Soho at all that night, if Levy had been killed in Bloomsbury? To put me off the scent?

Moray and Fripp? They hated Jews on principle. I was inclined to suspect Moray simply because I disliked him and he disliked Jews. But why would Moray want Levy dead? Had Levy found out something incriminating about him? That he frequented brothels, for instance? And how did Fripp and Moray know whether bombs had fallen in Soho on the night Levy went missing? It was entirely feasible that Moray might have been visiting a brothel in Soho that night, as he had been that day Pam and I saw him. But Fripp? I still thought that Moray's conversation with Fripp about attending a meeting with someone who had read *the* book in German was suspicious. Were the suspicious meetings taking place in Soho? What if Levy had discovered—

'I can hear your brain whirling around,' said Jim in a tone that brooked no nonsense. 'Lily, there's no mystery here and you're no Sherlock Ho—'

At that I whirled myself around, and shut him up by the simple expedient of kissing him. There was no more talk of Levy again that night.

The raiders came later in waves, crashing down on London and receding into the darkness, giving just enough respite to allow us to hope they had departed before returning in full force. I slept badly, tossing and turning to the sound of bombs, guns and fire-engine bells.

And I woke to the sound of Jim fiddling with the radio, which was emitting high-pitched squeaks rather than the morning news.

He'd made tea. I poured myself a cup and investigated his pantry. To my delight I found that Jim's weekly ration of bacon was untouched. Two rashers went into the frying pan and as I sniffed hungrily at the scent of the frying bacon I discovered a loaf in the bread bin. A couple of slices went into the pan with the bacon, and two more under the griller, and in my mind I sent thanks to Lord Woolton for not putting bread under the ration. When I discovered a small pot of raspberry jam, my joy was complete.

'There's a gremlin in the damn thing,' Jim called out.

I removed the toast from under the griller, placed the rashers on top and the fried bread beside them and opened the pot of jam.

'Breakfast is ready,' I called out.

'A veritable feast,' Jim said, as he sat down.

'Tell me about whatever it was you said was in the wireless,' I said as we ate.

'A gremlin? It's an imp. A sprite. They're to blame when things go wrong in your plane. I know for a fact that one of the blighters lived in my kite's centre of gravity because it used to hurl itself forward whenever I was about to land, which made the plane nose-heavy at the worst possible moment.'

I gave him a sceptical look over my sandwich.

256

'I'll have you know that all pilots believe implicitly in gremlins,' he assured me. 'They stiffen the controls. They jam the rudder or the ailerons. Gremlins even go so far as to dispel cloud cover when we need it the most.'

'Do the German planes have gremlins too?'

'Undoubtedly.' He smiled and took a sip of tea. 'The obnoxious little devils live in aircraft of all nationalities and wreak their havoc without regard to race, age or political persuasion.'

'I'm fairly sure they live in ambulances, too, then.'

He laughed. 'Probably.'

It had been easy to wake up with Jim, have breakfast with him, spend time with him. Celia might believe we were unsuited, but it didn't feel like it that morning. In fact, it felt quite the opposite.

CHAPTER TWENTY-NINE

In the station the following day I had just finished my first cup of tea for the morning when Moray opened the window into the office and called out that he needed an ambulance for a delivery of supplies to Great Ormond Street Hospital. Celia went to collect the chit, exchanging a few words with Moray as she did so. Moray nodded at her and looked up to address the room.

'Does anybody else want to attend Levy's funeral on Friday?' he asked.

'Will there be grog?' asked Sadler.

'You're not going,' said Moray. 'I've got Brennan, Ashwin, Halliday and Squire down for leave.'

'I think it's the right thing to do,' Celia told me as we headed off on the supply run.

It was a chilly morning and there was no wind. By the time we set off to return to the station after our delivery, the morning's mist was rapidly turning into fog.

'Looks like we're in for a genuine pea-souper of rich and ripe vintage,' said Celia.

She was right. Before long the Monster was engulfed in thick, reeking, khaki-coloured fog. It blotted out my vision, it closed my nose and caught in my throat. All sounds outside the ambulance were muffled and around us the ghostly traffic crept soundlessly. I slowed to walking pace and tried to use the white-painted kerb as a reference.

'I can't see a thing,' I said, groaning. 'You'll need to walk in front of the ambulance and warn me of obstacles.'

'I can't guide you that way,' she replied brusquely. 'It's dangerous to continue driving.'

So I turned into a narrow street, pulled up to the kerb and switched off the engine. We were now stranded in the noxious gloom. Although the windows were wound up tightly, even the small amount of polluted air that seeped into the cab was enough to make me cough and my eyes sting.

We were silent for a while as the fog swirled around the ambulance. My thoughts turned to Sadler's cruel stories on the night Levy failed to turn up. Perhaps he had been trying to confuse me with tall tales, when he knew all along that Levy was lying dead in Caroline Place.

'Ashwin,' I blurted out, 'do you know if Sadler has ever been investigated for black-marketeering or looting?'

'Yes. He was questioned by the police after Knaggs was caught looting, but nothing came of it. Moray told me. Why do you ask?'

I couldn't tell her the truth. 'I was wondering why he hadn't been hawking his French perfumes lately.'

'The perfumes he sells aren't really French. You do know Sadler is a wide boy.'

'Yes, of course I do. I've never bought anything from him, or from Knaggs.'

'If you want French perfume, I'd be glad to give you a bottle.'

My cheeks were on fire. 'That's very kind, but I—'

'Not at all. My pleasure. I'll drop it off at your flat.'

'No, really. I couldn't.'

'I've noticed that you like Je Reviens. I have a bottle I've barely touched.'

'Thank you,' I said weakly. What else could I do?

'I suppose Jim likes Je Reviens,' she said.

'I think so.'

'Lily . . .'

Her use of my first name surprised me. We all used surnames when on duty.

'I know you Australians think our class system is a load of old hat and your country is a democratic meritocracy. I'm not sure that is so, as I suspect a form of class system exists everywhere, but I do know that it's utterly rigid in this country.'

'I know, you're saying Jim is out of my class. I got the message the last time we had this conversation.'

'How much do you know about his background?'

'He's White Russian and has some sort of title that he refuses to use. A friend of his mother's paid his fees at Harrow and Cambridge, because the Revolution left his mother with very little money. But he became a barrister on his own merit, and I know that Jim isn't in the least concerned about the issue of class.'

'His mother is, let me tell you. And she is a very formidable woman.'

'You've said that before.'

'She scares the life out of me, to be honest.'

I laughed. 'What rot.'

Celia laughed as well. 'Actually, it's true.'

Outside, it appeared the fog was lifting somewhat. I hoped it was, as I did not want the conversation to continue.

'I think it's lifting,' I said. 'Should we try to get on?'

Without waiting for a reply I pressed the starter, rolled forward and turned into a main thoroughfare. I drove slowly, keeping my eyes riveted to the road.

'Turn left here,' said Celia.

With some relief I recognised the battered Doric columns of St Pancras Church. They had been badly hit by shrapnel, but somehow the church itself had escaped the bombs. It sat on the corner of Upper Tavistock Place, which meant we were nearly back at the station.

That evening I dressed with some trepidation. Jim was to pick me up at six and we were joining some of his RAF friends at the Hungaria restaurant. This would be the first time I had met any of his friends.

And there was also the frisson of excitement, for we would go first to his flat to drop off the small holdall that lay on my bed – the change of clothes and other necessaries I would need to again spend the night in Jim's flat.

'Living over the broom.' That was how the English referred to couples who lived together but were not married. No one could say that Jim and I were living over the broom; my shift work made that impossible and I would never do so anyway. I supposed that his class would call me his mistress. It did not feel that way to me. But at the same time, I did not really know what we were. We had never spoken of love – the closest either of us had come to a declaration were Jim's words that first morning. Nor had we spoken of the future – but how could anyone talk of the future when the present was so uncertain?

If I dared to think about what I really wanted, it was a fantasy. Celia would certainly call it a fantasy, and she would probably be right. In my fantasy, Jim would give up his English life and come to Australia. For a while I had loved being in London, but I didn't want to stay in Britain after the war. I wanted to return to my family and my friends and a country that I deeply loved. And more than that, I did not want to enter this rigid and prehistoric class system. If I married Jim, his and Celia's would be the class from which our friends would come.

My friends in England were other Australians such as Pam, or women like Katherine, who came from the same sort of middle-class background as I did. And even with Katherine, it was difficult sometimes to understand her views of the world and her acceptance of the rigid structure she was bound in.

I once read a newspaper article on the Japanese practice of bowing. It said that the Japanese know exactly how low they should bow to people according to age or station in life. It was crucial for your social standing to perform the correct bow. If you bowed too deeply to someone who merited only a shallow bob, or not deeply enough to someone who was due the full treatment, it was social death. Westerners always got it wrong, because it was not something that could be taught to you as an adult; it had to be learned at your mother's knee.

That was how I felt about the English class system. I was an outsider and I could not appreciate the subtle gradations of social standing given by accent or dress or schooling or family. How, therefore, could I ever really fit in? And did I want to? My mother had taught me to treat everyone the same and to face the world with kindness and pluck. Would that get me through if faced with women like Celia's sister? Or Jim's formidable mother? Or Celia, if we weren't in an ambulance in the Blitz together?

I had finished dressing, and regarded myself in the long mirror. My silk dinner gown looked well enough, though I really did not know if it was sufficiently *de rigueur* for the occasion. I dabbed some Je Reviens behind each ear and on each wrist. The bottle was getting low and I wondered if Celia had meant it about giving me one of hers. I slipped into my warmest coat – a heavy black wool I had bought in Prague, that completely covered my flimsy dinner gown – and slung my gas mask over my shoulder. Finally, I leaned towards the mirror in the tiny hallway to put on my lipstick.

'Bugger Celia Ashwin,' I said to my reflection. 'And bugger the English class system. I'll take it one day at a time.'

There was a knock at the door. Jim was punctual, as always. I opened the door, smiling.

CHAPTER THIRTY

'Where's your car?' I asked when we emerged on to the street. Jim gave a groan of annoyance.

'The blighter didn't wait. I arrived in a taxi and asked him to. Obviously had a better offer.'

'But where's your car?'

'Shredded a tyre yesterday. I put on the spare, but I can't replace the one that's shredded, because there's simply no rubber available. Anyway, it's impossible to drive on these roads. As soon as they clear them there's another raid and more tyre-shredding glass and debris. And it's only a matter of time before they abolish the basic petrol rationing for civilians.'

I laughed at his glum face. 'So where *is* your car?'

'Up on blocks in an underground garage in Mayfair. Next to a Rolls-Royce, I might add.'

'In elevated company then.'

'Yes. The Roller is up on blocks, too.'

He peered down the gloomy street. There were no cars or taxis to be seen. 'We could wait for a bus, or brave the Underground.'

'Have you been in the Underground after dark?'

'Recently? No. I use it in the daytime occasionally, but evenings I've been driving my car around.'

'Then I vote for the Underground,' I said. 'I think you need to see what's going on down there each night.'

'Why not? With luck we can catch a taxi near my flat. The Hungaria is in Lower Regent Street.'

It was raining steadily, so I pushed up my tartan umbrella as Jim unfurled his big black one and we walked down Gray's

Inn Road. Jim's flat was near Oxford Circus, so we could take the Piccadilly Line from Russell Square station and change at Holborn.

The rain had eased by the time I caught sight of the sandbags around the Underground entrance. Inside the station, a few people milled around in the dim light, laden with bags and blankets and pillows. These were the latecomers; people began queuing in the afternoon for a good spot on the platform. We bought our tickets and allowed ourselves to be swept along and down the precipitous stairs. The lift didn't operate at night.

The heavily laden figures around me brought back memories of Praha Hlavní Nádraží, the main railway station in Prague. Czech refugees, fleeing Nazi occupation, were far less orderly than this flood of humanity that swarmed in decorous uncertainty towards the platform.

The platform lights were dim, and revealed what looked like the result of some terrible catastrophe – a battlefield, or a city stricken by the plague. A path barely a yard wide allowed passengers to enter and leave the train and another yard of space beside the track was marked with a white line, but all the remainder of the platform was a mass of bodies. Londoners of both sexes and all ages sprawled around on coverlets or rugs with only some pillows for comfort against the cold concrete.

The men were mainly in shirtsleeves, having folded their coats for pillows, but most of the women were fully dressed. Some chattered together comfortably; others lay gazing mutely up at the curved ceiling. Most of the women appeared to be knitting. There were card parties and a game of chess, people reading newspapers. An elderly man appeared to be utterly engrossed with the subtleties of the Torquemada crossword puzzle in the *Observer*. Children were everywhere, playing cards or board games, or running around unchecked. Some of the smaller children were asleep, with arms flung out or clutching a favourite toy; in the platform light even their fresh faces appeared grey and hollow.

Jim looked quietly fascinated by the Tube shelterers, who in return regarded him with undisguised affection. Londoners loved RAF pilots.

'Shot down any Jerries?' asked a young boy, while a small girl stroked the arm of his greatcoat.

'A few,' replied Jim, to the boy's delight.

'In a Spitfire?' called out another boy.

'Hurricane.'

'Never mind,' said the boy, with real sympathy, 'maybe they'll let ya fly a Spitfire soon.'

We stepped past the shelterers to stand on the clear section at the edge of the platform.

'It's putrid down here,' observed Jim.

The air was indeed fetid and I glanced at the two hessian screens at either end of the platform, wondering how the sanitary facilities were arranged.

'I don't know if the ventilation system is working,' I said. 'The atmosphere is terribly thick. And it's so hot.'

Jim shrugged. 'Too many people and not enough trains coming through to move the air. It must be abominable when the trains stop running. Speaking of trains, here it comes.'

I felt the welcome rush of air through the tunnel, and a few seconds later the train roared into the station with a squeal of brakes. Its arrival produced no visible effect on the people lying on the platform, whether they were awake or asleep. We stepped hurriedly into the brightly lit carriage and sat down. In startling contrast to the packed horizontal humanity in the station only two or three people were sitting with us as the train roared off into the tunnel.

'The government has put in chemical toilets at Gloucester Road, so I suppose they're going into all the platforms,' I said. 'And there are plans to put first aid centres and refreshment services in all the stations.'

Jim gave a short laugh. 'All the comforts of home,' he said dryly. 'This has been an education.'

'Oh, there's more,' I said. 'The regulars all have their own spots that they come to each night, but the authorities are going to introduce ticketing to prevent the necessity for afternoon queues. That means a specific place on the platform for each ticket-holder.'

'Luxury,' he said. 'How on earth do you know all this?'

'My friend Pam,' I told him. 'She's a shelter officer at Gloucester Road Tube station.'

When we changed at Holborn, stepping over even greater numbers of people, I found myself looking out for any man handing out leaflets who might resemble Levy. I saw no one remotely like him, but what did that prove?

Meanwhile, women wearing green frocks with bright red kerchiefs on their heads and red armbands lettered 'TR' were moving around the platform. I assumed the letters stood for Tube Refreshments, because one carried a tray of food – buns and pieces of cake (1d); apples (1½d); meat pies (1½d); chocolate bars (2d) and packets of biscuits (2d); the other held a giant teapot from which she was pouring tea at a penny a pop.

Jim's face brightened when he saw them. 'At least they're feeding the poor blighters,' he whispered to me.

I thought of the incongruity of the people around us carrying out all the routine functions of their lives – eating, sleeping, socialising and using the primitive toilets – in such close proximity to hordes of others. No one seemed to be in distress or annoyed. In fact, many of them were smiling or laughing with their neighbours. Others sat quietly, or slept, although I couldn't comprehend how they could sleep in all the light and noise. A lone policeman patrolled, stopping now and again to have a quiet word with someone.

The escalator at Oxford Circus station was not running. Instead, it was packed with people, two to a stair. They would have an uncomfortable night's sleep I thought, as we carefully picked our way past them. Men were also lying on the narrow shelf behind the bannisters, sprawled out, head to foot, the entire way up.

Jim's lips made a hard, angry line by the time we emerged into the blackout gloom of Oxford Circus.

'Are you all right?' I asked, worried about his lungs. It had been a long and steep climb up to the surface.

'It makes me so angry,' he said, in a hissing whisper as we walked past the ruins of Peter Robinson's department store on our way to his flat. I had tight hold of his arm and we stepped carefully on the cracked paving.

'What does?' I had never seen him angry, so I found this mood interesting.

'People having to put up with that, night after night. There were thousands of people down there, in appalling conditions. And it's like that in all the Tube stations?'

'Welcome to London in the Blitz. Personally, I think it's a good solution to the problem of keeping safe from the bombs. Honestly, Jim, where else can they go? Pam says that in Aldwych Underground they've organised ENSA concerts, bunks and a library.'

Because of my job, I knew well that the Tube stations were not necessarily safe refuges. Only six weeks before, Trafalgar Square station had been hit; half a dozen or so shelterers had been killed and scores injured, but for reasons of morale the incident hadn't been publicised. Much worse, of course, had been the Balham station disaster two nights later.

Despite such dangers, every night thousands of Londoners sought the shelter of the Underground. Where else could they go? If they had no back yard they could not have their own Anderson shelter. There were not enough public shelters, and anyway, as these had often been built at street level people did not trust them in an air raid. It was an instinctive craving, I thought. When the raiders were in the sky, Londoners felt safer underground.

Jim had recovered his equanimity. 'It's funny how this war brings you face to face with other people – people you'd never have been so close to without the Blitz.'

'Well, there's a difference between us. I've always been face to face with all sorts of people. We're a lot more democratic in Australia, and I grew up in an outback pub, don't forget.'

He laughed. 'I had forgotten! Well, it's decidedly unusual in this country. I've a hunch that all this –' he waved a hand around us '– will do funny things to the world we've known in Britain. When it's all over I think people won't put up with the way things have been.'

'Some having a lot and others having very little?'

'No, not exactly. There will always be the very rich and the terribly poor. I'm talking about the heaving masses in between. I think that after we've been through all this together, ordinary people will expect a bit more from their country.'

'Fair enough. Good luck to them, I say. I'm on the side of the heaving British masses.'

'So am I,' said Jim.

'Not that I'll be here to see what happens to them.'

'Oh?'

'I'm going back to Australia as soon as the war is over.'

He murmured something in Russian. He might have been disappointed, but really, it was hard to tell.

At his flat I dumped my holdall and freshened up. Jim managed to find a taxi to take us to Lower Regent Street and the very smart Hungaria restaurant, where goulash and other peasant dishes were served at the cost of a royal banquet.

We entered the below-ground grill room to the gipsy music of a Tzigane orchestra. Flowery murals decorated the walls, but hanging among them were red and silver picks and shovels, mounted like military trophies. They were a nod to the grill room's reputation for being invulnerable. It was apparently bomb-proof, splinter-proof, blast-proof, smoke-proof and gas-proof. The decorations would have been more amusing if I had not seen so many people dug out of basement shelters and ruined buildings.

The restaurant was crowded with men and women in uniform, some men in evening dress and women in glamorous evening gowns. My oyster silk gown with its sequined shoulder straps, for which I had paid a month's salary in Prague, did not let me down. It clung beautifully, and when I emerged from the cloakroom I basked in the admiration in Jim's eyes.

There was an atmosphere of hectic gaiety in the place, fuelled by champagne, bright lights and frenetic music, but I thought it a little forced.

'Eat, drink and be merry,' I murmured.

Jim glanced at me and I did not finish the quote. The two couples we were joining were waiting at the bar. They all looked to be in their early twenties; the men were in Royal Air Force uniforms and the women in evening gowns. Jim threw me a broad smile, as though he had a surprise for me.

'What?' I said, smiling in return.

'Meet the Australian contingent in my squadron,' he said. 'Fred Harland and Mike Corrs. Fred's from Sydney, Mike from Brisbane.'

I stared at him, scarcely able to believe it. He'd brought me here to meet his Australian friends, not the group of upper-class nobs I'd been expecting. I beamed at Jim, trying to let him know how happy I was, before turning to the slightly built man with a sandy moustache and vividly blue eyes.

'G'day, Lily,' said Fred, giving me a nonchalant wave by way of greeting. I smiled in response, thinking how much I had missed the casual friendliness of my compatriots.

Fred was standing beside a tawny-haired woman in an emerald green dress. Her tan had not quite faded, and she was introduced as his wife, Frances.

'Jim tells us you're a Perth girl,' said Frances. 'One of my cousins lives there. Raves about the place.'

'Yes,' I said. 'It's—'

Before I could say more a dark-haired dreamboat with a movie star smile leaned in. 'I'm Mike. Good to meet you, Lily. This is my missus, Annette. We were married last month.'

Mike's wife was a tall, attractive girl, with ash-blonde hair and the exquisite creamy complexion that was never found in Australian girls.

'How do you do,' she said, then added, unnecessarily, 'I'm English.'

Over dinner we swapped stories of life in England in wartime.

'I hate the cold,' admitted Frances. 'And the way it gets dark so early here.'

'It'll only get worse,' I said and she gave a mock shudder.

'So you followed Fred from Sydney?' I asked.

She smiled. 'Couldn't let him loose on his own, and I can't stand being away from him. Only, now I'm here I've become shockingly superstitious.' She made a slight grimace. 'I can't help it – I think it comes from living in such uncertain times. If I put my left arm into a sleeve first, or my left foot into a shoe first, I'm unhappy for the rest of the day, thinking it will somehow affect how Fred flies.'

'I've told her it's all bulldust, but she's got this little ritual each time she waves me off,' said Fred, with an indulgent, if slightly exasperated smile.

'I knitted him a scarf, you see,' she said. 'And when he leaves me for the airfield I tie the scarf around his neck, right over left, and tuck it in.'

'And only then can I leave the bloody flat,' said Fred.

'I thought it was you pilots who were superstitious,' I said.

'Too right,' said Fred. 'I've seen men delay take-off until they've peed on the back wheel or –' he looked meaningfully at Mike '– spit on the rudder.'

Mike gave a shamefaced smile. 'Bit of spit never hurt the rudder. It chases away the gremlins.'

'Oh, don't start on those silly gremlins,' said Frances, to which all three men protested good-naturedly that she had obviously never flown a plane, or she would jolly well believe in them all right.

'Just about all of us have a lucky charm or a mascot,' said Fred. 'Mine is a little toy dog I won at Luna Park before I shipped out. I keep it in my map case.'

'What about you, Jim?' I asked.

He reached into his collar and pulled up the chain that held the gold and blue enamel cross he always wore. I had not examined it closely before, but now saw that it was beautifully wrought and obviously antique.

'My baptismal cross,' he said. 'I would never dream of taking off unless it was around my neck.'

'Lily, would you care to dance?' asked Mike.

I did, and Jim danced with Frances and Fred with Annette. Then Fred asked me and Jim asked Annette and Mike asked Frances. And so it went. We whirled around to the music of the excellent swing band, punctuated by the noise and reverberations of the guns and bombs from the raid outside.

'This place is amazing, you know,' Fred said, as we waltzed. 'It's so well-built that no one has to go to a shelter during a raid. And there's no need to go home at the end of the evening. Last time I was here the manager brought in pillows, rugs and screens, and Fran and I dossed down on the floor.'

Over dinner the conversation turned to the Blitz, which was still raging outside.

'It's funny to think that this Blitz on London might have saved the entire nation,' said Fred.

'Because it diverts attention from the airfields?' I asked, confused.

Fred nodded. 'You have no idea how close we came to losing the aerial battle with the Luftwaffe.'

'Surely not,' said Annette.

'All the advanced fighter fields were in shambles by early September,' said Mike.

'Keep it down,' said Jim. 'No need to broadcast it.'

I couldn't accept that. 'Surely we were hitting the Luftwaffe harder than it was hitting us.'

'Propaganda,' Jim replied, in a low voice. The other two nodded. 'The government upped the German losses by around a hundred per cent and decreased ours by around fifty per cent.'

'We were still winning, surely.'

'We had our backs to the wall and Fighter Command was simply waiting for the invasion,' he said wearily. 'We thought it likely they'd go for Dover, and we'd lost air control over the invasion area. In truth, we'd lost control of the air space over south-east England by then.'

'They didn't invade,' I said, a trifle belligerently, but in a low voice. We'd all be in trouble if we were overheard. 'Because of you pilots and how hard you fought, Germany couldn't invade Britain. So we won that battle. Churchill said so. *We won.*'

Jim exchanged looks with Fred and Mike. 'Yes,' he said. 'We won.' He also said, but not in words, 'At what cost.'

In the ladies' room a short while later, as Frances, Annette and I freshened our make-up, I asked Annette how she felt about going to Australia when the war was over.

'I'm looking forward to it. I'll miss my family, of course, but I'll be with Mike, and we want a big family of our own. I must say, the weather sounds divine.'

'Better than here,' said Frances.

'Do you think Mike would have remained in England if you hadn't wanted to leave?' I asked.

Annette leaned toward the mirror to apply her lipstick, rubbed her lips together and sat back with a smile. 'Probably, but he wants to go home to Australia more than I want to stay here in England. It's as simple as that.'

She gave me a sharp look. 'There's no reason why the woman should always follow the man though. Are you worried that Jim won't want to leave England?'

I felt myself flush. 'It's early days yet,' I murmured.

'Mike and Fred adore Jim,' said Annette. 'When he was flying with them they called him Dad, but really he was like an older brother, always looking out for them up there.'

'He's not at all stuck-up,' said Frances. 'I think he'd get on well in Australia.'

I made an excuse, picked up my evening bag and fled.

'Thank you for the Australian contingent,' I said to Jim in the taxi back to his flat. I was done in with dancing. We had finally left the restaurant when the All Clear had sounded around two o'clock. 'I really enjoyed meeting them.'

'They're the sort of people I like,' he said. 'Down to earth, confident and no hypocrisy about them.'

I smiled. 'I'm glad you like Australians.'

'Next time I'll introduce you to my British friends,' he said lightly. 'You'll like them. They're down to earth, confident and there's no hypocrisy about them. Even if they do come from the so-called upper class.'

I felt my cheeks flame. 'I didn't mean that only Australians could be . . .' I wondered why he would think so. 'Do you think I'm prejudiced against your class?'

He didn't answer for a beat or two, as the taxi took us through the practically deserted streets.

'I think you are homesick.' He looked at me intently. 'Lily, I could easily practise law in Australia, you know. After the war, I mean.'

'Oh, really?' I said lightly. Until Frances and Annette had mentioned it, I had never entertained the thought that Jim actually might choose to leave England and come with me to Australia. Now I felt confused. Was I just being contrary to be filled with a superstitious fear of making any plans for 'after the war'? Would it be tempting fate to do so? Levy's funeral was the next day. His death had made me all too aware that no one was safe in this Blitz.

'Lily—'

'There's no point thinking about such things right now. Not when everything is so uncertain. It's – it's bad luck.' I pushed aside the heavy curtain over the taxi's window and peeped outside. 'That was quick, we're almost at the flat.'

I glanced up at the low clouds above us when we left the taxi.

'We all welcome bad weather nowadays,' I said. 'Hoping it will keep the raiders away.'

'It won't,' he said, shining his torch at the keyhole. But he didn't put the key into the lock. 'We came so close to losing the air war with Germany,' he said, standing very still and looking down at his key.

'They didn't invade,' I said. 'Now they can't invade until next spring. And we'll be ready for them when – if they do.'

He gave a soft, bitter laugh. 'It was good old London that saved us. Hitler decided to annihilate London and that gave our airfields, our planes and, most of all, our pilots a rest. It was all we needed. Now we're rapidly getting back to strength. I think we can withstand invasion now, but God knows if we can save London unless we can figure out a way for our fighters to successfully attack the bombers at night.'

'Hitler won't annihilate London,' I said with certainty. 'He'll keep on hitting us but we can take it.'

Jim shook his head. 'For how long? It's been three months now. The destruction is appalling. People can't live like this, day after day, night after night, spending twelve, fourteen hours each day underground, emerging to find their homes and the places they love destroyed. Could London put up with this sort of bombing for four months?'

'We can. I know it.'

'Six months?'

'Yes.'

'What about a year of constant raids? I know you think London is too big to destroy but after a year it would be in ruins, and if London goes . . .'

I sang softly, 'There'll always be an England.'

'My cock-eyed optimist,' he said, and pulled me close for a kiss.

Later that night, as I lay beside him in the dark and listened to his soft, regular breathing, I thought again about what he had said. He was willing to come to Australia after the war. The obvious implication was marriage. Then I remembered his words about the Blitz on London. Could London take this sort of attack for many more months? And if London went . . .

It was madness to make plans in such times, when things were so uncertain.

CHAPTER THIRTY-ONE

David Levy's body lay in a simple wooden coffin that was nailed shut. The funeral ceremony was in Hebrew, but although the rituals were alien to me, the grief of the Levys was all too real. He was buried in the cemetery at Golders Green. I clung to Jim's arm as I watched his coffin being lowered into the grave. We sprinkled earth on top of it and I wept.

Maisie was in tears throughout and Squire left straight after the ceremony, perhaps uneasy at the thought of being surrounded by so many Jews. Celia was cool as ever, and dry-eyed.

A reception was held at the synagogue and Jim and I approached the Levys to offer our condolences. Mrs Levy was reclining on a small couch beside her husband, her legs still cased in plaster. They greeted us with warm dignity. After us came Celia.

'Ashwin?' Mr Levy seemed to be searching his memory. 'Are you related to Horace Ashwin, the politician?' He gave her a keen look.

Her composure did not falter. She said, 'He is my father-in-law. Cedric Ashwin is my husband.'

Mr Levy's expression became wooden and he made a half turn away from her, but I saw his wife's hand go out to his arm, urging him back. 'We thank you for coming, Mrs Ashwin,' she said, and her smile was so like Levy's that I wanted to weep again.

'My husband's . . . views . . . are not my own,' said Celia, faltering slightly for the first time. 'Your son was a wonderful ambulance attendant, kind, caring and competent. He will be much missed.'

She left soon afterwards.

The following week was one of busy night shifts with Celia. She was in a brittle mood and when she addressed me the cut glass of her accent was sharp enough to draw blood. We spoke little as we carried out our duties.

Daylight raids seemed to have ceased, but every night London had to cope with yet more death and destruction. After more than three months of blitzkrieg, we could no longer rely upon the big map in the common room to navigate the City and the East End; they had been so badly bombed that it was unclear where the normal ground level was situated amid the cliffs and slopes of rubble.

Saturday morning, as we drove back to Woburn Place towards the end of our shift, Celia seemed wrapped in her own brooding thoughts. At last she lifted her head and said, 'I'm sorry to have been such a wet rag all week.'

It was decent of her to acknowledge it, and I flashed her my best smile. 'That's all right, I've hardly been a barrel of laughs myself.'

'I've been turned down by the Wrens,' she said abruptly.

'I'm sorry to hear it,' I murmured. It was no surprise that Celia would want to join the women's navy – it was where all the posh women seemed to end up.

'It's Cedric, my husband,' she said. 'I'm sure that's the reason. I'm not considered . . . suitable, because of my fascist husband.'

'I am sorry, Ashwin. Might you have better luck with one of the other services?'

'No. The women I know in the ATS all seem to hate their duties and I can't bear the uniform of the WAAFS. I'm better off remaining in the Ambulance Service. Otherwise they may conscript me into the Land Army out of spite.'

'You're doing a wonderful job here,' I said.

She did not reply.

An hour later I was about to leave the washroom at the end of my shift when I heard Fripp's voice in the corridor.

'Are we meeting next week?'

Her hissing whisper was so ridiculously suspicious that I stood transfixed, my hand on the doorknob.

A voice answered her, too softly for me to hear what was said, or even be sure who spoke, though I thought it must be Moray, who would have been arriving around this time.

'All right,' said Fripp.

The doorknob began to turn. I ducked into a cubicle and closed the door and after a moment flushed the toilet. When I came out Fripp was combing her hair before the mirror. I smiled at her. She nodded in reply and gave me a closed lip smile. Excitement lurked in her gooseberry green eyes and I wondered if German literature was to be discussed at her mysterious meeting.

As they often did, my thoughts drifted to the night of Levy's disappearance, when Sadler had teased me by saying that Levy had been Blitzed in Soho. Fripp had been insistent that no planes had flown over Soho that night and Moray had agreed with her. The obvious conclusion was that they had both been in Soho that night, possibly together. And then suddenly, I could have kicked myself – how could I have not made the connection? Pam and I had watched Moray enter a building in Soho. We thought it was a brothel, but what if it was Moray's secret meeting place?

I went straight to the kitchen, where I found Maisie making tea.

'Do you know where Moray lives?' I asked. 'I was sure I saw him in Soho the other day.'

'He was bombed out a couple of months ago, but I thought he moved to a guesthouse close to the station.' She poured the tea from the large teapot into the rows of cups she had lined up. 'Actually, I've seen him in Soho, too.'

'I enjoy visiting Soho but it's not a very salubrious area to live in, I should think.'

'Oh, it's not all that bad,' she replied, in an obvious huff. 'The people are friendly, and parts of it are very nice indeed.' Her face was flushed and her lips pursed.

'Do you live there?' I asked, feeling the heat in my own face.

'In Frith Street.'

'Sorry. I really don't know that much about London and I spoke without thinking.'

She smiled. Maisie was never annoyed for long. 'There's always something to do in Soho, and the restaurants are marvellous. People always think of the Windmill, but it's a perfectly legitimate theatre. Actually, it's the only theatre in London that hasn't missed a performance yet. They've got six full-time bomb-spotters on the roof to give proper warning when the raiders are directly overhead. What's wrong with nudity anyway, if it's tastefully done?'

She left the kitchen and I heard her singing out that the tea was made. I picked up a cup, added my sugar and milk, and went back into the common room.

That night Jim and I went to the pictures in Leicester Square, and emerged from the cinema to find a raid in progress. We stood under the shelter of the cinema foyer and watched people dashing out into the square to pick up bits of shrapnel for souvenirs; a risky business, since the metal was still hot.

Afterwards, over supper at the Lyons, I told Jim what I had overheard Fripp say, and my suspicions about her meeting Moray in Soho. I immediately wished I hadn't spoken, for as usual he was annoyingly unimpressed.

'You can't even be sure she was talking to Moray, let alone what they were talking about.' He pretended to have had a revelation. 'I've got it. Fripp and Moray are having a torrid affair.'

'I wish you would take me seriously. There's something suspicious going on. I'm not an idiot.'

'I know you're not an idiot, but you've had some rotters in your station, a fraudster and a couple of wide boys, at least one of whom was a looter, and it's fired up your imagination. You really think there's a nest of fifth columnists in your ambulance station as well?' His expression was one of indulgent amusement. 'Honestly, Lily, if you carry on like this I'll expect one of Powell's hairy nuns to make an appearance.'

Infuriated, I battled on. 'We know there are fifth columnists in London, so why not at my station? Why does Moray spend so much time in Soho if he doesn't live there? It's suspicious. I think he's meeting Fripp and others in Soho, possibly in that place I saw him go into.'

He laughed. 'You think he's meeting Fripp in a brothel?'

'No, of course not. But—'

'There are many reasons a man like Moray might go to Soho. And as I said, you don't know who Fripp was talking to this afternoon, let alone why she is meeting anyone. I think you should do your job and leave the catching of any fifth columnists to the experts.'

I did not offer to stay at his flat that night.

The following Monday morning Fripp arrived at the station with freshly set hair and an air of fidgety excitement. Fripp was on the same schedule as me, and Moray worked days as the station officer, so I reasoned that any meeting would have to take place at night. Looking at her, I felt sure the meeting was to take place soon, perhaps that very evening. Jim was wrong, I knew it. I would show him that my suspicions were real, not fantasy.

I decided, as I sipped my first cup of tea, that I would follow either Fripp or Moray to find out where they held the mysterious meeting. If I lost sight of them, then I'd go to the building I'd seen Moray enter that day.

It was a slow shift that Monday, which meant we had to endure drills and first aid lectures. In the morning we sat through stirrup pump drill. Then it was respirator drill, followed by instructions on how to clean the ghastly things. After lunch was a lecture on dealing with fractures. We all knew how to perform such basic first aid but it was required that we undergo periodic retraining.

'Reassure the casualty if it appears he is conscious and able to understand,' said Moray reading from notes provided by the Ambulance Service.

And what if it's a woman who has been deafened by blast, I wondered.

'Tell the casualty that you'll be taking care of him. Loosen any restrictive clothing and—'

'What if you're biffed for taking liberties?' asked Sadler, to general laughter.

Moray ignored him. 'And remove any jewellery from the affected limb. Place the jewellery in the casualty's pocket and inform them that you are doing this because of potential swelling.'

Unless you're a looter, in which case put the jewellery in your own pocket, I thought, looking at Sadler.

I tried to keep Fripp in sight all day. At five o'clock she went to where the bicycles were kept, at one end of the basement garage. Moray joined the cyclists for a short chat about nothing much and then walked with Fripp as she wheeled her bicycle up the dark driveway from the garage to Woburn Place.

I watched them until they were swallowed up by the darkness at the entrance, then I tiptoed as close as I dared, almost to where Moray's torchlight illuminated a small circle near his feet at the top of the driveway. It also shone on the spokes of Fripp's bicycle, and her trouser legs. She was sitting on her bicycle and they were talking.

I took cover behind one of the thick concrete pillars that supported the garage roof near the entrance, where I would be out of sight if Moray shone his torch in my direction. It would be difficult to explain why I was loitering in the dark.

'So, I'll see you tonight,' Fripp said, and I could hear her excitement. It mirrored my own. I was right! They were meeting that evening.

'Be discreet, please, Nola.' Moray sounded peeved.

'And Mr—, I mean, my friend – he's coming too?'

'Mmmm.'

'I'll see you at seven, then.'

There was a squeak as she pushed off and rode away.

Moray turned and swept his torchlight behind him, across the garage floor and the pillar that concealed me. I leaned back and stayed absolutely still as the thin beam continued on past my hiding place. He did a couple more slow sweeps with the torch, then turned and walked quickly out of the garage on to the street.

My heart was thumping. I didn't dare follow Moray now, and Fripp was already gone. But if I was right, their meeting place was the basement flat in Soho.

I thought about alerting the police, but decided not to when I remembered Jim's amused scepticism. It was likely that the police would be just as unimpressed, because I simply didn't have enough evidence of wrongdoing yet.

Very well. I would go to the flat myself, well before seven o'clock, hide myself and see who turned up. At the very least I would discover if my suspicions were correct, that the flat was where Moray and Fripp were meeting. Maybe I would hear something. The blackout would be my cover. A faint prickle of nervous excitement ran over my skin. It was a reasonable plan, I thought. At worst, I would be embarking on a wild goose chase and I would spend a cold few hours in the dark. But I just might be able to expose a nest of fifth columnists and wipe the amused smile off Jim's face.

I walked to the garage entrance and stood for a few seconds in the darkness before I stepped out and was enveloped by the black velvet of a London evening in the blackout. I took one, two deep breaths as a moist breeze, smelling faintly of brick dust, cooled my cheeks. When I looked up, stars blazed overhead, and a crescent moon rode high in the sky. It partially illuminated my way to the crowded Russell Square Tube station.

I took the Tube to Tottenham Court Road and picked my way past the sprawled bodies on the platform to the stairs and up to the street. It was when I stood in the darkness at the entrance that an unforeseen problem with my plan became apparent. Clouds had moved in quickly, and now blanketed the moon. Everything looked completely different in the dark. I knew that Moray had entered a building that overlooked Soho Square, but my sense of direction was vague at the best of times and with no street signs to assist me, and in almost complete darkness, I was not sure I could even find Soho Square, let alone the building. And if I did find the building, how could I identify anyone in the dark?

Commuters brushed past me, their dimmed torches winking at the ground. I stood for a minute or so, wondering whether to slink back to Bloomsbury. But that would be a defeatist's way. I should at least try to put my plan into effect.

So I set off along Oxford Street. The first corner I reached I assumed was Soho Street, which should lead me straight to Soho Square. A passer-by confirmed that it was and I turned resolutely, giving myself a silent cheer.

A surprising number of people were abroad that night; their torchlights bobbed around me and anonymous dark bodies pushed past me as I carefully walked along the shattered pavements of Soho Street.

Without warning a stockinged leg appeared out of the darkness, lit by the beam of a torch. I let out a muffled cry of surprise as the creature addressed herself to me. ''Owbout it, love?' she said archly. 'Around the corner for a pound?'

'I'm – I'm not interested,' I squeaked. She must have mistaken me for a man, or more probably a boy, in my trousers and mannish overcoat.

She shone the torch at me and gave a shout of laughter. 'Be orf with ya, lad. Get home to mummy, quick as a wink. There's tigers 'round 'ere, an' we lurk in the shadows.'

I edged my way around her, giving her a wide berth but giggling to myself. Propositioned by one of those women. I wished I could share the story with Pam. What a lark!

Behind me I heard her try again.

''Owbout it love?'

A man muttered something and she shrieked with laughter.

'I throws the little minnows back,' she said. 'I prefer sharks, like you, darlin'. 'Owbout it? Paradise for a pound.' But the shark was not biting. I heard his footsteps behind me as I continued my careful walk along the street.

I found it easier to make my way if I ran my gloved hand along the walls of the buildings. I was managing fairly well until I banged painfully into the side of a surface shelter, at which I let out a word that would have shocked my mother.

A low chuckle sounded just behind me, obviously a man. I froze, trying to melt into the corner between the shelter and the building it adjoined. The light of a torch flashed into my eyes. I closed them, and put up a hand to shield my face. The light disappeared and the torch's owner walked past me without a word. I stood still as his low torchlight disappeared into the darkness. My heart was thumping wildly and I forced myself to calm down. If it was anyone I knew then surely he would have spoken.

Once his footsteps had faded away I edged around the brick obstruction, until I stood in front of a deeper patch of black that was, I thought, the square's central garden. If this was Soho Square, all I had to do now was follow the edges until I found the grand portico of the building I was looking for, although how I'd recognise it in the dark was still a mystery to me. *One thing at a time*, I said to myself. *One thing at a time, Lily.*

Pedestrians pushed past me as I began my groping journey, and one of these assured me that yes, I was in Soho Square. So far so good. I ran my hand along the railings that fronted the buildings and stopped to shine my torch at each entrance.

I was beginning to despair of identifying the building Moray had entered, when the wailing upward notes of the Warning siren rent the darkness like a trapped animal shrieking for help. As always, I shivered to hear it, then I jumped when a familiar screech sounded right behind me. *Surely that is Fripp?* I'd heard enough of her shrieks in the ambulance to recognise them. I stopped dead in my tracks and the woman cannoned into me before pushing away roughly. Thinking quickly, I switched off my torch, stepped back hard against the railings, turned my face away from her. 'Sorry miss,' I said gruffly.

'Never mind,' she muttered, and swung away from me to continue walking. I followed. She carried on for twenty yards or so, and then shone her torch at the building in front of her, revealing the deeply recessed and ornate portico I had been looking for.

I smiled into the darkness. *Thank you, Fripp*, I said silently. I was sure I would have found the building eventually, but she had made it much easier.

Stepping back, down from the white-painted kerb on to the darkness of the road, I watched her torchlight bob down the stairs that led to the basement flat. Two quick raps on a door, a pause and two slow ones. I moved closer to the top of the stairs and peered down. Torchlight flashed on to Fripp's face, the door opened more widely and she went inside. The door closed behind her.

Heavy footsteps were loud on the street behind me. Moray? I stepped back onto the road, and again watched as torchlight played on the portico and then illuminated the stairs to the basement flat. The man slowly descended. Two short raps, a pause and two slow raps. The door opened, torchlight flashed on to a pale face and the man was ushered inside. I watched the charade play out twice more, as a woman and then another man arrived and entered the flat.

I stood there, gazing into the darkness of the stairwell, deliberating on what to do next. I was right about the Soho flat. *Well done, me!* I imagined Jim's surprise when I told him about all this. And then I imagined his response, delivered in an amused tone: 'But you have no evidence as to what they are discussing in that flat. Perhaps it's entirely innocent. A Goethe appreciation society perhaps?'

The drone of bombers' engines and the thunder of guns now filled the darkness. In the distance was the scream and crump of falling bombs. I knew I should run to the surface shelter on the corner but I didn't want to move. Something reprehensible was going on down in that basement, I was sure of it. But what should I do about it?

I dared not go down the stairs and try eavesdropping through the door. Even if I could hear anything over the noise of the air raid, someone could emerge at any time to find me standing there.

According to the pamphlet about what to do if we found out anything suspicious, we were to go at once to the nearest police officer or military officer, with the facts – not surmise, just facts.

But what facts did I have to give? That a woman from my ambulance station who had expressed defeatist and perhaps fascist views was meeting her friends in a flat in Soho? Jim's doubts were likely to be shared by the police. Fripp's father was high up in the War Office, Moray was station officer of the Bloomsbury auxiliary ambulance station. I would need good evidence to convince the authorities that Fripp and Moray were acting against Britain's interests.

I stood there for what seemed an eternity as the raid raged on. The sky roared with the sound of aircraft and guns, and the ground shook with the impact of bombs. To my relief, they were falling some distance away, and the mobile gun unit was not close enough for shrapnel to be a problem.

In my head I kept running through how I could explain my suspicions to the police, but each time I heard Jim's calm, lawyerly voice dismissing them as fantasy. And I wasn't even sure where the nearest police station was.

I was still dithering when the door to the basement flat opened and torchlight shone on the stairs. I hastily stepped back into the darkness of the road as four, maybe five, people emerged. One couple made short goodbyes and disappeared into the night. The other couple lingered.

'Not much to discuss tonight,' said a man's voice. It was not one I recognised. 'I think he wanted us out of there.'

Then the woman spoke, and it was Fripp. 'It's upsetting that Moray thinks we need to stop meeting for a while,' she said.

'We'll lie low, but keep gathering information, like he says,' he replied.

'You don't think . . .' Her voice rose. 'I have a lot to lose if any of this gets out. And my father—'

'Don't worry. Moray's just being cautious.'

'I'll miss our meetings,' said Fripp, now in a coy voice.

'They're not social occasions.' The man's reply was curt. 'I'll be off then. Goodbye.' He walked away into the night.

Fripp stood for a second or two, then flinched at the sound of a falling bomb and scurried off towards the shelter.

Mitchell. The name suddenly came to me. Mr Mitchell was the man who read the book in its original German. That was something. And I knew that the meetings weren't social occasions and that Mr Mitchell and Fripp and Moray were gathering information and Fripp's War Office father was involved. None of that is innocent, Jim. Surely even you would find that suspicious.

As I watched Fripp's torchlight fade into the darkness I came to a decision. I would tell the police about my suspicions. If the meetings were innocent, then Fripp and Mr Mitchell and the others would spend an uncomfortable hour or so being interviewed and they would be released. But if they were indeed fifth columnists – and I felt more strongly than ever that they were – then the authorities needed to know.

*   *   *

I was just turning to walk away when the nightmare began. A hand clamped over my mouth and pulled my head sharply backwards as my arm was twisted painfully behind my back. I tried to kick and twist out of his hold, but my attacker was taller and stronger than me and had me off balance. He dragged me with him down the stairs, and tossed me through the open doorway, where I landed heavily on a bare wooden floor as the door slammed shut. For a moment I lay there, dazed and gasping for breath. A light was switched on and I had to shut my eyes against the sudden brightness. When I opened them, Moray was standing between me and the door.

I pushed myself to my feet and glared at him, which he seemed to find amusing. He moved towards me, and I backed up into a sparsely furnished living room, glancing around as I did so, looking for a way of escape. An open doorway to my left led to a small kitchen. The door to the right was shut. I could see no obvious way out, so I decided upon righteous indignation.

'How dare you?'

Moray gave me his wolfish smile. 'There is nothing I can say that will not sound as if we are in a bad American gangster movie. Try to understand, Lily, I—'

'I understand very well that you're a traitorous Nazi bastard.'

He shrugged, seemingly unconcerned.

'We'll talk later. For now, I must ask you to rest quietly in the bedroom. I am expecting an important guest and it would be very foolish of you to let him become aware that you are here in the flat.' He looked at me and frowned. 'Very foolish indeed. Can I trust you to remain silent? Otherwise I won't hesitate to tie you up and gag you.'

'What are you going to do with me?'

'Absolutely nothing . . . if you promise to keep your mouth shut while my guest is here. If you do not give me your word, then you will be tied up and gagged. I mean that. Will you give me your word that you will keep quiet?'

I nodded. Moray was far too strong for me to tackle on my own. There appeared to be no one else in the flat, and no one had appeared on the street for some time when I was keeping watch. An air raid was in progress, and people were sensibly in shelter. If I screamed, no one would hear me. Moray would probably hit me and then he would gag me and tie me up as he had threatened. I would go along with him for the time being and try to escape while he was with his mysterious guest.

He opened the door to my right, switched on the light, and gestured for me to go inside.

'Remember,' he said lightly. 'Not a word or a sound. It would be difficult to explain your presence and I really don't want to have to try.'

I backed away from him into the room.

'Oh, and by the way, there are bars over the window, so there's no escape that way.'

He pulled the door shut behind me and I heard the sound of a key turning in the lock. For a few seconds I simply stood there with my back to the door, listening to the drone of bombers overhead and the thumping of the guns.

'Idiot,' I whispered. 'Fool to come here without letting anyone know. What on earth am I going to do?'

I had mentioned the flat in Soho to Jim, but I hadn't been specific as to where it was. No one would know where to look for me if I disappeared. Like Levy had disappeared. I tried to swallow, but my mouth was suddenly very dry. Levy. Had he been here too? And suddenly I remembered the thing I had heard, weeks ago, that Fripp said to Moray, it was in the same conversation as her mention of Mitchell. How could it have slipped my mind?

Something like, 'I almost fainted when Sadler mentioned Soho.' Sadler had been saying Levy was blitzed in Soho. And why would she have nearly fainted to hear him say that? Because Levy had been *here*? Had been *killed* here? I felt very cold. Deep in my bones I felt cold. And I knew I was right. I had been a fool not to see the connection before. It was time I began using my brain.

I sat down on the bed and took stock of the room. The bed was under the window, which was small and narrow and high up, and covered by a thick blackout blind. The window was the only possible means of escape. Moray might have been bluffing when he said it was barred. I should check, but how? The bedroom contained a wardrobe, a mirrored dressing table and an iron-framed bedstead. I could pull the bed away from the wall and move the dressing table to rest under the window, then climb up to the window.

My thoughts were thrown into disarray when I heard two short knocks, followed by two long knocks. Moray's guest was arriving. I whirled around to put my ear against the door.

'*Heil Hitler.*' It was a man's voice, low and authoritative.

'*Heil Hitler,*' replied Moray.

CHAPTER THIRTY-TWO

My limbs suddenly felt like cotton wool. My legs gave way and I found myself on the floor, slumped against the door, taking fast, shallow and unsatisfying breaths as my heart thumped painfully. I berated myself, told myself I was stupid, needlessly reckless. How could I have got myself into such a fix? Trapped here while Moray sold out his country, and at his mercy once he had finished his dirty business?

I didn't know whether Moray was a German spy or a British fifth columnist, but he had killed Levy and now he would kill me. Perhaps quite inadvertently, while pursuing other investigations, Levy had discovered that Moray was holding these meetings. Moray had struck him down and then dumped his body in Caroline Place.

'I was right, Jim. I was right all along,' I whispered, but much good it would do me. I had discovered his dirty secret, and now Moray would murder me, just as he had murdered Levy.

Well, I would not give up my life without a fight. Moray would find out that I was tougher than I looked. Growing up in Kookynie had taught me skills I would never have learned in the city. How to deal with snakes and spiders and drunks and amorous drifters. Dad had decided I needed to know how to defend myself when I was twelve, after an encounter with an inebriated swagman who had spent too long on his own. No harm had been done, because Chas Willis, our barman, heard my yelp and was there quickly enough, but my father had made it his job to teach me the dirtiest tricks that an Irish-Australian former goldminer, shearer, roustabout, lumper, cane-cutter, professional boxer now turned pub owner had picked up over the years. My mother never really forgave him.

'Violence should always be a last resort,' Dad had told me. 'Try to run away, or talk your way out of it first. But if you need to fight, there's no point in the Marquis of Queensberry Rules. You're a little thing and any fellow you're up against will have the advantage of height and weight.'

'So what can I do?' I had asked.

'You need to use your brains and you need to be willing to hurt the chap – really hurt him. Gouge his eyes. Grab his groin and twist hard, real hard. Trouble is, most females can't bring themselves to do that.'

My father's advice was to get in quickly with a low, dirty blow to the groin and then run as fast as possible while the attacker was incapacitated. If a quick escape was impossible, then, while the villain was doubled over, hit him on the head, with something weighty enough to render him unconscious, and then escape.

I stood up and carefully examined the room for a weapon.

Perhaps the bed could be dismantled. I managed to unscrew one of the bed knobs but the rest remained solidly in place and parts of it were rusted together. I put the bed knob aside, in case I could find a use for it. Next I examined the wardrobe. It was empty, save for some cheap wooden coat hangers. I took one out and weighed up its usefulness. It might do to poke out an eye.

When I was twelve I had thought I could do anything. At twenty-five I was not so sure. Could I really gouge eyes, hit Moray hard enough to knock him out? Could I kill him? I stared at the coat hanger and tried to imagine thrusting it into his eye.

If it meant that I could live, and unmask Moray as a Nazi, I thought, then I would have to give it a go.

I found big, abstract notions such as freedom and democracy difficult to weigh up, but I had seen in real life how the Nazis had treated men, women and children in Prague. Here in London

I had seen Messerschmitt dive-bombers strafe civilians. Moray had killed Levy, my dear friend, a much better man than Moray. If I had to do it to survive, I thought grimly, I could kill the brute.

I put the coat hanger next to the doorknob.

The only other piece of furniture in the room was the dressing table. I pulled open the drawers. They were empty. I removed the smallest drawer, which was quite heavy. Perhaps I could smash it into Moray's face or groin.

The drawer went next to the other objects on the bed. I sat beside them, waiting for Moray's guest to leave. I would attack the moment Moray came through the door.

For another ten minutes or so I sat listening to the drone of German aircraft punctuated by the thunder of the guns. There was nothing to be heard in the flat. Occasionally the room shook as a bomb fell in the distance. As time passed, the buoyancy that had been generated by my preparations ebbed away. Eventually I sighed.

'You can't do it, Lily,' I said softly to myself.

My father was right. This plan would work only if I was willing to gouge Moray's eyes or attack him like a mad woman. The problem was that, although I was fairly sure I could fight in my own defence, I was not sure I could attack. And I knew that if I tried to attack Moray and failed, it would all be so much worse. Besides, my plan was doomed to failure if Moray came into the room holding a gun or a knife.

I stood up and strode around the room, trying to think of something that would get me out of this mess alive. I stopped my pacing in front of the wardrobe, which stood next to the door. It was a big, solid piece of furniture and it was empty. A new plan presented itself. If I really put my back into it, I could push an empty wardrobe across the door. Moray and his Nazi friend would not hear a thing over the air raid racket.

At the very least, I would buy myself some time.

I put my back against the side of the wardrobe and used my legs to shove it towards the door in a series of jerks. It moved fairly smoothly on the wooden floor and the drone of the bombers and percussion of bombs masked the scraping sounds.

And as I was pushing, a second plan presented itself. Even if the window was barred, as Moray had said, if I moved the bed and pushed the dressing table under the window I could lift the blackout blind. Once the air raid ceased, then people would be on the street. The bright light in the room would be a beacon to any passing ARP Warden. When he ordered Moray to turn out the light, I could scream blue murder and be saved.

With a last jerk, the wardrobe settled into place in front of the door. As I took a moment to exult in how easy it had been, I heard voices. It seemed that Moray's guest was leaving. Two more *Heil Hitlers* were followed by the noise of a door shutting. After a moment Moray knocked on the door.

'Lily,' he said.

I didn't answer.

He turned the key in the lock, and the door banged fruitlessly against the back of the wardrobe.

'What have you done?' His voice was sharply annoyed.

'You can't come in.'

He pushed the door a few times and to my horror, the wardrobe moved slightly. I pushed it back into place.

'Lily, this is not what it seems.'

'Oh? It's not? *Heil Hitler* is the new English greeting, is it?'

Bang. He was putting more effort in now, and the wardrobe shuddered and moved forward slightly. I put my back to it and pushed it firmly against the door.

'I can keep this up all night,' I said.

'So can I,' he replied. 'But all I need to do is take the door off its hinges. A hammer will make short work of the back of the wardrobe, or whatever it is you've put there.'

It was no idle threat. The back of the wardrobe was thin plywood and a hammer would indeed make short work of it.

'I'll remove the blackout blind,' I yelled. 'A warden will come pretty quickly, I'm sure, with the light spilling out on the road.'

He did not reply. In a few moments the room went dark. I realised that he must have removed the fuse.

'Stupid girl,' I muttered. 'Stupid.'

'It's stalemate, Lily,' he said. 'Will you just listen to me? It's not what you think.'

'I heard more than enough when that man arrived. I know what you are, you filthy traitor. I know you killed Levy.'

'I didn't kill Levy,' he said, 'and you have no idea what I am.'

I made no reply. Moray called out my name a few more times but I said nothing. And I heard nothing more.

It was black as pitch in the bedroom. I felt my way to the bed and groped around for my handbag, and in it, my torch. I felt safer, somehow, with its slim light for company, and prayed the battery was good for a while longer. I sat down in front of the wardrobe and rested against it.

'Lily?' Moray was back. 'I'm going to tell you something very secret. Lives depend upon you keeping this secret.'

'I won't believe anything you say,' I said. 'I heard you. Heard you *Heil Hitler*, you Nazi swine.'

'Lily, I'm a British Intelligence agent.'

I laughed out loud. 'Yes, and I'm Mata Hari.' It was not the best retort, but it was the best I could do, and it shut him up.

Time seemed to slow as I waited in the dark by the wardrobe. At one-thirty, by my watch, the All Clear sounded. Not long afterwards Moray knocked on the door.

'Lily?' his voice was a hissing whisper.

'What?'

'I *am* a British agent, and some Intelligence officers will be arriving soon to verify what I'm telling you.'

'As if I'd believe your Nazi mates pretending to be army officers.' But I was beginning to feel confused. Would he be saying all this if he intended to kill me?

'British Military Intelligence set me up as the Gestapo's contact in Britain. My role in the Ambulance Service is simply my cover. I control the activities of Nazi sympathisers in this country. It means we're able to neutralise their threat to the war effort.

'Hah. Nothing you could possibly say will convince me.'

'I thought you might say that. So they're bringing your pilot friend along with them. He knows all about the project.'

CHAPTER THIRTY-THREE

An hour later, Jim was on the other side of the door telling me that Moray was indeed a British Intelligence agent whose mission was of the utmost importance and would I please push the wardrobe out of the way and let us all talk about this like civilised people.

He took a while to convince me.

'You can't think I'm a traitor, Lily.'

'I don't.' Somehow, deep in my bones I knew that Jim was no traitor. 'You may be acting under duress, though.'

His voice thrummed with indignation. 'There is nothing anyone could do to me or threaten me with that would cause me to betray you or my country.'

'But—'

'My commanding officer is here with me, as is Moray's superior. Please open the door, Lily.'

Now I felt sick with thinking that all along Jim had been lying to me. He had known about Moray, and he had lied to me. I pushed the wardrobe away from the door and prepared to face him.

Ten minutes later, Major Whitehead was handing me a cup of tea. He was big and hearty, with a cheerfully lined face and intensely blue eyes. Beside him was a slim man with a small moustache who was dressed in RAF blue and had introduced himself as Wing Commander Maine.

'So Mr Moray had you convinced that he was a bad sort, eh?' said the Major. 'He's convinced a lot of people of that, which is exactly what we need him to do.'

I glanced at Moray, who had been chatting to Jim.

'How did you know I was outside the flat?' I asked him.

'I was behind you when you got onto the Tube train. I thought someone was listening when the ridiculously indiscreet Fripp was talking to me. You left the station like a woman with a mission, and I followed you from Tottenham Court Road. I was on tenterhooks throughout the meeting, expecting you to burst in with a couple of burly policemen. I crept up the stairs behind Fripp and the others, wondering if you were still there. You were, and I acted quickly. I'm very sorry if I hurt you when I dragged you in here.' He threw me a sharp glance. 'But however did you know about this place?'

'I saw you coming in here some weeks ago. I was with a friend, across the square, on our way to a cafe.' I felt my cheeks burn. 'We thought you were going to a brothel.'

He gave a bark of laughter. 'Some of these flats are used for such purposes. After you'd had your run-in with Edna I flashed my torch in your face, just to make sure it really was you and I took advantage of your confusion to get ahead of you and into the flat.'

'Edna?'

He gave me his wolfish grin.

'Oh, *that* woman,' I said, still embarrassed about the incident.

Jim looked at me quizzically.

'I was approached by one of those – those women that hang around in the streets here.'

'What?' He seemed to be repressing laughter. He looked at Moray. 'One of the girls approached Lily?'

Moray laughed. 'Who scuttled away like a frightened rabbit. Edna thought she was just a lad.'

I wanted to thump them both, laughing at my situation. How alone I had been in the bedroom, wondering if I was going to be murdered. From the heat in my face my cheeks must have been beetroot red, but I managed to say, maintaining a last shred of dignity, 'You know that woman's name then?'

'I do not know her professionally, I assure you. But I'm here often enough to have got to know most of the girls.' His smile broadened. 'I'm a happily married man, Lily. My wife's in the country with our three children.'

'And your name's not Jack Moray?'

'Nothing like it.'

I looked at Major Whitehead.

'Mr Moray has made contact with scores of fifth columnists all over Britain,' he said. 'This has been a highly successful strategy for us.'

'Actually, we've been rather shocked by the numbers of people who've approached him wanting to give assistance to the Nazis,' said the major. 'Some have proffered information that would have been very useful indeed to the Germans.'

I felt dizzy. Britain was at war. German bombers had killed thousands of civilians in the Blitz. Our armies were fighting for their lives, and yet there were British citizens willing to assist the Nazis?

'What sort of people would commit treason to help Germany defeat us?' I asked.

'All sorts,' said Moray, 'but I've found it's mainly those who hate Jews. Most of the people I've encountered have never been members of a fascist party, but they hold such extreme anti-Semitic feelings that they think a British victory would mean victory for the Jews. So they give their support to Hitler.'

'But that's madness,' I said. 'What could possibly make them hate Jews so much?'

'I don't know, Lily. There's a long history to anti-Semitism. I can't find a reason really, other than people hate those who are different.'

'And that's why you were so horrible to Levy? To convince us you were anti-Semitic, fascist.' I looked at him. 'You did a good job of it.'

He held my gaze. 'I liked David Levy and I am very sorry about his death.'

'And you had nothing to do with it?'

Moray shook his head in mock bewilderment and looked across at Jim.

'She's like a terrier, isn't she? After a rat.'

I broke in. '*She* needs to know for sure,' I said, annoyed. 'And if the analogy fits . . .'

He looked at me. 'I had absolutely nothing to do with David Levy's death and I have no idea how he ended up in the flat in Caroline Place. I can only presume his death was as the inquest found it. On the night Levy died I was at a meeting here with Fripp and some others.'

'People from the station? Was Ashwin one of them?'

'Ashwin has never approached me with regard to assisting Germany. I can't tell you any more, Lily. You saw Fripp come here tonight, which is unfortunate. I can't give you any more information.'

'But what's going to happen to Fripp? Will she be arrested? Are you just going to let her keep spreading her traitorous information and defeatism?'

'Fripp will be dealt with at the appropriate time, but if you give me away to her, or to anyone else, by even the slightest hint, it could jeopardise the complete operation. You do understand? If you cannot guarantee this, we will have to transfer you out of the station.'

'I understand. I won't say a word.'

Major Whitehead made a gentle throat-clearing noise. I looked at him.

'We need you to sign some documents, Miss Brennan.'

I signed all the documents Major Whitehead put in front of me. And in so doing I gave my binding word to take the secrets I had learned that night to my grave, or risk imprisonment or worse.

The five of us climbed the steps and stood together in a dark and silent London. It was around three o'clock and thick clouds formed a cloak over the city. The raiders had disappeared.

'Don't come to work today,' said Moray. 'I'll find cover for you.' He said goodbye and walked off briskly along the street.

Major Whitehead led the rest of us around the corner, where a large saloon was parked with a driver from the women's army service at the wheel. Jim gave her my address and she drove us to Bloomsbury through the usual maze of detours.

'Not much damage here tonight,' said the major, twisting around to address us from the front seat.

The wing commander snorted softly. 'They tend to become a trifle lost when there's thick cloud cover like this. I expect we'll find that the outer suburbs have had a rough time of it.'

Jim saw me to my door.

'Do you want me to stay?' he asked.

I shook my head. I was still angry about all his lies and I found it hard to speak to him.

'I couldn't tell you anything. Lily, you must understand that.'

'But you lied to me. I accepted everything you said, because I never thought you would lie to me.' I understood why he had done so, but I was not sure how we could move on.

'Lily, I had no choice.'

I opened the door and went inside, feeling lost and very alone.

Katherine sat down with me at lunch in the service restaurant, later that day.

'I'm on night shift,' she said, yawning. 'Why are you here? I thought you were on days this week.'

I shrugged. 'Took the day off. I needed a break'

She nodded sympathetically. 'It's been a rough few weeks for you.'

How easily I had lied to her. What else could I do? I had signed the forms which compelled me to lie. Katherine had believed me because she assumed I would never lie to her. Jim had had no choice either, so why was I so upset about it?

'You seem rather down in the dumps,' she said. 'Man trouble?'

I shrugged.

'Well he's a darling, and he's crazy about you. Has something happened? Some old girlfriend crept out of the woodwork? Some reason why he can't make an honest woman out of you?'

'No, nothing like that.'

'You like him, don't you?'

'Yes,' I sighed.

'For goodness' sake, Lily, what's the matter? This is like pulling teeth. Tell me, truly, do you think he's going to propose?'

'That's the problem, Katherine, I think that is exactly what he is going to do.'

'Marry the man, Lily, and get on with your lives together. If you love him, take the leap.'

'I do love him, but I can't.'

'Yes you can, silly. Marriage is the usual outcome. Why wouldn't you?'

'He's too posh for me.'

'What *is* his title?' she asked. 'You've never said.'

'I don't know. He won't talk about it.'

She threw me a considering look. 'You'd be mad to let him go.'

'But I want to go home to Australia after the war. I don't want to live in England.'

'He's a barrister, isn't he?'

'Yes.'

'Then he can do his barristering just as well in Australia, can't he? He wasn't born in this country. His mother lives in France, you said. It seems that his ties to Britain are slight. I suspect he'd be happy to leave if you don't want to stay here.'

'He said he would leave. Said he'd go to Australia.'

'Then what's stopping you?'

I couldn't tell her. I knew exactly what was stopping me. It was fear. Everybody insisted I was so brave, but I feared saying yes to a man who might despise my background, look down on my family when he met them. I feared discovering things about him I might not like. I feared tempting fate in wartime

302

by committing myself to a future with Jim, and I feared ending up like Betty Wilkinson, who had married in the firm belief that a bright future lay ahead. Fate had struck her down. I was afraid of fate. My fears were childish and silly, I knew that, but they were also almost overwhelming. I couldn't tell Katherine all this.

'I'd rather keep things as they are,' I said lamely. 'Jim won't push me, I'm sure he won't.'

At the ambulance station the following morning I felt an almost complete sense of disconnection from the people around me. Moray sent me out with Celia to ferry supplies between hospitals and transfer patients. It was mindless duty and I spent the time brooding on what I had learned of the world around me, of the British, even of Jim. Everything felt dirty, as if I had indeed been infected by the kind of defeatism Fripp peddled. *What are we fighting for?* I wondered. *What did Levy die for?*

As we were returning to the station, Celia said, 'If you're staying in this evening, I'll bring you that bottle of perfume.'

'That's very kind of you, but really there's no need.'

'I'd like to. Say nine o'clock?'

I shrugged.

We entered the common room to the sound of Powell blathering on with her usual nonsense.

'I swear it's all absolutely true. It's called the Eagle's Nest because it's on top of a mountain. It's a glass-sided building and there's nothing in it but a huge telescope. Hitler sits alone there and gazes out over the world and sky, plotting what he's going to do.'

Like Lucifer in 'Paradise Lost', I thought, as I sat down next to Armstrong. I murmured, 'Here matter new to gaze the Devil met Undazzled; far and wide his eye commands.'

Did Hitler watch Powell through his telescope, I wondered, spouting nonsense about him here in London?

Armstrong gave me a suspicious look. I smiled at him and he looked away, blushing. The boy seemed harmless enough, but he had disliked Levy. Could he . . .

As Powell continued speaking I had a sudden fearful thought. How did she know so much about Hitler? She might seem to be a fluffy-haired woman with little brain, but who knew what she got up to in her spare time. Was anything as it seemed? Was anyone?

'And he has a special astrologer,' she droned on, 'who's like a German Rasputin. He mixes a special red elixir of life and he drinks it every day, to keep young.'

Who drinks the stuff, I wondered, Hitler or the German Rasputin? Powell really did need to take more trouble with her pronouns. I laughed to myself. Powell was no fifth columnist; I'd stake my life on it.

Obviously pleased with the attention she was commanding, Powell continued her story. 'They watch the stars together, and the astrologer plots out what Hitler should—'

Celia's clear voice cut through Powell's chatter.

'All of that tripe comes from a book called *I was Hitler's Maid*. Complete rubbish. Honestly, Powell, you do say the silliest things. Hitler is no Satan, or mystic or fairy-tale monster. He's a common megalomaniac whom the German people were stupid enough to put into a position of too much power.'

Powell sniffed, but it shut her up. Fripp threw Celia a frown, but Celia soon stared her down.

I looked at Fripp. Here was a woman who was quite ready to sell out her country, who had flirted with the man who 'read the book in its original German'. I itched to slap her. My thoughts wandered into a reverie of Fripp being publicly humiliated for her traitorous intent, paraded through London on her way to incarceration in the Tower along with Celia's wretched husband, as jeering Blitz victims pelted her with rotten fruit . . .

'Brennan.' Moray's voice interrupted my thoughts.

He was leaning through the doorway to the office looking at me. 'Brennan. In here now, please.'

I walked into the office. He asked me to shut the door and sit down.

'You can't look at Fripp like that,' he said.

'Like what?'

'As if you want to see her hung, drawn and quartered. People are noticing.'

'Sorry.'

'And you were staring at the others in the common room as if they were all a bunch of potential fifth columnists.'

I squirmed in my chair.

'Brennan, your expressive face is part of your charm.' He paused and started again. 'That's why I insisted that Vassilikov be under orders to reveal nothing to you about my mission.'

I wanted to speak, but he went on, 'I also suggested he try to dissuade you from further investigation.' Moray gave a quick laugh. 'Silly of me, in hindsight. I should have realised that nothing would stop you investigating Levy's death, and it was fairly clear that you suspected me.'

I didn't say anything for a while, then, 'I suppose I wanted it to be you, or Sadler, or anyone really. That would have meant that Levy's death was more than one of countless utterly pointless Blitz deaths.'

'You loved him very much.'

I began to remonstrate as I always did, but stopped at the look in his eyes.

'Yes,' I admitted. 'I loved him very much. But not in the way people think. David Levy was my dear friend and a wonderful man and he deserved better than a lonely death in a bombed building.'

How odd it was to be sharing such confidences with Moray. He was silent for a beat or two, watching me. Then he looked down at his messy desk. 'Lily, you won't like this but I really think you need to be transferred to another station. Do you have any preference as to which?'

'Please don't do that.'

He looked up. 'The endeavour I'm engaged in is too important to take account of your feelings. I can't risk you giving anything away. I'm sorry.'

'Am I really that transparent?'

'I can't take the risk. If Fripp leaves this station then you can return, but I can't have you working with her.'

'May I go to Berkeley Square, then? My friend Katherine is a deputy station officer there.'

'Done,' said Moray, and he smiled at me.

I began to pick at my nails. They were filthy and the cuticles were cracked.

'Ashwin says I have no future with Jim,' I said, 'because I can't hide what I feel. Apparently those in her class are able to do that.'

'The upper class in this country is trained into that from childhood. It allows them to forge and command empires, poor sods.'

'It's your class, too.'

Moray shook his head. 'I'm a grammar school boy; I didn't attend a public school.' I must have looked quizzical, because he added. 'The fact that I went to a good grammar school may impress some people in this country, but it certainly does not impress those in Ashwin's class.'

'Oh, I see what you mean,' I said slowly. 'I went to a private school in Perth, which means I'm considered posh by a lot of people at home. But I was a boarder from the country and the daughter of a publican to boot. The girls from the old Perth families looked down on country boarders and especially looked down on me.'

'And I thought there was no class system in Australia.'

'It's nothing like it is here.'

'I have a feeling that things will change in this country once we've won the war. I think the old British class system is in for a battering.'

'That's what Jim thinks, but Ashwin says it's still very rigid and I'll never fit in.'

'I'll tell you straight that you'll never fit in if you *try* to fit in. Just be yourself, Lily. The people who are worth knowing will respect you for it.' He looked at me keenly. 'Don't ever be ashamed of who you are or where you come from. Then they really will despise you.'

'I'm not! And I never will be. Besides, I don't intend to remain in England once the war is over. Australia is my home.' I stood to leave the office.

'Just a minute, Lily.'

I looked at him, but he seemed strangely reluctant to speak. He frowned at his desk and then looked up at me.

'My skill, if you want to call it that, is to be able to pick the people who are willing to turn hate into action. I knew from the first time I met Fripp that her hatred of Jews ran so deep that she would take risks to help Germany win this war.'

'What about Sadler?'

He replied firmly, 'Sadler is a petty criminal with an eye on the main chance, but he would never actively work against Britain. He thinks he has something over me, because he knows I'm often in Soho. His remarks to you about Soho on the night Levy was missing were a warning to me.'

'A warning?'

'He thinks I'm running a prostitution racket and he's been attempting to blackmail me.'

I could not help laughing. Moray did not laugh with me.

'What are you going to do about it?'

'It won't be long before Sadler finds himself conscripted into a job he really won't enjoy.' Moray looked hard at me. 'If it helps, I can tell you that the only one from this station who is in my group is Fripp.'

307

It did help to know that.

'Stick with your pilot, Lily. He's a good man. Ignore Ashwin.'

'I'll try. But she knows Jim's world much better than I do.'

'Ashwin only sees what she wants to.'

'She's frightfully brave, but she does take stupid risks.'

Moray leaned forward across the desk to stare into my eyes. 'It's easy to get the wrong impression of people, and because of that, to misinterpret what they do and why they do it.' He gave a quick laugh. 'For a while I thought that Levy might be queer.'

'What?'

'He showed no interest in you or Maisie Halliday, except as friends, and you're both very attractive women. He also ignored Ashwin completely whenever she was in the room. Never looked at her. Ashwin is gorgeous. Although Levy may have disliked her because she was married to that fascist, no man who was interested in women could ignore Ashwin so completely as he seemed to do.'

'I really don't think that Levy . . .' And yet, it had always surprised me how uninterested Levy had seemed in me or Maisie or Ashwin or any woman really.

Moray went on as if I'd not spoken. 'Only, one evening I caught Levy watching Ashwin surreptitiously. And he was watching her in a way that made it clear he was not homosexual, if you get my meaning.'

I stared at him, unsure what he was trying to tell me.

'And Ashwin,' he continued, 'would never look at Levy. Now that might be because he was Jewish, but it's telling that her risk-taking coincided with Levy's disappearance. It began just after he went missing.'

Now I was utterly confused. 'What do you mean?'

'What I mean is, if you want to know what happened to Levy, perhaps you should talk to Ashwin.'

CHAPTER THIRTY-FOUR

'What do you think he meant?' I asked, after I had settled Jim on to my couch with his brandy. He had come at my request and I had treated him to a mediocre dinner in the service restaurant. Now we were waiting for Celia to arrive with the perfume. I wanted him with me when I asked her about Levy. He had agreed to ask the questions if I felt it was too much for me.

'He meant exactly what he said. Simply that you should talk to Celia.'

'But do you know what he was getting at? Was he saying that Celia killed Levy?'

'You know perfectly well he did not say that, Lily.'

'Not in so many words, but he was awfully enigmatic. Jim, do you know something about this? About Levy's death, I mean. Is there something you're holding back?'

He looked up, and held my gaze. 'I swear I know nothing about David's death. I did lie to you about Moray, but that was because I was ordered to do so. I hated lying to you, but there was nothing else I could do.'

I opened my mouth to say – what? – but he stalled me, saying, 'I hate lying, especially to you. But I can't promise not to lie if it is crucial to my intelligence work.'

I stared at him, wondering how to respond. How could I remain angry when we were at war and he was involved in secret and possibly dangerous work? Work that was often based on lies.

'I can accept the need to keep your duties secret,' I said eventually, 'but no other lies.'

He reached out for my hand and squeezed it. 'No other lies. Ever. You have my word.'

I nodded, accepting his promise.

He released my hand and sat back in his chair. 'For what it's worth, and it's only a guess, I'm fairly sure I know what Celia will say. I think what we have here is a tragedy, not a murder.'

I jumped at the knock at the door and I went to open it. Celia was standing there, holding the bottle of perfume.

'Please come in,' I said. I meant a polite request, but it came out like an order. 'If you don't mind,' I added limply. 'Jim's here. We – we'd like to talk to you.'

The light faded from her eyes. She held out the small bottle. I took it from her and she entered without a word.

'Would you like a glass of brandy?' I asked.

'Why not?' she replied. She swallowed it in a single gulp, as if it were medicine, and it brought some colour into her white face. She held out the glass for a refill and I poured some more of Lady Anne's brandy into it.

'This is good stuff,' she said, taking a sip. 'Fire away. Isn't that what they say in the American movies? As if one were facing a firing squad.'

Jim seemed rather to admire her insouciance. He smiled a little, then sighed. 'Celia, it's clear that you've guessed what we want to know. Why don't you tell us what happened that night?'

She raised an eyebrow. 'The night David died?'

'Yes.'

'Unburden myself? Admit my guilt?'

'Is there any guilt?' I said, startled.

She took another sip of brandy and then looked up into my eyes.

'Oh, yes,' she said. 'There's guilt. It began with kindness. David Levy was kind to me. In the end it killed him.'

I stared at her, my heart thumping.

'Would you care to explain, Celia?' Jim's voice was soft, but somehow as probing as a lancet.

She glanced at him and then looked at me.

'How was he when he was with a patient?' she asked me.

'Very gentle,' I replied. 'Sweet.'

She laughed, but there were tears in her eyes. 'You saw the other side to the obnoxious man he could be in the station.'

'Yes,' I agreed. 'He didn't like many of you very much. So he didn't show you what a funny, intelligent and caring man he really was.'

She shook her head. When she spoke it was in a level, rather monotonous tone.

'I came off my bike when I was cycling home one evening. The Warning had just sounded and I was going too fast. David saw it happen and came over to offer me help. I had sprained my ankle.' She looked up at me. 'Do you remember?'

I nodded, and glanced at Jim. 'She came to work on a crutch with the ankle bandaged. It was not long after the Blitz started in early September.'

Celia put down the brandy and spoke again in that low, dreary voice. 'He helped me over to the side of the road, dealt with my bike, and palpated my ankle to see what the trouble was. We had just agreed that the ankle was probably sprained when the guns started up and all at once the raiders were overhead.

'The Blitz had only been going for a couple of days. We had seen what the bombs could do and we knew the danger of being caught in the open in a raid. I began to cry, which I never do. I can only suppose it was because my ankle was hurting like hell and I couldn't get up and run away on it. And also because the planes were so loud and bombs were dropping close by. And he – and David had been so very kind, which I had not expected.'

She was holding her hands in fists and her nails were digging into her palms. When she released them I saw spots of blood welling.

'Celia – your hands.'

She glanced down at her hands. 'Pain helps,' she said, dismissively. 'It makes me feel something.'

311

Perhaps my horrified pity showed in my face, because she raised one shoulder in a shrug and said, 'It's proof.'

'Proof of what?' asked Jim.

'That I've not really been dead these last weeks.' Her voice was now musing, reflective. 'If I can still bleed, I must be alive.' She made a sound of contempt.

'What happened, Celia?' There was no sympathy in Jim's voice.

'Let me tell it my way. This is my confession and I'll tell it as I will.'

'Tell it then,' he said.

'The raid had started in earnest so David put me on my bicycle and he wheeled me to a public shelter as I perched on the saddle. It was a nightmare. Bombs were falling close by, screaming as they fell. David was calm, kind. Protective of me.' She closed her eyes. 'Guiding me through hell.' She opened her eyes. 'I need a cigarette.'

Jim shrugged. 'I don't have any.'

When she glanced at me I said, 'I don't smoke.'

She shuddered. 'I need a cigarette,' she repeated.

'Sorry Celia,' said Jim. 'Just tell us what happened.'

She drew a long breath, as if she were inhaling smoke. When she exhaled she seemed calmer. 'When we reached the shelter he carried me inside and stayed with me throughout the raid.' Her mouth twisted into a tight smile. 'I saw how the women in that shelter looked at him, which surprised me. You see, I'd put him into a compartment – Jew – and I'd never really looked at him before. I'd worked with the man for months, and I'd never bothered to look at him properly.'

The smile morphed into an expression of distaste. 'I'm – I hate what I am.'

Her voice faded into silence.

'What happened, Celia?' Jim's voice was calm, expressionless.

'Everything changed, once I really looked at him . . .' She glanced up at me again, and said quickly, almost fiercely, 'And he looked at me, and it was as if everyone else had faded away and only he and I existed in the world.' She laughed a little, mirthlessly. 'It sounds so very . . . trite, when you put it into words, but that's how it started.'

'What?'

'Our affair. Our version of *Romeo and Juliet*. Our madness. David's death.'

'Where did you go to be together?' asked Jim. 'To carry on this affair.'

She looked up at him with contempt. 'Where do you damn well think?'

'The flat.'

'It belongs to a friend who scuttled away to Canada for the duration. I had a key from before the war that I had somehow never returned. It was close to the ambulance station, but far enough away to be safe.'

'Safe?'

Celia looked at Jim and her lip rose in a sneer. 'I'm married to a well-known fascist. David is – was – Jewish. Neither of us wanted to be found out. He insisted on secrecy just as much as I did, for the sake of his parents.' Her voice became softer. 'Neither of us could really believe what had happened.'

'Couldn't believe that you'd fallen in love?' Jim was looking at her intently and Celia's face became flushed.

'I suppose love is a word for it,' she said. 'It wasn't entirely lust, anyway. We laughed a great deal, talked about all sorts of things. I – I craved him. He said he felt the same.' She looked at me, a query in her eyes. 'Is that love, do you think?'

'Yes,' I said. 'I think it is.'

'You must have known it couldn't be kept secret forever,' said Jim.

She raised her shoulder and grimaced. 'We were living one day at a time. We were together just over nine weeks. That has to do for a lifetime.'

She sat in silence for a moment.

'What happened, Celia?' Jim asked.

Again she seemed to withdraw into her memories. A shudder began at her shoulders and swept through her. When she looked at me, for the first time since I had met her I saw real emotion in her expression. It wasn't pleasant. It was horror.

'David was epileptic,' she said to me. 'Did you know that?'

'Yes. That's why they refused him in the armed services, and why he couldn't drive the ambulance.'

'He told me about it early on, but I found it hard to believe. He seemed so – vibrant.' Again she paused, and took a deep breath as if she couldn't get enough air into her lungs.

'He had some sort of a fit,' she said softly. 'That night. When he fell, his head struck the side of a small table. There was blood on the back of his head. I waited with him until the convulsions had ceased and he was in a deep sleep. I checked his breathing—'

'Was it stertorous?' My words were like a sharp bark. 'How bad was the head injury? Was he clammy to touch? Did you check his pulse?'

She ignored me.

'He seemed to be sleeping peacefully. I washed away the blood, put a pillow under his head, covered him with a blanket and I left.'

'You left him there on the floor?' I was horrified, and then angry. 'You left him?' I repeated, in a colder voice.

'I left him lying on the floor with a pillow under his head, covered by a blanket. I was already late for an important family engagement that I couldn't miss without difficult explanations I was unwilling to make.'

I stared at her. 'How could you do that? How could you just leave him there? If you'd stayed then perhaps . . .'

She made an expression of distaste. 'Look at you, Lily Brennan, staring at me with those big brown eyes and passing judgment in that way you do. Always so willing to judge, aren't you?'

'Oh, yes,' I said. 'I'm so very middle class. I have feelings and—'

'Lily,' said Jim sharply. I looked at him and he was shaking his head at me.

It was as if cold water had been thrown on to me. I sat for a second or two, furious that he should defend the woman who had left Levy to die alone. I looked up to glare at him, but he shook his head again and glanced at Celia.

I followed his gaze. Celia was sitting on her chair in a pose of utter rigidity; her long neck was all ropey sinews, and her jaw clenched so tightly that her lips were pulled back almost in a snarl. When she spoke her voice was high and strained.

'I had a family gathering that I had to attend and for which I was already late. David was aware that I had to rush off after – after our meeting. He had told me when we first – he told me that if he ever had a fit I should leave him to regain consciousness alone.'

'Was that the last time you saw him?' asked Jim. There was a stiff, impassive expression on his face.

The barrister is at work, I thought, cross-examining. His manner was coolly detached. No emotion allowed in a courtroom.

'No,' said Celia. 'I returned later that night, some time after midnight. David had told me that he would sometimes sleep for hours after a grand mal fit and I wanted to make sure that he was well.'

'What did you find?'

'He was stone cold. You know how it takes some of them, as if they're just asleep. He looked as if he was asleep, but he was dead. I felt for his pulse, shook him, tried to breath air into his lungs. None of it worked. Eventually I just sat back and looked at him. I couldn't believe it. It was a nightmare, but it was real.'

Although she stared at Jim, it was clear that she was seeing another scene. She seemed to squint, as if looking at something that pained her.

'He was so beautiful, as if he was sleeping peacefully. I found myself holding his cold hand and repeating, over and over, *Please just wake up, Please just wake up, Please . . .'*

And, at last, the dam broke. She covered her face with her hands to hide the cataract of tears as gasping sobs racked her body. Celia's hands were white, long fingered. Beautiful hands. Only, in our line of work we couldn't keep our nails looking pretty. Her nails were short and faintly lined with grime and her cuticles were as cracked as mine were.

Her sobs slowed, and eventually ceased. She pulled out a handkerchief and mopped her eyes and face.

'I am so very sorry,' she said. She looked up at me. 'I left him there, to die alone.'

Jim reached over and touched her shoulder and she turned her head to look at him.

'I was at the inquest, Celia. I heard the pathologist's evidence. The blow to his head when he fell caused his death. There was a massive internal bleed. You couldn't have saved him.'

'I left him to die alone. That's why Lily looks at me with such loathing. She's right to do so.'

Her eyes were red and swollen and there was a world of misery in them, but she sat up straight, shoulders back, chin up to face full-on whatever was set against her. It was her only defence, I thought. It was her carapace, her armour against the judgment of people like me, but it could not protect her from her own sense of guilt.

I leaned towards her, as Jim had done, and she flinched slightly as I took hold of her hand.

'I don't loathe you,' I said.

She clutched my hand in a hard, convulsive movement and stared into my eyes.

'The raiders came over when I was there with him,' she said. 'I couldn't leave him again, so I stayed beside him, despite the bombs. When the place came down on us I hoped that I'd die, too. I hoped we'd be found together, both dead, and damn the consequences.'

I imagined the scene as the raiders roared in low, the screaming swish of the falling bombs and the terror of the explosions. I wondered if Celia had been knocked unconscious for a moment before waking to the awful realisation that she had survived and Levy was still lying dead beside her.

'Why didn't you tell anyone where he was?' I asked. 'I mean, tell them earlier than you did?'

She let go of my hand to sit up in her chair. Her back was straight and eyes held mine steadily. 'When I realised that I was alive and – shockingly – unharmed, I thought it would be best to leave David to be found by the rescue crew. I thought they would find him quickly and his parents would be spared the scandal of him having been with me – Cedric Ashwin's wife – when he died.'

'But two weeks went by,' I said. 'I don't see how you could leave him there for so long.'

At this she seemed to deflate. Her shoulders drooped and her hair fell across her face as she stared down at the floor.

'When there was a second bombing raid on the flat a week later and still no one found him, I thought that it was a sign that he should remain buried there. I suppose I wasn't thinking clearly. It was when you told me about his mother that the fog cleared. I realised then that she deserved – that she should have a body to bury. So I telephoned the police.'

Celia took a breath, pushed her hair back from her face and sat up straight in her chair. She looked at Jim.

'What now?'

'The coroner's jury found his death was due to misadventure caused by enemy action,' said Jim slowly. 'From what you've told us, although death by accident is probably more appropriate, death by misadventure is an entirely proper verdict in the circumstances. I see no purpose in telling the police any of this.'

Celia stood and began to pace the room, much as Mr Levy had done when Jim and I visited him at the Dorchester.

'I was eighteen when I married Cedric,' she said. 'A half-formed creature, who accepted without question the views I had heard expressed around me all my life. It was this war, my work in the Ambulance Service, David . . .'

She stopped in front of my bookcase to stare down at the books. Her hand brushed gently over my books. 'Would you believe that David and I discussed books? We talked of books, so many things. He thought there was more to me than . . .'

She pulled her shoulders back and raised her chin, stood tall and proud. 'I wrote to Cedric. I told him that I would be seeking a divorce, because I no longer accept any of the beliefs he holds. I told him I would swear to my adultery.'

The agitated pacing began again, punctuated by abrupt remarks. 'He wrote back, says he won't divorce me. I don't know what to do. I can't go back to him.'

I drew in a shaky breath.

'Levy's parents, do you think . . .' I began.

She turned and came to stand in front of me. Her eyes were red and puffy, but her face was otherwise composed.

'You wonder if I should tell David's parents what really happened?'

I gave a slight shrug. 'I don't know. I think if I were them I would like to know the truth. But maybe it would simply upset them to no purpose.'

We both glanced at Jim, who seemed troubled. 'Celia,' he said, 'I really don't think that you need—'

'Oh, I think I probably do need,' she snapped. 'We all know that confession benefits the confessor more than the one to whom the awful truth is divulged. The question is, will it help them to know?'

I said, slowly, 'I couldn't sleep some nights, thinking of Levy's horror at being caught in a raid. I'm relieved to know that he didn't suffer.'

She looked away, towards the bookcase. 'And you think that Mrs Levy would find relief in that as well?'

'I think she might,' I said.

The following day Jim took Celia Ashwin to visit Mr and Mrs Levy in their suite at the Dorchester. He then withdrew. All he could tell me when we met at his flat that evening was that Celia had stayed an hour with them and when she emerged it was clear that she had been crying.

'But how did she seem?' I asked.

'Reserved as ever. Not desperate or unhappy, though.'

'And the Levys?'

'They thanked me.'

'And that's all you're going to tell me?'

'It's all I can tell you. I think it went as well as it could.'

CHAPTER THIRTY-FIVE

I left the Bloomsbury auxiliary ambulance station the week after my attempts at spy-catching had come to such an ignominious conclusion. As I had requested, Moray arranged for me to join the Berkeley Square depot, which was one of four big posts in the London area and where Katherine was a deputy. It was very different from the little Bloomsbury station. Nearly two hundred people worked from Berkeley Square, including members of rescue and first aid squads.

The atmosphere at the station was jolly and the personnel were as diverse as they had been at Bloomsbury, with Oxford and Cambridge graduates, artists, actors, typists, peeresses, shop girls and a man who used to run one of the smartest hairdressing salons in London.

The station officer had worked for Cook's tours before the war; he knew even more than Levy had about the topography of London and loved to tell stories about the city.

Staff at Berkeley Square were expected to work twenty-four hour shifts on alternate days. Bunks were provided so we could catch up on sleep during quiet times, and food was available at any hour.

'Settling in?' Katherine joined me for lunch in the depot's canteen a week or so after I had started there.

'Actually, yes. I'm settling in better than I had hoped. I like Nella Flintcroft very much, by the way.' Flintcroft was my new ambulance attendant, a chirpy twenty-three-year-old from Birmingham. Like me, she had been a teacher in peace-time.

'Good. I thought you'd like Flintcroft. She's brand new to the work and you can teach her the ropes. And how's that sexy pilot of yours?'

'Still around.' I smiled. 'And still sexy. We're off to dinner at the Ritz tomorrow night.'

Katherine laughed. 'It's become rather a joke, this dinner at the Ritz he keeps promising you. You've not made it yet.'

'I have high hopes for tomorrow,' I said. 'We'll be among the angels dining at the Ritz. Just like in the song.'

She laughed. 'And nightingales will sing in Berkeley Square. Tell you what, I'll lend you my blue velvet evening gown. It's miles too long for you, but I'll tack it up and I promise it's grand enough for the Ritz.'

I met Maisie for lunch the following day.

'It's not nearly so much fun now you've left the station,' she said. 'I'm paired with Ashwin now.'

I had not seen Celia since she revealed the truth about herself and Levy, and I wondered if she was avoiding me.

'I can't say I like Ashwin much,' said Maisie. 'I think she's a very hard woman.'

'She doesn't give much away,' I said, 'but she's not hard.'

Maisie grimaced. 'I'm sorry. That was unkind of me. Ashwin can't help being so posh.'

'Give it time,' I said. 'She's actually rather nice when you get to know her.'

Maisie's look was frankly disbelieving, and I changed the subject.

After lunch I went to the hairdresser, where I paid more than I could afford to have my hair washed and styled and my nails manicured. I wanted to look my best for dinner at the Ritz.

I emerged from my bedroom wearing my best silk slip. I was also wearing coral lipstick, lashings of mascara and a touch of Pam's blue eyeshadow.

Katherine and Pam glanced up from where they were sitting cross-legged on my rug, tacking up the hem of Katherine's evening gown by a good six inches. Katherine bit off the thread she'd been using and stood up to shake out the thick velvet skirt. I well knew that to be lent her velvet evening gown was a singular honour. It was a beautiful gown, sapphire-blue with a daringly low décolletage, straight elbow-length sleeves and a flowing skirt decorated with silver cut-out embroidery. There was silver embroidery also on the sleeves. With the girls' help I eased myself into the gown and Katherine buttoned up the back.

'How do I look?' I gave a twirl and enjoyed the sensation of velvet swishing about my legs.

'About sixteen,' said Katherine.

I poked out my tongue at her.

'I take it back,' she said. 'Closer to twelve.'

Pam glanced at her watch, and jumped up with a squeal. 'Golly, I'd better get a move on. I'm on duty tonight with Betty.'

'How is she?' I asked. 'I've not seen her for weeks.'

'She's much better. I think all she needed was to feel needed. She's marvellous in the shelter, especially with the children.' She laughed, somewhat sheepishly. 'I'm simply not a motherly type. They give me the willies, those children, with all their noise and neediness and always runny noses. I hand them over to Betty and she seems to enjoy it. Everyone's happy.'

'I hear it's different with your own,' I said.

'Gosh, I hope so,' said Pam.

'Don't you need to be at the shelter?' I said.

'Tell me all about it tomorrow,' she said, and ran out of my flat, slamming the door behind her.

Katherine came over and adjusted the fit of the gown. I felt like I had just acquired a fairy godmother.

To my delight, when I arrived at his flat and removed my coat, Jim actually blushed. I took it as a compliment. He made me a cocktail and we chatted about my day, but he seemed preoccupied.

'Jim, is something the matter?' I asked.

He held out his hand and when I came across to him, he pulled me down to sit next to him on the couch.

'Lily,' said Jim. 'Let's get married.'

He was pale but his gaze was steady and his face very serious.

'Oh Jim, I don't know,' I said, and he winced. 'It still seems so early, there's so much we don't know about each other, about what will happen in the war.'

His eyes became shadowed, and his jaw tightened. 'You became engaged to that naval lieutenant after knowing him only a few weeks.'

I shook my head. 'Exactly. And that was a mistake. I was naive then, immature. I didn't know him at all.'

'It was only a year ago, Lily, and you do know me.'

'It was a *hundred* years ago. It was before the Blitz. We're both all keyed up about the war and Levy's death. Either of us could be killed or wounded; anything could happen. This is no time to make such huge decisions.'

He shook his head. 'Marry me, Lily, and we can chance it together. I won't ask you to stay here. I'm happy to come to Australia after the war, make our home there.'

I was running out of arguments. There remained the question that most haunted me. I had to ask it.

'Why do you want to marry me, Jim?'

'I want to marry you because I love you. I want to share all my life with you, not just the days and nights you can spare me. I want to have a family with you.'

'We're like Ashwin and Levy,' I said, hesitantly, though my heart exulted to hear him say he loved me. 'Celia and David loved each other, but they knew it would never work. It's like that with us. We're just too different.'

'That's not true. How can you think such nonsense?'

'It's not just me. Celia told me that you and I have no future because we're like fish and fowl. She should know.'

He seemed to consider this. 'I suppose I'm the fowl.'

'What? Why would you say that?'

He touched his nose. 'This bally thing. It's always described as hawkish or beaky.'

I laughed without thinking, and felt better for it. 'So that makes me the cold fish?'

He smiled. 'Never that.'

'I need time.'

'Of course. But, just tell me . . .' He looked away and said, lightly, as if the answer was of no consequence. 'Do you love me?'

'Yes,' I said. He looked at me then, held my gaze steadily, smiling. 'Yes,' I repeated. 'I love you.'

The sky was clear with a few small clouds and the moon was a bright crescent in the western sky. The moon, together with the bluish 'star-light' of the filtered street-lamps, illuminated our way as we walked along Riding House Street. An air raid was in progress, and the planes were loud overhead, but no bombs seemed to be dropping in our area.

We were hoping to find a taxi near Broadcasting House. It was a chilly night, and I had belted my heavy coat over Katherine's gown for warmth. Our breath puffed white before us with each exhalation.

The walls of All Souls Church loomed, and I ran my gloved hand along the dressed stone. Jim's torchlight had just picked out the chipped stone steps of the church's semi-circular portico when we both flinched at the shrieking, whistling noise of a large bomb falling. I instinctively crouched down as protection against blast. Jim crouched beside me, his arms around my shoulders. *This is it*, I thought. *This is death.*

The noise filled the air for a few seconds and then abruptly ceased, as if it had been cut off in mid-air. I leaned into Jim, my heart thumping wildly, but the explosion I expected did not come.

After a few seconds came the sound of something clattering along a roof in the square ahead. The Germans usually dropped incendiary bombs to 'light up' the raid, and I assumed it was the canisters of phosphorus hitting the roof of Broadcasting House.

'Incendiaries,' I said. 'We may be able to assist in dealing with them.'

We walked on closer to the square and I waited for the little bombs to hit the road, but there was nothing to be heard.

'That's odd,' I said, peering at the dark bulk of the BBC building across the square. 'It certainly sounded like incendiaries, but where are they?'

I stepped back and Jim's arms folded around me.

'Can't see any taxis,' he murmured into my hair. 'We could walk down to Regent Street.'

'It's strange that there are no incendiaries,' I repeated uneasily, over the low roar of the bombers. He didn't seem to realise how odd this all was. What had happened to the bomb we heard falling?

Footsteps sounded behind us.

'What's all this then?'

We swung around to see a policeman walking towards us. The moonlight illuminated the white 'P' on his steel hat.

'I don't know what's going on,' I said to him. 'We heard incendiaries dropping, but where are they?'

'Look,' said Jim.

A large, dark and shiny object rolled silently out of the gloom of Langham Place, heading for Broadcasting House. It had almost reached the lamp post in the middle of the road opposite the Langham Hotel, but then it appeared to hesitate and retreated into the shadowy darkness from where it had come.

'What was that?' I hissed.

'I think it's a taxi, miss,' said the constable.

'But it was silent. This doesn't make sense.'

The sound of footsteps came from the direction of Broadcasting House, and out of the shadows strode two more policemen.

'That you Bill?' said our policeman. 'Syd?'

'We were told by a gentleman over there that there's something peculiar on the road,' said one of them.

'We saw it,' said our policeman. 'It came in from Langham Place.' He gestured towards where the object had retreated. 'Funny thing is, it made no noise.'

'We'll check it out,' they replied.

They disappeared into the gloom.

'Look,' Jim said, and pointed up.

A large mud-coloured cloth, at least twenty-five feet across, was falling softly and silently into the square. It gently collapsed on to the road and disappeared into the darkness of the tarmac about forty feet away from us. I had a mental image of the children's game of drop the hanky, only this handkerchief had been dropped by a giant.

'What was that?' I asked, fear making my voice shrill.

'They've been doing repair work on Broadcasting House,' said the policeman. 'Looks like a tarpaulin has come loose.'

'Maybe,' said Jim. 'I don't like it.'

I was still loosely wrapped in his arms and I felt the tension in his body.

A shout rang out from Langham Place and the two policemen came running out of the darkness. They shouted again. It was unintelligible to me, but Jim whirled around, took firm hold of my arm and pulled me along behind him as he ran at breakneck speed along Riding House Street back towards his flat. I could hear his laboured breathing and I felt the fear in his hard, painful grip on my arm as I struggled to keep up in my high heels.

A loud swishing noise came from behind us, almost as if a plane were diving through the air with its engine off, or a gigantic fuse was burning.

It all made sense to me now. I had the calm realisation that, although we were almost certainly going to die, I had been

trained for exactly such an event. I would do my best to survive
and to keep Jim alive. Twenty-two seconds. That was the time
we had until detonation and a blast that could explode lungs and
tear heads from bodies and destroy everything around us.

'Down,' I shouted, dragging on his arm to make him stop.
'We need to get down. *Now*!'

He stopped running. His breathing was laboured as I tugged
him into a low crouch.

'Flat down,' I shrieked. 'We need to lie flat. And grab
something, or we'll be blown on to the railings or walls.'

'The lamp post,' yelled Jim, pulling me over to it.

I stretched out flat on the pavement with my head towards
the swishing noise and I grabbed tight hold of the post and shut
my eyes. Jim lay on top of me, covering my body entirely with
his, painfully crushing me into the tarmac as he took firm hold
of the post.

My world had contracted into mere sensation: the taste of
blood from where I had bitten my cheek, the smell of Jim's
woollen greatcoat and the damp tarmac under my face, the
heavy weight of Jim's body on mine.

'I love you,' said Jim.

The world exploded into a blinding wild white light. A
colossal rush of air lifted his body up and away from me for a
few terrifying seconds. I held tight to the lamp post with all my
strength, holding on against the blast wind. Jim's body landed
back on top of me with a thump and I felt the tension in his
muscles as he clung doggedly to the post. His body pressed
down on me, pushing me onto the road.

Then followed a great roar, as if my handkerchief-dropping
giant were now an enormous lion bellowing its rage. An
excruciating pain filled my ears, closely followed by a high-
pitched whine, loud and unceasing, that blocked out all
other sounds.

I had lost my hold on the post and now clung to the kerb,
but the weight of Jim's body anchored me in place. I felt him

shudder violently, as if something had struck him. It caused us both to lurch sideways, but Jim's grip on the post held. My fingers were cramping as I continued to clutch the kerb. Jim's body lurched again as something else struck him, this time with greater force. Now he was a limp, dead weight on top of me. His hands must have fallen away from the lamp post, because then we were apart and he was swept away, leaving me open to the elements, at the mercy of the blast wind. My hands lost their grip on the kerb. I scrabbled at the concrete, but my grip faltered and I, too, moved along like so much flotsam. But the force of the blast must have been weakening, because my progress was a stately, inexorable sweep along the road. A body – Jim's body? – bumped me. I tried to grab him, keep him with me, but he slipped out of my grasp away into the darkness. After a minute, or an hour, or an eternity, all movement finally ceased and I was still.

Again, my world was purely sensation. Darkness. The scent of cordite and smoke. The taste of blood. A ceaseless, maddening whine that drowned out all other noise. Pain in my head and my legs and my chest. Pain in my face and my arms. When I tried to move, my body would not obey me.

Jim. Where was Jim? *Shout, Lily.* I opened my mouth and I cried out, but I heard no sound other than the ringing in my ears. I pushed up, to kneel on the road. My coat and Katherine's gown were in tatters, but held in place by the belt. The light of a torch was in my eyes. Someone was helping me to stand upright. It was a woman, an ambulance officer. She was speaking to me, but I heard nothing.

I looked around, desperate for Jim. My heart gave a thump as I saw him lying face down on the road, about ten yards from me, apparently unconscious. *Not dead*, I prayed. First aid workers fussed over him, but he seemed as floppy and unresponsive as a rag doll. *Please not dead.* His greatcoat had been ripped into shreds by the blast, and most of his clothes were gone. One arm was at an unnatural angle. By the aid workers' torchlight I saw that the bare skin of his back and his legs was blackened. Blood trickled from a wound on his head. The team placed him face down on a stretcher and carried him away. *Please Jim, don't be dead.*

A nurse wearing a steel hat took hold of my face and turned it towards her. She shone her torch into my eyes, palpated my body. She said something I could not hear over the ringing in my ears. I touched my ear and shrugged. She mimed an enquiry into my health.

'I'm fine,' I said, although I heard no words. I looked at the retreating ambulance. 'Is he alive?'

She nodded, but did not smile and her gaze seemed to slide furtively away from mine. She propped me against the wall of a building, leaving me there while she went to assess other casualties.

The whine in my ears seemed to have intensified, which added to my feeling of unreality as I looked around me. I was in a scene from Dante's *Inferno*, illuminated by a reddish-yellow light. The air was hot, and reeking black smoke billowed from blazing buildings. Some distance in front of me a car burned. Pieces of brick, masonry and glass of all sizes lay strewn as if by my roaring, handkerchief-dropping giant. Black shapes were dotted around, some crouched over other black shapes, others standing still or moving about in a seemingly aimless manner. Fire engines arrived; water flowed from their hoses. I heard nothing over the constant whine that filled my ears.

The nurse in the steel hat returned and walked me to the first aid post in Broadcasting House. Briskly efficient women bathed my face and used tweezers to pull pieces of stone and tar out of my skin. I wondered if I would be scarred for life, and if Jim would mind. Then I remembered. He might be dead, or dying at this very moment, and time seemed to stop.

I was somewhere else and someone was forcing me to sip a hot sweet liquid, but my whole body seemed to be shaking, and it spilled out of the cup and down my chin. Someone forced the cup back to my mouth and tipped it up so that I had to drink. I opened my eyes and looked up, and it was Katherine, holding an empty cup. She tried to smile and said something I could not hear.

'Where am I?' I had no idea how loudly I was speaking.

From the movement of her lips, she might have been saying Middlesex Hospital.

'How is Jim?' The world seemed to stop as I waited for her response.

She shook her head.

My whole body seemed to clench as darkness rose up and enveloped me and I fell into blessed oblivion.

I was drifting upwards, and as I gained a sort of consciousness my thoughts wandered from one subject to another in sharp flickers of memory. The wind cutting a flat swathe through a field of wheat . . . red dust swirling . . . the green flash of cockatoos against a sky of burnished blue . . . the campfire scent of bacon and damper on a cold desert morning . . . my infants' class, laughing at a story I told . . . a dozen red roses in a blue lustre bowl . . . the melancholy refrain of *Valse Russe* . . . the long tapered fingers of Jim's hand on my arm.

Jim. I could see his face so vividly I had to open my eyes.

I was lying in a bed, between white sheets that smelled of carbolic. My limbs felt heavy, my head ached and my face, arms and legs stung as if badly grazed. My ears reverberated still with the endless ringing. My chest hurt when I breathed. I lay still, unwilling to worsen the pain.

Jim. Is Jim alive? I must have cried out, because a doctor came to my bedside and spoke to me. I looked at him, uncomprehending. He mouthed, 'Morphine?'

I shook my head in a very small movement. 'Flight Lieutenant Vassilikov.' I could not hear my words, only the dreadful whine. I tried again. 'Jim Vassilikov?'

The doctor shrugged and mimed incomprehension. I did not know if he could not understand me or if he had no news of Jim's condition. I found myself crying, weeping silently, and I tried to push myself up, to make him understand and answer me. The doctor said something to someone behind him. I felt the prick of a hypodermic needle and I fell into darkness again.

CHAPTER THIRTY-SIX

When I opened my eyes again my ears were still ringing, but more softly than before. I rolled my head to the left and counted four beds. To the right there were two more. On the small table beside the bed was a carafe of water, a glass and a straw basket filled with grapes. Celia Ashwin was sitting next to me, reading a newspaper.

'Jim,' I said. It was a scratchy sound and muffled, but I could hear it. 'How is Jim?'

Celia looked up. 'Broken arm,' she said, in her usual cool, dispassionate tone. 'Head injury that will probably cause some scarring. They're worried about some residual deafness in one ear. The previous lung injuries were exacerbated, which is a shame, but they think he'll recover nicely and be discharged next week.'

My eyes filled with hot tears. 'Thank you. It was a parachute bomb, wasn't it?'

'Yes.'

'Did many die?'

'Five, including a policeman. Luckily you and Jim were shielded somewhat from the blast. You know Jim saved your life?'

I nodded. He had anchored me, prevented me from being blown against a railing or a wall, stopped the blast from exploding my lungs or my body being torn apart.

'Would you care for a drink of water?'

I nodded and she held my head steady as I sipped.

'How long have I been here?'

'It's Friday afternoon. You were injured Wednesday night – broken ribs, mild concussion – so you've been here a day and a half. You became very agitated yesterday, and they kept you doped up.' She raised an eyebrow. 'I've been spending time between both your bedsides. The grapes are from the Levys. They asked me to send you their good wishes.'

'The Levys? Asked you?'

'I've been helping Mrs Levy in her charity work with Jewish refugees.'

I had a sudden suspicion that I was in a dream. Nothing was making sense. Celia saw my expression and raised an eyebrow.

'Atonement,' she said, in a very matter of fact way. 'Mrs Levy understands my need to atone.'

'But—'

'And I'm useful to her because I'm efficient and I have good contacts.'

'But you didn't kill him,' I blurted out. 'Why do you need to atone?'

'Because I was a craven coward who left him alone.' She shrugged and looked down to rummage around in her handbag. A lipstick and compact appeared in her hand and she spent a minute or so refreshing her lipstick, which I suspected was to avoid looking at me. When she had finished she turned to me again. She seemed composed.

'Did you know that some Jews believe that the soul hovers over the body it has left for three days?'

I shook my head.

'They think that in that time the soul is lost, confused and so they set someone to watch over the body until it is buried,' she said. 'It is never left alone.'

'But, Celia—'

'I left David alone in those ruins for more than two weeks because I was afraid of my family, of Cedric, of society – oh, of everything really. I let his family and his friends suffer dreadfully, not knowing what had happened to him. So, now

333

I'm trying to atone by assisting his family in their war work – by assisting his people who are war refugees.' She laughed a little, self-consciously. 'Helen won't speak to me, of course, and Cedric wants me locked up as a mad woman, but he still won't divorce me.'

'You are happier, though?'

She smiled. There was a clear, unaffected humour in her smile and although I saw grief still in her eyes, the bitterness had gone.

'Actually, I am,' she said. 'Selfish as ever, I find it helps me to be helping people who are worse off than I.' A shadow passed over her face. 'The stories I've heard.' She looked at me with a savage intentness. 'We simply *must* defeat the Nazis, Lily.'

Celia gave me her lopsided smile. 'I've monopolised the conversation and I do beg your pardon. Are you well enough to walk? If you are, I can take you to see Jim.'

'Yes, please.' I raised my hand to my cheek. 'My face. How is my face? Will I be scarred?'

She passed me the compact and I stared at my red face, pocked with red marks from where the gravel had been removed. It looked unfortunate, but it was not too disfiguring.

'Would they mind if I put on some powder?' I asked.

Celia shrugged. 'I won't tell on you. Here. Let me do it.'

Once my face looked less raw, and my lips were the pretty coral colour of Celia's lipstick she helped me to sit up. I swung my feet out of the bed and she was waiting with a dressing gown.

'I was wrong,' she said, as she held it for me to shrug into. I waited for her to explain what she meant.

'I don't know if David and I ever really had a chance, but you and Jim do. Life is uncertain, Lily. And that's why we must grab hold of what we want and damn the consequences. Don't let fear destroy your chance at happiness.'

Jim lay white and still in the narrow bed as I limped through the ward doorway, supported by Celia. His head was bandaged and his left arm was in a plaster cast. An oxygen mask covered his face. When he saw me he pulled it to one side and said, in a rasping whisper, 'Sight for sore eyes.'

They had been his words when I visited him in hospital before, when I had been accompanied by Levy.

I managed a smile and sat down on the hard chair next to his bed. Celia murmured something and left us.

'We must stop meeting like this,' I said. 'And for the record, let's forgo dinner at the Ritz.'

He smiled and held out his hand. When I took it he squeezed it gently.

On Christmas Eve it snowed, and there were no bombs. Nor were there bombs on Christmas night, or the day after. Word on the street was that a deal had been brokered with the Germans: if we didn't bomb them during the festive season, they wouldn't bomb us.

Jim remained in hospital for Christmas, and Katherine and I went to Gloucester Road Tube station to celebrate with Pam and Betty and their hordes of tube shelterers. Despite the surroundings, we all had a marvellous time. As I sang carols, ate the meagre dinner among the many laughing people, stood for the loyal toast and joined the deafening cheers for 'the King, God bless him' and for Churchill, I thought that Hitler's plan to destroy London's morale had been a dismal failure.

'Not even the sound of a plane,' said Pam at breakfast on the day following Boxing Day. 'If this keeps up I may recover the roses in my cheeks.'

'They'll come tonight,' said Katherine.

'Pessimist,' said Pam.

'Near full moon,' replied Katherine. 'They won't waste it. We'll be in for it in the next few nights.'

Katherine was right, of course.

Jim was discharged on the twenty-ninth of December. His arm was still in a cast and he was pale and thin, but otherwise seemed well enough. My scars were healing also and I had made up my mind about my future.

'Now you listen to me, Jim Vassilikov,' I said in a brisk voice, after I had settled him on my sofa. 'No more shilly-shallying. I think we should be married as soon as possible. And although I would prefer to return to Australia after the war – if you want to stay here in England, I will.'

Jim smiled. 'I told you, I would be delighted to live in Australia. But, ah, there *is* something I forgot to tell you.' He was frowning slightly, but only slightly.

'What?' I looked at him suspiciously, but he seemed calm and unperturbed. 'Are you teasing me?'

'You will need to convert.'

'Convert to what?'

'The Russian Orthodox Church.'

I stared at him. 'Or you won't marry me? You *are* teasing me.'

'Of course I'll still marry you – I think we should be married right away, in the registry office, this week, preferably. But we would not be considered legally married by my family – and more importantly, our children wouldn't be considered legitimate by them – unless we also marry in an Orthodox ceremony. If they ever want to use the title – well, they couldn't really, unless we marry in the Church – in my Church, I mean. Is it a problem for you?' He added lightly, 'I seem to find it is important to me.'

'I'm C of E, but I'm not very . . .' I let my voice die away as I considered what it would mean. I knew nothing about the Orthodox religion. I would have to take lessons, I supposed, with a black-bearded patriarch. Would I need to learn Russian? Could I just swap over like that?

And then, all at once, my worries disappeared. Why not? It was the same God, after all.

'She's apples,' I said, in a broad Australian accent, which made Jim laugh. 'What is your Russian title, anyway? You've never told me.'

He bowed his head to me. 'I am Prince Ivan Mikhailovich Vassilikov of Russia.'

I blurted out the first thing in my head. 'It's a joke. Isn't it? You're teasing me, because I told you my dog was called Prince.'

His expression was unreadable.

'My father was a prince – it's a fairly common title in Russia – but he wasn't a royal prince. He was a Georgian nobleman, a Cossack if you will. It's my mother who's the Romanov.' He spoke in a detached style, as if he were reading from a guidebook.

'Your mother is a Romanov?'

'My mother is a great-granddaughter of Tsar Nicholas I, so she's a member of the Romanov dynasty. But by marrying my father, who was effectively a commoner despite his title, she renounced her dynastic rights.'

I swallowed a laugh. 'So you're not in line for the Russian throne.'

'No.'

'Well, thank God for that!' I said, and he seemed to relax at last.

'So that's your mysterious title,' I said, lightly, taking hold of his hand. 'You won't expect me to curtsy, will you. I'm—'

'I know. Believe me, I know very well that you're Australian and Australians don't go in much for nobility, except for the British royal family.'

'Too right.' Then something occurred to me. 'Are you related to the British monarchy?'

'George III was my great-great-great-great-grandfather. But that side of the family stayed in Germany. I'm barely related to King George VI.'

'Oh.' I suddenly felt lost, unsettled and unsure again. Out of my depth.

Jim looked away, down at his right hand as it tapped the side of the sofa, playing his imaginary piano. I knew him well enough to know that it meant he was in as much turmoil as I was. His left hand was still clasping mine though. I squeezed it hard.

'Jim, we really are so different. Our backgrounds . . .'

'Flying fish,' he said.

'I beg your pardon?'

'Fish that fly. To take Celia's very trite analogy to a logical conclusion, why can't we meet halfway, like flying fish?'

I laughed. 'That's silly.'

'Not wanting to marry me because of my accident of birth is silly. I don't use the title and it does not define me. My mother may not be thrilled, if that is what worries you, but we rarely see one another. You're not marrying my mother. She may even decide to visit us in Australia: who can say what miracles may happen when fish are flying.'

'I want to believe you,' I said. 'But—'

'We found each other, Lily,' he said, and there was a quiet intensity in his voice. 'How remarkable is that? Think about it. We were born in the same hour, eight thousand miles apart, and we found each other here in London in the middle of a war.'

He withdrew his hand from my clasp, leaving my hand suddenly cold.

'Now try to think about what it would be like to live your life without me,' he said. 'I – I can't imagine life without you. Not now that I've found you.'

In my mind, the words of a Shakespeare sonnet came unbidden: *For summer and his pleasures wait on thee, And, thou away, the very birds are mute: Or, if they sing, 'tis with so dull a cheer, That leaves look pale, dreading the winter's near.*

I breathed a laugh. I knew what it would be like to live my life without him. It would be like winter. A cold, dark, wet English winter, one without an end.

'Marry me, Lily.'

'I think I've been subtly manoeuvred,' I said.

'Here.'

He handed me a small leather box, decorated with gold leaves and flowers. When I opened it there was the ring. A sapphire surrounded by eight diamonds.

'Let's see if it fits,' he said.

It did.

* * *

The Warning went at six o'clock that evening. Its mournful wail rose and fell in the clear cold night air to be superseded almost immediately by the roar of planes coming in low. Under a full bombers' moon London lay open, beautiful and as vulnerable as an anaesthetised patient stretched out on an operating table. The white-painted kerbs, the shadows of the grand buildings and the twisting Thames all conspired to guide the raiders straight to the heart of the capital.

By ten o'clock, when Jim and I stood on my small balcony, the eerie red glow from the south-east was like a perverted sunrise. The air was hot – in mid-winter! It felt singed and with every breath we inhaled ashes. The smell of burning was almost overpowering. The sound of fire engine bells tore the night, competing with the sound of bombers and guns.

'What is happening?' I said.

Jim shuddered and rubbed his eyes in a weary gesture and looked again at the glow in the east.

'The City is burning,' he said. 'My God, Lily, it's an inferno. We're looking at another Great Fire of London.'

I wondered if St Paul's – if the City – would survive the holocaust of flame that lit the night sky with such an infernal brightness.

It is madness to plan for a future in such times, I thought. And yet that was exactly what we were doing. I reached out for his arm.

'Come inside,' I said. 'This ash is bad for your lungs. Whatever it is, London will survive it. And we'll have time enough tomorrow to see what has happened.'

Together, we had all the time in the world.

ACKNOWLEDGEMENTS

As always, this novel would not have been written without the support and assistance and research skills of my wonderful husband, Toby.

Thanks also to my fabulous agents, the ever-supportive Sheila Drummond in Australia and Anna Carmichael in London. Thanks to the team at Ebury Press, especially Gillian Green, Emily Yau and Josephine Turner. And to Justinia Baird-Murray for the lovely cover and Charlotte Cole for her sympathetic editing.

I owe a great debt to my dear friends in Iffley, Oxford: Venetia, Alice and Steve, Jan and Jonathan and Brenda and Sam, who welcomed a couple of Aussies to their golden city, and made them feel as if they belonged. And to John and Rosemary, Kate and Jonathan, and Jock and Jill – still friends so many years after our Tuscan adventure. Many thanks to the amazing staff at the Bodleian Library and the Oxford Central Library – every book imaginable about the Blitz was mine for the asking. Thanks to my dear friends, Felicity and Philip McCann, who generously allowed us to stay in their lovely home when we were back in Perth. Janet Blagg (as always) helped so much. Lovely Lisa Fagin Davis reassured me when I was panicking about the Jewish bits. My friends, all of you, thank you so much.

Finally, this novel is also dedicated to the 'ambulance girls' who risked their lives and who lost their lives, racing through falling bombs to help the victims of the Blitz. I am in awe of their immense courage and grace under fire.

341

FURTHER READING

When writing this novel I tried to ensure that my depiction of the London Blitz was as accurate as possible. I spent many happy hours researching at the Bodleian Library in Oxford and I can't possibly acknowledge all the books and articles I read and the internet sites I visited, but the following stand out as invaluable in my depiction of London during those dark days:

Beardmore, George. *Civilians at War: Journals 1938–1946*. London: John Murray, 1984.

De Courcy, Anne. *Debs at War 1939–1945: How Wartime Changed Their Lives*. London: Weidenfeld & Nicolson, 2005.

Freedman, Jean R. *Whistling in the Dark: Memory and Culture in Wartime London*. Lexington: University Press of Kentucky, 1999.

Gardiner, Juliet. *The Blitz: The British Under Attack*. London: Harperpress, 2010.

Hartley, Jenny. *Millions Like Us: British Women's Fiction of the Second World War*. London: Virago, 1997.

Hodgson, Vere. *Few Eggs and No Oranges: A Diary Showing How Unimportant People in London and Birmingham Lived Throughout the War Years*. London: Persephone, 1999.

Howard, Elizabeth Jane. *Slipstream: A Memoir*. London: Macmillan, 2002.

Kushner, Tony. *The Persistence of Prejudice: Anti-Semitism in British Society during the Second World War*. Manchester: Manchester University Press, 1989.

Lefebure, Molly. *Murder on the Home Front: A True Story of Morgues, Murderers and Mystery in the Blitz*. London: Sphere, 2013.

Nicholson, Harold. *Diaries and Letters*, London: Fontana, 1969–1971.

Nixon, Barbara. *Raiders Overhead*. London: Lindsay Drummond, 1943.

Raby, Angela. *The Forgotten Service: Auxiliary Ambulance Station 39, Weymouth Mews. London*: Battle of Britain International, 1999.

Sweet, Matthew. *The West End Front: The Wartime Secrets of London's Grand Hotels*. London: Faber and Faber Ltd, 2011.

Waller, Jane, and Vaughn-Rees, Michael. *Blitz: The Civilian War 1940–45*. London: Optima, 1990.

Wyndham, Joan. *Love Lessons: A Wartime Diary*. London: Heinemann, 1985.

Ziegler, Philip. *London at War 1939–1945*. London: Sinclair-Stevenson, 1995.